Nick Kennedy was spectacular, Sammy thought.

Broad shoulders, beautiful biceps, enough hair on his chest to be sexy without him looking like a total gorilla and a definite six-pack.

Mr December was going to be the best page on the calendar. He could probably sell the calendar all by himself.

But now he'd said there was no wife or girlfriend, she couldn't help wondering: How come a gorgeous man with a good brain and kind eyes was single? Was it because he was a workaholic and his girlfriends tended to get fed up waiting for him to notice them? Or had she missed some major personality flaw?

"What?" he asked, clearly noting that she was staring at him.

"Nothing," she said, embarrassed to discover that her voice was slightly croaky. She really had to get a grip.

The last thing she needed was for her skittish model to work out that she was attracted to him.

But a girl could dream.

FALLING FOR
MR DECEMBER

BY
KATE HARDY

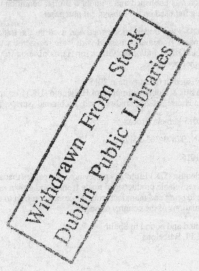

MILLS &
BOON

Published in Great Britain 2015
by Mills & Boon, an imprint of Harlequin (UK) Limited,
Eton House, 18-24 Paradise Road, Richmond, Surrey, TW9 1SR

© 2015 Pamela Brooks

ISBN: 978-0-263-25175-3

23-1015

Printed and bound in Spain
by CPI, Barcelona

Award-winning author **Kate Hardy** lives in Norwich with her husband, two children, one spaniel and too many books to count! She's a fan of the theater, ballroom dancing, posh chocolate and anything Italian. She's a history and science geek, plays the guitar and piano and makes great cookies (which is why she also has to go to the gym five days a week. . .).

To Fi, my best friend, with much love.

CHAPTER ONE

SAMMY LAUGHED AS the penny finally dropped. 'So you want me to photograph naked men for you?'

Ayesha, who chaired the Friends of the London Victoria Hospital, squirmed and stared into her latte. 'Put like that, it sounds terrible!'

'I know what you meant. Do it *artistically*,' Sammy said, still smiling. 'A calendar of hot men to raise funds for the cancer ward. It's a great idea. So do you have a bunch of sexy doctors lined up to pose for me?'

'A couple,' Mari, the vice-chair, said. 'But we were thinking maybe we can include other people who've been involved with the ward.'

'Cured patients, so you can say that this is what a cancer survivor looks like? That could work well.' And, for a cause like that, Sammy would seriously think about going public and baring her own leg, if they couldn't get enough models.

'We were thinking relatives of patients,' Ayesha said. 'Ones with high profiles locally. We've got an actor, a musician, a chef, a gardener…'

'So I could maybe shoot them in their own locations, doing their job. That'd work really well,' Sammy said.

'And they're all happy about posing naked—provided I preserve their modesty?'

'Ye—es,' Ayesha said.

The hesitation told her everything. 'You didn't actually tell them it meant posing naked, did you?' Sammy asked.

'We're going to,' Mari said. 'We can talk them into it.'

'As I'll need signed model release forms before I can let you use the photographs, I'm afraid you'll have to do that.' Sammy looked at her diary. 'If you're using the hospital as a location, I could shoot the whole lot in a day, but if I need to go to different places then I'll have to work out a schedule based on the locations and the availability of the models.' She scribbled some notes down on a pad. 'These are the best times for me to do it, but I can also work round a couple of other things if you need me to. Talk to your models and let me know where and when you want me to do the shoots.'

'Sammy, you're a star. Thank you so much,' Ayesha said.

Sammy shrugged off the praise. 'It's the least I can do. If it wasn't for the treatment I had here when I was a teen—' and again two years ago '—then I wouldn't be here. And this means I can give something back.' She smiled. 'This is going to be fun. And we're going to raise a ton of money for the ward.'

Nick folded his arms and looked at his sister. 'All right, Mandy. Out with it.'

'Out with what?' she deadpanned.

'Amanda Kennedy, I've known you for thirty-five years.'

'At least one year of which you wouldn't remember, because you were a baby at the time,' she retorted.

'Agreed,' he said, 'but I can always read your expression. So don't ever take up playing poker, will you?'

She sighed. 'I guess.'

Nick had known that tonight wasn't just about his sister giving him an update on his nephew's cancer treatment. Despite going through a messy divorce, Mandy still believed in love and happy endings. And all too often she tried to fix him up with someone she thought would be his perfect date. Nick had stopped believing in love years ago, and he'd learned the hard way that you couldn't be successful both in love and in your career. So after the break-up of his marriage he'd gone for the safe option and concentrated on his career.

No doubt this was another of Mandy's friends who really needed a plus-one for a dinner party and he'd fit the bill perfectly. OK. He'd help out, but he'd make it clear that he wasn't looking for a relationship. Nowadays he didn't do anything deeper than casual dating.

Then his sister said something he really hadn't expected. 'The Friends of the Hospital are doing a calendar to raise funds for the ward.'

He didn't need to ask which ward. The cancer ward. The one that had treated his nephew Xander for osteosarcoma. Well, he could do something to help there, too. 'If they're looking for a sponsor to cover production costs, count me in.'

Mandy reached across the table and squeezed his hand. 'Aww, Nick. I knew you'd offer to help before I could ask you. But they already have a sponsor for printing costs.'

'OK. What else do they need to cover? Distribution? Warehouse? Paying the photographer?'

'Um—not that, either. The photographer's doing it for nothing.'

'Then what?'

She took a deep breath. 'They want you to be one of the models.'

'Me?' He looked at her, totally shocked. He knew his sister had been under a lot of stress recently, but had she gone temporarily insane? 'Why?'

Mandy raised her eyebrows. 'Need I remind you that you actually got approached by a model agency when you were seventeen?'

'And I didn't take up their offer.' He might have considered it, to fund his way through university; but a couple of weeks later their parents had split up and life had disintegrated into chaos. Nick had forgotten all about the modelling offer and retreated into his studies. Concentrating on his books was what had got him through all the upheaval of his parents' divorce. Just as concentrating on his job had got him through the misery of his own divorce.

'Seriously, Nick—will you do it? They're looking for people who are connected with the ward.'

As Xander's uncle, he definitely had that connection.

'And they want people with interesting jobs.'

'A barrister isn't that exciting,' he said.

'Yes, it is. You look like a film star in your wig and gown.'

He rolled his eyes. 'Mandy, I'm just an ordinary guy.'

'Like hell you are. Apart from the fact that you're my little brother, which would make you special in any case, can I remind you that you're one of the youngest ever barristers appointed to being a QC?'

He grimaced. 'Why would anyone be interested in that?' About the only people who would even know what a QC was were people who had needed to brief one. Or maybe fans of certain types of TV crime drama.

'And you'd be helping raise money for the ward. Money they really need for new equipment.'

That was an unbeatable argument, and they both knew it. How could he possibly say no? This was to help other kids who were in Xander's position. And a little voice in his head added selfishly that maybe if he did it, then that would persuade Fate to give Xander a break and keep him in remission. And for that Nick would do almost anything.

'Will you do it?' she asked.

He closed his eyes briefly. 'All right.'

She smiled. 'Good. Thank you. I'll give your phone number and email to them, then—I'll do that now, if you don't mind, because they're waiting on my answer.'

'OK.' But Mandy was still hiding something, he was sure. 'And the rest of it?' he asked.

She blinked. 'What do you mean?'

'You're holding something back.'

She shrugged and tapped a message into her phone.

'Just save us both the time and tell me the rest of it, Mandy,' he said, leaning back and eyeing her over his glass of water.

'OK.' She sat back in her own chair and looked at him straight. 'Since you ask, you're going to be naked.'

'What?' He'd just taken a sip of water and he nearly choked on it. Naked? He must've misheard. No way would his sister have done this to him.

'You won't be *showing* anything,' she said.

'Define naked,' he said grimly.

'In court. Wearing your wig and robe.'

He shook his head. 'I'm afraid I can't do that, Mandy. The Head of Chambers would never agree to it.'

'Um, he already has.'

He blinked hard. Was he hearing things? Leo had already said yes? But—how? 'You what?'

'I talked to your clerk this morning,' she said. 'And he thinks it's a great idea.'

Now Nick was beginning to understand all the knowing smiles that had greeted him all afternoon. The news must've gone round chambers in ten seconds flat—gossip that juicy would never be ignored. And they'd all known that he didn't have a clue what was going on, making it even more fun for them.

'So what exactly did Gary say?' he asked, keeping his voice low and even and meanwhile planning how he was going to make his clerk grovel hugely in the morning.

'He put me through to your Head of Chambers. Then I told Leo all about it and he said he thought it was really a good idea, too. And he's getting clearance for us so you can do the shoot in the local court. He says he'll cover any photographic permission costs at the court himself.'

'Oh, good God.' With his boss on side, there was no way Nick could get out of it. He covered his face with his hands. 'Please tell me this is some weird, surreal dream. Please tell me it's a nightmare and I'm going to wake up. Preferably right now.'

'Nick, I've already told them you said yes,' Mandy said plaintively.

'That was before I knew I was going to be naked. This is a seriously bad idea, Mandy,' he said softly. 'I'm a senior barrister. I have to respect the dignity of the court. Which doesn't mean posing naked—or near-naked—for a calendar shoot, no matter how noble the cause is.'

'But Leo said it would be OK. And… Nick, we need you,' Mandy pleaded. 'And it's not as if you're the only one with a responsible job. One of the surgeons at the hospital is doing it.'

'Which is publicity for his own place of work.'

'And I think there's an actor and a musician on their list. And a chef.'

'All of whom would get a career boost from the publicity,' he pointed out.

'Please, Nick. For me. And for Xander.'

'It doesn't look as if I've got much choice,' he said grimly. 'But promise me you'll never, ever pitch a stunt like this again.'

'I promise. I'm sorry, Nick.' She bit her lip. 'But the ward needs the money.'

Lack of money meant lack of equipment. Which in turn meant that some kids wouldn't get the treatment they so badly needed. And that meant that those kids might even die.

Which was Nick's worst nightmare regarding his nephew.

And he was in a position to change that. To give more kids a chance of life—the same amazing chance that Xander had been given. All he had to do was pose for one little picture that would help to publicise the cause and encourage people to donate.

One little *naked* picture.

It really went against the grain. But far worse was

the thought of his nephew dying and the way it would shatter all their lives and devastate his elder sister.

'All right,' he said, blowing out a breath. 'But I need to double-check this with Leo myself, first, and make sure that he's absolutely clear on all the details. And if he changes his mind and says that I can't do it, then I'll sell calendars by hand for you—and I'm very persuasive, so I'll sell tons of them to everyone in the whole of Inner Temple and Middle Temple. Plus I'll also give a personal donation to match those sales. Double.' Time *and* money. They'd be a good alternative to posing naked for a calendar, wouldn't they?

And hopefully he'd be able to persuade his Head of Chambers that having one of his barristers naked and in the focus of the press might not be such a good idea…

CHAPTER TWO

AND OF COURSE Leo still said yes. Even when Nick pointed out exactly what was involved.

So, two weeks later, Nick found himself heading to the local Crown court. Leo had arranged for Court Number Two to be used outside the normal court working hours, though there was still a chance that Nick might bump into someone he knew who'd want to know what he was doing hanging round the court building when he wasn't in a trial—especially when he looked as scruffy as he did right now.

S. J. Thompson, the photographer, had sent him a couple of very business-like texts to arrange the photo shoot and explain that Nick needed to dress casually and remove anything that might cause a mark on his skin—socks, collars, waistbands and the like—at least two hours before the shoot.

For putting him through something as embarrassing as this—not to mention the teasing he knew he'd get from his colleagues when the calendar actually came out—Fate had *better* keep Xander safe, Nick thought grimly.

When he got to the court, carrying his court attire in its usual boxes, there was nobody waiting outside. The only person he could see in the lobby was a woman who looked to be in her late twenties or so, wearing black trousers, a black silky short-sleeved top and black shoes. Her blonde hair was cropped so short as to be almost a military cut. She didn't look remotely like the man Nick was here to meet.

She looked up from her book, then closed it, stood up and walked towards him. 'Nick Kennedy, I presume?'

He blinked. Was she the photographer's assistant or something? 'Yes.'

'Thank you for being on time. I'm S. J. Thompson—though you can call me Sammy, if you like.' She held out her hand for him to shake.

'*You're* S. J. Thompson?' Even as the words came out, he realised how dim they sounded. And how stupid of him to assume that the use of initials meant that the photographer was male.

She gave him a slight smile. 'I'm afraid so.'

Clearly he wasn't the first to have made that mistake. 'I—er—nice to meet you,' he said, feeling totally wrong-footed.

And, when he shook her hand, awareness zinged through every pore. Sammy Thompson was the most striking woman he'd met in a long time. And that severe haircut only served to highlight how pretty and feminine her face was. There was nothing masculine at all about her. Her mouth was a perfect rosebud, and he found himself wanting to trace her lower lip with his fingertip. Worse still, he could picture himself doing that before leaning in and kissing her. Lightly at first, a touch as light as a butterfly's wing, and then deepening the kiss as she responded...

He shook himself mentally. Oh, for pity's sake.

This was *business*. OK, maybe not the normal kind of business he'd conduct here in the court, but it was still business. And he wasn't exactly known for having ridiculous flights of fancy.

But he did feel uncomfortable right now.

It was nothing to do with sexism—as far as he was concerned, it was how you did your job that mattered, not what your gender or your sexual orientation or your religion was—but Sammy's gender made this situation a little more difficult. Because it meant that now he was going to be stripping off in front of a woman he'd never met before.

Either his doubts showed on his face or she was used to this reaction from the people she photographed, because she said softly, 'It's not going to be as bad as you think. And, if it helps, remember that I'll be seeing you simply as a life model rather than as an actual person. I don't tend to hit on my models.'

'I—yes. Of course. Sorry.' How long had it been since he'd felt in a whirl, like this? He was never this pathetic and woolly. And he really hoped he didn't look as if he was staring at her. He forced himself to look away. 'I believe we have Court Number Two booked.'

'My equipment's already in there, though I haven't set it up fully yet,' she said. 'Once we've decided precisely where you're going to stand, it won't take me long. Oh, and we really ought to cover the legal details now.'

Legal details? That got his attention.

'Firstly, I have public liability insurance, which covers any damage to person or property while we're in the location—not that there will be any—and secondly I'll need you to sign a model release form,' she said.

'It's pretty standard wording, but I'd still prefer you to read it thoroughly before you sign it.' There was just the slightest twinkle in her sea-green eyes as she added, 'Though I guess in your case I don't really need to tell you to ask me to explain any legal wording you don't understand.'

'Quite,' he agreed, trying to sound cool and professional. Even though Sammy Thompson was making him feel decidedly hot under the collar. What was it about her that made him feel like this?

'Shall we?' She gestured for them both to go in to the court room, and put a note on the door saying *Filming in progress: do not enter.*

'I take it you've worked in here before, or at least somewhere like this?' she asked.

'Yes.'

'Good. Then you'll be comfortable with the setting,' she said approvingly.

True, but he really wasn't comfortable with what he was about to do. 'Usually I'm fully dressed when I'm in this room,' he said.

She indicated his cases and suit carrier. 'This lot contains what you wear in court, I assume?'

He nodded. 'I brought all of it because I wasn't sure what you'd need.' Though he knew it would be a lot less than he would prefer.

'OK. Talk me through it,' she invited.

He took his work clothing out of the cases he'd brought with him, piece by piece, and laid each one in turn on the judge's bench. 'Tunic shirt, waistcoat, pinstripe trousers and frock coat.'

'You don't wear a normal business suit under your lawyer's gown?' she asked, sounding surprised.

'I did before I took silk,' he said. 'That is, before I became a QC—a Queen's Counsel.'

'Which is a senior barrister, right?'

'Yes. So that's why I wear the frock coat.' He took out the gown. 'And this.'

'And that gown's silk, I assume?' she asked.

'Yes.'

'May I touch it?'

He frowned. 'Why?'

'So I can move it about and see how the light affects it,' she said. 'Obviously I'll be careful with it. One of my best friends is a wedding dress designer, and I've taken most of the shots for her portfolio and website, so I understand how to handle material without marking it.'

'Ah. Of course.'

His fingers brushed against hers as she took the gown from him, and it felt as if pure electricity were running through his veins. What on earth was the matter with him? He never reacted like this. Especially to a complete stranger.

Maybe he was overreacting because he hadn't dated in a while, and his body's natural urges were making themselves felt because Sammy was really attractive. Well, tough. This was business and he really didn't have time for this. Behave, he told his libido mentally. You know relationships are a disaster zone.

She peered at the material carefully from several angles, then nodded in seeming satisfaction. 'OK. Do you wear lace at your collar, or am I thinking of something else?'

'That'd be ceremonial legal dress,' he said. 'Normally in Crown court a male barrister wears a wing collar that attaches to the shirt, and court bands.' He took them out of their cases for her.

'So the bands are the things that hang down like a two-pronged white tie?'

Despite himself, he smiled. 'Yes. Actually, they're symbolic. The Lord Chief Justice said back in the sixteenth century that they were two tongues. One for the rich, for a fee, to reward our long studies; and one without reward to defend the poor and oppressed.'

'I like that,' she said. 'So you defend the poor and oppressed?'

'I'm usually a prosecutor,' he said, 'but English barristers can defend as well as prosecute. I guess in either case I'd be defending my client's interests, and it's not for me to call them poor or oppressed.'

Sammy liked that little bit of humility. Given that Nicholas Kennedy QC was a top barrister, she'd half expected him to be a bit on the arrogant side, but she instinctively liked the man she'd just met. He had kind eyes, a deep rich brown. And, even though he clearly wasn't very comfortable with the idea of being part of a shoot for the charity calendar—especially now he knew the photographer was female—he'd obviously made a promise to someone and had the integrity to keep that promise.

She could see exactly why the committee had asked him to pose for their calendar. Talk about photogenic. His bone structure was gorgeous. He could've been a model for a top perfume house, advertising aftershave. It was rare to have that kind of beauty teamed with an equally spectacular intellect. And it made him almost totally irresistible.

But she was going to have to resist the pull of attraction. She was here to work, not to drool over the eye candy. Right now she was supposed to be putting the man at his ease. And hadn't she just told him that she never hit on her models?

Well, this wasn't going to be a first for her.

Be professional, she reminded herself. She wasn't going to let herself remember the little shiver of desire that had rippled down her spine when he'd shaken her hand. Or wonder how that beautiful mouth would feel against her skin. She was going to focus on her job.

Besides, he was probably committed elsewhere. He wasn't wearing a wedding ring, but that didn't prove anything. A man that beautiful would've been snapped up years ago.

'Your hair's very short,' she commented. 'Do you have a military background, or is the haircut necessary because you have to wear a wig in court?'

'It makes the wig a little more comfortable, yes,' he said. 'Speaking of which…' He took out the wig next.

There were short, neat rows of curls all the way round the pale grey wig, and two tiny tails hanging down at the back with neat curls at the ends.

'The wig is what everyone associates with lawyers in court,' she said. 'You'll definitely be wearing that, and probably the gown—though I might do some shots without the gown as well.'

'What else do I get to wear?' he asked hopefully.

'Not the trousers, the coat or the shirt, I'm afraid. Even though they're nicely cut and made from good material.'

He flinched.

'You can wear the collar and tie thingies.'

She could see in his expression that he was dying to correct her terminology—but he didn't. Clearly he was resisting the temptation to be nit-picky and was trying to be co-operative. Teasing probably wasn't the kindest or most appropriate thing she could do right now.

'Thank you. I think,' he said.

She smiled. 'As I said, to me you'll be simply a life model.'

But she needed him to relax so the strain wouldn't show on his face when she photographed him. Given what he did for a living—and that he'd agreed to wear some of his court dress for the shoot—she guessed he'd be more comfortable talking about his work. 'Talk me through the court layout, so I can decide where to put you.' Even though she knew perfectly well where she was going to ask him to stand. She'd done her research properly, the way she always did before she took a portrait.

'Right in front of us is the judge's bench.'

'Where he bangs his gavel, right?'

He laughed. 'I think you've been watching too many TV dramas. English judges don't use gavels.'

She knew that, but he didn't need to know that she knew. It looked as if her plan to make him more comfortable was working. Except, when he laughed like that, it made him look sexy as hell—and that made it much more difficult for her to keep her part of the bargain, to be detached and think of him as a life model.

Not that Sammy was looking for a relationship right now. She was too busy with her job, and she was fed up to the back teeth with dating Mr Wrong—men who ran for the hills in panic, the second they learned about her past, or who saw themselves as her knight in shining armour and wrapped her so tightly in cotton wool that she couldn't breathe. None of them had seen her as a woman.

Then again, she wasn't really a whole woman any more, was she? So she couldn't put the blame completely on them.

And after Bryn had finally been the one to break her heart, Sammy had decided that it would be much easier to focus on her family, her friends and her job and forget completely about romance.

Though the wedding she'd photographed a couple of months ago had made her feel wistful; now both her best friends were loved-up and settled. And although she was really happy for both of them, it had left her feeling just the tiniest bit lonely. And the tiniest bit sorry for herself. Even if she ever did manage to meet her Mr Right, there was no guarantee of a happy ending. Not if he wanted children of his own, without any kind of complications. She couldn't offer that.

She pushed the thought away. Enough of the pity party. She had a great life. A family who loved her—even if they were a tad on the overprotective side—friends who'd celebrate the good times with her and be there for her in the bad times, and a job that really fulfilled her. Asking for more was just greedy.

'No gavel, then. So what else am I looking at?'

'OK. In front of the judge you have the clerk of the court, the usher, and the person who makes the sound recording of the trial or a stenographer who types it up as the trial goes along. They face the same way as the judge.' He walked over to the benches facing the judge's bench. 'This is where the barristers sit, though we stand when we're addressing the court. The defence barrister is nearest to the jury—' he indicated the seats at the side of the room '—and the prosecution barrister is nearest to the witness box. The solicitors sit behind the barristers, and at the back is the dock where the defendant sits. Over there behind the witness box you have the public gallery and the press bench.'

'So it'd make the most sense to photograph you where you'd normally stand in court,' she said. Exactly where she'd always planned for him to pose—and where her equipment just so happened to be waiting. 'OK. Can you stand there for me?'

'Dressed like this?' he asked.

She smiled. 'For the moment, yes—though if you wouldn't mind putting on your gown, that'd help with the light meter readings.'

He shrugged on his gown and went to stand at the barristers' bench. She noticed that he was looking nervous again.

'You're really not going to end up on the front page of the newspapers with headlines screaming about "top barrister flashes his bits",' she reassured him. 'The point of the calendar is to sell gorgeous men posed artistically.' And Nick definitely fitted the bill on both counts. 'If the bench doesn't cover your modesty, so to speak, then you can hold a bunch of papers in a strategic place. Don't you normally have a bunch of papers with you in court, tied with a pink ribbon?'

'A brief,' he said. 'It's the instructions from my client. The defence has a pink silk ribbon and the prosecution uses white.'

Though he still didn't look convinced about the shoot.

She sighed. 'Look, just stand there for a second.'

As he did so, she took her camera body out of its carrying case, fitted a lens so she could take a quick photograph, then came over to show him the digital picture on the screen. 'This obviously isn't a proper composition—for the real one I'll be quite a bit more nit-picky about the lighting and the lens—but it should be enough to prove to you that your dignity will remain intact. OK now?'

'Sorry.' He blew out a breath. 'I know I'm being ridiculous about this. I guess this just isn't the normal sort of thing I'd do in a day's work.'

'That's pretty much what everyone's said so far.' She grinned. 'Well, except for the actor. He didn't mind stripping off, but I guess he'd done it a few times before. All in the name of art, of course.'

'Of course,' Nick echoed, still looking uncomfortable.

'And what you do in court—you have a persona, and that's a bit like acting, isn't it?'

'A bit, I suppose,' Nick said. 'But, as I said, at work I'm normally wearing quite formal dress—not standing in the middle of the room, almost naked.'

'For what it's worth,' Sammy said, 'I think what you're doing is really special. It takes guts—everyone's happy enough to put their hand in their pocket and donate money to a good cause, but you're doing something out of the ordinary. Something that's going to make a lot more of a difference. And I bet whoever you're doing this for is hugely proud of you.'

'My sister,' he said, 'and my nephew.'

'The ward treated your nephew?' she asked softly.

He nodded. 'Xander's in remission at the moment.'

She guessed the bargain he'd made in his head: if he

did this to help raise money, then Fate might smile on
his nephew and keep him in remission. She knew her
own sister had made the same bargain, and it was why
Jenny had her hair cropped at the same time as Sammy
did, every two years.

She wondered briefly why Xander's father hadn't
offered to do the calendar shoot. Or maybe it was just
that Nick had a more photogenic job. It was none of her
business, anyway. She was just here to do the shoot.

'OK. I'm happy with that position. Now, there aren't
any windows in here; plus we've got a notice on the
door, so nobody's going to walk in on us. It's quite safe.
So, while I'm setting up properly here, do you want to
lose the clothes?'

No, Nick didn't want to lose the clothes. At all.

But he'd promised he'd do it, and he wasn't going to
break his word. 'What do you want me to wear out of
the court dress?' he asked, drawing on his usual court
demeanour and trying to sound as if he was completely
unflustered.

'Wig, collar and bands, and we'll try some shots
with the gown and some without,' she said. 'I take it
you followed my instructions to avoid marks on your
skin?'

'Yes.'

'Good. Let's do this.'

Nick felt incredibly self-conscious stripping off. Putting on the collar and bands without his tunic shirt felt
weird. Though the silk gown was soft against his skin,
and he gathered it in front of him to cover himself and
went to stand by the bench.

'We'll do some shots sitting down, first,' Sammy

said. 'I guess you need some papers spread out on the bench in front of you.'

Luckily he'd thought to bring a brief with him. He fetched it and sat down.

'Do you wear glasses?' she asked.

'No.'

'Pity. I should've thought to bring some frames with me.'

He frowned. 'Why do you want me to wear glasses?'

'To make you look clever.'

He wasn't sure if she was teasing him or not. Then he looked her straight in the eye and saw the mischievous twinkle. 'Very funny.'

'Yes, m'lud—or should I say Your Honour?'

He rolled his eyes. 'That's what I'd say to the judge. You'd refer to me as My Learned Friend.'

Her mouth quirked, and heat flooded his body. That impish smile transformed Sammy Thompson to a pure beauty.

And this was totally inappropriate.

He damped his feelings down. For all he knew, she was married or involved with someone. OK, so she wasn't wearing a ring, but that didn't mean anything. And he wasn't looking for a relationship anyway; the disintegration of his marriage to Naomi three years ago had put him off the idea of opening his life to someone else ever again. The one woman he'd thought was different. The one he'd thought had supported his ambitions and understood him. Yet it had all been a sham. That wasn't a mistake he intended to repeat. Even if he did find Sammy Thompson attractive, he wasn't going to act on that attraction. Dating seriously wasn't something he did any more.

He focused on posing for Sammy and following her instructions. He stood up, changing position when she told him to.

'OK. Now you can lose the gown for the next set of shots.'

'Are you quite sure about this?' he asked, wishing he were a hundred miles away.

'Tell you what, shy boy,' she drawled. 'Do the rest of the shoot for me without making any more fuss, and I'll buy you dinner.'

He blinked. Was she asking him out? 'Dinner? Why?'

'Because I've already shot two other models for the calendar today and I didn't have time for lunch, which means that right now I'm starving—I'll apologise now in case my stomach starts rumbling during the shoot. So I think we should have dinner while we look through the shots and you tell me which ones you approve to put forward to the Friends of the Hospital,' she said. 'Unless you have a girlfriend or a wife who'd have a problem with that, in which case please call her now and ask her to join us, because I really don't want to have to wait for too long before dinner.'

He shrugged slightly. 'No wife. No girlfriend.' And this was feeling more and more like agreeing to a date. Something that pushed him even further outside his comfort zone. He paused. 'Would it be a problem for your partner if you ate with me?'

'Not if I had one, because this is my job.'

So she was single. Available...

He squashed those thoughts. No, no and no. He didn't date any more. Not seriously.

'The quicker we get this done, the quicker I get food,' she continued, 'and the less likely it is that I'll get grumpy with you. You need to focus, m'learned friend. Lose the gown. And think yourself lucky.'

'Lucky?' He very nearly had to shake his head to clear it. Was she talking about *him* getting lucky?

'You're Mr December. I could've made you wear a Santa hat. Or pose holding a bunch of mistletoe. Or—' She flapped a dismissive hand. 'Insert a cheesy Christmassy pose of choice.'

Ah. *That* kind of lucky. Nothing to do with sex, then.

And would his head please, please start playing by the rules and stop thinking about lust and other inappropriate things? Because right now he was naked, and it would be impossible to hide his physical reaction to her.

'Noted,' he said dryly. He took off his gown, folded it neatly, and set it on the bench where it would be out of sight of her camera.

Wearing just his barrister's wig, collar and bands, Nick Kennedy was spectacular, Sammy thought. Broad shoulders, beautiful biceps, enough hair on his chest to be sexy without him looking like a total gorilla, and a definite six pack.

Mr December was going to be the best page on the calendar. He could probably sell the calendar all by himself.

But now he'd said there was no wife or girlfriend, she couldn't help wondering: how come a gorgeous man with a good brain and kind eyes was single? Was it because he was a workaholic and his girlfriends tended to get fed up waiting for him to notice them? Or had she missed some major personality flaw?

'What?' he asked, clearly noting that she was staring at him.

'Nothing,' she said, embarrassed to discover that her voice was slightly croaky. She really had to get a grip. The last thing she needed was for her skittish model to work out that she was attracted to him. And Nicholas Kennedy was bright. He couldn't be more than five or six years older than Sammy's own thirty years, and he was at the top of his profession. Scratch bright: that kind of background meant he had to be super-bright. So he'd be able to work it out quickly.

She got him to do a few more poses. To her relief, he'd relaxed enough with her by now to trust her, even when she moved round and took some shots from the side and some others from the back. And, oh, his back was beautiful. She'd love to do some proper nude studies of him. In a wood, looking for all the world like a statue of a Greek god.

Not that he'd agree to it. Not in a million years.

But a girl could dream…

'OK. That's a wrap. You can get dressed now,' she said, 'and by the time I've loaded everything on to my laptop we'll be ready to go to dinner.'

'The stuff I was wearing is hardly dressy enough for going out,' he said.

She laughed. 'As I wasn't planning to take you to the Dorchester or Claridge's, I think you'll be just fine.'

She put the memory card in the slot on her laptop and downloaded the photographs while she packed away the rest of her equipment. Once she'd finished downloading the pictures, she saved the files. 'Is it OK for me to turn round now?' she asked with her back still towards Nick.

'Sure.'

Rather than putting on the ratty T-shirt and tracksuit

bottoms again, he was wearing the white tunic shirt—without the collar—the waistcoat and his court trousers.

Sammy's heart skipped a beat. Right now, with his formal dress very slightly dishevelled, he looked as sexy as hell. She could imagine him with the shirt undone, especially as she'd actually seen his bare chest. If his hair was ever so slightly longer and someone had ruffled her hand through it to suggest that he'd just been thoroughly kissed, he'd look spectacular. In fact he'd go straight to number one in the Sexiest Man in the World list. She itched to get her camera out again. And this time she'd make him pose very differently.

'OK?' he asked.

No. Not OK at all. She was all quivery and girly, and that really wasn't good.

So she'd have to fall back on acerbic humour to hide how she really felt. 'Sure. Lucky, lucky me—I get to have dinner with a half-dressed man.' Her mouth quirked. 'Are you really so vain that you couldn't go out to eat in an old tracksuit and T-shirt?'

'I'm not vain,' he protested. 'I just feel a little more comfortable in this than I do in the scruffy stuff.'

'It'd serve you right if I took you to a fast-food burger restaurant now—and then you'd really look out of place,' she teased.

'I'll bluff it. There's nothing wrong with burgers.'

Did he really expect her to believe that? She'd just bet he was the kind of guy who went for fine wines and Michelin-starred dining. 'When was the last time you went to a fast-food place?' she challenged.

'Last weekend, with my nephews,' was the prompt reply. 'Next question?'

Ouch. She'd forgotten about his nephews. If they

were teens, like her own nephews, then she knew he'd be very familiar with fast-food places. She screwed up her face. 'OK, now it's my turn to apologise. Blame my rudeness on low blood sugar. Because I am a grumpy, starving photographer right now.'

He smiled, and she wished she'd kept her mouth shut. Stuffy and uncomfortable, she could deal with, but relaxed and sexy was another kettle of fish entirely.

Right now, Nick Kennedy could be very dangerous to her peace of mind.

'Let's go and eat,' Nick said, 'and you can show me how much of an idiot I've made of myself.'

He hadn't made an idiot of himself at all. He was utterly gorgeous and he'd be the star of the calendar—even more so than the actor and the musician who'd posed for her earlier in the week, because they were aware of how pretty they were and Nick wasn't. But Sammy knew she needed to keep her libido under control. She'd learned her lesson well, after Bryn.

No.

More.

Relationships.

Make that underlined and with three exclamation marks. And covered in acid yellow highlighter to make sure she didn't forget it.

'My car's outside,' she said.

'So is mine.'

She took a coin from her purse. 'Let's toss for it. The winner gets to drive. Heads or tails?'

'Heads.'

It was heads.

'My car, then,' he said.

'Do you mind if I bring my equipment with me?' she

asked. 'I'd prefer not to leave it unattended, even if it's locked out of sight in my car.'

'It would make more sense,' Nick said, 'if we got a takeaway and ate it at my place. Then neither of us would have to worry about leaving expensive work equipment unattended in the car.'

'Why your place and not mine?'

He coughed. 'Because I just won the coin toss.' He paused. 'You can ring my sister and ask her to vouch for me, if you're worried about going to a stranger's flat.'

'A stranger who's willing to put himself out of his comfort zone to help raise money for an oncology ward, and whose day job means he skewers the baddies in court and gets them sentenced for their crimes? I think I'll be safe enough with you,' Sammy said. Plus all her instincts were telling her that Nick was one of the good guys, and her instincts—except when it came to dating—were pretty good. 'But I'll follow you in my car. That makes more sense than getting the Tube back here afterwards.'

'You won't have to get the Tube back here. I'll give you a lift.'

'So you're going to drive home, then back here, then home again? That doesn't make sense either.' She took her phone out of her bag. 'Give me your address, just in case I get stuck in traffic and can't follow you over a junction or something, and end up having to use my satnav.' She tapped in the details as he dictated them. 'Great. Let's go.'

'Can I carry anything for you?' he asked.

She indicated his armful of boxes and carriers. 'I think you've got enough of your own, and anyway I'm used to lugging this lot about.'

'Fair enough.'

She took the notice off the court door, told the security team that it was fine to lock up, and packed all her equipment into her car. And all the time she was berating herself mentally. She must be crazy. Why hadn't she just done what she'd agreed with her other models and emailed him a choice of half a dozen photographs that she could go on to present to the calendar committee? Why was she letting him review the whole shoot with her?

The truth was because she wanted to spend more time with him. Because she was attracted to him.

But she also knew that her relationships were a disaster area. She had a three-date rule, because agreeing to more than that risked her having to tell the truth about her past—and in her experience men reacted badly to the information. Besides, she was pretty sure that Nick Kennedy was a total workaholic who wouldn't have time for a girlfriend—that was still the only reason she could think of why someone as gorgeous and good-hearted as him would be single—so it was better not to start anything. So she'd be sensible and professional when they looked at the photographs. They'd grab some food; and then she'd say a polite goodbye and never see him again.

Pity.

But, since Bryn, Sammy had learned to be sensible. It was the safest way.

And she was never getting her heart broken again.

CHAPTER THREE

As HE DROVE back to his flat, Nick wondered if he'd just gone completely crazy. Why on earth had he invited Sammy Thompson back to his flat?

Then again, she'd had a fair point about not leaving expensive equipment unattended in a car. Horsehair wigs and silk barrister gowns weren't exactly cheap, either, and he wouldn't want to leave them in his car—just as she clearly hadn't wanted to leave her camera equipment in hers.

Out of the few dates he'd been on since the end of his marriage, he hadn't invited a single one of his girl-friends back to his flat. And he was far too sensible to invite a complete stranger back to his flat.

Yet that was exactly what he'd just done. Today was the first time he'd met Sammy. He knew practically nothing about her, other than that she was a photographer and she'd been commissioned to shoot the calendar by the Friends of the London Victoria.

Then again, he had good instincts—except perhaps where his ex-wife was concerned, he admitted wryly—and he'd liked Sammy immediately. She was business-like and capable, and she had a sense of humour that appealed to him.

And he was going to have to ignore the fact that she was utterly gorgeous. Slender yet with curves in all the right places, maybe six inches shorter than his own six foot one, and she was strong enough to carry heavy boxes of photographic equipment around without it seeming to bother her. Her bright blonde hair—which he was pretty sure was natural rather than dyed—was cut in a short pixie crop that framed her heart-shaped face, and her sea-green eyes were serious when she was working and teasing when something amused her.

Then there was her mouth. A perfect cupid's bow. A mouth that he'd wanted to trace with the tip of his finger before exploring it with his own mouth…

This was bad. He hadn't waxed poetic over anyone like this for years—maybe not since he was a teenager. So he'd better get it into his head that Sammy Thompson was simply the photographer who was working on the charity calendar, and he'd probably never see her again after today. Except maybe if the ward held some kind of launch event when the calendar went on sale and they both happened to attend it, and then they could just be polite to each other.

Be professional, he told himself. Treat her as if she's a client, or a colleague. Keep it business-like, choose the photographs, and then you can just let her walk out of your life and go back to what you normally do. Work, being there for Mandy and the boys, and more work. A perfectly balanced life.

Sammy was glad that she'd taken Nick's address and put the postcode into her satellite navigation system before they left the court's car park, because as she'd half expected she ended up losing him at a junction.

Following the satnav's directions, she ended up driving through one of the prettiest tree-lined streets in Bloomsbury, where the five-storey town houses all had wrought iron railings, tall white-framed sash windows that would let huge amounts of light flood into the rooms, and window boxes full of bright, well-manicured geraniums. She could see Nick's car towards the end of the street, and thankfully there was a parking space on the road behind it. Nick himself was waiting for her by his car.

When she climbed out of her car, Nick handed her a parking permit to place inside her windscreen. 'I'm sorry I lost you at that junction,' he said. 'I did slow down, but I couldn't see you behind me.'

'No worries,' Sammy said with a smile. 'That's precisely why I took your address.'

'Come in,' he said.

'And you don't mind if I bring all my stuff in?'

'That's fine.' He was still laden with his own cases, but even so he picked up the heaviest of her boxes and took it to the door of the Georgian house on the corner.

It was exactly the kind of building that made Sammy itch to get her camera out. The front door was painted black, with white columns and narrow bands of stucco either side to turn the entrance from a rectangle to a perfect square. Above the entrance was a filigree fanlight, the pattern within the arched window reminding her of a spider's web. The door knocker, handle and letterbox were all shiny brass, the front doorstep was scrubbed clean, and on either side of the step there was a bay tree in a black wooden planter, its stem perfectly straight and its leaves clipped into a neat ball.

Everything was discreet, tidy—and clearly wealthy

without being ostentatious about it. It was a house that had been looked after properly.

Clearly her interest showed on her face, because Nick smiled. 'You like the architecture?'

'It's gorgeous,' she said. 'I have to admit, architectural detail is one of my biggest weaknesses. Especially windows like that one.' She indicated the fanlight above the front door.

'Come on up and I'll give you the guided tour.' And then he looked slightly shocked, as if he hadn't meant to say that.

Tough. He'd said it now, and Sammy wasn't going to pass up the chance to look round such a gorgeous building.

'My flat's the ground floor and first storey,' he said.

'Not the whole house?'

He smiled. 'I live on my own, so I don't really need a whole town house. The flat gives me enough room for work, guests and entertaining.'

Though even a flat in a building like this—and in an area like this—would cost an eye-watering amount, Sammy thought. Especially a duplex flat. It would be way out of her own price range.

'Let's base ourselves in the kitchen,' Nick said. 'We can order some food, and then I'll show you round.'

'Sounds good to me.'

Nick's kitchen was small, but perfectly equipped. It had clearly been fitted out by a designer and it was the kind of shabby chic that didn't come cheap, with distressed cream-painted doors and drawer fronts, light wood worktops and pale terracotta splash-backs and floor tiles. There was a terracotta pot of herbs on one of the windowsills, and an expensive Italian coffee-maker and matching kettle, both in cream enamel; apart from that, everything was tucked neatly away.

Either Nicholas Kennedy was a total neat freak, or he didn't actually use this room much himself, she thought.

She set her boxes on the floor next to the light wood table at one end of the kitchen and put her laptop on the table itself. 'Is it OK to leave these here?'

'Sure.' Nick opened a drawer and brought out a file. Sammy had to bite her lip to stop herself grinning when she realised that his takeaway menus were all filed neatly in punched plastic pockets. She'd bet they were in alphabetical order, too.

Clearly he didn't have a clutter drawer with menus and all sorts of bits and pieces stuffed into it, unlike everyone else she knew. He was a neat freak, then. But that didn't mean he was totally buttoned-up. After all, he'd agreed to do a naked photo shoot. Someone totally stuffy would've refused to do that.

'Would you prefer Indian, Chinese, or Thai?' he asked.

'I eat practically anything,' Sammy said, 'except prawns. Fish, yes; crustaceans, no. Other than that, anything you like, as long as it's here as soon as possible.'

'Because you're starving. Noted.' He gave her a slight smile. 'How about a mix of Chinese dishes to share, then? And I promise, no prawns.'

'That'd be lovely.'

'Crispy duck?'

'Love it. Thank you.'

She set up her laptop while he was ordering their meal.

'They'll be here in forty minutes,' he said. 'OK. I promised you a guided tour.'

Sammy didn't quite dare ask if she could bring her camera. 'Lay on, Macduff,' she said with a smile.

'Living room,' he said, showing her through the first door.

Like the hallway, it had a stripped pale wooden floor. There were two huge sash windows dressed with floor-length dark green curtains; the walls were painted dark red and there was an antique-looking glass chandelier hanging from the high ceiling. It looked more like the effort of a designer than personal choice, Sammy thought.

The sofas were all low, upholstered in dark green leather and looked comfortable, and there was a light-coloured wooden coffee table in the middle of the room, set on a green silk patterned rug. There was a black marble fireplace with a huge mirror above it, reflecting the chandelier and the state-of-the-art television and audio-visual centre. Between the two sash windows, there was an enormous clock with a white face and dark roman numerals. There were plenty of silver-framed photographs on the mantelpiece, which she assumed were of his family.

But what really grabbed her attention was the painting on the wall. It wasn't exactly out of place, but she would've expected the designer to choose a couple of period portraits or maybe some kind of still life, to go with the rest of the decor. This painting was a modern landscape of a bay at dusk where the sea, cliffs and sky blurred together in the mist. It was all tones of blue and grey and silver—really striking. 'That's beautiful,' she said.

'Yes. I liked it the moment I set eyes on it,' he said.

So this was his taste rather than his designer's? She liked it. A lot.

Just as she had a rather nasty feeling that she could like Nick Kennedy rather a lot, if she got the chance. He was more than easy on the eye, and she liked what she'd learned about him in the short time she'd known him.

He ushered her in to the next room. 'My office.'

It was another room with dark red walls and stripped wood floors, but this time the curtains framing the two huge sash windows were cream voile and the patterned silk rug in the centre was dark red. The chandelier was wrought iron, and one wall was completely filled with books, most of which she guessed would be legal tomes. There was a desk against the opposite wall, teamed with what she recognised as a very expensive office chair— the kind she'd dreamed about owning but couldn't justify the price tag—and a state-of-the-art computer sat on his desk.

She could imagine him working here, with a bunch of papers spread out on the desk, his elbow resting on the table and his hand thrust through his hair while he made notes with a fountain pen. Because Nicholas Kennedy was definitely the kind of man who would use a posh pen rather than a disposable ballpoint.

'Dining room,' Nick said, showing her the next room.

Like the other rooms, the dining room had stripped floors; but it was much lighter because the walls were painted cream rather than dark red. There was a huge mirror above the white marble fireplace, reflecting the light from the sash windows and the antique glass chandelier. A light-coloured wooden table that seated eight sat in the centre of the room, teamed with matching chairs upholstered in cream-and-beige striped silk, which in turn matched the floor-length curtains. The silk rug here was in tones of cream and beige. She loved the room; she could just imagine sitting on the window-seat with a book, sunning herself while she read.

And there was another striking piece of art on the wall—a close-up of a peacock with its tail spread, and it looked as if it was painted in acrylics. 'The colours are glorious,' she said softly, enjoying the splash of orange among the turquoise, blues and greens. And it was so very different from the other picture; clearly Nick's taste was diverse.

But the artwork that really made her gasp was in his bedroom. The room was large, but for a change not painted dark red; it had blue and cream Regency striped wallpaper, floor-length navy curtains, stripped floors and a dark blue silk patterned rug to reflect the curtains.

She couldn't take her eyes off the black and white photograph that had been sliced vertically into three and framed in narrow black wood: a shot of the steel and glass roof of the Great Court at the British Museum. 'That's one of my favourite places in London.' And she had quite a few shots of that roof in her own collection. 'I adore that roof.'

'Me, too,' he said. 'It's the pattern and the light.'

'Did you know that no two panes of glass in the roof are the same?' she asked.

'No, but now you've said it, I'm going to have to look.'

'There are more than three thousand of them,' she pointed out. 'And the differences are tiny. It's only because of the undulations.' But the sudden light in his eyes now they were talking about art made her wonder. 'Did you ever think about being an artist or an architect rather than a barrister?'

He smiled. 'Absolutely not. I can barely draw a straight line with a pencil.' And then he changed the subject, making her wonder even more. 'Given that I already know you're starving, can I make you a coffee and offer you some chocolate biscuits to tide you over until the takeaway arrives?'

'That would be lovely. Thank you,' she said. 'Your flat's beautiful. Though I wouldn't have put you down as someone who'd choose dark red walls.'

'An interior designer organised most of the place for me just before I moved in,' he admitted. 'Maybe my living room and office are a little dark.'

Just a tad, but she wasn't going to be rude about it. '"Strikingly masculine" is probably the official phrase,' she said with a smile.

He ushered her back to the kitchen. She sat at the table and opened the file of photographs on her laptop while he made the coffee; and then he brought over two mugs of coffee and a plate of really good chocolate biscuits.

'Help yourself,' he said. 'And don't be polite. You said you'd missed lunch.'

'Thank you,' she said gratefully, and devoured two. 'These are scrumptious.'

'They're my sister's favourites,' he said. 'I keep a stock in for her.'

Nick was the kind of man who paid attention to details and quietly acted on them, she thought. She'd just bet he had a stock of his nephews' favourite treats, too. And the coffee was better than that served in most up-market cafés; though, given that posh coffee machine sitting on his kitchen worktop, it wasn't so surprising. If you had an expensive machine, it stood to reason that you'd use good coffee in it. 'Would you like to see the photographs now?' she asked.

'Sure.' He viewed them in silence, then nodded with what she was pretty sure was relief. 'You were very discreet. Thank you.'

'The point is to raise money, not to embarrass people,' she said softly. 'And it's meant to be fun, so I think we should discount this one, this one and this one—' she pointed to them on the screen '—as you look very slightly uptight in them.'

'Agreed,' he said. 'I have to admit, picking out your own photographs is a bit…' He grimaced.

'It makes everyone squirm. It's much, much easier to look at someone else's photographs and choose the best ones in a set than it is to choose your own,' she said.

'Which ones would you choose?' he asked.

'Honestly? This, this and this.' She pointed them out. 'Mainly because of the expression on your face. You look more relaxed here.' And really, really sexy, which was the whole point of the calendar. Selling pictures of hot men to make money for the ward. Not that she was going to say it; she knew it would make him uncomfortable.

'OK. I'm happy with those ones,' he said.

'Great.' She took the model release form from her bag. 'So we'll put the shot numbers in here.' She wrote them down. 'Would you like to check that you agree with the numbers before you sign?'

He smiled. 'You sound like a lawyer.'

'I sound like a professional photographer who likes to get things right,' she corrected.

He checked the numbers on the form against the numbers on her laptop, then signed the form. 'I'm impressed with what you did. Can I see any of the other calendar shots?'

Sammy shook her head. 'Sorry. Only the Chair of the Friends and the committee members she chooses to work with her on the project can see them until the proofs are printed,' she said.

'Fair enough. I was just curious.'

'About the other models?' she asked.

'About your work,' he said, 'given the way you re-acted to that picture of the British Museum's roof.'

'Ah. If you want to see my portfolio, that's a differ-ent matter entirely.' She pulled up a different file for him. 'Knock yourself out.'

He looked through them. 'You've got a real mixture here—lots of people and a few landscapes.'

'They tend to go with profiles of people in maga-zines and Sunday supplements,' she said. 'That's my bread-and-butter work. So if the profile is of someone who's set up an English vineyard, I'd take a portrait of that person and then whatever else is needed to illus-trate the interview or article. Say, the vineyard itself, or a close-up of a bunch of grapes, or the area where the wine's produced or bottled.'

'What about the photographs you take for you?'

'What makes you think I don't take these ones for me?' she parried.

'Apart from the fact that you admitted that they were work, it was the look on your face when you saw the house—as if you were dying to grab your camera and focus in on little details. Particularly the fanlight win-dow.'

'Busted,' she said with a rueful smile. 'Architecture's my big love—I never wanted to be an architect and create the buildings myself, but what I like is to make people focus in on a feature and see the building in a different light instead of just taking it for granted or ignoring it entirely.' And, although she'd never normally show her private shots to someone she barely knew, something about the way Nick looked at her made her want to open up. She went into another file. 'Like these ones.'

'They're stunning,' Nick said as he scrolled through them. 'And I mean it—I'm not just being polite. I'd be more than happy to have any of these blown up, framed and hung on my walls.'

She could see in his face that he meant it. And it made her feel warm inside. Some of her exes had scoffed at her private photography, calling her nerdy and not understanding at all what she loved about the architecture. And others had wanted her to give it all up so they could look after her—because a cancer survivor shouldn't be pushing herself to take photographs from difficult positions. Hanging off a balcony to get a better angle for her shot really wasn't the sort of thing a delicate little flower should do.

She'd wanted a relationship, not a straightjacket. And being protected in such a smothering way had made her feel stifled and miserable, even more than when the men she'd dated had backed off at the very first mention of the word 'cancer'.

'So when do you take this kind of shot?' Nick asked.

'When I get a day off, I walk round London and find interesting things. And sometimes I go to the coast—I love seascapes. Especially if a lighthouse or a pier's involved.'

'And you put your pictures on the internet?'

'I have a blog for my favourite shots,' she admitted.

'So did you always know you wanted to be a photographer?' he asked.

'Like most kids, I didn't have a clue what I wanted to do when I grew up,' Sammy said. 'Then, one summer, my uncle—who was a press photographer before he retired—taught me how to use a proper SLR camera.' Nick didn't need to know that it was because she'd been cooped up in one place, the summer when she'd had treatment for osteosarcoma; she'd been bored and miserable, unable to go out with her friends because she had been forced to wait for the surgical wounds to heal and to do her physiotherapy. Uncle Julian had shown her how she could get a different perspective on her surroundings and encouraged her to experiment with shots from her chair. 'I loved every second of it. And I ended up doing my degree in photography and following in his footsteps.'

'A press photographer? So you started out working for a magazine?'

'For the first couple of years after I graduated, I did; and then the publication I worked for was restructured and quite a few of the staff were made redundant, including me. That's when I decided to take the leap and go freelance,' she explained. 'Though that also means I don't tend to turn work down. You never know when you're going to have a dry spell, and I like to have at least three months' money sitting in the bank so I can always pay my rent.'

'And you do weddings as well?' He pointed to one of the other photographs.

'Only for people close to me. That one's Ashleigh, one of my best friends, on Capri last year.'

'It's a beautiful setting.'

'Really romantic,' she agreed. 'The bridesmaid is my other best friend, Claire. She and I went to the Blue Grotto, the next day. It was for a commission, I admit, but I would've gone anyway because the place is so gorgeous. You had to lie down in the boat to get through the entrance, but it was worth the effort. The light was really something else.' She flicked into another file and showed him some of the photographs. 'Look.'

'I like that—it's another of the sort of scenes I'd like to have on my wall,' he said.

She nodded. 'Like that misty seascape in your living room. That's the kind of thing I like to shoot at dawn or dusk. If you do it with a long exposure, the waves swirl about and look like mist.'

'That's clever,' he said.

She smiled. 'No. That's technique. Anyone can do it when they know how.'

When their food arrived, Sammy put her laptop away while Nick brought out plates and cutlery.

'Would you like a glass of wine?' he asked.

She shook her head. 'Thanks for the offer, but I'm driving so I'd rather not. A glass of water's fine, thanks.'

He poured them both a glass of water from a jug in the fridge—filtered water, she thought. Nick Kennedy clearly dotted all his I's and crossed every T.

'Help yourself,' he said, gesturing to the various dishes in the centre of the table.

'Thank you.' She noticed that he eyed her plate when she'd finished heaping it. 'What?'

'It's refreshing, eating with someone who actually enjoys food.'

'That sounds as if you've been eating dinner with the wrong kind of person,' she said dryly. 'Most people I know enjoy food.'

'Hmm.'

She finished stuffing one of the pancakes with shredded duck and cucumber, added some hoi sin sauce and took a taste. 'And this is seriously good. I haven't had crispy duck this excellent before. Nice choice, Mr Kennedy.' She paused. 'As we're going halves on this, how much do I owe you?'

'My house, my hospitality, my bill,' he said. 'No arguments.'

'Thank you.' Though there was more than one way to win an argument. Maybe she could print one of her seascapes for him, the one he'd really liked, to say thank you for the meal. 'So you like modern art rather than, say, reproductions?' she asked.

'Some. I'm not so keen on abstract art, which probably makes me a bit of a philistine,' he admitted.

'No, you like what you like, and that doesn't make you a philistine—it makes you honest,' she said. 'And your taste is quite diverse. I'm assuming they're original artworks, given that one of them is acrylics?'

He nodded. 'I like to support local artists where I can. There's a gallery not far from my chambers. The gallery owner gives me a call if something comes in that she thinks I'll like.'

'That's fabulous. It means both the artist and the art-lover win. Well, obviously, and the gallery owner, because she gets her commission.'

'Something like that.' He paused. 'Can I ask you something personal?'

Her heart skipped a beat. From his body language

and the way he'd relaxed with her, she had a feeling that the attraction was mutual. Was he going to ask her out?

And, if he did, would she have the courage to act on that attraction and say yes?

'Sure,' she said, affecting coolness.

'Your hair,' he said. 'What you said about me being in the military—is that why your hair's so short, too? You spent time in the Forces?'

The question was so unexpected that she answered it honestly before she realised what she was saying. 'No. I have a crop like this every two years.'

He blinked. 'Why two years?'

She could try and flannel him and say that it was a fashion statement, but he was observant. She was pretty sure he would've picked up the cues. 'Because it takes that long for my hair to grow twelve inches.'

He looked puzzled. 'Why do you need to grow your hair twelve inches?'

'Because seven to twelve inches is what they need for wigs,' she said softly.

The penny dropped immediately. 'You donate your hair?'

She nodded. 'There's a charity that makes wigs for kids who've lost their hair after chemotherapy. My sister Jenny and I have our hair cut together every two years. We normally get people to sponsor us as well, and the money goes to the ward so they can buy things for the kids. You know, things to keep them occupied and cheer them up, because being stuck in hospital isn't much fun—especially when you're a kid.' The hair cut before last had been on the actual day of Sammy's test results. She and Jenny had celebrated the news with a hair cut and a bottle of champagne.

'That's a really nice thing to do. I take it your sister's your connection to the ward?'

'Uh-huh,' Sammy said. It wasn't a total fib. Her sister was one of the connections. Just Sammy herself happened to be the main one. Not that Nick needed to know that.

'So that's why you're taking the photographs.'

She nodded. 'I take photographs for the ward every Christmas—so the families do at least get to have some Christmas pics together with their children, and with Santa for the younger ones. That's why Ayesha knew I was up to the job and would waive my fee, because I always do where the ward's concerned.'

'I assumed you were a photographic student who wanted to do it for his portfolio, and you'd been interviewed with half a dozen others.'

'No,' she said. 'Though you have a point about the portfolio. Maybe I should've given someone else the chance to work with me.'

'But then your styles would've been different,' he said.

'I guess. But I ought to think about that in future.'

When they'd finished their meal, Sammy refused the offer of more coffee. 'I'd better let you get on.'

Which Nick guessed was a polite way of saying that she needed to get on. And now, he thought, this was where she left and they'd say a polite goodbye, and they'd never see each other again.

Except his head and his mouth were clearly working to different scripts, because he found himself asking, 'When's your next day off?'

'I'm actually on holiday at the moment,' she said.

'I'm doing the last four shoots for the calendar tomorrow and the day after, but other than that my time's my own.'

'You're using your holiday to shoot the calendar?' And yet she'd said she was a freelance who never turned work down. Her time off must be precious.

She shrugged. 'It's not a big deal.'

But she wouldn't meet his eye. And she'd said that her sister was her connection to the ward. So maybe she'd made the same kind of silent bargain with Fate that he had, Nick thought—do the job and it'd keep her loved one safely in remission.

'So, thanks for dinner. And for being patient at the shoot,' she said. 'I know it can be a bit wearing, being told exactly how to stand and moving your head or your shoulders just a fraction.'

'You were very professional and made it easy,' he said, meaning it.

This was his cue to say goodbye. But his mouth had gone into reckless mode. 'Would you spend the day with me on Sunday?' he asked. 'Maybe we could have lunch, and you could show me some of the places you really like in London.'

'Urban hiking, one of my American friends calls it.' She smiled. 'I'd like that. OK. But there's a string attached.'

He frowned. 'What?'

'You bought dinner tonight, so I'm buying lunch on Sunday. No arguments.'

He wasn't surprised; Sammy had already struck him as someone who was seriously independent. He wasn't going to argue for now, but he'd find a way to get round her reservations on Sunday. 'OK. What time?'

'Half past nine?' she suggested.

'OK. It's a date.'

Even though he'd promised himself he wouldn't date again. Because Sammy Thompson intrigued him. And he wasn't quite ready to say goodbye to her yet.

CHAPTER FOUR

'So how was the photo shoot?' Mandy asked.

She sounded ever so slightly guilty, Nick thought. 'It was fine,' he reassured his sister. 'The photographer was nice. She put me at my ease, and she let me choose the shots to give to the committee.'

'*She?* But I thought…' Her voice trailed off.

'So did I,' Nick said wryly.

'Oh, no. It must have been so embarrassing, taking all your clothes off in front of a woman you'd never met before.'

Nick laughed. 'She was at pains to tell me before the shoot that she saw me only as a life model, not as a person.'

'Right.' Mandy sounded intrigued. 'So was she young? Old?'

'It's immaterial, Mandy. Don't even think about trying to match-make.' And no way was he admitting to his elder sister that he was seeing the photographer for lunch on Sunday. It probably wouldn't come to anything, anyway. By then his common sense would be back in place. He and Sammy would have a nice walk through the city together, talk about art and architecture, have lunch, and then not see each other again.

Except Nick discovered the next morning that his common sense was very far from being back in place. When he walked into the narrow lanes off Fleet Street to his chambers, he found himself looking at the buildings with a photographer's eye.

Sammy would love this area, he thought.

And she'd really love the hidden gem in the middle.

He couldn't resist texting her.

I have a bright idea for Sunday.

Details? she texted back.

Just bring your camera. Which Tube line are you on?

There was a short pause before she replied: Northern.

Meet you at Embankment Tube station at 9.30? he suggested.

Her reply was a smiley face and a slightly sassy note.

Hope good coffee is involved.

He grinned and typed back: It will be.

On Sunday, Sammy felt ridiculously nervous. This was her first date in months—and it was with someone whose working life and whole lifestyle were so very different from her own.

She'd liked Nick Kennedy instinctively. She was attracted to him. And it was definitely mutual.

But how would he react if she told him she'd had osteosarcoma as a teen?

She didn't think he'd be one of the men who ran

for the hills—his nephew had the same condition, so he'd understand instead of panicking at the c-word. But would he be overprotective, the way her family was, making a big deal out of every twinge she felt and worrying that it might be the first sign of something more sinister?

And, if he was close to his nephews, did that mean he liked kids? That maybe he'd want some of his own, some day? That could be a problem, because—thanks to the demands of her treatment—she might not be able to have kids in the future. There were possibilities, but no actual definites, because she'd had to have her eggs frozen before her first chemotherapy—and IVF didn't come with a cast-iron guarantee that it would work.

Part of her wanted to make up an excuse and call the whole thing off. Not because she was a coward, but because over the years her boyfriends' reactions to the complications had worn her down. It had left her feeling less of a woman and more of a freak.

Though part of her was intrigued by Nick. He was a man with a buttoned-down, highly respectable job, and yet he'd actually posed naked for a charity calendar. That took guts; and it also hinted at an unconventional streak.

So maybe this could even be the start of something good. She'd have to take that leap of faith and try to trust that it wouldn't go the same way as her last few relationships had.

Maybe Nick Kennedy was different.

But, until she knew him a little better and could work out what his reaction would be, she'd keep quiet about the fact that she'd had bone cancer and was in remission.

* * *

Nick's heart skipped a beat as he saw Sammy at the Tube station. Again, she was dressed completely in black, though this time her T-shirt was more of a vest top, in a nod to the warm September weather, and she wore a silver necklace decorated with deep green beads that matched the studs in her ears.

And she looked stunning.

Not that she seemed to realise she was turning heads. That was something else he liked about Sammy Thompson. She was just herself, comfortable in her own skin. And that in itself made her easy to be with.

He greeted her with a kiss to her cheek. 'So you're being the Mysterious Woman in Black again?' he teased.

She smiled at him. 'I never thought about it before but, yes, I probably do wear too much black. Sorry. I guess it's a hangover from art college.'

'Don't apologise. Actually, it suits you,' he said. 'And I like your jewellery.'

'The green stuff? It's malachite,' she said. 'One of my art school friends became a jeweller when she graduated. I love Amy's work—all the strong lines and the colours. She uses very different semi-precious stones, too.'

'My sister likes that kind of thing, and she's got a birthday coming up. Perhaps you can give me your friend's details and maybe she can design something for me,' he said.

'Sure I can. Remind me when we stop for coffee—and I haven't forgotten that you promised me good coffee.'

'I did indeed.' He smiled at her. 'Shall we?'

Together they walked out of the Tube station, then headed down the Embankment with the Thames on their right.

'So where are we going?' she asked as he turned left and took her into a maze of narrow passageways.

'This is Inner Temple—one of the Inns of Court,' he explained.

'Where you work?'

He was pleased that she'd realised that. 'Yes. We're not going to my actual office, but I thought you'd like to see some of the area around it.' He led her into a court-yard. All the way round, there were dark brick buildings with tall sash windows and stone doorways. At each end of the courtyard was a white stone arched entranceway, and in the middle were trees, slatted benches and stone troughs containing bright pink geraniums.

'This is absolutely gorgeous,' she said. 'Is it OK to take photographs here, or do I have to ask permission from someone?'

'It's fine as long as they're not for commercial use—then you'd need to talk to the media relations team first,' he said.

'Do you mind…?'

'Be my guest,' he said with a smile. He watched her as she looked around the courtyard and bent down to take various shots, moving position to change the angle of whatever had caught her eye. It had never occurred to him to do that; whenever he'd taken a photograph, he'd just framed a snap in the viewfinder.

Which was probably why his photographs were snaps and hers were a true art form.

'This was a really good choice, Nick,' she said. 'I like this place. A lot.'

And he thought that she might like what he was about to show her even more. 'Come this way,' he said, and led her through the archway. In the next courtyard was a church built of honey-coloured stone; part of it was completely round, with a smaller round tower perched on top.

'This is the original Crusader church in London—one of the four remaining round churches in England,' he said softly. 'And the reason I brought you here now is so you can explore it as much as you like before the Sunday service starts.'

'I had no idea this was even here,' she said, looking entranced. 'So we can actually go inside?'

He nodded. 'And it's got the Templar effigy tombs. I think you'll like them.'

She did. Not just the round church itself, but also the way the blues, purples and reds from the sunlight coming through the stained glass windows shone onto the dark marble pillars surrounding the Templar effigy tombs. This was her idea of the perfect day—and it had come from a very unexpected source.

'That's William Marshal. He served under four English kings, and was the regent for Henry III,' Nick explained as they stood in front of the tombs. 'Next to him is his son William.'

Stone effigies that were nearly a thousand years old, darkened by age, portraying knights wearing their mail armour, holding a shield and sword, with dogs at their feet. Sammy was entranced by them, particularly the little dogs, and took plenty of detail shots.

'I love this church. It's so peaceful,' she whispered. 'Though inside it doesn't look as old as it actually is.'

'It was badly damaged in the second world war during the Blitz,' Nick whispered back, 'so it had to be restored. But I can show you something really, really old.'

It turned out to be a Norman doorway with a rounded decorated arch, with beautiful geometric ironwork spreading across the wood. Again, Sammy took plenty of photographs, focusing on the details that caught her eye.

'Come with me,' Nick said, and took her into the gardens.

There was a long, tree-lined avenue that Sammy found irresistible, and she made him pose in the centre of it.

'This is the Broadwalk,' he said. 'The London plane trees were planted here in Victorian times.'

And in the Peony Garden there was an ancient wall and an iron railing with wisteria tumbling down it. 'It's amazing that these gardens are smack in the middle of the city and only a few steps away from the Thames,' Sammy said. 'They're stunning. I thought I knew London pretty well, but I had absolutely no idea they were here.'

'Most people don't—though the gardens are open to the public,' Nick said, 'and it's the perfect place to chill out on a summer lunchtime. If I'm not in court, I'll sometimes eat a sandwich out here. It's a good place to think, too, when you're stuck on some knotty legal problem.'

Sammy found the brass sundial in the centre of one of the gardens equally fascinating. 'Why is there a Pegasus in the middle of the sundial?' she asked.

'It's the symbol of Inner Temple. It's said that it was chosen for Robert Dudley.'

'The guy Elizabeth the First was in love with?'

'At the time, he was her Master of the Horse,' Nick said. 'He took part in the Christmas revels here in the middle of the sixteenth century, and his followers all wore the symbol of Pegasus. It's thought to come from there.'

'It's a beautiful piece of brasswork,' she said. 'Though I still think Dudley was a bit of a baddie. It was a little bit too convenient how his wife fell down the stairs and broke her neck. So did Amy Robsart trip or was she pushed?'

'We'll never know the truth,' Nick said.

She paused. 'Would you have defended Robert Dudley in a court of law if he'd been up on a charge of murdering his wife?'

He didn't hesitate. 'If I was asked to, yes.'

She looked at him. 'Would you defend someone you absolutely knew was a criminal?' Because that was something she really couldn't get her head round. 'How could you defend someone you knew was guilty?'

Nick smiled. 'That's the first question everyone asks a barrister. First of all, in law, everyone is presumed innocent unless proven guilty. Secondly, everyone has a right to representation and we're not allowed to refuse to represent someone just because we don't like them, or because we don't believe in their case,' he explained. 'Barristers work under strict rules of ethics, and we're subject to the law. So if my client's guilty, I can't say in court that he's innocent, and I can't call anyone to give false evidence on his behalf, because that's perjury— I'd be struck off.'

'So would he get away with it?'

'It's the prosecution's job to prove the case to a jury

so they're absolutely sure that the person in the dock committed the crime. The jury has to hear from both sides for the justice system to work properly,' Nick said. 'So as a barrister I care about my client having the same human rights and entitlements as anyone else.'

OK, so Nick was professional. But what about the ethics he'd spoken of earlier? What about doing the right thing? 'But if they'd admitted to you that they'd done whatever they'd been accused of?'

'Then I would advise them to plead guilty to the charge, because the truth would come out in court,' he said simply.

'And if they said they were still going to plead not guilty?'

'Then I could walk away, because my first duty is to the court. And I could also refuse to take the case if I was going to be a witness in the case, because there would be a conflict of interests.' He shrugged. 'Though sometimes innocent people appear guilty, and sometimes guilty people appear innocent, so it's really important that both sides are heard properly and all the evidence is put to the jury so they can reach a verdict.'

'So you wouldn't try to get your client off if they were guilty?' That made her feel better about the situation.

'Guilt isn't actually that black and white,' he said.

She frowned. 'How do you mean?'

'OK. Supposing I have a client—let's call him Tom—who's been accused of taking an expensive pen from a shop.'

'That's theft,' Sammy said promptly.

'Only if he intended to deprive the shop-owner of the pen permanently and dishonestly. Supposing he'd taken it accidentally and was on his way to give it back? Or maybe someone had threatened him—if he didn't take the pen, then that person would hurt someone he loved, which means he took it under duress. Or maybe,' Nick continued, 'Tom's only nine years old—which means he's under the age of criminal responsibility. Or he has dementia, to the point where he's not responsible for his actions and didn't realise he'd taken the pen.'

Sammy looked thoughtfully at him. 'So if Tom did take the pen, in those cases he wouldn't actually be guilty of theft.'

'Exactly. Guilt's a really tricky question,' Nick said. 'As I said, it's important that all the facts are known so the jury reaches the right verdict. Both sides have to be heard for the system to work properly.'

'You really love your job, don't you?' she asked. She could see his passion for it in his expression and hear it in the way he talked about it.

'Guilty as charged,' he said with a smile. 'Though not everyone gets that.'

If you had workaholic tendencies, it could play havoc with your relationships if your partner didn't understand how important your job was to you. Sammy knew that from experience. Was that why Nick was single? Because his girlfriends got fed up with coming second to his job all the time? Not that it was any of her business. She wasn't going to be pushy and ask. 'I really love my job, too,' she said, smiling back. 'There's nothing wrong with that.'

'I'm glad you get it,' he said softly. 'And there's something else I wanted to show you.' He took her back through to the maze of buildings.

'Old-fashioned street lamps,' she said with delight

when they came to a stop in front of one. 'They're gorgeous. I love that shape—like the lanterns you see on Christmas cards. I can imagine people bustling past wearing top hats and capes and crinoline dresses.'

'Absolutely right, because this is the Victorian bit. These are working gas lamps,' he said. 'It's really atmospheric at night—like being back in Dickens' time. In fact, there are several bits of Middle Temple that he described in his books.'

With the stucco-fronted buildings and the narrow passageways, she could imagine it. 'This is amazing. You work in such a beautiful area, Nick.'

'I'm very privileged,' he said. 'And I promised you good coffee. Do you think it's too early for brunch?'

Sammy glanced at her watch. 'Whoops. Sorry. I had no idea I'd spent so much time photographing things. I'm afraid I can get a bit carried away. I...' She blew out a breath. 'Sorry.'

'Hey, no need to apologise. It was my idea to bring you here, and I'm really glad you liked it as much as I hoped you would,' he said, his eyes crinkling at the corners.

'Coffee and brunch,' she said, 'is a great idea. And, remember, we had a deal. It's my bill. No arguments.'

He looked as if he wanted to protest but, to her relief, he nodded. 'OK. Let's go this way.'

Nick had had a feeling that Sammy was going to be stubborn about paying her share. So had her ex been the controlling type who never listened to her? He couldn't think of any reason why someone as vibrant and gorgeous as Sammy Thompson would still be single, other than that someone had let her down. Badly.

His own track record wasn't great. And he didn't believe in love. So it wasn't fair of him to let this continue, see where things took them—because the chances were that she'd end up hurt. They'd have lunch and then he'd find a nice way of saying goodbye. Because, after all, it wasn't her fault; *he* was the problem.

He walked alongside her, half lost in thought. His hand brushed against hers once, twice, making his skin tingle. The third time, he ended up catching her fingers loosely between his. She didn't pull away, but she didn't look at him or make a comment, either.

Shy?

Weirdly, he felt the same. Like a teenager holding hands with his girl for the first time. And it was a very, very long time since anyone had made him feel like that. Enough to make him rethink his earlier decision. Would it be so bad, seeing where things went? Would it necessarily mean that one or both of them would get hurt? Could he take the risk?

Eventually they reached the café he'd had in mind. 'Is this OK with you?' he asked.

She looked at the menu in the glass case by the door. 'Very OK, thank you. Though it's going to be quite hard to choose, because I like absolutely everything on the menu.'

Again, he found her attitude to food so refreshing; his last couple of dates had been with women who were so focused on watching what they ate that they forgot to enjoy it. Meaning that he hadn't enjoyed his food, either. And he'd made polite excuses not to see them again.

The waitress greeted them as they walked through the door, showed them to a quiet table for two, and took their order for coffee while she gave them time to browse through the menu.

In the end, Sammy sat back in her chair and sighed. 'I just can't decide between the hazelnut waffles with berries and Greek yoghurt, or the eggs Florentine—or the scrambled eggs with smoked salmon and sourdough bread,' she finished, looking rueful. 'And I don't quite have room for all of them.'

'There are two ways of sorting that out,' he said.

'Which are?'

'Either we come here for brunch again and the next time we choose whatever we don't have today,' he said. 'Or we order two different dishes and share them.'

Or, better still, do both. Because, the more he got to know Sammy, the more he liked her and the more he discovered that he wanted to spend time with her. Even though this wasn't the way he normally did things.

'If we share,' she said, 'what do you suggest?'

'The smoked salmon and the waffles.'

'Done,' she said. 'And freshly squeezed blood orange juice as well as the coffee.'

'Sounds perfect,' he said.

When the waitress came back, Sammy ordered for them. Nick wasn't quite used to that, but he rather liked her independent streak.

She sighed happily once she'd taken a sip of her juice. 'This is almost as good as Venice.'

'Venice?'

'When we had breakfast on the Grand Canal,' she said. 'It was amazing. We sat there watching the gondoliers at the stand next to us. One of them noticed and actually serenaded us—we loved it.'

'Who's "we"?' he asked.

'Me, Claire and Ashleigh. Claire and Ash knew each other from school, and I met Claire at art school—she was studying textiles and I was studying photography. We were the Terrible Trio.'

'Were?' he prompted.

'They're the ones in the wedding pictures I showed you. The bride and the bridesmaid in Capri—that was Ash getting married last year, and Claire got married in the spring this year.' She shrugged, and gave him a super-bright smile. 'Obviously I still get to spend time with them when I'm in London. But we won't be going on holiday together any more, just the three of us.'

Something she'd clearly miss. Meaning that Sammy was feeling just a little bit lonely right now? he wondered. He felt lonely, sometimes. When he woke at three in the morning, the bed feeling way too wide and nobody to cuddle up to. And then his father's words from all those years ago would echo in his head. *Love's not reliable, the way work is. Give your job your heart and you'll get to the top. Give love your heart and it'll just cheat on you and break you.*

With age and maturity, Nick had come to realise that his father had been speaking from hurt and anger at the disintegration of his marriage. And Edward Kennedy had never recovered from the divorce—he'd buried himself in work, and moved to Brussels to take his career ambitions further when Nick was halfway through his degree. Edward had done well for himself and reached the top of his particular tree, but Nick often thought his father was lonely and there was a gap in his life.

It wasn't the kind of life Nick wanted for himself—all work and no love. He'd wanted to have both. He'd met Naomi and she'd seemed to understand his drive to be the best at what he did. She'd encouraged him. He'd thought he had it all.

But then he'd come home early and found out that his marriage wasn't what he thought it was. His father's words had turned out to be all too true: because she'd cheated on him and broken his heart. Just like the way his mother had done to his father. Or maybe some of that had been his own fault, for paying too much attention to his work and not enough to his wife—even though at the time he'd thought she was OK with the hours he worked.

He pushed the thought away. Not here. Not now.

When their food arrived, Nick noticed that Sammy went straight for the waffles.

'Aren't you supposed to eat the savoury stuff first and then the sweet?' he asked.

She shook her head. 'Haven't you heard? Life's short, so eat dessert first. It's a good philosophy.'

He thought of Xander and guessed that she was thinking of her sister. Wanting to push away the sadness, he said, 'Can I be nosey and look at the photographs you took earlier?'

'Sure.' She took her camera out of her bag and handed it to him. Again, their fingers touched and adrenalin rippled through him. From the brief widening of her eyes, Nick thought it might just be the same for her, too. Instant attraction. Something he had a feeling neither of them really had time for. And yet something about Sammy made him want to explore this thing between them further. Even though he didn't do love any more. Or maybe it would be different with Sammy, because she loved her job as much as he loved his. And she was direct. He didn't think she'd say one thing and mean another, the way Naomi had.

'These photographs are amazing,' he said. 'I'd never really noticed the kind of details you picked out. The stonework, the windows, the ironwork. You've made me see my workplace in a completely different way.'

'It's what I do,' she said simply. 'The same as you made me think a bit differently this morning, when we talked about people being innocent or guilty.'

'It's what I do,' he said. 'Sammy, are you busy this afternoon?'

'I've got nothing planned. Why?'

He decided to take the risk. 'Because I've really enjoyed spending time with you and I'm not really ready for that to end just yet.'

'Oh.' There was the faintest slash of red in her cheeks. 'Me, too,' she said, her voice ever so slightly croaky.

'Given that we're just round the corner from Trafalgar Square, I'm tempted to suggest going to the art gallery,' he said. 'But it kind of feels wrong to take a photographer to an art gallery.'

She laughed. 'Don't worry about that. I never need an excuse to go to the National Portrait Gallery. That's not work. It's pure pleasure.'

'And you love your job anyway,' he finished.

'Like you. And I'm guessing you get nagged by your family as much as I do about overdoing things,' she said.

'My sister's favourite words are, "You work too hard."' He rolled his eyes. 'But how else are you really going to be good at your job and get to the top of your profession unless you put the hours in?'

'Absolutely. I guess in some areas you could get to

the top by nepotism, but it wouldn't mean that you were any good at your job,' she mused. 'And I want to be the best photographer I can be.'

Her views were so like his own. Nick had a feeling that he'd just met the one woman who might actually understand him. Then again, he'd made that mistake before. He'd thought that Naomi had encouraged his ambitions—to the point where he'd considered easing back on his hours to spend more time with her and start a family. And yet he'd ended up making the same error as his dad and his sister. He'd put his trust in someone who seemed to see things his way on the surface, but had a hidden agenda. Someone weak, who'd lied to get her own way.

'Nick?'

'Sorry. Wool-gathering.' He forced himself to smile. 'Let's go to the gallery.'

When she excused herself to go to the toilet, he asked the waitress for the bill. Except he discovered that Sammy had beaten him to it and already paid it on her way to the ladies'.

'Thank you for brunch,' he said when she came back to their table.

'Pleasure. But it was my turn anyway,' she said, 'because you bought the takeaway, the other night.'

He couldn't argue with that. But it was refreshing to be with someone who believed in fair shares instead of expecting to be treated all the time.

On the way to the National Portrait Gallery, they ended up holding hands again. This time, Sammy slanted Nick a sideways glance, at exactly the same time that he looked at her.

She burst out laughing. 'Is it just me, or do you feel seventeen again?'

'Something like that,' he said, and tightened his fingers round hers. 'I feel as if I should have greasy hair that's badly cut, acne, and be quoting terrible poetry at you.'

She laughed. 'I bet you were a beautiful teen.' And then she blushed. 'Um, that's with my photographer's head on.'

'I'll accept the compliment very happily,' he said. 'For the record, I bet you were a beautiful teen, too.'

'Nah. I was very ordinary,' Sammy told him with a grin.

He didn't believe that at all.

They spent the afternoon wandering round the gallery, and Sammy taught him how to read a portrait. 'The whole point of a portrait is to tell you about the subject. With the older paintings, the background's important and you need to look at what the person chooses to be painted with. In modern photographic portraits, you try to stop the background noise coming through and concentrate on your subject.'

There was a mischievous glint in his eye. 'I love it when you talk technical.'

She grimaced. 'Sorry. I can be very boring on my pet subject.'

'I'm not bored in the slightest. This is totally new stuff to me.' He smiled at her. 'Besides, I rambled on enough about law earlier.'

When she'd said how she loved her job, too. She'd understood something about him that Naomi never had. And it was crazy that it made him feel so warm inside.

'Do you have any portraits on display here?' he asked.

She laughed. 'Sadly, I'm not *quite* in the same league as David Bailey or Lord Lichfield. Maybe one day.'

'What's your favourite portrait you've taken?' he asked.

She looked thoughtful. 'I can probably name you half a dozen. But my absolute favourite is probably Freddy, the free runner.'

'You mean, one of those people who run around London and jump off rooftops?' he asked.

'According to Freddy, it's all about expressing yourself without limiting your movement—but yes, that's what it looks like. To get the interview and the portrait, the journalist and I went with him on a free run. He said you know who you are when you know how your body moves and what you're capable of doing. That if you learn to overcome obstacles in your environment you'll also learn how to overcome obstacles and stress in your daily life—and that fascinated me.'

'So you actually did the jumping off roofs bit with him?' Now that he hadn't expected.

'Not with my camera, no—the insurance would never have covered that kind of risk.' She smiled. 'But I did have a go when the journo looked after my camera.'

He raised an eyebrow. 'So are you brave, or are you a thrill seeker?'

'Neither,' she said. 'Life's short, so it's always worth taking the chance to experience something new, even if it seems a bit scary at first. Because that way you push yourself beyond your boundaries and you live life to the full—you don't get left with a pile of regrets at the end.'

'That's a good philosophy,' he said. 'So what's on your bucket list?'

For a moment he thought he saw her flinch. But it must've been his imagination. Or maybe it was a phrase that made her think about her sister. 'Sorry. That could've been phrased better.'

'Things I really want to do before I die.' She pursed her lips. 'Top of my list would be the chance to go to the edge of the earth's atmosphere—the bit where you see the blue curved line of space and all the blackness above. I'd love the chance to see that for myself and photograph it.' She looked straight at him. 'How about you? What's on your list?'

'Most of the places I want to see are in the middle of political turmoil right now,' he said, 'so it's not sensible to travel there. But on the doable list, I'd love to see the whales and polar bears in Canada. And see the Northern Lights.'

'Book the trip,' she said immediately.

Yeah. Except he wanted to share it with someone. 'When work isn't quite so busy,' he said, knowing that it was a feeble excuse.

'Being busy at work is fine,' she said softly. 'But it's important to remember to take time to play as well. To give yourself a chance to refill the well.'

Clearly his expression said that he thought that was totally flaky, because she grinned. 'I just believe in living life to the full. Work hard and play hard.'

He persuaded her to let him buy her coffee and cake in the gallery's café. When they'd finished, he said, 'May I see you home?'

'Thank you, Nick, but I'm an adult. I'm perfectly capable of getting myself home.'

There was a slight edge to her voice that surprised him. He'd thought they'd had a good time together. Clearly it was time to back off. 'Sorry. I was brought up to be a bit old-fashioned.'

'Courtesy—yes, I can understand that. Sorry for biting your head off.' She took a deep breath. 'Let's just say in the past my family's tried to wrap me up in cotton wool, and that drives me crazy.' There was a flash of panic in her eyes, gone so fast that Nick thought he might've imagined it. And then Sammy added, 'I guess it comes from being the baby of the family.'

Nick was the baby of the family, and nobody had wrapped him in cotton wool. When his mother's affair had come to light, his sister Mandy had been away at university and Nick had been left alone with his father—who'd been too hurt and angry to put a filter over his words. Edward Kennedy had said an awful lot of bitter, unhappy things that the teenaged Nick could've done without hearing.

He shook himself. Now wasn't the time to dwell on that. 'A photographer who's actually tried free running and dreams of going to the edge of space is the last person who'd want to be wrapped in cotton wool,' he said.

She looked relieved that he actually understood her. And then she looked him in the eye. 'We could always go for the compromise.'

'What's that?'

'Walk me to the Tube station?' she suggested.

'Works for me,' he said.

And he was pleased that this time she was the one to tangle her fingers with his as they walked.

At the entrance to the Tube station, he turned to her.

'I've had a really nice day. Thank you.' He bent his head, intending to kiss her politely on the cheek—but somehow his lips ended up brushing against hers. Once, twice. Clinging. Exploring the softness of her mouth, the sweetness.

And it made him feel as if an electric shock had run through him.

When he pulled back, he could see the shock and surprise in her own eyes, so clearly it had affected her in the same way.

'Nick. I…' The words dried up and she shook her head helplessly.

'Yeah. Me, too,' he said softly. And, because he could see just the faintest bit of panic on her face, he backed off. 'See you later.' Even though he had the strongest feeling that he might not. And he didn't look back once as he headed on the half-hour walk back to his flat.

Sammy really hadn't expected that kiss. She didn't think Nick had intended to kiss her like that, either. He'd probably been aiming for her cheek—just as she'd been doing. Except then they'd both turned the wrong way and their mouths had accidentally collided.

She brooded about it all the way home.

Part of her didn't want to risk another relationship where she'd get let down.

And yet she'd told him her view on life. *It's always worth taking the chance to experience something new, even if it seems a bit scary at first. Because that way you push yourself beyond your boundaries and you live life to the full—you don't get left with a pile of regrets at the end.*

Dating Nick Kennedy was a scary prospect. One she wasn't sure she was brave enough to handle. What if he was disgusted by her scars and it made him back away? He wouldn't be the first. And, even if he wasn't repulsed by her leg, would she be enough of a woman for him? It was a bone-deep fear that she hadn't even discussed with her sister and her best friends. She knew they'd tell her she was being ridiculous and they were probably right, but that didn't shift the fear. The fact that she'd have difficulty conceiving—that if she met someone who wanted to have a family with her, they'd have to go through IVF using her frozen eggs, and there was no guarantee it would work—made her feel less of a woman. In her head, she knew it was stupid, but in her heart she couldn't help worrying about it.

But, if she walked away from Nick, would she end up with a pile of regrets?

Was this sudden burst of loneliness just a reaction to the fact that Claire and Ashleigh had both got married and she was the only one of the Terrible Trio who was single now? Or was it something more?

There was only one way to find out.

She texted him.

Very carefully.

Thank you. I had a really good time today.

He took his time in replying.

Me, too.

Was he being polite? Or was he being wary, given that she'd bitten his head off so unfairly?

Bravery time again. And this would be their second official date, so it was safely within her three-dates-and-end-it rule. She could do this. Keep it casual. Unthreatening. She tapped into her phone.

Maybe we could do something next week, if you're free.

That was the crunch suggestion. If he made an excuse and backed off, so would she. If he didn't…then maybe they could have some fun together.

He took even longer replying, this time. And she only realised how tense she was when her phone beeped and she saw his message.

Day or evening?

Either. I'm still on holiday next week. Nothing planned.

His reply was swift.

Am in court for at least three days but can do evenings.

Good. How are you with heights?

Instead of texting her, this time he called her. 'What do you have in mind? Is this something to do with free running?'

'No. Just heights. Something off my bucket list that I hope you'll enjoy.'

'The top of the Shard?' he suggested. 'Sure. Heights aren't a problem.'

'Not the Shard. Something else,' she said. 'Dress casually. I'll text you with the times and directions when I've booked it. *Ciao*.'

And then she hung up before she made a fool of herself.

CHAPTER FIVE

ONCE SAMMY HAD booked tickets for the outing she'd planned, she sent Nick a cheeky text.

M'learned friend, do you possess such a thing as a pair of jeans?

Clearly he was in court, because he didn't reply until lunchtime. And then he called her rather than texted her. 'Of course I own a pair of jeans, Sammy. Why?'

'Because I need you to wear them when you meet me on Thursday night. Trainers would be good, too, but they're not essential.'

'Jeans and trainers? Why? What are we doing?'

'Something fun,' she said. 'Because as I told you before, I believe in working hard, but I also believe in playing just as hard.'

'Fair enough. Are you at least going to tell me the location, or am I supposed to be developing my mind-reading abilities?'

She laughed. 'North Greenwich Tube station. And that's all you need to know for now. I'll text you the time.'

'Hmm,' Nick said, but she could hear the smile in his voice.

* * *

When Nick met Sammy on Thursday evening, she did a pirouette in front of him. 'I hope you notice that I'm not wearing black today,' she said.

She was wearing faded jeans, which clung to her like a second skin, a hot pink T-shirt, and canvas shoes that matched her T-shirt. And Nick was slightly shocked to realise how much he wanted to carry her off to his flat and peel her clothes off her. Very, very slowly.

'You look very nice,' he said, hoping that his thoughts weren't showing on his face and that she hadn't developed mind-reading skills. 'So where are we going?'

'The O2 Arena. We're booked in for the sunset climb,' she told him. 'I've already bought the tickets and this is my idea, so don't even *think* about offending me by offering to pay. Got it?'

'Yes, ma'am,' he said, saluting and clicking his heels together.

'Good. I'm glad you know your place, m'learned friend.'

And he loved the teasing glint in her eyes. With Sammy, he was starting to rediscover his sense of fun—something he'd lost after the break-up of his marriage, except for the time he spent with his nephews. 'So we're actually walking over the top of the Dome?'

'Yep. You were the one talking about bucket lists. This happens to be on mine. One of my best friends is totally scared of heights, but you said you were OK with them, so I thought I'd dragoon you into doing it with me.' She paused and frowned. 'Oh, wait. You haven't done this already, have you?'

'No.' Though this was definitely something that his nephews would love to do, he thought. Maybe it was something he'd suggest doing with them. Maybe he'd ask Sammy to join them—though he didn't know whether she actually liked children. Plus it was way too soon to suggest meeting his family. This was, what, their second date? Yeah. Way too soon. They needed time to get to know each other, first.

Live for the moment, he reminded himself. 'I'm looking forward to this.'

'Me, too.' She looked gleeful. 'This is going to be huge fun.'

He agreed. Particularly because he was going to be sharing the experience with her.

After a safety briefing with the guides, they joined the rest of their group in putting on their climb suits and boots. Next they put on a harness with a latch that they'd been told to clip to the walkway; and finally they climbed the stairs up to the suspended walkway.

The person at the front of the line stumbled partway up the steep incline, and the walkway rippled with the impact. The person in front of Sammy stopped dead, clearly worried, and Sammy had to stop short.

Nick almost collided with her and rested his hands on her shoulders to steady them both. 'OK?' he asked Sammy.

'I'm fine,' she said. 'Apparently this happens a bit, especially on the way down. I'm sure we'll both be fine.'

The gradient levelled out, and finally they found themselves in the viewing platform on the centre above the Dome. Sammy took her mobile phone out of her pocket and took snaps of the panoramic view. Nick recognised the cable car, Canary Wharf, the Shard and the Gherkin, along with Royal Greenwich and the sculpture at the Olympic Park.

But best of all was the sunset, just to the side of the buildings of Canary Wharf. He could see exactly why this had been on her bucket list. It was a photographer's dream view.

'This is an amazing view,' he said.

She beamed. 'I hoped it would be like this—and I love the way all the skyscrapers are lit up, too, now it's dusk. Hey, can I take a selfie with you?'

He laughed. 'That sounds *really* weird coming from a professional photographer.'

'Don't knock it. A good selfie can still be a good shot. If you hold your arm out far enough and zoom in, then you're not going to end up with a bulbous nose or big ears.'

'Bulbous nose?'

She laughed. 'Like that shot where the monkey stole that camera from the photographer and managed to take a selfie. I've seen a few of those in my time.' She took a few snaps of them together on the edge of the walkway, with the iconic masts from the Dome sticking out on either side of them. And Nick enjoyed the fact that he got to put his arm round her, even if they were both in climb suits and he wasn't actually touching her skin.

'So now we're up here,' Sammy said to their guide, 'do we get to do the James Bond bit now, minus the bullets?'

'Sliding down the side of the Dome, you mean?' He laughed. 'I'm afraid that would be a no.'

'Pity,' she said, and clipped her harness back on the walkway to start the descent.

At the bottom, once they'd changed out of their climb suits and boots and walked away from the area, Nick teased, 'What with your yen for outer space, the free running stuff and now this, I think you were totally bluffing about bravery and you're really a thrill seeker at heart.'

'No. The free running stuff was work, anyway, and I haven't actually done it since. I just think it's a good idea to get out of your comfort zone every so often, because life is short and you need to appreciate every second of it,' she said. 'In fact, I have a very good idea right now…' She stood on tiptoe, cupped his face with her hands, and pressed her mouth to his.

Her lips were warm and soft and she tasted of strawberries. And Nick couldn't help responding, wrapping his arms tightly round her and nibbling at her lower lip to persuade her to deepen the kiss.

Sammy Thompson made his head spin.

And he couldn't remember the last time he'd reacted so strongly to someone. He'd always thought of himself as careful—that he'd get to know someone over a few months before going to bed with them. But Sammy made him want to take all his brakes off and he wanted to make love with her right now. He wasn't sure if that was more exhilarating or frightening.

'Great idea,' he said when she finally broke the kiss. 'Apart from the fact that my head's totally scrambled now, thanks to you.'

'So you're outside your comfort zone?' she asked.

'Yes and no.' He stole another kiss. 'I think I could get to like this very much indeed. You?'

She fanned herself. 'I don't normally do this sort of thing with complete strangers.'

'We're not complete strangers now. Plus you've seen me naked,' he pointed out, 'which puts you at rather an unfair advantage.'

To his amusement, her face went bright scarlet, clashing with her T-shirt. 'Nothing untoward was on show when you modelled for me,' she reminded him.

'I was naked, so it still counts. And I think this means I need to get to see you naked, to even things up.'

Her eyes were sparkling. 'Oh, do you now?'

He pulled her closer and nibbled her ear. 'That was the best idea I've had all day.' She was still deliciously pink. And he noticed that she wasn't making excuses and backing away. Anticipation skittered through him. Were they both about to break their own rules and fast-track to the next stage?

'I think we should feature you on the front cover of the calendar,' she said thoughtfully. 'Because, with your bare chest and your abs, we'll sell tons of copies for the ward.'

Which answered his question. This was teasing banter, not a statement of intent. Best to keep it playful, then. He groaned theatrically. 'OK. Shutting up now. Do you have to rush off, or shall we have dinner?'

'Dinner would be good,' she said. 'Shall we go to one of the restaurants here?'

'Here's fine. And dinner's on me, seeing as it was my idea and you bought the tickets to the climb.'

'Thank you,' she said with a smile.

They went to one of the bars inside the Dome, and looked through the menu.

'You're going to choose dessert first, aren't you?' he asked.

She wrinkled her nose. 'Yes, but it looks as if most of the puddings on the menu are chocolate.'

'Problem?' he asked.

She nodded. 'I hate chocolate puddings.'

'You don't like chocolate?' He was surprised. Every female he knew loved chocolate.

'No, I love chocolate,' she said, 'but I don't like chocolate puddings or chocolate ice cream. And I already know that makes me weird. I've been told that often enough.'

He grinned. 'Someone rather wise once told me that you like what you like and it doesn't mean you're a philistine—or, in this case, weird.'

She laughed back, clearly recognising that he was throwing her words back at her. 'I guess.'

She chose the salted caramel cheesecake—the only non-chocolate pudding on the menu—and they ordered a mix of sharing plates between them: ginger and lemon chicken, pulled pork, sweet potato fries, quinoa salad and stuffed peppers.

'What do you want to drink?' he asked.

'They can apparently mix a cocktail to suit you,' she said. 'And I'm really torn between a glass of Prosecco and a cocktail.'

'You could always have a cocktail based on Prosecco, and that way you get the best of both worlds,' he pointed out. 'Why not ask the barman? And I'll join you.'

Once they'd told the bartender what they'd chosen to eat, and Sammy explained that she wasn't much of a spirits drinker, he made them a cocktail of Prosecco mixed with ginger liqueur and limoncello.

'Excellent choice, m'learned friend,' she said to Nick with a grin after the first sip. 'I like this.'

'Me, too,' he agreed.

The food was just as good but the company was even better. Nick found himself relaxing with Sammy, laughing and talking about a complete mixture of subjects. Every so often, his fingers brushed against hers as they chose something else from their sharing platter, and adrenalin fizzed through his veins.

Plus there were those kisses. He couldn't get them out of his head. Her mouth was beautiful, her lips soft and warm, and he wanted to kiss Sammy again. Explore her. Find out where she liked being touched, where she liked being kissed. What made her curl her toes with pleasure.

There was definitely something special about Sammy Thompson. But would she be prepared to take a chance on him? Nick still hadn't worked out why she was single. She was bright, she was charming, and she made him see the world in a slightly different way. Someone, he guessed, must have hurt her and made her wary of relationships.

But maybe she could learn to trust him.

And maybe he could learn to trust her.

Because she wasn't like Naomi. Sammy struck him as very straightforward and honest. She wasn't the sort to spin a web of lies and turn someone into the bad guy when he hadn't actually done anything wrong.

After their meal, they walked hand in hand back to the Tube station. 'Sammy, I know you're old enough and tough enough to look after yourself, but this time will you please let me see you home to your front door?' he asked. At her raised eyebrows, he gave her a rueful smile. 'OK, I admit—it's because I've enjoyed tonight and I want to spend a few more minutes with you, and seeing you home feels like a good excuse.'

'And once you see me to my front door, then I'm supposed to invite you in for coffee?' she asked.

'It's not essential,' he said, 'though it would be nice.' He paused. 'And, if you offered, I'd accept.'

'Even though the coffee's not going to be made with a posh Italian coffee machine like yours?' she tested.

He laughed. 'You could give me a chipped mug of decaf instant coffee made with long-life milk that was almost out of date and that would be absolutely fine.'

She laughed back. 'No way—with a coffee machine like yours, you're used to the best and you might even verge on being a coffee snob. And none of my mugs are chipped, thank you very much.'

But she agreed to let him walk her back to her front door. It turned out that she lived in a small flat in Camden, among a row of terraced houses painted ice cream colours. Cute—and the area suited her, he thought. Vibrant, with something interesting round every corner.

'I'll give you the guided tour of the flat,' she said. 'It's going to take us all of two minutes—and that's provided I talk a lot while I show you round.'

He smiled. 'Sounds good to me.'

She hadn't been exaggerating that much; her flat was compact and much, much smaller than his. All the floors were stripped and varnished wood, but that was the only thing their flats had in common. Her walls were all painted cream and the windows had neutral-coloured roman blinds rather than floor-length curtains. Though he guessed that made it easier to focus on the artwork; there were framed photographs grouped together on the walls that seemed to have either a similar theme or a similar colour.

'Are these all your own pictures?' he asked.

She nodded. 'I change them round every so often.

But it's nice to use the shots rather than just leave them languishing out of sight on my hard drive.'

Her kitchen was open plan. 'I guess it's fairly self-explanatory—I use the dining table as a desk as well as to eat,' she said.

'It's a nice room,' he said. 'Comfortable.' The other half of the room was the living room and contained a sofa, a stereo system, a bookcase, a cupboard where he guessed she kept most of her photographic equipment, and a small television.

Her bathroom was only just big enough to contain a bath with a shower over it, the toilet and a sink; there wasn't a window, but the room was small enough for the overhead light to keep things bright. Her bedroom was equally bijou, with just enough room for a double bed with an iron frame, a small pine bedside cabinet, and a matching chest of drawers and wardrobe.

And he suddenly had the clearest picture of being in that double bed with her, curled up together and talking after they'd made love. Her face would be flushed with passion and her eyes sparkling. And he couldn't resist spinning her into his arms and kissing her until he felt dizzy.

'Well, now,' she said when he broke the kiss, sounding flustered.

'Sorry.'

She lifted an eyebrow. 'Are you?'

'For kissing you, no,' he admitted. 'For being pushy, yes.'

She smiled and stroked his face. 'I don't think either of us knows how to handle this. I don't usually invite men home after a second date. But here you are.'

'I don't usually invite complete strangers home, either,' he said. 'But I invited you back to my place after the shoot.'

She laughed. 'You don't strip off in front of strangers, either. But you did for me.'

It would be oh, so easy to pick her up and carry her to her bed. Suggest that he stripped for her again. Better still, suggest that she undressed him. Very slowly. With a lot of kissing in between.

But rushing things would just make life way too complicated.

He needed to cool things down. As in right now, before he did something reckless and they both got burned. 'Talk to me,' he said. 'Tell me about your job. Does it mean a lot of travelling?'

'I go wherever the photograph needs to be taken,' she said, ushering him back to her living room and then switching on the kettle to make coffee. 'Sometimes it's in London, but often it's further afield.' She lifted a shoulder. 'I've done some work in LA, some in New York, and some on various film locations. The best bit is when I get a chance to explore while I'm away and take some shots for myself, too.'

'Like your architectural stuff?'

She nodded. 'And seascapes.'

'So do you have a dark room and an office somewhere?' he asked.

She shook her head. 'Most of my work is digital, so I don't really need a dark room. But occasionally I borrow my uncle's, if I've been experimenting with arty shots and want to do it the old-fashioned way. There's something special about watching the shot develop on the paper.'

'And is it like they show you in the movies, with trays of liquids and a red light?'

'It's called a safe light, and it can be brown or red,' she said. 'Basically, ordinary light will ruin any unexposed film or photographic paper, whereas safe light means that you can see what you're doing but it won't wreck your work.'

'Sounds like a sensible solution,' he said.

'Though you don't have to have a special room to be a dark room,' she said. 'My bathroom doesn't have an outside window, so in theory it wouldn't take much to turn it into a dark room, provided I block out all the light round the door. And I could use my bath as a bench for the chemicals.'

He looked at her, surprised. 'But wouldn't they ruin your bath?'

'No, because you wash the chemicals away too quickly for them to do any damage—besides, the bath is the same kind of plastic as the trays.'

'So how does it work?'

'Basically you have four trays set up,' she explained. 'You expose the photographic negative onto the paper—the length of time you expose it controls what you see on the final image—and then you put the paper into developer trays so you can actually see the image. Once it looks exactly how you want it, you move the paper from the developer tray to the stop bath, so the picture doesn't develop any more. From there you move the paper to the fixer so you can look at the image in normal light later without it being ruined; and finally you rinse the paper in water to get rid of the last bits of chemicals.'

'And then you peg it up on a line to dry?' he asked.

'Just like in the movies. Yup.' She smiled. 'Actually, I love making black and white prints. I could take you to Uncle Julian's and show you how it's done sometime, if you like. It's magical when you see the image emerging, like a ghost at first and then getting stronger. And it's fun playing about with different contrasts, and different sorts of paper.'

'No. You have a passion for your job,' he said softly, 'and it shows.'

And he really wanted to see that passion in her eyes again.

Except he wanted to be the one to put it there. Like he had when he'd kissed her a few minutes ago.

When she finished making coffee, she came to join him on the sofa and set her mug on the floor. And that was the perfect cue for him to slide his arm round her shoulders. From there it was easy to twist round to face her, and to brush his lips against hers. Her mouth was soft and sweet and giving, and she slid her hands round his neck to draw him closer.

The next thing he knew, he was lying full length on her sofa, she was lying on top of him, and his hands were splayed against her back, underneath her T-shirt.

Her skin was so soft, so warm. Touching wasn't enough. He wanted to see, too.

Which was crazy. He never behaved like this, so out of control. He didn't do love. And he didn't want to hurt Sammy. He should back off. Now.

Except he couldn't.

He blew out a breath. 'Sorry. I'm taking this a bit too fast again.'

Her face was flushed and her eyes were sparkling. 'You and me both.'

'I'm sorry. I don't normally behave like this,' he said.

'Neither do I.' Her face was rueful. 'I might say outrageous things, but I don't tend to walk the talk,' she admitted.

'There's just something about you that makes me want more than I should ask for,' he said softly, holding her closer because he wasn't quite ready yet to relinquish the feel of her skin against his fingertips.

'Me, too. But, Nick, this probably isn't a good idea. Our lifestyles are too different.'

'Actually, they're probably too similar,' he corrected. 'We're both workaholics.'

'I guess so.'

He stole a kiss. 'So maybe it could work between us. But I agree. We need to cool this very slightly. Much as I'd really like to scoop you up and take you to your bed right this very minute—and believe me I've wanted to do that all evening—I can't do that, because I don't actually carry condoms around with me.'

'I don't have any either.'

His heart skipped a beat. Was she saying that, if she'd had condoms, she would've been fine with him taking her to her bed? For a second, he couldn't breathe.

'Rain check,' she whispered, and climbed off him.

The sensible thing, Nick thought, would be for them to sit at opposite ends of her sofa. Except her sofa was so compact that even when they tried it in tacit agreement, they were still close enough to touch.

Take it down a notch, he told himself, and took her hand instead.

'I'm trying to take it slower,' he said by way of explanation.

She smiled. 'OK. Let's pick a safe subject. We did something on my bucket list this evening. What's on yours, apart from polar bears, whale-watching, the

Northern Lights and some places that are too dangerous for tourists?'

Making love with you.

Not that he was going to say that out loud.

And he was still a bit stunned that she'd actually remembered what he'd told her.

He thought about it for a while. 'A proper afternoon
tea in a very posh hotel,' he said. 'With a cake stand
and a silver teapot and someone playing the piano in
the lobby.'

'Oh, come off it,' she scoffed. 'You're a barrister
and you work in the middle of London. You must've
done that before.'

'Actually, no. My clients don't generally tend to take
me to tea at a posh hotel,' he said mildly, 'and in the af-
ternoons if I'm not in court then I'm in my chambers,
up to my eyes in paperwork. If I'm *very* lucky I might
be able to sweet-talk my clerk Gary into making me a
mug of tea—but usually we take turns, so whoever puts
the kettle on in the kitchen usually checks to see who
else wants a cuppa.'

'Seriously? You don't have a secretary?'

'Barristers have clerks,' he said. 'The clerks are responsible for the admin and business activities of the
chambers. So Gary would do some secretarial things,
like arranging meetings, invoicing solicitors for fees
and planning case timetables in detail, but he also looks
after three more barristers as well as me. He doesn't
have time to wait on my every whim—and he wouldn't
do that anyway,' he admitted with a grin. 'If I asked
him to go and put the kettle on, he'd tell me I was old
enough and ugly enough to make my own cuppa, he
was already busy making phone calls on my behalf,

and his is white with three sugars while I'm at it, thank you very much.'

'Right.' She smiled as if she was imagining the scene, then looked at him. 'I can't believe you've never had a proper posh afternoon tea.'

'I take it you have, then?' he asked.

'Oh, yes.' Her eyes lit up. 'Birthdays, red letter days, and any other time I can find an excuse to do it.'

'Seriously?'

'Provided the cake isn't chocolate. Then I have to talk people into swapping with me. But posh tea, dainty finger sandwiches, scones with jam and clotted cream, yummy little savouries… Yeah, I love all that. It's so decadent and such a treat. Like going out for breakfast. I think I'd rather do that than go out for dinner, even. It feels more special.'

He'd enjoyed sharing brunch with her. And he had a feeling that this particular item on his bucket list would be even more enjoyable if he shared it with her, especially as she sounded so enthusiastic about it. 'Right then, Ms Thompson, would you like to come to afternoon tea with me?'

'Thank you, m'learned friend, I would,' she said.

'Good. When?' He took his phone out of his pocket and checked his diary. 'This weekend?'

Sammy grabbed her phone to check her diary, too. 'Sorry, I can't. I'm in Somerset doing a shoot with an organic cider producer.'

'OK.' He checked the next week. 'How's Wednesday afternoon looking for you?'

Sammy nodded. 'I've got a planning meeting at one of the magazines in London that morning, so Wednesday afternoon is pretty much perfect for me.'

'Great. I'll book something tomorrow and let you know where and what time,' he said. 'Call me if there's a problem and we'll reschedule if we need to.'

'OK. That sounds good.'

'And I'd better let you get on.' He stood up, and she saw him to the door.

He kissed her goodbye, being careful to keep his libido in check. 'See you on Wednesday,' he said.

And he could hardly wait.

CHAPTER SIX

WEDNESDAY.

A seriously posh hotel.

For afternoon tea.

Panic flooded through Sammy the more she thought about it. Given that kind of venue, she could hardly turn up in her usual black trousers. But a business suit with opaque tights wouldn't be appropriate, either; they were having an Indian summer, even though it was late September. Wearing a floaty cotton dress meant having bare legs or wearing the sheerest tights; and either of those options would mean that the scar on her left leg would be clearly visible.

Even though Nick would probably be too nice to ask her what had caused the scar, she'd know that he was wondering about it. Or maybe he'd recognise it as something that he'd seen before, on his nephew's leg. And in the end she'd cave in and tell him that she'd had a strange bony lump on her shin as a teen, and when it had been investigated the doctors had told her that she had osteosarcoma.

Bone cancer.

Chemotherapy had shrunk the tumour before the operation, and the surgeon had been able to take out the tumour from the bone and put in a metal prosthesis. Sammy knew she'd been one of the lucky ones, able to have bone-sparing surgery rather than an amputation. She'd done every single breathing exercise and every single physiotherapy exercise to the letter after the operation. She'd been through more chemotherapy to mop up any last bad cells after the operation and she'd attended every single one of her regular check-ups. And she was hugely grateful that she'd come through it.

She was strong. She had the full support of her family.

And when she'd met Bryn, she'd thought she'd finally found someone different.

But instead he'd gone on to break her heart. He'd asked her to marry him just before she'd had her scare, two years before. And then he'd ended it the day she'd got the results. He'd admitted that he couldn't cope with the prospect of her having cancer again, but he hadn't wanted to be the bad guy who'd dumped the cancer patient. Instead, he'd waited until they knew she was clear—and then he'd dumped her.

Just as well they hadn't actually chosen the engagement ring.

Sammy had walked away with her head held high and her heart feeling as if it had been ground into sand. And she'd promised herself she'd never make the mistake of getting that close to anyone again. Yet, right now, she was taking a huge risk. This would be her third date with Nick—and she didn't have an exit strategy in place.

She dragged in a breath. Nick's nephew had been diagnosed with osteosarcoma, so maybe Nick would understand more than the average person.

But what if he didn't?

What if it made him back away? What if she repulsed him?

Even Bryn—who'd been engaged to her—hadn't coped with her scars. Not really. They'd always made love with the lights off, and he'd been careful never to look at her leg or touch it. She'd pretended that it didn't matter…but it had.

And it mattered now.

She really wasn't ready to tell Nick about her past yet.

She didn't want to call off their date, either; given that she'd already told him how much she liked going out for afternoon tea, she knew he wouldn't believe a feeble excuse. And, being a lawyer, of course he'd ask questions.

Probing ones.

Ones where even a silent reaction would help him to see the truth.

Sammy still hadn't worked out how to deal with the situation by the time she met up with her best friends for a long-planned evening with pizza at her flat.

Except Ashleigh and Claire had known her for long enough to guess that something was wrong.

'Spit it out,' Claire said.

'What?' Sammy asked, feigning innocence.

'You're very quiet. Which isn't you, unless you're concentrating on a shoot. So talk to us,' Ashleigh said. 'That's what best friends are for. To listen, to tell you when you're being an idiot, and to give you a hug when you need one.'

Sammy actually felt tears pricking her eyes at

Ashleigh's words, and was cross with herself for it. For pity's sake. She wasn't one of those people who bawled their eyes out at the drop of a hat.

'Did you find another lump?' Claire asked softly.

'No. Why does everyone *always* assume it's the cancer come back, if something's bothering me?' Sammy asked, losing her cool.

Ashleigh and Claire immediately put down their cutlery, stood up and enveloped her in a hug.

'We're not assuming anything,' Ashleigh said, stroking her hair. 'But we've known you for years, we can see you're upset, and we want to be here for you.'

'It's just something stupid.' Sammy swallowed hard to keep the tears back. She wasn't weak. She was independent and strong. She could do this.

'Then it's something we can help you with—and make you laugh about,' Claire pointed out. 'Don't push us away. There's a fine line between being independent and being too stubborn, you know.'

She and Ashleigh returned to their chairs, but each of them kept hold of one of Sammy's hands.

'I don't know what to wear on a date,' Sammy muttered.

'OK,' Ashleigh said carefully. 'Where are you going, and is it a first date?'

'Afternoon tea at a posh hotel.' Sammy knew this was something she should have told them about before. Because they were her best friends and they had her best interests at heart. They wouldn't judge her. They never had. 'Third date.'

Claire and Ashleigh exchanged a glance. 'Is there going to be a fourth?' Claire asked.

Was she going to break her three-date rule for Nick?

'I don't know.' She wanted to. And she didn't. All at the same time. 'It's driving me crazy,' she admitted.

'Tell us about him,' Ashleigh said.

So Sammy found herself spilling the beans. How she'd taken Nick's photograph for the charity calendar, then ended up having dinner with him—which didn't count as a date, because then that would mean that afternoon tea was the scary fourth—and they'd seen each other a couple of times since.

'Does he know about your leg?' Claire asked.

Sammy shook her head. 'It hasn't been the right time to talk about it, yet.'

'If he's involved with the calendar, he must have a connection to the ward,' Ashleigh suggested.

'Yes. His nephew had osteosarcoma,' Sammy said.

'So he'll understand,' Ashleigh reassured her. 'If you're even thinking about a fourth date with him, Sammy, it's serious. So you're going to have to tell him.'

'And you have to do it before you end up naked with him and he sees the scar,' Claire added.

Ice slid down Sammy's spine. 'Because you think he'll reject me when he sees it?' That had happened before. A mistake she'd made three times until she'd learned to keep it to herself. Until Bryn, who'd made her trust him...and then let her down even more than the run-for-the-hills boyfriends.

'No, of course not. I mean because when you have sex with him for the first time you want to enjoy it, not worry about having to explain your medical history to him beforehand,' Claire said, rolling her eyes.

'And if you think he's not going to see you for who you are, then you shouldn't be thinking about having sex with him anyway—because in that case he's not good enough for you,' Ashleigh added firmly.

'I know.' Sammy rubbed a hand over her short crop. But even if her hair had been at its longest, she wouldn't have been able to hide behind it because her best friends knew her so well. 'He's a good man—he's ethical and honest.'

'Unlike a certain person I'd like to stake out in a field of fire ants while he was covered in honey,' Claire said darkly. Sammy knew she was referring to Bryn.

'Why can't you wear your usual black trousers, maybe with a top that's a bit more dressy than usual?' Ashleigh asked.

'Because it's the kind of place where I need to wear a dress.'

'Where are you going?' Claire asked.

When Sammy told them the name of the hotel, they both whistled.

'The afternoon tea there is meant to be amazing,' Ashleigh said. 'You have to go and tell us so we can live vicariously through you. Don't chicken out.'

The problem was, Sammy wanted to chicken out. This was the third date. Crunch time. And she knew she was making a fuss about what to wear so she could avoid facing the real reason why she didn't want to go—that she was afraid it would all go wrong and she'd end up hurt again.

'Actually, you can wear a dress, Cinderella. Because your fairy godmother just happened to get some new material delivered last week that would be perfect for you,' Claire said. 'It's purple and I think it's got your name written all over it.'

Her best friend was going to make her a dress, especially for her date? 'Claire-bear, I can't ask you to—' Sammy began.

'You're not asking, I'm offering,' Claire cut in. 'In fact, I'm telling you.'

'If you make me a dress,' Sammy said, 'I'm paying for it, and I don't mean mates' rates.'

'What, like you let me pay you for my wedding photographs and all the shots you took for my website— *not*?' Claire scoffed. 'No. I'm doing it because I want to make you a dress. Just occasionally, Sammy, it's nice to be able to do something as a treat for one of my best friends, OK? So shut up and say yes instead of being over-independent.'

'OK. And sorry. And I really, really appreciate you,' Sammy said.

Claire cuffed her arm playfully. 'So you should, Sammikins. I was thinking an empire line maxi dress, with a V-neck, in two layers—plain underneath and chiffon on top.'

It always amazed Sammy how Claire could see the perfect dress for someone whenever she looked at them. And Claire's creations were stunning. Ashleigh's wedding dress had been amazing.

'You've got heels to go with it?' Claire asked.

'Just because I tend to live in trousers, it doesn't mean I don't own any pretty shoes,' Sammy said.

'Good. Bring them tomorrow night for your fitting so I can make sure the hem's right,' Claire said.

'And what about jewellery?' Ashleigh asked. 'Because Mum had a string of black pearls that'd look fabulous with what Claire's just described. I'll bring them with me tomorrow.'

Sammy had to swallow the lump in her throat.

Ashleigh's parents had been killed in a car accident eight years ago, so for Ashleigh to offer to lend her friend something so very precious… 'Thanks.'

'Hey.' Ashleigh hugged her. 'You're worth it.'

'You do know that when you two start having babies, I'll take portraits of the babies every single month for you. As a best friend gift,' Sammy said. The same way she'd done their wedding photographs and had refused to take any payment for even the photographic paper.

'Godmother gift, not just best friend,' Claire corrected. 'And I'm really glad you brought the subject up, because…' She paused for dramatic effect. 'Well, there's something I need to ask you both. Sean agrees with me. Will you both be godmothers?'

Sammy's jaw dropped. 'Oh, my God. You're actually having a baby?'

'In six months' time,' Claire confirmed.

'Oh, that's fantastic.' Sammy hugged her. 'I'm so pleased for you and Sean.'

Ashleigh coughed. 'Seeing as we're doing news, I guess I have a little announcement, too.'

'What?' Sammy stared at her in amazement. 'You and Luke, too?'

'In six months' time, too.' Ashleigh nodded. 'And I'll be looking for you both to be godmothers as well.'

'I'm the only one of us who can drink alcohol now, or I'd rush out and buy a bottle of champagne,' Sammy said. 'Both of you, expecting at the same time. That's *amazing*. Such brilliant news.'

'So, if this thing works out with your barrister, you're absolutely not allowed to get married to him until after we've had the babies,' Claire said, 'because I'm not planning to walk down the aisle behind you in a maternity matron of honour dress.'

'Seconded,' Ashleigh said. 'And we are so drinking champagne at your wedding. Which we can't do when we're pregnant.'

'Two babies,' Sammy said, beaming at both of them. 'That is, I'm assuming neither of you are having twins?'

'Not me,' Claire said.

'Just one baby here, too. But we're waiting until the baby's born to find out if we're having a girl or a boy. Luke and I agreed we wouldn't ask,' Ashleigh said.

'That's fabulous. Really fabulous.' Sammy was thrilled for her friends, she really was.

But at the same time there was a tiny chunk of ice in the middle of her heart.

One of the downsides of having chemotherapy at sixteen was that she'd had to have some eggs frozen in case she wanted to have children when she was older. But there were no guarantees that IVF would work— and she knew that could be a deal-breaker for any potential partner.

Including Nick. She thought about Nick. She had no idea whether he wanted children or not, and she couldn't think of an easy way to ask him. In any case, it was way too early to ask him right now. They'd only been out together twice. So she'd have to add it to the list of difficult conversations they'd need to have if things worked out between them. Cancer, fertility…no wonder her exes had panicked and run. And she was pretty sure that Nick had some issues, too. No way could someone with such a good heart and a keen intellect—perfect partner material—be single at his age without some emotional baggage.

Or maybe she was over-thinking it and she should just treat this whole thing as a chance to have some fun.

Whatever, she knew that she had to tell him the truth about herself.

But not just yet…

The following evening, Sammy met her best friends at Claire's shop for the dress fitting. She put on the high heels she planned to wear with the dress, and Claire adjusted the hem.

'You look a million dollars,' Ashleigh said, and looped the black pearls round Sammy's neck.

'Totally stunning,' Claire agreed. 'Your barrister isn't going to know what hit him.'

And there wasn't a single inch of leg displayed above Sammy's ankle. The dress was floaty, feminine and gorgeous, and Sammy didn't quite recognise herself in the mirror.

'Thank you. Both of you.' The lump in her throat made her voice all croaky.

'Hey. We want to see you as happy as we are,' Ashleigh said softly. 'Which doesn't mean we're trying to marry you off—you don't have to be married to be happy. But I know you've been lonely since Bryn.'

'Hey. I have a brilliant family and the best friends I could ask for,' Sammy said. 'Asking for more is greedy.'

'No, it's not,' Claire said. 'You deserve it. Enjoy your date.'

So what would his mysterious Woman in Black be wearing today? Nick wondered. Something dressy, given their surroundings. But he was pretty sure it would be black.

As he became aware of someone entering the room, he looked up from checking the emails on his phone and did a double take.

Not black, then.

And very, *very* dressy.

He'd never have believed that Sammy scrubbed up so well. She took his breath away. She was wearing only the lightest make-up, but that dress…

He stood up when she walked over to their table. 'You look amazing,' he said.

She blushed. 'Thank you.'

'Really amazing,' he said, sitting down again after the waiter had seated her.

'And note that I'm not wearing black,' she said with a self-deprecating smile.

He smiled. 'I'd guessed that you'd wear a little black dress. I'm glad I was wrong.'

'I did tell you that my best friend's a dress designer. And she's amazingly talented.'

'I'll second that,' he said.

The waiter ran through the list of teas. 'I'd recommend one of the black or green teas with the sandwiches and savouries,' he said, 'and then a fruit infusion with the sweet selection.'

'That sounds perfect,' Sammy said. 'Could I have Earl Grey, please?'

'And for me, too,' Nick said.

'I've never been here,' she said when the waiter had gone. 'Claire and Ash—my best friends—would love this. It's like a proper Regency drawing room. And there's even a pianist.'

Nick raised an eyebrow. 'He could be playing this one especially for you right now.'

'Debussy's "Girl with the Flaxen Hair".' She smiled back. 'Maybe.'

'Not a fan of Debussy?' he asked.

'Beethoven all the way for me,' Sammy said.

Romantic. Why didn't that surprise him?

The waiter brought over their tea in a silver pot, and a sage-and-cream striped porcelain tray to match their cups, saucers and tea plates, filled with a selection of sandwiches and savouries.

'I'm really glad I skipped lunch,' Sammy said. 'I don't know where to start. The sandwiches—smoked salmon, roast beef, ham, or cucumber and cream cheese?'

'I'd say the Welsh rarebit first, as it's hot,' Nick suggested. 'Then maybe we should start at one end of the tray of sandwiches and work our way through.'

'Great idea. This is such a treat. Thank you so much for inviting me.'

'I can't think of anyone I'd rather share this with,' Nick said. And he realised how true it was. He enjoyed Sammy's company hugely. Strange that this was only their third official date. It felt as if he'd known her for years and years. He was comfortable with her, felt that he could be himself—and that was such a rare feeling. Something that made him want to take things a lot further between them. Because maybe Sammy was the one he could learn to trust. The one who'd help to mend his heart again.

Once they'd finished the savoury platter, he excused himself and had a quiet word with the pianist.

When the waiter brought the fruit teas—lemon verbena for him and strawberry and rhubarb for Sammy—

with the three-tiered cake stand containing the sweet selection, Sammy looked at Nick with slightly narrowed eyes. 'Did you just say something to the pianist?'

'I might've done,' he said, lifting one shoulder in a shrug.

'The Moonlight Sonata is my favourite piece of music in the world,' she said softly. 'And it's perfect right now. Perfect music, perfect food—and perfect company.'

His thoughts entirely. He gave her a tiny bow. 'Why, thank you, ma'am.'

They made short work of the scones with clotted cream and jam, the lavender shortbread and the tiny rich selection of pastries.

'Oh, yes—a verrine,' Sammy said, looking at the shot glass filled with panna cotta. 'I love it when I get a commission in Paris. It means I get the chance to go to a certain patisserie and have one of their deconstructed desserts.'

'Want to swap mine for your super-chocolatey brownie?' he asked.

She blinked. 'You remembered that I don't like chocolate cake?'

'Of course.' Why was she so surprised? Or maybe she'd just dated the wrong kind of man in the past. Someone who was selfish and never put her first. That would explain why she was single: dating someone selfish would definitely put you off relationships. Naomi had put him off relationships just as badly.

'I've really enjoyed this,' she said when they'd finished. 'Though I don't think I'm going to eat again for a week!'

'Agreed. Though could I tempt you to a glass of wine back at my place?' he asked.

She smiled. 'I'd like that.'

He ordered a taxi to take them back to his flat.

Nick already had half a dozen bottles of his favourite white wines chilling in his wine cooler; he swiftly opened one and poured them both a glass.

'This is lovely,' Sammy said when she'd taken a sip. 'What is it?'

'Montrachet,' he explained. 'It's one of the grand cru chardonnays.'

'It's gorgeous. Really smooth.'

He hooked up his phone to his stereo system, and set some Beethoven piano music playing. And when Sammy put her wine glass on the low coffee table, she ended up curled against him on the sofa, with her head resting on his shoulder.

They didn't even have to talk; and it felt so good, just being together. She felt more relaxed with Nick than she ever had with anyone else—even in the early days with Bryn, before he'd killed her love stone dead and broken her heart.

She knew she ought to tell Nick about her past and explain about her leg; but she just couldn't find the right words, and she didn't want to spoil what had been such a perfect afternoon.

She reached up to trace the curve of his mouth with a forefinger. 'I really enjoyed today.'

'Me, too,' he said.

Even though she knew it was being greedy, wanting something she couldn't have, she couldn't resist stealing a kiss. He responded instantly, wrapping his arms tightly round her and kissing her back.

Everything about this man felt right.

But the fear was still there. Would she repulse him? When push came to shove, would he too think she wasn't enough of a woman for him?

'Nick, I really have to go,' she said softly. 'I've got a train to Edinburgh at the crack of dawn tomorrow, and it's a four-and-a-half-hour journey.'

'Can I drive you home? I've only had one glass of wine, so I'm below the limit for driving. And yes, I know you're perfectly capable of taking the Tube,' he added swiftly, 'but you're wearing high heels and that gorgeous dress and it won't be much fun keeping the hem out of the way on the escalators.'

True. And she liked the way he was thinking of her. 'Thank you. That would be nice,' she said. Plus it meant she got to spend just a little bit more time with him.

'So what are you doing in Edinburgh?' he asked as he drove her home.

'I'm taking a portrait of a sculptor for one of the Sunday magazines. Actually, it's someone whose work I've admired for a while, so I'm really looking forward to meeting him,' she said. 'What about you?'

'Preparing for a trial which starts next week and might go on for a fortnight or so. How long are you away for?'

'Three days,' she said. 'Shall I call you when I get back?' And maybe on that long train journey she'd find the right words to tell him about her leg. And, if they managed to negotiate that and come out the other side in one piece, maybe they could do Date Four. Take another step towards a real relationship.

'I'd like that,' he said. He parked outside her flat.

'And I'm guessing you have to pack, check over your equipment and charge up various batteries.'

'Something like that,' she said.

'Then I won't ask to come in for coffee.' He cupped her face in his hand and kissed her goodnight so sweetly that she felt the tears prick her eyelids. 'Sleep well,' he said softly.

'You too,' she said, and stole a last kiss before climbing out of his car.

There was a message on her phone when she got up the next morning. Short, sweet and to the point: Safe journey.

Have a good day in chambers, she typed back.

She could really get used to dating Nick Kennedy.

But before she got too comfortable she really had to tell him the truth about herself...

CHAPTER SEVEN

WHILE SAMMY WAS in Edinburgh, she had a chance to explore some of the shoreline of the Firth of Forth; the sculptor whose photograph she was taking was inspired by it, and took her and Ben, the journalist, for a short drive from the city down to Yellowcraigs. They headed off the beaten track, down through a pretty village to the parking area, and then walked out to the beach.

The long, sweeping cove was beautiful. 'I love this sky. I could take your picture here,' Sammy suggested.

'Or on Fidra.' Jimmy McBain pointed to the island. 'I thought we could get a boat over there this morning.'

'Sounds good to me.' Sammy smiled at the journalist. 'OK with you, Ben?'

'I'm not the world's best sailor,' the journalist admitted, 'but I'll give it a go.'

'Just as well I told you to bring your walking boots in a plastic bag,' Jimmy said with a grin. 'And we'll cheer you up when we get back with a wee dram.'

Sammy took a few shots of Jimmy on the beach while he chatted to them about the area.

'So why is the name Fidra familiar?' Ben asked.

Sammy knew the answer to that one. 'Robert Louis Stevenson spent his holidays there as a boy.' When Ben still looked puzzled, she said, 'Pieces of eight? Long John Silver?'

'Oh—*Treasure Island*.'

'That's the one,' Jimmy said, looking pleased. Sammy took a few more shots of the cove while Jimmy was talking to the skipper of a boat, and she thought of Nick and his misty shoreline painting. He'd love it here, she was sure. On impulse, she took a snap of the island on her phone and sent it to him.

Guess where I am?

Clearly he was in chambers rather than in court, because he answered straight away.

I thought you said you were going to Edinburgh?

I did. We're half an hour or so's drive away. This is the island of Fidra.

Fidra?

She smiled.

Tsk. You must've read Treasure Island when you were a kid?

That's Treasure Island?

Jimmy the Sculptor says that's what inspired Robert Louis Stevenson. I think you'd like it here. Ice creams, cafes, miles of sand, and apparently just down the road is biggest colony of puffins on the east coast.

Sounds great, was the response.

Had they been dating long enough to think about going away together? She typed, Wish you were here, then stopped herself. She did wish that she were sharing this with Nick, but was telling him a step too far? She went to delete the message but accidentally pressed the wrong button and sent it instead.

Oh, no.

This time, there was no reply.

Well, it served her right for being way too forward. Of course it was too soon to think about going away together. How ridiculous of her to think otherwise.

Thankfully right then they had to get on the boat, and after that her time was caught up taking photographs, so it stopped her brooding about the situation.

Then her phone beeped on their way back to the city.

Sorry about earlier. I was called back to court so my phone was off. Wish I was there, too.

It made Sammy feel all warm inside.

And it clearly showed on her face, because Jimmy patted her arm. 'Message from your man, was it?'

'Yes.'

'He's a lucky lad. You'd have plenty of admirers up here, even though your haircut's…well.' He rolled his eyes. 'You'd be a bonnier lass if you'd let it grow.'

She smiled back. 'It's short right now because I donate my hair to make wigs for children who've had cancer.'

Jimmy whistled. 'So you've a good heart, too. That's rare. Bonny, and with a good heart.'

'And it'd make a great story,' Ben said, looking interested.

'Agreed. I can get you some people to interview, if you like,' Sammy said. 'Especially as I happened to shoot a calendar which is going to raise money for the cancer ward. You could maybe do an article on that. Hot men stripping off to raise money.'

'It'd be a good human interest story.' Ben held her gaze. 'And I can start by interviewing you.'

She shook her head. 'I'd rather stay behind the lens.'

He could see that she meant it and he left it there rather than nagging, but Sammy found herself thinking about it on the way back to London, the next morning. Maybe if she went public about her experience, it would help someone else to get through their own situation. And talking to Ben about it might be a good test run, something that would give her the courage to talk to Nick.

'Ben—did you mean it about that interview?' she asked.

'Which one?' He groaned. 'Sorry. My brain is totally scrambled. Never let me agree to drink with a Scots guy again.'

'Or a cider producer in Somerset—I'm sure you had a hangover after that interview, too,' she said with a grin. 'I mean the article about the charity calendar and why I donate my hair.'

'Yes, I meant it. Though give me a while for my brain to unscramble so I can work up some decent questions.'

'Sure. I'll get you a cup of tea and a bacon sandwich from the buffet.' And she'd better hope that her courage didn't fail her in the time between now and when her colleague had recovered from his hangover.

It didn't. And Ben was incredibly kind with his questions.

'I had no idea that you'd been through all that,' he said when he'd finished the interview.

'I don't talk about it because I don't want cancer to define me,' she said simply.

He nodded. 'I admired you before, because you're always so professional and you deliver every single time. But knowing you had to cope with all that as well— you're really amazing, Sammy.'

'That isn't why I told you. It's not about my ego. I want to give other people some hope so they know you really can come out the other side of the experience and it'll be OK,' she said. 'Though is there any way you can do the piece without actually revealing who I am?'

He raised an eyebrow. 'You think people might not want to hire you because you're a cancer survivor?'

'Some people don't react so well,' she said. Personally as well as professionally. Not that she wanted to explain that.

Ben gave her a pithy response about precisely what that kind of people could do.

'I still have to earn my living,' she said.

'I'll talk to my editor and see if we can find a way round it,' he said. 'But thank you. Now I know your story—well, I'm really proud to call myself your colleague.'

'And friend,' she said. 'Now shut up before I start being wet.'

He grinned. 'That's the last word I'd ever use to describe you.'

Talking to Ben had been so easy.

But was that simply because he was a journalist, used to asking questions and teasing the real story out of reluctant interviewees? Would it be as easy, talking to Nick?

Ben was her colleague. Her friend. She'd known him for years. There was no way that her past could change their relationship.

Whereas Nick was…

Help.

Not her lover. Not yet. Though she wanted him to be. 'Boyfriend' sounded twee. Partner? They hadn't been together that long. But she really felt she'd clicked with him. While she'd been away in Edinburgh, she'd really missed him, and it had shocked her how much she'd wanted to share all her new experiences with him. Had he missed her? Or had he been so busy that he'd barely registered her absence?

She was probably over-thinking things again.

Why couldn't she be like she was in every other area of her life? Why couldn't she just step up and do it? Tell him?

'You are such a coward, Samantha Jane Thompson,' she told herself grimly.

Back at her flat, she found a rectangular parcel waiting for her. It had fitted perfectly through her letterbox, and she recognised the box as one from a very exclusive chocolatier.

There was a note with it in bold script that was clearly from a fountain pen:

Welcome home. Missed you.

So he *had* missed her as much as she'd missed him. And what a welcome home. She hardly knew where to start when she opened the box; they were glorious, and each one was a treat. Best of all was the dark chocolate violet crème.

She glanced at her watch. It was a Saturday, but Nick had said that he was preparing for a trial. He was probably knee-deep in paperwork. Better not to disturb him, then. She texted him instead of calling.

Thank you so much for the chocolates. They're sublime. Might not be any left by the time I see you! *insert guilty smiley*

When he didn't reply, she knew that her guess about him being really busy was right. But, to her surprise, he called her at half past five.

'Hey. So did you find any treasure on your island?'

'I took some good shots, if that counts.' She laughed. 'And thank you for the chocolates. They're amazing. Though, um, there aren't many left to share with you.'

'My pleasure. Besides, they're meant for you, not for sharing.' His voice was full of warmth. 'I just wanted to welcome you back.'

And how. Which gave her the courage to suggest Date Four. Something she hadn't done in a long, long time. 'Are you busy tonight, or do you want to do something?'

'Aren't you tired after that long train journey?' he asked.

'A bit,' she admitted, 'but if you're not busy maybe we could have a quick drink or something.'

'I really missed you,' he said softly. 'How about we compromise and I'll come over to you with a takeaway?'

She'd been away for three days so she hadn't had a chance to restock her fridge, apart from the carton of

milk she'd grabbed at the train station. She padded over
to it and glanced inside. 'It seems I have a bottle of Prosecco in the fridge,' she said. She opened the freezer
door. 'And some posh ice cream.'

'Perfect. I'll order something to be delivered to yours
and be with you at seven.'

'Sounds good to me.'

At precisely seven, her doorbell rang. She opened
the door and greeted Nick with a hug. 'Hey.' Then she
stepped back and took in his appearance; he was wearing an expensively cut wool suit, a handmade white
shirt and an understated silk tie.

'I feel very scruffy compared with you,' she said. 'I
wish now I'd changed.'

'Instead of working?' He smiled. 'You had a long
journey and it was sensible to dress for comfort.'

'I can change now.'

'Too late. Dinner's just arrived,' he said, indicating the white van emblazoned with the name of a Thai
restaurant that had pulled up outside her flat. 'Perfect
timing, too.'

Over dinner, she showed him some of the shots of
Fidra.

'That beach looks amazing,' he said.

'It's gorgeous. That sweeping cove…'

'Maybe,' he said, 'we could go there together sometime.'

Maybe. If he still wanted to know her, once she'd
told him about her past.

But for a workaholic like Nick to suggest taking
some time away… 'I'd like that,' she said.

They ended up stretched out on her sofa, all warm
and smoochy. Sammy's legs were entangled with his,

his hands were flat against her back underneath her T-shirt—and how good his skin felt against hers—and her arms were wrapped round his neck.

It would be oh, so easy to suggest that they moved from her sofa to her bed, where they could shut the world away. Where they could take the time to explore each other, discover where each other liked being touched and kissed.

Except…she still hadn't told him.

And letting him find out by seeing her scar—or, worse, touching it by accident—would be totally wrong.

'Sammy? Is everything OK?'

Clearly he'd picked up on her tension.

'Just tired,' she fibbed. 'It's been a long few days with a lot of travelling.'

Nick kissed her gently. 'I'd better go and let you get some sleep.'

Now. Tell him now. Don't be such a coward. He's not going to run for the hills. He's not going to react the way Bryn and the others did.

'Sorry,' she said, chickening out.

'It's fine. I'll call you tomorrow.' He gave her a last lingering kiss. 'I'll see myself out. Sweet dreams.'

And, even though she was tired, she couldn't sleep. She lay there in the dark, regretting her cowardice. Why was it so hard to tell him the truth?

Over the next couple of weeks, Sammy and Nick spent as much time together as they could. The more she got to know him, the more she liked him, and she hoped it might be the same for him. They had similar tastes in music; they both liked complicated whodunnit dramas—though he always made some comment about

the legal bits being wrong—and they both liked outrageous stand-up comedy and long walks on the beach and browsing through little art galleries.

This could be perfect. With Nick, she felt as if she really fitted.

All she had to do was tell him.

The truth, the whole truth and nothing but the truth. How hard could it be?

She even practised it in front of the mirror. *Nick, there's something I need to tell you. I'll understand if you want to call the whole thing off, but fourteen years ago I had...*

Six letters.

Two syllables.

A word that could explode someone's whole world and leave nothing but rubble.

Three dates on the trot, she tried to tell him—and failed.

Then he said to her, 'On Saturday, Mandy's going on a spa day with a couple of her friends—it's a birthday present from them. I promised her I'd look after the boys for her.' He paused. 'I was wondering, would you like to spend the day with us?'

He wanted her to meet his family?

This was serious.

And this was his nephew who'd had osteosarcoma.

Oh, help. She really, really needed to tell him about her past, but she still hadn't found the right time or the right words to tell him.

There was a wary look in his eyes; clearly he was half expecting her to refuse. It would probably be sensible to refuse, yet at the same time she didn't want to hurt him. How could she throw the offer back in his face? She had a feeling this wasn't the kind of thing he suggested very often.

'Actually,' she said, 'I like kids very much. I have two nieces and two nephews myself, and my family's really close. How old are the boys?'

'Xander's twelve and Ned's eight.'

'Good ages,' she said. Stupid. Any age was a good age. 'My nephews are very slightly older.' And now she was babbling. Focus, Sammy, she told herself. 'Maybe we could go to the park if it's a nice day, or somewhere like the Natural History Museum if it's wet.'

'That's a great idea,' he said. 'I'll pick you up.'

Tell him. Tell him now.

'Nick…'

'Yes?'

For a split second, she glimpsed vulnerability in his face.

No, she couldn't tell him right now.

'What?' he asked.

She thought on her feet. 'Please don't think I'm being nosey here, but I just need to know if there are any topics of conversation I ought to steer clear of on Saturday?'

He nodded. 'Xander's a bit sensitive about his leg. And we don't talk about their father.'

She winced inwardly. 'I take it from that, he let them down?'

'Big time,' he said, his face tightening. 'Mandy doesn't want anyone to badmouth him in front of the boys, in case he ever decides to come back into their lives, but…' He looked grim. 'I can't ever see that happening. Warren the Weasel walked out on them the day they got Xander's diagnosis, eighteen months ago, and they haven't seen him since.'

Sammy sucked in a breath, shocked beyond measure. She could just about get her head round the reasons why someone might not be able to cope with their partner's diagnosis and walk away, but to do something like that to their child… 'That's pretty rough on your sister and the boys.'

'Yeah.' His lip curled. 'Warren's the most selfish man I've ever met. He hasn't even sent the boys a birthday or Christmas card since he left. Mandy's been trying to keep the lines of communication open and she takes them to see his parents. Warren's mother always makes excuses for him, saying he's "sensitive"—' Nick made exaggerated quote marks with his fingers as he said the words '—but he's certainly not sensitive to his sons' feelings. Or to his ex-wife's. The only people he cares about are me, myself and I.' He blew out a breath. 'Thankfully Mandy had the sense to divorce him for unreasonable behaviour, and he had the sense not to dispute it.'

With a hotshot barrister as an ex-brother-in-law, Warren would have been very stupid indeed to try to contest a divorce petition, Sammy thought. And it sounded as if Nick seriously disliked the man.

'I'm sorry,' she said.

Nick shrugged. 'It's not your fault.'

'I know, but still a horrible situation for you all to deal with.' She took a deep breath. 'And that's empathy speaking, not pity.' She'd had enough pity after her diagnosis to last a lifetime; no way would she ever give pity to someone else.

He drew her into his arms and held her close. 'Thank you. It's appreciated.' He sighed and brushed his mouth against her hair. 'We're not very good at marriage in my family.'

So was this the reason why he was single? Because he'd been so badly bitten that he didn't want to risk falling in love again? Not sure what to say, she stroked his face.

'Sorry. I shouldn't burden you with my woes,' he said, looking guilty.

'No, that's fine. And it's not going any further than me.'

He kissed her lightly. 'I know. And thanks. Again.' He grimaced. 'I guess you ought to know what you're getting yourself into. My parents split up when I was seventeen. My sister—well, I've told you about the weasel she married. And I'm divorced as well. So we're not a good bet, the Kennedys.'

'Or maybe you haven't met the right person for you yet.' She worked it out. He would've been in the middle of his exams when his parents split up. A really vulnerable, impressionable time.

'Maybe,' he said. 'Dad kind of buried himself in work after my mother left.'

Not 'Mum', she noticed. It sounded as if he wasn't close to his mother. Did he blame her for the divorce? But asking felt too much like prying.

'Do you see much of your parents?' she asked carefully.

'Dad lives in Brussels, so we don't see him that often.' He gave her a rueful smile. 'He specialises in European law. I guess he hoped I'd follow in his footsteps, but I like London too much.'

'What about your mother?'

He shrugged. 'She's even further away, in Cornwall.'

She frowned. 'How can Cornwall be further away from London than Brussels?'

'It's quicker to get the Eurostar to Brussels than to drive to the far depths of Cornwall,' he said.

She had a feeling that there was a bit more to it than that, but pushing would be unfair. 'So they don't get to see much of their grandchildren, then?'

'No. Which is a shame, because Mandy could've done with their support after Warren left. Dad's very busy in Brussels, and our mother has her B&B to think about. But Mandy knows she can always rely on me, even though I'm the baby of the family.' He smiled. 'And it's not a burden—not at all. Xander and Ned are nice kids. Plus it means I have a cast-iron excuse to see all the superhero films at the cinema, because I can take them.'

'Sounds good. I do something similar with my nephews and nieces,' she said lightly.

Guilt seeped through her. Nick had been open with her. She really ought to tell him what he was getting into, too. The spectre of cancer, fertility issues, the fact she wasn't really a whole woman…the Sammy Thompson he'd met was a fake.

But the words dried up in her throat when she tried to utter them.

She'd tell him.

Soon.

And was it so wrong to want to feel like a normal person without complications for just that little bit longer, instead of turning into Sammy-the-cancer-survivor?

CHAPTER EIGHT

SATURDAY DAWNED BRIGHT and sunny. Although it was the beginning of October it was still really warm.

Nick called Sammy's landline. 'We're outside in the car,' he said.

'Great. I'm coming out to join you,' she told him.

To her secret amusement, although he was wearing jeans he was also wearing another of those white hand-made shirts; she guessed he was always going to have that touch of formality.

The boys were both sitting in the back of the car. Sammy could see the family resemblance to Nick in their dark hair and dark eyes. She was curious as to how he was going to introduce her to them: as his friend or as his girlfriend?

'Boys, this is my friend Sammy,' he said. 'Sammy, these are my nephews, Xander and Ned.'

Friend, then—which was sensible. Especially given the situation with their father; Nick obviously wouldn't want to introduce the boys to a string of 'aunties', feeling that they'd had enough change in their life already. She could understand that.

The boys chorused hello, both looking slightly shy.

Sammy smiled at them. 'It's very nice to meet you

both. Nick says we're going to the park—is that OK with you?'

Ned looked thrilled. 'They have a really cool zip-wire at the park.'

'That sounds like fun,' she said. 'Are adults allowed on it?'

'You like zip-wires?' Ned asked, his eyes round with surprise.

'I love them,' she said. 'Race you?'

'You're on,' Ned said with a grin.

Nick drove them to a park that the boys clearly knew well. There was a play area with a massive slide wide enough to take four people at a time and a low zip-wire, and the boys spent most of their time there. Sammy raced Nick down the slide and joined the boys on the zip-wire.

Then she noticed a stall selling water pistols and nudged Nick. 'My brothers, sister and I loved that sort of thing when I was a kid. I bet the boys will, too.'

He raised his eyebrows. 'You're challenging us to a water fight?'

'Ah, no. I was thinking me and the boys versus you.'

'Three against one? That's totally unfair.' But he was laughing, so she was pretty sure he was up for it. 'Where are we going to get water from?' he asked.

She gestured to the kiosk at the other side of the playing field. 'I'm pretty sure they'll sell bottled water. That'll do the job.'

'Hmm.'

'Ned, Xander—team huddle,' she said, beckoning the boys over.

'Team huddle?' they asked, mystified, but went with her.

'Water fight. Us versus Uncle Nick,' she explained economically. 'What do you think?'

'Yeah,' they chorused, each pumping a fist into the air.

She bought four water pistols and two large bottles of still water, and she enjoyed charging round with the boys and doing her best to soak Nick with water. Though she noticed that Xander was looking tired at almost the same time as Nick clearly did, because Nick stopped dead and said, 'Right, time for a truce.'

'Not a chance,' she said.

He came over to her and lowered his voice. 'They've been running around like mad and Xander's in danger of overdoing it. He needs to rest.'

She murmured back, 'I know. Trust me.' Then she turned to Xander. 'I've been thinking—with three of us, we're getting in each other's way. I reckon we need a master strategist to direct us, and I think out of the three of us you'd be the best one to do that.'

The boy looked slightly suspicious. 'Master strategist? Really?'

'Really,' she confirmed. 'Come and sit down here by this tree so you've got the best view of the field. Now, imagine you're the shepherd, Ned and I are the sheepdogs, and Uncle Nick's the big fat sheep who's about to get a bath.'

'And?'

'So you need to direct us,' she said. 'And if you do it right, then we win and your Uncle Nick gets totally soaked.'

Xander stopped looking suspicious and grinned. 'Let's do it.'

She and Ned followed Xander's shouted directions, and finally managed to soak Nick from head to foot.

'OK, I surrender,' Nick said, laughing.

And, with that white shirt and his jeans plastered to his skin so the outline of his pectorals and gluteus maximus were perfectly defined, he looked utterly gorgeous. Sammy had already noticed how many female heads he was turning during the water fight, and several more seemed to be showing interest in a hot, wet man.

'We won, Sammy!' Ned crowed. He rushed over to her and hugged her.

'That's because we had a great strategy director,' she said, and high-fived Xander and then Ned, who both beamed at her.

'Not that brilliant,' Nick said calmly. Before Sammy realised what he was planning to do, he'd picked up all four water pistols and soaked her. 'Revenge,' he said with a grin, 'is sweet.'

'Oh, you monster—you'd already surrendered so that's totally cheating,' she said, laughing. 'For that you can buy me an ice cream, and I'm going to sit down here and get Xander to protect me.' She took one of the water pistols from Nick, refilled it, and handed it to Xander. 'You're my bodyguard.'

'Cool,' Xander said.

'Can we have ice creams, too? A whippy one with a chocolate flake?' Ned asked hopefully, adding belatedly, 'Please?'

'Whippy ice cream with a chocolate flake—is there any other kind?' Sammy teased.

'Hint taken.' Nick rolled his eyes. 'Come on, Ned. Let's go and queue up.'

Xander had gone quiet, she noticed. 'Are you OK?' she asked softly when Nick and Ned had left.

The boy sighed. 'I just wish… I hate my stupid leg. I know you're just being nice about letting me rest.'

'Hey. We needed you as our strategy director,' she said. 'And now to protect me against sneaky water attacks from Nick.'

'I'm twelve, not a baby like Ned—I knew what you were doing. But my leg had started hurting a bit so I went along with it.' Then he glanced at her. 'Sorry, Uncle Nick and Mum would be mad at me for being rude to you.'

'You're not being rude, just honest—and if your leg starts aching of course it's going to make you feel fed up and grumpy.'

'It aches nearly all the time,' Xander said with a sigh. 'They had to take part of my bone away, so there's a metal thing in my leg they have to expand when the rest of my bones grow.'

'Meaning you don't have to have lots of operations, just the one? That's really good,' she said.

He blinked at her. 'Uncle Nick says you know someone who had what I did. That's why you photographed him and everyone else for the calendar.'

'I do.' She paused. This was a huge risk—but it might help the boy to feel a bit happier. 'Want to know a secret?'

'What sort of secret?'

'A really, really big secret. But you have to promise not to tell anyone,' she warned.

'Cross my heart and hope to die,' he said, making the sign of a cross over his heart with his fingertip.

Sammy glanced over towards Nick. He and Ned

were in the queue at the ice cream van so they probably couldn't see, but even so she shifted so she could hide her legs from Nick's view in case he turned round, and pushed up the left leg of her jeans to her knee.

Xander's eyes went wide. 'You've got a scar in the same place as me.'

'Yes, and for exactly the same reason,' she said softly. 'But I was a little bit older than you—I was sixteen when I had my op.'

'Did it hurt?'

'My leg?' At his nod, she said softly, 'After the op, yes.'

'Does it hurt now?'

'No.'

'And you had to have more than one op?'

'Luckily not, because I'd pretty much stopped growing at sixteen—but some of my friends did.' She swallowed hard. 'This is your and my secret, Xander, OK?'

'OK,' Xander said.

'Good. And it's important to do your exercises, even when they're boring and even when they hurt a little bit.'

'Why?' he asked.

'Because it means you get strong,' she said. 'And, next time you think you can't do something and your leg's holding you back, remember that I go all over the world in my job. It doesn't hold me back.'

'Have you been to Australia?' he challenged.

'And America, and Japan.' She paused. 'And I climbed Mount Kilimanjaro three years ago.'

His eyes went wide. 'Really? You climbed a mountain? Even after...you know?'

'Yup. I can show you the photographs. I went as the

team photographer, but obviously I had to go where they went, so that meant climbing with them.'

He looked impressed. 'That's *so* cool.'

'I know. Though I guess I should admit that it isn't the climb that's the hard thing—it's not like rock-climbing where you see people sticking an axe into the cliff or what have you and hauling themselves up. It's the altitude that makes it difficult. The air's really thin, so you have to walk incredibly slowly or you can't breathe and get dizzy. And sleeping on the hard ground for five or six nights really makes you ache all over. But it was worth it. The views were amazing.' She high-fived him. 'And if I can do anything I like after having osteosarcoma, then so can you. Never, ever let your cancer define you. Because you're more than that.'

For a second, his eyes glistened with tears, but he blinked them away. 'Thanks, Sammy.' His voice was a little hoarse.

'Any time,' she said. 'And any time you want to talk to me, you can—I'll keep whatever you tell me confidential. Uncle Nick's got my phone and email.'

'Thanks—it's really nice having someone who understands.'

Sammy had the strongest feeling that he wanted to tell her something. So she waited, knowing from experience as a photographer that people always filled a silence if you gave them the time.

And he did.

'Uncle Nick always makes me stop and rest before I'm really ready.'

'It's because he loves you,' she said gently, 'and he worries about you, and he's scared you'll overdo it and give you a setback.' Just what her family had said to her, when she'd finally lost her temper with everyone and yelled about how being wrapped in cotton wool drove her crazy.

'But I won't overdo it—I'm *twelve*, not stupid.'

'He knows that,' she said, 'but sometimes when you love someone and you're scared for them, that kind of stops you thinking straight.'

'So what do I do?'

'Tell him,' she said simply, knowing that she was the biggest hypocrite in the world—because she hadn't told Nick what he really ought to know, had she? 'Sit down with him and tell him what you told me. Tell him you're doing all your exercises and you want to get strong, so you're not going to overdo it because you know that'll mean you have to wait even longer before you're fully recovered. Promise him you'll always say when you're tired or you've had enough, and then he'll relax a bit.'

'Is that what you did?'

'Eventually. After a big fight.' And even now she knew she sometimes overdid the independence bit, but she couldn't help it.

Xander nodded. 'I love Uncle Nick. He's a better dad to me than...' He dragged in a breath. 'I'm not supposed to talk about that, either.'

'That your dad left?'

He nodded. 'I hate him. He left us when Mum really needed him. She still cries when she doesn't think I can hear her. I used to think it was my fault for getting sick, but Uncle Nick said it wasn't that at all. I once heard him call my dad a—well, he's right, but Mum would kill me if I used that word.'

Sammy's heart bled for him. She still couldn't get

her head round how anyone could be so selfish as to put themselves before their child, especially when their child really needed them. She gave him a hug. 'Xander, if I had a magic wand, I'd fix this—but people are complicated. Maybe your dad was just really scared.'

'Uncle Nick's scared. Mum's scared. Ned's scared. But they didn't leave.' He lifted his head. 'Did your dad leave you when you got cancer?'

'Nope. But some of my boyfriends did.'

'Because they were scared?'

'Something like that.'

'Then they were weasels and you deserve better,' Xander said. 'That's what Uncle Nick says about Dad to Mum.'

'When he thinks you can't hear?'

The boy nodded. 'And because she'd yell at him for using the other word.'

She ruffled his hair. 'I take it they don't know you have ears like a bat, then.'

Xander smiled. 'No. I sometimes think I'd like to be Batman, though.'

'You and me both. Though I'd rather be the Black Widow.'

'In the Avengers? Yeah. She's awesome.'

They were still laughing when Nick and Ned came back with the ice creams.

'What's so funny?' Nick asked.

'We're talking about superhero movies,' Sammy said.

'Sammy wants to be the Black Widow,' Xander informed him.

Nick stood so that the boys couldn't see him and mouthed, 'That works for me—she's hot.'

Sammy had a hard time keeping a straight face and dealing with the rush of heat that went through her.

'I want to be Spiderman,' Ned said.

'And I'm Batman,' Xander said. 'Who would you be, Uncle Nick?'

He sighed. 'You've already bagsied both my favourites.'

'You can be Robin,' Xander said kindly.

Nick shook his head. 'No. I think I'll be Iron Man.'

Sammy shifted so that only Nick could see her face, caught his eye, and mouthed, 'Works for me—*he's* hot.' She had the satisfaction of seeing colour slash across Nick's cheeks. Yeah. Two could play at that game.

And she pushed away the fact that she still hadn't told him the truth.

They went to a fried chicken place for lunch on the way home. Nick turned to Sammy when the boys were out of earshot. 'Thank you—you found a nice way to make Xander rest and not feel that he was missing out. And I apologise. I thought at first you were pushing him too hard.'

She nodded grimly. 'A word to the wise—don't wrap him in cotton wool, because he'll resent it later. You need to find a way of keeping him right in the middle of things and yet resting at the same time.'

'That sounds like experience talking.'

'Uh-huh.' She certainly couldn't tell him what Xander had confided in her, as she'd promised to keep it to herself.

'Would this be your sister who was wrapped in cotton wool?' Nick asked softly.

No, it had been her, for the first week. But, after that huge fight, Sammy's family had learned to support her instead of smothering her. Most of the time. She knew they still panicked, which was why she didn't always tell them if she felt any kind of twinge in her leg. 'I'd rather not talk about it,' she said.

'Your sister's not…?' He stopped and winced. 'I'm sorry. I didn't mean to rip the top off your scars.'

'My sister's fine. Now let's change the subject. I'm sorry for soaking you.'

'I got my own back.'

'Yeah, and your car's a bit soggy.'

'It'll dry,' he said. 'Thank you. You're good with the boys.'

'I'm an aunt of four,' she reminded him, 'so I jolly well ought to be good with kids by now.' She pushed back the surge of longing. She had to be realistic and recognise that she might have to content herself with being an aunt or a godmother. But she'd deal with it when she had to.

'My ex wasn't good with kids,' he said. 'She never really enjoyed spending time with the boys.'

Because she wanted kids of her own and his attention had been focused on them? Sammy wondered. 'That's a shame,' she said.

He gave her a thin smile. 'Yeah. There wasn't a maternal bone in Naomi's body.'

Ah. So she'd got it wrong and Nick's ex hadn't wanted kids. And it sounded as if it had been an issue between them. Maybe one of the issues that had led to their divorce.

Did Nick want children? Sammy wasn't brave enough to ask—because she knew this might be the deal-breaker for their relationship. If he wanted kids and she couldn't give them to him, what then?

Sammy was still damp by the time they got back to his sister's house.

'I can't make you sit around in wet clothes,' Nick said. 'Look, you're about the same size as Mandy. I can go and get something for you to change into. She won't mind.'

Sammy went cold—supposing he brought down a skirt? Something that would show him her scar? That wasn't the way she wanted to tell him. And she wished she'd been brave enough to tell him before. 'No, it's fine,' she said with a smile. 'I'll soon dry out in the back garden.' She indicated the patio table and chairs. 'Do you have a pack of cards?'

'We do,' Xander said, and went to fetch them while Nick organised drinks.

Sammy shuffled the cards. 'This was my favourite card game when I was your age. It's called Cheat— you go round in turn and put down the next named card. So if I start with an ace, Xander would put down a two, Nick would put down a three, and Ned would put down a four.'

Ned frowned. 'But that doesn't sound like fun.'

'Oh, yes, it is,' she said. 'Because you put the cards face down on the table, and nobody knows if I've put down say four aces, or four completely different cards.'

'So if you put down three fives and I don't have any sixes, I put down a card and pretend it's a six?' Xander asked.

'Exactly. And if I've got four sixes, I know you haven't put down a six, so I'd say Cheat and you'd have to pick up all the cards on the table. But if I've got three sixes and someone else has got one six, we won't know if you're cheating or not…unless you giggle and give yourself away.' She smiled. 'Uncle Nick should be good at this. He'll be able to see if people aren't telling the truth.'

He did. And Sammy let him win the first round.

And then she played the way she had with her family, half a lifetime ago. As a total card sharp. With a grin, she put down her last cards, saying, 'Three fours.'

Nick frowned. 'Hang on, you laid down three fours last time it was fours—and there aren't seven fours in a pack of cards.' He pointed a finger at her. 'Cheat!'

She turned over the last three cards, one by one. The four of diamonds, the four of clubs and the four of hearts.

'But—how?' Nick asked plaintively.

She laughed. 'Because I cheated massively last time and you didn't spot it.'

'You're really good at this,' Xander said admiringly.

She winked at him. 'My dad taught me how to play when I was Ned's age—and I have two big brothers and a big sister, so I had to learn to be really good at this or they'd sit on me.'

'Really sit on you?' Ned's eyes went wide.

She laughed. 'No, not *really*, but when you're the littlest it's hard to come last all the time, and I always knew if they were being kind and let me win.'

'I don't like it when Xander lets me win,' Ned confided in a whisper.

She ruffled his hair. 'Then, young Spiderman, let me give you some tips…'

Mandy came back just before tea time.

'Thank you so much,' she said to Sammy, shaking her hand. 'I feel so guilty about dumping my parental responsibilities on Nick and on you, especially as I hadn't even met you!'

'Not at all,' Sammy said firmly. 'Apart from the fact that it's your birthday weekend, I had a really good afternoon and your boys are lovely. And it's tough being a single mum. Having a break means you're refreshed and can enjoy the kids more.'

Mandy blinked. 'Wow, that's… I'm not used to people being that understanding.'

Sammy smiled. 'Remember, I'm a photographer. I've met an awful lot of people and heard an awful lot of life stories over the years.' She blew on her nails and polished them against her T-shirt. 'Very wise that makes me, young Padawan.'

Mandy laughed. 'If you're Yoda, then how old does that make me?'

Sammy laughed back. 'About the same age as my oldest brother, I'd guess. Which is—ooh—*ancient*.'

Mandy grinned. 'I like you. Would you stay and have dinner with us?' She wrinkled her nose. 'Though I guess you'd want to spend some time alone with Nick.'

'If you're offering me just about anything followed by birthday cake that isn't chocolate,' Sammy said, 'I'm all yours. *And* I'll do the washing up.'

'Deal, even though I'd always pick chocolate cake first,' Mandy said with another grin. 'I take back what I said. I *really* like you.'

Sammy smiled. 'If you're like your brother and your sons, then I like you, too.'

'I like your hair—it's a pretty radical cut, but you've got the bone structure to get away with it.'

'Thank you,' Sammy said, 'but I don't have it cut this short for fashion.'

'What, then?'

'Didn't Nick tell you? I grow my hair and donate it every two years, when it's long enough to make a child's wig,' Sammy explained.

'A kid who's had chemo?' Mandy swallowed hard. 'Xander lost his hair when he had chemo.'

'That's the downside of chemo—but he's doing just fine,' Sammy said softly. 'Thanks to you, he's really well adjusted.'

'I hope so.'

Sammy saw the sheen of tears in Mandy's eyes and hugged her. 'Sorry, I didn't mean to make you cry.'

'It's not you—it just catches me unawares sometimes. I never met anyone who donated hair before. Maybe that's something I can do in the future,' Mandy said thoughtfully.

'My sister's a teacher. She makes everyone in the staff room sponsor her before we have our hair cut,' Sammy said.

Mandy nodded. 'I could do that, too.'

'And if you don't want to do it on your own, join us—except it's going to be another two years before our hair's long enough to do it again.'

'I'll do it next week,' Mandy said. 'And then I'll join you in two years.'

'It's a deal,' Sammy said.

She enjoyed sharing pizza, garlic bread and birthday cake with Nick's family. Later that evening, Nick took her home. 'Thank you,' he said as they sat in the car outside her flat. 'You've been brilliant.'

'I had a great day,' she said. 'I loved the zip-wire. And the water fight.'

His eyes went hot. 'Yeah. Me, too.'

She kissed him. 'You have no idea how many of the mums were ogling you.'

'You have no idea how many of the dads were ogling *you*,' he countered. 'You're a natural with kids.' He paused. 'I probably shouldn't ask you this, but would you think about having your own, some day?'

'Maybe,' she said carefully. And this really was the crunch question, as far as she was concerned. Now he'd brought it up, she'd have to be brave and ask him. 'What about you?'

'Some day.' He looked sad. 'I wanted them about five years ago, but my ex wasn't keen.'

'Is that why you broke up with her?' She realised how bad that sounded and clapped her hand to her mouth. 'Sorry. I was being intrusive. You don't have to answer that.'

'No, that's fine. And no, it isn't why we broke up. You could say that my job got in the way.'

From the look on his face, Sammy was pretty sure there was more to it than that, but now wasn't the time to pry. 'I'm sorry,' she said again.

'It wasn't your fault, so there's no need to apologise.' He leaned forward and stole a kiss. 'But every cloud has a silver lining. It means that you and I got to meet.'

'There is that to it.' But he definitely wanted kids, and she might not be able to do that. She needed time to think. Time to work out how to tell him the truth about herself. She kissed him lingeringly. 'I would invite you in, but—'

'—you've got an early start tomorrow?' he guessed. 'Even on a Sunday?'

'That's the thing about being a freelance—you never

really know what hours you're going to work from week to week,' she said lightly.

'Yeah. Call me later,' he said softly, 'and maybe we can do something when we're both free.'

'Great idea.' She stroked his face. 'Thank you for letting me share today with you.'

'My pleasure.'

Mandy called Nick later that evening. 'I really like her, and so do the boys. They haven't stopped talking about her since she left.'

'Uh-huh,' Nick said, knowing that there was going to be more.

'She's a million miles away from Naomi—that one would never have had a water fight with the boys.'

No. Naomi had never really taken to them. 'Or ganged up on me so blatantly,' he said. 'You know the three of them soaked me in the park?'

'Suck it up and deal with it, you big baby,' Mandy said, laughing. 'But, seriously, Nick, Xander thinks she's amazing. She had a chat with him in the park— he wouldn't tell me what she said, but his attitude's changed. He said he wasn't going to let cancer define him.'

'Sammy's sister had cancer,' he said.

'The one who donates her hair for wigs, too?'

'Yes,' he said.

'And I bet Sammy was there for her every step of the way.' She paused. 'Nick, I know how you feel about relationships, but I'm telling you now that Sammy's different. She's a keeper.'

Yeah, he knew.

But sometimes he thought he could see something in

Sammy's eyes—something she was holding back. He really wasn't sure if she felt the same way about him that he was starting to feel about her.

Did he have the spirit to risk his heart again?

And, knowing that relationships weren't his strong point, was it fair to her?

CHAPTER NINE

LATER IN THE WEEK, Sammy had a girly pizza night with Claire, Ashleigh and her sister Jenny. She ended up telling them about the interview she'd given Ben. And admitting that she'd met Nick's family.

'Have you told Nick about your leg, yet?' Claire asked.

'I've tried telling him a few times,' Sammy said miserably. 'But I keep chickening out at the last minute. And what if he reacts badly when he realises I've kept it from him all this time—especially as I've had loads of chances to tell him the truth?'

'He might be a bit upset at first that you kept it from him,' Jenny said, 'but then he'll think about it and realise that it's a hell of a thing to tell someone. And then it will be fine.'

'Hmm.' Sammy wasn't so sure.

'Give him a chance, Sammy,' Ashleigh urged. 'Tell him.'

'I'll do it when I get back from New York next week, I promise,' Sammy said.

And she really meant to do it.

Except, when she got back to the airport, Nick was waiting for her right by the arrivals gate. Seeing him so unexpectedly totally threw her.

He took her suitcase and the heaviest of her photo-graphic boxes from her. 'How was your flight?'

'Fine.' She frowned. 'Hang on, what are you doing here?'

'The trial finished at lunchtime and I had some time to kill. I thought you might like a lift home.'

She knew part of that was a fib—following one trial, Nick would be in the middle of doing prep work for the next one, so he'd clearly taken time off just to meet her here—but it was so good to see him.

'Did you eat on the plane?' he asked.

'I had a sandwich, so I'm fine.'

He gave her a sidelong look. 'I've never seen you in a business suit before.'

'I'm not always a complete scruff,' she said. And she was very glad that she was wearing thick opaque tights, to hide her scars and avoid any awkward questions.

'No, I didn't mean that,' he said. 'I'm just used to you wearing black trousers. Smart ones.' He stopped and kissed her. 'You look fabulous. And I've missed you.'

'I've missed you, too,' she admitted, kissing him back.

He loaded her luggage into his car and drove her back to her flat.

'Do you want to come in for a coffee?' she asked.

'I'd love to.'

Her heart hammered. She was going to tell him now. Give him the choice to walk away, the way Bryn and the others had, or to accept her for who she was.

She slid her jacket off and hung it over the back of a chair, switched the kettle on and practised the words in her head. *There's something I need to tell you. Nothing to worry about. Just so you know, nearly half a lifetime ago I had osteosarcoma, but I'm absolutely fine now.*

But when Nick had put the visitor parking permit inside his windscreen, he walked back into her kitchen and kissed her stupid, and all the words flew out of her head.

She kissed him back, loving the way his mouth teased hers, warm and coaxing and sexy as hell.

'You make me feel light-headed,' she whispered.

'That's how you make me feel, too.' He drew her closer. 'Sammy. I know this is soon, I know it's crazy, but I've never felt a connection like this before. Not even with…' He shook his head, clearly not wanting to talk about his ex. 'This is ridiculous. In court, I'm articulate and I'm never stuck for what to say. Right here, right now, I'm making a total mess of this.' He brushed his mouth over hers. 'What I'm trying to say is, I want you. I really, *really* want you. And right now there's nothing more I'd like than to carry you to your bed.'

The smouldering heat in his eyes knocked every bit of common sense out of her brain. She'd never been looked at with such desire before. The feeling was heady, and she gave in to her body's urging. How could she possibly resist? She couldn't think about anything else other than what he'd just said and how much she wanted that to happen, too. 'Then what are you waiting for?' she asked, sounding a little hoarse.

He gave her the most sensual smile she'd ever seen, scooped her up and carried her to her bedroom.

When he set Sammy down on her feet next to the bed, her heart felt as if it were hammering so hard against her ribs that the whole world could hear it.

'Curtains,' she whispered. She switched on her bedside lamp, closed the curtains and walked back to him.

'I'm all yours,' he said softly. 'Do what you will with me.'

Need throbbed through her. She'd never wanted anyone so badly in her entire life. With shaking hands, she removed his tie, then slowly unbuttoned his collar. And then she dealt with each button on his shirt in turn.

He really was beautiful. And she couldn't resist skimming her fingertips over his pectorals and down to his abs.

'When I was photographing you for the calendar,' she said, 'I really wanted to photograph you for myself.'

'Oh?' He looked interested.

'In a green glade somewhere,' she continued.

'Wearing what?' he asked.

She grinned. 'The same as any other Greek statue.'

He raised an eyebrow. 'Just a fig leaf?'

She laughed. 'No fig leaf. You have beautiful musculature.'

He frowned. 'Are you telling me you're seeing me as a life model?'

'Right now, no.' Her voice went husky. 'I'm seeing you as my lover.'

'Good.' He stole a kiss. 'I'm looking forward to learning what you like. What makes you smile. What makes you see stars.'

'I like the sound of that,' she said.

He kissed her, then undid her own white shirt, exploring and touching and teasing as he uncovered her skin. He traced the lacy edge of her bra. 'I like this,' he whispered.

'Good.' She unbuckled his belt, her hands shaking as she undid the button of his trousers; she slid the zip down and helped him ease his trousers off.

He kicked off his shoes and got rid of his socks, then kissed her again. 'I think we're a little mismatched here, Ms Thompson.'

Sammy spread her hands in invitation. 'All yours.' She smiled. 'What's the phrase you used? "Do what you will with me."'

The heat in his eyes took her breath away.

He unzipped her lined skirt and let it fall to the floor next to his trousers.

And then, as he started to roll the waistband of her tights downwards, her common sense came back.

It felt as if someone had tipped a whole bucket of ice-cold water over her.

She couldn't do this.

Not now.

Maybe not ever.

Memories echoed in her head. The disgust in her last boyfriend's eyes when he'd seen her leg. The way Bryn had always insisted on having the light off, as if he couldn't bear to see her skin. He'd said it was because he hadn't been able to bear to think about her being in pain, but she'd known the truth. Her scar had repulsed him.

She knew Nick wasn't Bryn. In her head, she knew he was a good man. That he'd understand.

But the fear was too strong. She really, really couldn't do this.

'Sammy?' Nick stopped, clearly seeing that she was upset.

She shook her head. 'I can't do this. I'm sorry. I thought I could. But I can't.'

'What's wrong?' He curled his fingers round hers. 'Tell me.'

That was the point. She couldn't. Every single time she tried, her throat felt as if it had filled with sand. And she sure as hell wasn't going to show him. Apart from being unfair to him—it would come as a total shock—she couldn't bear to see the disgust or the pity in his face when he saw her leg.

Right now, she felt totally inadequate. She'd so wanted to do this. She'd so wanted to be *normal* and to make love with the most gorgeous man she'd ever met. But she wasn't normal, she never would be, and she knew she could never have the uncomplicated relationship she'd longed for.

And the panic flooding through her was far, far stronger than the voice of reason.

'I can't do this, Nick.' Her breath hitched. 'You have to go.'

He shook his head, his dark eyes filled with concern. 'Sammy, I can't just leave you on your own when you're upset.'

'Please, Nick. Just go.' She dropped her gaze. 'It's not you. Nothing you've done. It's me.' She was too scared to face the fear, too pathetic and weak and snivelling. She pulled her hand away from his and crossed her arms over her breasts.

'Sammy?'

'Please, just go,' she repeated.

She couldn't look at him. But she could hear the puzzlement in his voice, the concern. 'Sammy, you're clearly upset and I'm really not happy about leaving you on your own like this when something's obviously badly wrong. Can I ring someone for you? Your sister? Your friend who made you the dress?'

Why did he have to be so nice about it? Why couldn't

he just lose his temper and storm out? Why couldn't he be one of those horrible men she'd dated before?

Holding the tears back took so much effort. 'I can't do this, Nick. I just can't. I can't be with you.' She'd been stupid and selfish to think that this would work. 'This thing between us isn't going to work. It's not you, it's me.'

'But why?'

'It just *is*. I'm sorry. I really wish it could be different.' That at least was true. 'But we can't be together any more. It's over.'

'But—I thought we were getting closer.' His voice was full of hurt. 'You met my family. We…' He stopped.

Yeah. They had been getting closer. She really liked his family. And they'd just been about to make love.

But this wasn't fair of her. Even if he could cope with her being a cancer survivor, there were the complications. The fertility issues. She knew he wanted kids of his own, and she might not be able to offer him that. She'd been unfair and selfish to let things go this far. She should've stuck to her rules and ended it at the third date. Before either of them got hurt.

'I'm sorry,' she said. 'Please go, Nick.'

Nick dragged his clothes on in silence, too stunned to say any more.

Sammy had ended their relationship.

Just when he thought they were moving closer to the next stage. To making more of a commitment to each other.

They'd almost made love, for pity's sake.

There was clearly something very badly wrong,

something that had upset her, but she obviously didn't trust him enough to tell him what it was. Which made him feel like something that had just crawled out from under a stone.

Pain lanced through him. It looked as if he'd made the same mistake all over again. He was pretty sure that, unlike Naomi, Sammy wasn't having an affair and using his workaholic tendencies as an excuse to make him the one at fault for the break-up. But, just as he had last time, he'd invested more of himself in the relationship than his partner had. Sammy had made it clear that she didn't feel the same way about him that he felt about her.

Right now she couldn't even bear to look at him.

Feeling horrible, he left in silence and drove back to his flat. It was an effort to concentrate, and a couple of taxis beeped their horns at him for not driving on the second that the traffic lights had turned green. And he was none the wiser by the time he got home. Why something that had felt so special had just dissolved into nothingness. But he'd just have to suck it up and deal with it. He'd done it before and survived.

He tried calling her the next day. If nothing else, just to be sure that she was OK—because he was pretty sure that he'd seen fear in her face. Something was wrong, he was sure.

But she didn't answer her phone or return his messages.

Just silence.

And he wasn't pathetic enough to keep trying to talk to her when his attentions weren't welcome.

Over the next week and a half, Nick buried himself in work—that, at least, would never let him down. And he stonewalled any questions until people finally stopped asking him if everything was OK.

It wasn't OK.

But it would be.

Eventually.

Sammy's eyes felt three times the size of normal—she'd cried for so long. But she knew from experience that the best way to deal with heartache was to concentrate on her work and not leave even the tiniest moment free for the pain to make itself felt.

Though she had to tell a white lie at her photo shoot, the morning after she'd broken up with Nick. 'I've got conjunctivitis,' she said, 'so I need to wear dark glasses.'

Her eyes were sore and puffy, all right. But from crying, not from an eye infection.

It felt as if she'd made the biggest mistake of her life.

But she knew she'd done the right thing in the long run.

She just hoped it would stop hurting soon.

'I know something's wrong,' Mandy said. 'I'm your big sister. You can't fob me off with any more excuses. And Danica next door is babysitting the boys, so I can stay here until you finally tell me what's wrong.'

Nick sighed. 'OK. Sammy and I have split up.'

'What? But why did you dump her? Sammy was lovely,' Mandy said.

'I didn't dump her. She dumped me.' Nick shrugged.

'No *way*,' Mandy said, sounding shocked. 'The way she was with you—I could see how much she thought of you. You must've got it wrong.'

'She said it wasn't working for her. And you can't

force someone to feel something they don't.' He looked away. 'At least I didn't make a total fool out of myself and tell her how I felt about her before she dumped me.'

'Oh, Nick.' Mandy hugged him. 'Are you sure you're not just being a typical bloke and totally misreading things?'

'Pretty sure,' he said dryly. He wasn't going to tell his sister the circumstances. Some things weren't for sharing. 'She was quite clear about it.'

'I'm sorry. I really hoped…'

'Yeah, I know.' So had he. 'Plenty more fish in the sea.'

'Except you're not going to even put out a single line, let alone a net.'

'Hey. I have a great family, a job I love, and friends. I don't need anything more,' Nick said lightly.

And if he told himself that enough times, he'd believe it.

'What do you mean, you've split up? You're telling us he turned out to be another Bryn?' Ashleigh said.

Sammy looked away.

'You *did* tell him about your leg?' Claire asked.

'No.'

'So you dumped him without even talking about it?' Ashleigh asked, her voice filled with disbelief. 'Sammy, are you nuts? You broke your three-dates rule for him. Which means he was special.'

'He is.' Sammy bit her lip. 'It was the right thing to do. Now he's got the chance to find someone without any complications.'

'You mean, you were too much of a coward to give it a chance to work,' Claire said. When Sammy flinched, she continued, 'And yes, Ash and I can tell it to you this straight, because we're your best friends and we love you, and you've just done the most stupid thing *ever*.'

'Talk to him,' Ashleigh urged. 'Tell him you made a mistake. Tell him everything.'

Sammy shook her head. 'It's a bit late for that now.'

'It's never too late,' Claire said. 'Look, you've got the calendar launch next week. He's one of the models, so he's bound to be there. Talk to him then.'

Except Nick wasn't at the launch.

Xander, Ned and Mandy were there, but Mandy gave her a cool look and steered the boys away before they could talk to her.

And Sammy felt like the nastiest woman in the world.

She felt even worse when her phone pinged with a text from Xander.

You're not the Black Widow. You're one of the weasels.

He was absolutely right.

She went home on her own.

And then she cried herself to sleep all over again.

CHAPTER TEN

'TEA?' GARY SMILED broadly at Nick and placed the mug on his desk. 'Oh, and you might like to see this.' He handed over a press cutting. 'It's about your calendar. Which is selling like hot cakes from the clerks' room, I might add. We're getting people from every set of chambers around here coming in to buy them.'

Nick rolled his eyes. 'The next person to ask me if I'll strip off in the middle of their court case is going to get pushed into the nearest puddle.'

'Hey.' Gary punched his arm awkwardly. 'They're only teasing. What you did is pretty awesome. I'm not sure I'd have the guts to do it. Is your nephew doing OK?'

'Yeah, he is. Thanks for asking.'

'Are *you* OK?'

Nick gave his clerk a pointed look. 'I will be, if people will let me get on with my job.'

'Got it, boss.' Gary sketched a wry salute and left Nick's office.

Nick ignored the article for a while. But curiosity eventually won, and he picked it up to look at it.

It was pretty standard stuff: how a group of people connected with the oncology ward had stripped off for a charity calendar to raise money for new equipment and treatment. And it came with a montage of photographs from the calendar—including his own page. Mr December.

He was about to drop the cutting in the bin when something in the last paragraph caught his eye.

About the woman who'd photographed the calendar.

Who was a cancer survivor.

What the hell…?

He sat up, slapped the cutting back on his desk and read it more closely.

When he'd finished, he just stared at the page, stunned. He'd had absolutely no idea that Sammy had had osteosarcoma as a teen.

Why hadn't she told him? Especially when she knew that his nephew had the same condition? Did she really think it made any difference to the way he'd treat her?

The article implied that not everyone in Sammy's past had reacted well to her medical condition. OK, some people were ignorant. But, for pity's sake, she *knew* him. Surely she'd known that he wouldn't react badly? That he would never have pushed her away or made her feel ugly or anything less than beautiful? That for him, beauty was skin deep and that it was who you were rather than what you looked like that mattered?

Nick thought about it.

And then he thought some more.

He remembered that day in the park. He'd asked Sammy afterwards if she wanted children; and he'd told her that he wanted kids of his own.

According to the article, she'd had chemotherapy before and after the surgery. He didn't know that much about the side-effects of cancer treatment on women—

thankfully none of the women in his life had been affected by it—but he was pretty sure that it could make
having children difficult. A quick bit of research on the
internet told him that, yes, fertility could be a problem,
depending on whether or not she'd had some eggs frozen before the treatment.

It's not you, it's me.

Her words took on a slightly different meaning now.
Maybe she'd ended things between them not because
she wasn't interested, but because she thought that having a family would be too complicated, she knew he
wanted children, and she didn't want to stand in the
way of his dreams. She'd pushed him away, but maybe
she'd broken up with him as the ultimate in self-sacri-
fice rather than actually rejecting him.

She hadn't given him the chance to discuss it with
her. But maybe, if she'd been hurt badly before, she
found it difficult to trust. As difficult as he did.

Even though part of him was hurt and angry that she
hadn't trusted him, a deeper part of him understood
why. Maybe he should cut her some slack. Give her a
chance to tell him herself.

When his session in court had ended, in the middle
of the afternoon, Nick called her. The line went straight
through to voicemail: meaning that she was busy, or she
was avoiding him. He wasn't sure which. Either way,
he'd leave a very clear message, so she'd be left in no
doubt. 'Sammy, it's Nick. I saw the article your friend
wrote about the calendar. About you. If you don't call
me back, I'll come and sit outside your flat until you
get home, and I don't care if I have to sit there for a
whole month before you turn up. Because we really,
really need to talk.'

* * *

'Answer it, you chicken,' Sammy told herself when she saw Nick's name on the screen of her mobile phone.

But she didn't quite have the nerve.

She listened to the voicemail he left her, though.

It seemed that Nick wanted to talk to her. And he wasn't planning to take no for an answer.

She dragged in a breath. He'd read the article, so he knew the truth about her now. She had absolutely no idea what was going through his head. But she knew that she owed him an explanation at the very least.

Time to be brave.

She picked up her phone and called him. 'It's Sammy, returning your call,' she said, careful to keep her voice neutral.

'We need to talk, and I'd rather not do this on the phone. Can we meet this evening?' he asked.

Sammy noticed that her hand was actually shaking. 'I—um…'

'A neutral place,' he said softly. 'Remember that place where we had brunch, just off Fleet Street?'

'Yes. I remember.'

'Shall we meet there?'

'OK. What time?'

'Any time after six is good for me.'

'Six, then,' she said. Better to get it over with as soon as possible than to wait and worry herself stupid about it.

'I'll see you there at six.'

The phone went dead. Either he was busy, or he was seriously fed up with her. Or maybe both.

Sammy just about managed to focus on her work for the next couple of hours, and then she headed for the café where they'd met before. Nick was already there—and her heart skipped a beat when he met her gaze.

Seeing him again made her realise just how much she'd missed him.

But she'd messed this up big time.

This was going to be closure, and nothing more, she reminded herself. *Don't think that this is fixable. Because it's not. Your role today is to apologise for not telling him, explain, and then walk away. Don't sit there vainly wishing and hoping for things you can't have.*

'Thank you for coming,' he said when she reached his table. 'What would you like to drink? Wine? Coffee?'

'Mint tea, please,' she said.

He ordered her a mint tea and himself a coffee.

Something about his message had really bugged her. 'Would you really have sat outside my flat for a whole month?'

'I would've camped on your doorstep,' he said. 'I might not have been very fragrant if you'd kept me waiting for a whole month—but yes, I would've waited.'

For the first time since he'd called her, hope flickered in her heart. So was he saying they still had a chance?

The waiter brought their drinks over before she could ask. And then it wasn't appropriate to say anything. This was a discussion they needed to have in semi-private.

'Why didn't you tell me?' he asked gently when the waiter had gone to look after another table of customers.

'And you've seen the article?' It was a rhetorical question. She already knew he had. But she couldn't think of what to say, and it was the only thing that came into her head.

'I've read it,' he confirmed. And she could hear the hurt in his voice. 'Why didn't you tell me?'

'I was going to.'

'We almost made love, Sammy,' he said softly, 'and you didn't tell me—but now I know why you never wear a short skirt unless you're also wearing thick opaque tights. Why you asked me to leave, instead of doing what we both really wanted to do.'

'Yes.' And now she felt miserable and stupid. Why hadn't she been brave enough to tell him? They'd both missed out on something that could've been amazing. All because she'd been too scared.

'You told me that your sister was your connection to the ward—that she was the one with cancer.'

She shook her head. 'No. I told you that my sister donated her hair, the same as I do. You just assumed that she was the connection to the ward, not me.'

'You obviously realised that, but you still didn't correct me.'

'And a lie of omission is just as bad as a full-on lie, I guess.' She sighed.

'Why didn't you tell me? That's what I don't understand.'

She shrugged slightly. 'Because I've found that people treat me differently when they know.'

'Xander has the same condition. Did you see me treating him any differently from the way I treat Ned?'

'No. Well, you're a bit more protective with him.'

'Which is only natural.' He glanced at her. 'Did Xander say that to you?'

'I'd rather not answer that.'

Then another thought occurred to him. His sister had said that Xander's attitude to cancer had changed since he'd talked to Sammy. 'Does Xander know about you?'

She nodded. 'I asked him not to tell anyone.'

He frowned. 'I don't get it. Why did you tell him and not me?'

'Because I wanted him to see that there was hope on the other side of the op, and having osteosarcoma didn't mean that he'd end up never being able to do anything again. I wanted him to see that not being able to play football with his mates is just temporary, and having to rest would give him a chance to find other things he likes doing just as much.'

'Mandy says he sees things differently, so obviously we have you to thank for that. I think you're right— he did need to hear something like that from someone who'd been through it,' Nick said, 'but I still don't get why you think *I'd* treat you differently.'

'I know you're not like my exes. Some of them walked away because even the word "cancer" brought them out into a cold sweat.' She paused for a moment. This wasn't something she found easy to talk about, but she knew she owed Nick the full truth now. 'Except Bryn. He was the one I thought was different,' she said softly. 'He was the one who asked me to marry him.'

Nick waited. Clearly he knew that trick too, she thought wryly.

'Two years ago, I had a scare. I found a lump in my breast. Most people my age would've just assumed that it was probably a cyst and not worried themselves stupid from the time they discovered the lump until the time they got the results back, but once you've had osteosarcoma you have a different perspective,' she said.

'Even though I had chemo before and after the surgery, it doesn't mean that they managed to zap every single bad cell. So there's always a chance that the cancer will come back somewhere else in my body. You need to understand that.'

'But you have regular check-ups, yes?'

She nodded. 'They're annual, now. I have my check-up in the morning; then, in the afternoon—if I'm clear—my sister Jenny and I go out for champagne to celebrate. Every other year, we have an appointment afterwards at a salon so we can donate our hair.'

Then he asked the crunch question, his voice so gentle that it made her want to cry. 'And was the lump cancer?'

'No. It was a cyst. I had a scan and the doctor took some fluid out of it, so they could tell me straight away it was benign. Obviously they tested the cells to make absolutely sure. But it went away by itself.'

'That's good—right?' he asked.

She swallowed hard. 'That's when Bryn broke our engagement—as soon as he knew I was OK. He didn't want to be the bad guy who dumped the woman who had cancer.'

Nick raised his eyebrows. 'But it was fine to dump you when he was sure the cancer hadn't come back?'

She nodded. 'He said he couldn't cope with the fear that it would come back in the future.'

Nick said something very pithy, and she flinched.

'It's true,' he said, 'and he wasn't good enough for you. He was one of the weasels and you had a lucky escape.'

'Xander said I was a weasel,' she said miserably.

Nick frowned. 'When?'

'At the calendar launch. And he's right. I hurt you, and I'm sorry.'

'You're not a weasel,' he said. 'And Xander—'

'—was covering your back,' she said. 'Because he loves you and he knew I'd split up with you.'

'I guess.' His frown deepened. 'I'm still trying to get my head round the fact that you think I'd be as weak and selfish as your ex. You know how I feel about Mandy's ex walking out on them when Xander was diagnosed. I'd never, ever do that to anyone I loved.'

'I know—and I panicked. I'm sorry,' she said again. 'I know you're not like them. But I… I tend to push people away when I get scared. My family and my best friends yell at me all the time for being too independent. Claire—the one who made me the dress—says there's a fine line between being independent and being too stubborn.'

'She has a point,' he said.

She bit her lip. 'I know. I guess…' She sighed. 'The men in my life either run for the hills or they wrap me in cotton wool, and that just makes me more stubborn and more independent. I'm sorry.'

'You're not the only one to blame. I should've pushed you harder and not taken your silence for an answer. I let you walk out of my life because I thought I'd made the same mistake all over again, too,' he said. 'That I felt more for you than you felt for me.'

She frowned. 'But I broke my three-date rule for you. Doesn't that tell you something?'

'What three-date rule?' he asked, looking surprised.

'I never date anyone more than three times. Then I don't have to tell them about my past. I can pretend I'm normal. That I'm a real woman.'

He stared at her as if she'd just grown another head. 'How do you work out that you're not a real woman? Because you look perfectly real to me.'

'That's not what I mean,' she said miserably. 'It's complicated.'

'I'm used to complicated situations in court,' he said softly. 'Try me.'

'Do you have any idea how hard this is to talk about?'

'Having not been through cancer myself, no. But I guess it's as hard as I find talking about my marriage. And I told you about that.'

'That she broke up with you because you're a work-aholic.'

He grimaced. 'I guess that's the anodyne version.'

She frowned. 'What's the real version?'

'If I tell you,' he said, 'then you come clean with me. All of it.'

She took a deep breath. 'All of it. OK.' She bit her lip. 'I know I'm being a coward and putting it off, but... you, first?'

He reached over and squeezed her hand. 'You've been through the kind of hell most people can't cope with—and you still smile your way through life, living it to the full. You're no coward, Sammy. But, OK, me first. I thought Naomi liked our lifestyle—I worked hard, so did she, and we had a nice flat and good holidays and a decent standard of living. I knew my dad had made that mistake with my mother, focusing on his job and leaving her to be practically a single parent as well as having her own career, and I'd got to the stage where I'd started wanting a family of my own. So I came home early one night. I intended to take her out somewhere to spoil her, tell her that I was going to cut back a bit on my hours and put her first, and suggest that maybe we could start trying for a baby.'

Everything Sammy wanted.

And something she might not be able to have.

She pushed the thought away and listened to him.

'I heard voices when I got home. I thought maybe Naomi was home early and listening to the radio, or watching something on the TV.' He looked away. 'And then I walked into the bedroom. She wasn't alone.'

His ex had been having an affair?

It must have cut him to the quick.

Especially as he'd said that his mother had had an affair and his parents had split up during his late teens. It must have brought all that misery back, too.

'Her lover did the decent thing and left us to talk. And Naomi told me she'd started seeing him because she was lonely, fed up with waiting for me to come home late from the office, and our marriage was over.' He blew out a breath. 'And yet she'd always encouraged me to work late, to go for every case that would move my career forward. It was only later that I worked out she'd done that to cover her tracks and make it easier for her to see the other guy. But my job was the perfect excuse for me to be the one at fault.'

'That's…' This time Sammy was the one to make a pithy comment.

'Yeah.' He looked away. 'She lied to me.'

She reached across the table to squeeze his hand. 'And I lied to you, too. By omission, but it was still a lie. And I pushed you away without giving you a chance— just like she did.'

He said nothing, clearly not trusting himself to speak.

'I'm sorry I hurt you,' she said. 'It's not that I don't trust you. I know you're a good man, Nick. You're honourable and decent. All I can say in my defence is that I was scared.'

'We've both made bad choices in the past. That doesn't mean we'll make a bad choice this time,' Nick said.

'OK. Let me ask you straight. Can you cope with the fact that I'm in remission, but one day the cancer might come back?'

'Yes.'

'How?' she asked, wanting to believe him but not quite able to.

'Because one day you might be knocked over by a bus, or have a piano dropped on your head, or be struck by lightning,' he said. 'You can't live the rest of your life worrying about something that might not happen. Yes, there's a chance it might come back. But there's also a chance that it might not.'

'You need to be realistic about this,' Sammy said. 'Because there's more of a chance of me getting cancer again than there is of me having a piano dropped on my head. Quite a big chance.'

'It doesn't make any difference to me,' he said. 'In English law, there's the eggshell skull rule. You take your victim as you find them.' He flapped a dismissive hand. 'Well, not that you're my victim, but you get what I mean.'

'Yes.' She smiled.

'And, for the record, I'm not going to wrap you in cotton wool. I remember you telling me not to do that to Xander, and I thought you were speaking about the way people treated your sister.'

'It was the way people treated me,' she said. 'And it drives me nuts.'

'No wrapping in cotton wool, either. So that's the first elephant down,' he said. 'Want to tackle the second? Because I have a feeling that this one's the really big one. The mammoth, you might say.'

'Second?'

'This thing about not being a real woman. I'm hazarding a guess here, but I read up on the side-effects of chemotherapy.'

So he knew?

'You once asked me if I wanted children,' he said, 'and I told you that I did. But when I asked you, you fudged the issue. Is that because you don't want children, or because you don't think you'll be able to have them?'

'I do want children. I had some of my eggs frozen before the first chemo.' She dragged in a breath. 'But there's no guarantee that IVF will work. So I might not be able to have children.'

'There are other ways,' he pointed out. 'If we want children and IVF doesn't work, then we can foster or we can adopt. Or we can just enjoy being an aunt and uncle. I have two and you have four, right? I reckon that makes a five-a-side football team with one in reserve.'

Her eyes filled with tears. 'Would that be enough for you? Being an uncle and maybe a godfather?'

'If I have you in my life, yes.' His dark eyes held hers, and she knew that he meant it. Truly.

A tear spilled over her lashes and he brushed it away. 'Don't cry. I never want to hurt you, Sammy. And, believe me, as far as I'm concerned you're all woman. I don't get how you can think otherwise. Unless your ex said that—and you already know that the man's worthless and his views aren't worth listening to, yes?'

'I guess.' The wobble in her voice was obvious to her own ears. It was something she found it so hard to get her head around. 'I can't make any promises that this is going to work,' she said, 'but maybe we can start again and see how it goes?'

'Learn to trust. Together. That works for me,' he said.

She took a deep breath. 'OK. Then I think the first thing is…well, not something I want to do in the middle of this café.' A hurdle she should've tried to overcome long, long before. And one that would have to be cleared right now before they could move forward. 'Your place or mine?'

'Mine's nearer,' he said.

'Your place, then. Which Tube station?'

'The Tube changes from here are a bit messy. Actually, it's just as quick to walk—unless you want to get a taxi?' he suggested.

She shook her head. 'Walking's fine.'

He paid the bill, and they walked back to his flat hand in hand. They didn't say much on the way. Sammy grew more and more nervous, the nearer they got to his flat, but she knew she had to do this.

'What would you like to drink?' he asked when he closed his front door behind him.

'I don't want a drink.' She shook her head. 'We need to go to your bedroom.'

He sucked in a breath. 'Sammy?'

'With the curtains closed and the overhead light on full. In fact, every single light in that room on full,' she said. She remembered where his room was; she took his hand and led him there.

He guessed what she was going to do. 'Sammy, you don't have to do this.'

'Oh, but I do,' she said. 'This is the third elephant. The last one. And it's bigger than a mammoth. Getting on for Amphicoelias size, I'd say.'

'Amphicoelias?' He looked mystified.

'You don't know the name of the biggest sauropod ever? And you an uncle of two boys. Tsk. You need to bone up on your dinosaurs.' Her tone was light, but her hands were shaking as she undid the button of her jeans.

'Sammy.' Gently, he put his hands over hers. 'Do you trust me to do this?'

The lump in her throat was so huge that she couldn't speak, just nodded.

Slowly, he undid the zip, drew the denim down over her hips, then knelt down and drew the material down her thighs to her knees.

She flinched.

He leaned back and looked up at her. 'Do you want me to stop?'

She shook her head. 'No.'

'No?' His voice was so gentle. But there was no pity in his eyes. Just empathy. He understood, and he'd let her take this at her pace.

'And yes,' she admitted. This terrified her. The moment when things between them would change. When he'd start to pity her and want to protect her. When he'd see for himself that she wasn't a real woman.

As if he could read her mind, he said, 'It's really not going to make a difference between us. But you're right—I do need to see this for myself. And then I need to prove to you that it won't change a thing.'

She closed her eyes. 'Then do it.'

Gently, he pulled the jeans down to her ankles and helped her step out of each leg.

She still had her eyes closed.

Then she felt him kiss her shin. Her left shin. The scar. All the way from the bottom to the top, his mouth soft yet very sure.

A tear leaked out and slid down her face; she couldn't stop it.

'Sammy,' he said, his voice husky. 'You're so brave and so incredible and so amazing. And this is just one little part of you. The part that makes me proud, because you've been through so much and you haven't let it hold you back.' He pressed another kiss to her scar, then got to his feet; she felt him cup her face with his hands.

'Open your eyes,' he said softly. 'Open your eyes and look into mine.'

It was one of the hardest things she'd ever done. If she looked into his eyes now and saw the slightest jot of pity, then she'd walk away. She'd have regrets, but she'd still walk away, because this was a deal-breaker.

'Do it,' he said.

She held her breath and opened her eyes.

But there was no pity in his gaze, just understanding. And something else she didn't quite dare name, but she really hoped she wasn't wrong about it.

'You're brave and you're beautiful, and I love you,' he said. 'Yes, we'll have a few bumps in the road ahead of us—everyone does—but we'll face them and we'll deal with them as and when we have to. Together.'

'You love me?' she whispered.

'I love you,' he confirmed. 'I think I fell for you the day I met you. The day you bossed me around and made me strip in front of you—and then you made me talk to you until I was comfortable about what I was doing. And you had dinner with me without being fussy about what you ate. And I knew you were straightforward and honest.'

'But I lied to you,' she said.

'No, you just didn't correct me when I made a wrong assumption,' he said, 'and you didn't tell me about the thing that really scared you. And although I admit I was hurt when I found out, I understand now why you kept it from me—and it's not a problem for me any more.'

'Thank you.'

He kissed her lightly. 'We've got a chance, Sammy. Let's take it.'

She stroked his face. 'For me, it was when you let Ned soak you in the water fight. You didn't care about your dignity. You just wanted the boys to have fun.'

He coughed. 'Is that a roundabout way of saying…?'

She blinked. 'I didn't say it already?'

He looked pained. *'Sammy.'*

She smiled. 'I love you, too. Though I'm still scared it's all going to go wrong.'

'We've both been here before and it's gone wrong,' he said, 'but it doesn't mean that it'll be like that this time. Let's give it a go—see if we can help each other learn to trust again.'

'I'd like that.'

'Starting now,' he said.

'With me half-naked and you fully dressed?' she protested.

'I think we've been here before. Or something like that. Except this time I hope you're not going to ask me to leave.'

'We're in your flat. I can hardly ask you to leave.'

'Then tell me you're not going to walk away,' he said. 'Because right now I need to be close to you. I want to make love with you. And I want to prove to you that you're all woman. You're all the woman I'll ever want or need.'

She didn't need a second prompt. She leaned forward, kissed him, and began to undo his shirt.

CHAPTER ELEVEN

Two months later

NICK SET A mug of tea down on the bedside cabinet next to Sammy and placed the Sunday newspapers on the bed next to her.

'Are you quite sure you have to work today?' she asked, patting the pillow next to her invitingly. 'I was thinking we could have a lazy morning in bed, then go and look at the Christmas lights this afternoon. Hot chocolate, mulled wine, Christmas gingerbread, that sort of thing...'

'I definitely have to work, so we need to take a rain check.' He leaned over and kissed her. 'But I'll text you when I'm nearly done and you can come and meet me. We'll eat out tonight—my treat,' he said.

She smiled at him and kissed him back. 'That sounds lovely, but will you be able to get a table anywhere? Most places will be booked up for office Christmas parties.'

He grinned. 'I'm sure I can find something.'

'Trust you, you're Mr December?' she teased.

'Something like that.' His eyes crinkled at the corners. 'I love you.'

'I love you, too. See you later.'

Sammy spent the morning in bed reading the newspaper, had a light lunch and pottered round her flat in the afternoon.

Her phone pinged at three with a message.

Meet me at Temple Church and bring your camera.

Odd, she thought, or maybe Nick had found out that there was some kind of exhibition or a carol concert on today and wanted to make up for the fact that they hadn't been able to do anything Christmassy today. She locked the front door behind her, caught the Tube to Embankment, then headed for Inner Temple on foot.

As the sun set by four o'clock in December, it was starting to get dark by the time she got to the complex of buildings around the church. She couldn't resist pausing by the gas lamps and taking a few shots; she remembered Nick saying that it was like being back in Dickens' time with the streets lit by gaslight, and he was absolutely right. The light was different—much softer. All they needed was a sprinkle of snow and a few actors from a period drama walking around in crinolines or top hats and tailcoats, and the Inns of Court would look just like an old-fashioned Christmas card.

She headed to the church. It looked beautiful, with a Christmas tree scenting the air and the organ playing 'Silent Night'. But if there was a carol concert on today, it couldn't be for a while yet; the place was virtually empty, apart from a couple of stray tourists.

As she walked in, the music changed. Was the organist playing Moonlight Sonata or was she imagining it? Were they even allowed to play secular music on a church organ? she wondered.

And there definitely weren't any signs up about a carol concert today. Sammy looked around the church for Nick, but she couldn't see him. Maybe he'd been caught up with a phone call or something. Well, at least this was a nice place to wait for him. And with beautiful music playing, because it was definitely Beethoven.

When she went to take another look at the Crusader tomb effigies, a church official came over to her.

'Ms Thompson?'

'Yes.' She looked at him in surprise. How had he known her name?

'I believe there's a message for you,' he said.

From Nick? she wondered. But why hadn't Nick just called her mobile phone?

The church official gestured to the effigies and Sammy realised that propped against the little stone dog that had captured her imagination last time was a cream vellum envelope—and her name was written on it in bold black ink. She recognised the handwriting as Nick's.

Why would he leave her a note here? And why next to the little stone dog?

'Thank you,' she said, and opened the envelope. It contained a cream vellum card. On the front, there was a brief message.

Life's short—eat dessert first.

Something she'd said often enough to him. Hmm. So were they meeting somewhere for dessert rather than a full meal? Well, that was fine by her.

She opened the card, and inside there were directions to go to the café where they'd had brunch. The place where they'd talked over all the misunderstandings and agreed to start again.

Maybe he was going to meet her there, then. But it was strange that he'd asked her to come here to the church first.

'Thank you,' she said to the church official.

She also stopped by the organist, because she was starting to suspect something. 'Thank you,' she said quietly. 'The Moonlight Sonata is my favourite piece of music, and I have a feeling that you might have been asked to play it especially for me.'

The organist smiled. 'I was, my dear. And it was my pleasure. I love Beethoven, too.'

Her favourite piece of music, the Crusader tombs and the café where they'd had brunch. What was the connection? Or was Nick doing some kind of treasure trail?

She dropped some money into the church donation box on her way out, and headed to the café, intrigued. What was Nick up to?

Icicle lights were hanging everywhere on shop fronts along the Strand, and she knew that if she peeped in at Somerset House there would be skaters in the ice rink in front of a massive Christmas tree. As she passed the entrance, she could hear 'All I Want For Christmas Is You' belting out, and she could smell hot chocolate.

This was definitely something she needed to take Nick to in the future, she thought. Somewhere they could both play hard, after a day's work.

'Good evening, Ms Thompson,' the waiter said when she walked in to the café.

She wasn't even going to ask how the waiter knew her name. Nick had clearly given directions of some sort. 'Good evening,' she replied.

'Come this way,' the waiter said, and seated her at a small table with a candle in the centre, next to a sparkly reindeer with a red ribbon round its neck, and a miniature Christmas tree decorated with red and gold baubles. Though only one place was set, and there was no sign of Nick.

'Mr Kennedy says to have dessert on him,' the waiter told her.

'Dessert?' So was this going to be a mince pie, or Christmas pudding with brandy sauce? she wondered.

'He was very specific,' the waiter said. And Sammy couldn't help smiling when he brought out a tiny hazelnut waffle, finished with berries and cream, together with a small coffee. Not Christmassy, but just what they'd enjoyed on their first visit here.

'Thank you,' she said, and texted Nick.

The waffle's a very nice touch—but what are you up to?

Wait and see, he replied.

So you *are* up to something...

This time, he didn't reply. OK. If he wanted to be mysterious, she'd let him have his fun. Because this was turning out to be just as fun for her, too—trying to guess what his next move was.

She enjoyed both the waffle and the coffee. When she'd finished, the waiter handed her another cream vellum envelope. This time, she was directed to the National Portrait Gallery, to one of the portraits that Nick had really liked when they'd visited together.

She loved walking through Trafalgar Square; the massive Christmas tree next to the fountain was lit with vertical strands of white lights, and the fountain itself was lit up, the jets spraying higher than usual. The trees in Trafalgar Square and St Paul's Cathedral were two of her favourites in London, and she had plenty of shots of both in her portfolio—even so, she couldn't resist taking just a couple more.

Almost as soon as she walked into the art gallery and found the painting Nick had specified, one of the curators came over to her. 'Ms Thompson?' he asked.

'Yes.' She smiled, now absolutely sure that Nick had planned some sort of treasure trail for her. Something based on their dates, unless she was missing something.

'I have a note for you,' the curator said.

It was another vellum envelope, although this time the message was written on the back of a postcard of the portrait she'd been directed to rather than on plain cream card. The directions were to the gallery's café, and the message read:

I'm not going to make you climb over the Dome tonight as the sun's already set—but I thought you might like these.

So this trail of his was definitely based on their first few dates, she thought with a smile. Her table in the café was specially reserved for her, set with a single red rose in an exquisite crystal bud vase. After the waiter had seated her at the table, he brought over a glass of champagne and two tiny squares of toast with Welsh rarebit. Just like the afternoon tea they'd had together at the posh hotel.

'Enjoy, ma'am,' he said with a small bow.

'Thank you,' she said, and ate the Welsh rarebit before it went cold, then called Nick.

His phone went straight through to voicemail.

She sighed and left a message. 'Nick, thank you. It's very nice having a backwards dinner, complete with champagne, but it would be even nicer if I got to share it with you. Where are you?'

A few seconds later, her phone beeped with a reply. Patience...

So he *was* there. Just not answering her. 'Arrgh,' she said, rolling her eyes, and sipped her champagne.

When she'd finished, a man wearing livery and a peaked cap came over to her. 'Ms Thompson? Please come with me.'

The next stage of Nick's trail, she thought. So wherever she was going next was clearly by car, because this man was definitely dressed as a chauffeur.

Not just a car, she discovered: a limo. Very shiny, very black, and very swish. Which, she supposed, went perfectly with a chauffeur.

There was another envelope in the car.

I do hope you meant it when you said you're not scared of heights.

Hmm. Nick had already said they weren't going to walk over the Dome tonight, so what did he have in mind?

She had no clue as the car drove along the Victoria Embankment; they were driving in the opposite direction to the London Eye, so he couldn't have meant that. But then the driver turned along London Bridge, and she could see the lights from the bridge, the riverfront buildings and the fairy lights on the trees all reflected in the dark water of the Thames. London by night was beautiful—but she'd always thought that London by night at Christmas was even more magical.

And finally the driver pulled up outside the tallest building in London—the Shard, its very top storeys lit up with the nightly-changing Christmas light show.

Now she understood what he meant about heights.

Hopefully this meant that Nick would be at the top, waiting for her.

The driver opened the door for her and ushered her inside.

She was met at the doorway by someone that she assumed was part of the attraction's PR team. 'Ms Thompson?' the man asked.

'Yes,' she said, wondering quite what was coming next.

To her surprise, he handed her a filled water pistol, together with another of the vellum envelopes. The note said:

Choose your target carefully.

She remembered the day they spent in the park with Nick's nephews and smiled. Was he planning to have another water fight with her?

'This way, please, Ms Thompson.' The man took her to a corridor. Set in the middle was a table, with three photographs set on a small ledge. As a nod to Christmas, all the photographs were decked with a sprig of holly, making her smile. The first photograph was of Nick wearing his full barrister garb; the second was Nick wearing a suit, and the last one was Nick in jeans.

Which one was she supposed to shoot?

This was a tough decision. The barrister garb was linked to the very first day she'd met him, albeit he hadn't worn much of it; the suit was what he wore whenever she met him from work; and he'd worn jeans to the park when she and the boys had ganged up on him and soaked him.

She tried to second-guess him. A barrister would be super-protective—so Nick, knowing how much over-protectiveness drove her crazy, would want her to take that target down…right?

She aimed the water pistol at the photo of Nick in his barrister dress and knocked it over.

There was another small vellum envelope underneath the photograph. She read the message:

Good choice. Now go to the lift.

So she had got it right. That was a relief.

'Um—could you direct me to the lift, please?' she asked.

'Of course, Ms Thompson,' the PR man said.

As soon as the lift doors opened, Sammy saw tasteful Christmas decorations—swathes of beautiful greenery. But there was also a handmade sign bearing a photograph of a pile of fluffy cotton wool balls, with a red X scrawled through it in pen, and she burst out laughing before grabbing her phone and calling Nick.

This time, he actually answered his phone.

'So are you telling me this is a cotton-wool-free zone?' she asked.

He laughed. 'Got it in one.'

'Where are you?'

'Not far now,' he said. 'Pay attention.'

'Yes, m'learned friend.'

He laughed again and hung up.

She wasn't quite sure what he had in mind but she was enjoying this. He'd clearly spent time setting this up and she loved how very personal it was.

The lift stopped halfway up the tower, and the PR man said, 'You need to get out at this floor.'

Nick wasn't at the top?

'OK,' she said.

But just outside the lift was another table. This one had three cards on it.

The first was a gorgeous shot of lightning—one she would've loved to have in her own portfolio. Inside, he'd written:

Chance of being struck by lightning—roughly one in a million.

To her amusement, he'd listed the source so she could look it up and prove it to herself.

The second was a picture of a piano. Inside, he'd written:

Chance of a piano falling on your head—apparently this is an old movie trope and there aren't any actual recorded cases of a piano being dropped onto someone's head.

Trust him to investigate it thoroughly and debunk the myth. She couldn't help smiling.

The third was a picture of a bumpy, lumpy road leading to the brow of a hill. Inside, he'd written:

Chance of having rough times ahead—one hundred per cent, but I'll be there to hold your hand through whatever comes. Without cotton wool. Just as I know you'll be there for me.

There was a huge lump in her throat.

He really meant this.

They'd be there for each other, no matter what lay ahead.

'Ms Thompson?' the PR man said. 'We need to go up.'

'Yes.' She smiled at him, swallowed hard and put the cards in her bag.

Another corridor stop: and this one also had cards on the table. A picture of the edge of space.

I can't promise you this right now, but once it's commercially available...

She smiled. She'd so hold him to that one.

A picture of the Northern Lights and polar bears.

Alternative suggestion to the edge of space, from my bucket list.

And finally a picture of a lighthouse.

You said you liked these. You, me, a bottle of champagne and a spa bath on New Year's Eve. How about it?

Sammy grinned. She was totally fine with that. She scooped up the cards and put them in her bag, too.

'Ms Thompson,' the PR man said, gesturing back to the lift.

This time, the lift went straight to the top—and when the doors opened Nick was right there, waiting for her.

'You,' she said, 'are amazing, Mr December.' She walked over to him, wrapped her arms round him and kissed him.

'You're pretty amazing yourself,' he said.

'I can't believe you did all that for me. And what if I'd picked the wrong target with the water pistol?' she asked.

'I had a contingency plan,' he said.

'Which was?'

'I put exactly the same message under all three,' he confessed with a grin.

She laughed. 'Nick, that's cheating.'

'Cheating?' He coughed. 'And who is the queen of a certain card game?'

'Got it.' She smiled at him. 'That treasure trail you made is like everything we've shared together, squished into a single afternoon.'

'And you liked it?'

'I *loved* it,' she said. 'I really appreciate the time and effort you put in to this.'

'Good,' he said, 'because there's something I need to say.'

She went very still. After all this, surely he hadn't changed his mind? He wasn't going to walk away from her, like Bryn had? 'What?'

'Look down from the viewing platform.' He indicated the edge.

She took his hand and walked over to the area he'd indicated. When she looked down, she saw five words spelled out in fairy lights on the roof of one of the nearby buildings.

Sammy, will you marry me?

'Nick, I...' She could barely get the words out.

He dropped to one knee beside her and took a box from his pocket containing the most beautiful, simple, solitaire diamond. 'I talked to your friend Amy about the kind of design you'd like, so I really hope you like this.'

And now she definitely couldn't speak. The ring was perfect.

'I love you, Sammy Thompson,' he said. 'I want to grow old with you, if we're lucky enough. I want to live with you and make love with you and laugh with you. Life's not always going to be full of sunshine, but I reckon we can weather the storms together. Will you please do me the honour of being my wife?'

Realistic, practical and totally honest. She knew he'd be there for her—just as she'd be there for him. And she too wanted to grow old with him, live with him and make love with him and laugh with him. 'Yes,' she said simply.

He kissed the back of her ring finger, then slid the diamond onto it. 'I'm very glad you said yes.'

'You really thought I might say no?'

'It was a risk,' he said.

'Someone wise told me the risk was one in a million for a lightning strike. Impossibly tiny for a piano falling on your head. And a hundred per cent for life not always going your way in the future—but we have each other,' she said softly.

'We have each other,' he said.

He gestured upwards, and she realised that they were standing right underneath a ball of mistletoe. 'Well, now. A Christmas proposal deserves a proper Christmas kiss, I think,' she said and kissed him lingeringly.

'And now...I promised you dinner.'

He'd said that he'd be able to find them a table, even though most places would be fully booked with Christmas parties. And she couldn't wait to see what he'd arranged. She smiled. 'You've organised dinner up here?'

'Sort of,' he said. 'Come this way, Mrs Kennedy-to-be.'

They went down one floor in the lift, and he led them into a dark room.

'She said yes,' he said into the darkness.

And then the lights came on, what seemed like a thousand party poppers went off along with much shrieking and cheering, and she realised that all their family and friends were there, ready to celebrate their engagement. Nick had clearly set this up and sworn everyone to secrecy, because she hadn't had a clue.

And smack in the middle of a table—right next to a Christmas tree covered in icicle lights and gauzy ribbon and silver baubles—was a really huge, really swish engagement cake.

'Cake first,' Nick said.

He didn't need to say the rest of it. They both already knew.

She smiled at him. 'Always.'

* * * * *

"You haven't changed your mind, have you?"

"No." In fact, now that he'd laid out his plan she could see the enticing future. As odd as it was to be snuggled with Scott on her sofa, she wondered if it was exactly where they were meant to be.

When he looked at her his eyes had darkened and his lips were curved in a sexy smile. Something had changed between them.

His mouth was hot, hungry on hers. His hand moved under the hem of her dress, onto her thigh. She shivered as she imagined his hands moving higher. . .

"Does this feel good to you?" she asked.

"It feels. . .good. Right."

"To me, too," she confessed. "Maybe the strange part is that it *doesn't* feel weird."

After a moment he nodded. "I think I'd better go."

She blinked. "You're leaving?"

"It's either that or I'm going to get you out of that pretty dress. And I'm not sure we're ready for that step yet."

She walked him to the door and smiled, giving in to an impertinent impulse. "Scott? For the record you wouldn't have to try very hard. With the dress, I mean."

She shut the door and leaned against it. What had she gotten herself into?

* * *

Proposals & Promises:
Putting a ring on it is just the beginning!

THE BOSS'S
MARRIAGE PLAN

BY
GINA WILKINS

Published in Great Britain 2015
by Mills & Boon, an imprint of Harlequin (UK) Limited,
Eton House, 18-24 Paradise Road, Richmond, Surrey, TW9 1SR

© 2015 Gina Wilkins

ISBN: 978-0-263-25175-3

23-1015

Harlequin (UK) Limited's policy is to use papers that are natural, renewable and recyclable products and made from wood grown in sustainable forests. The logging and manufacturing processes conform to the legal environmental regulations of the country of origin.

Printed and bound in Spain
by CPI, Barcelona

Author of more than one hundred titles for Mills & Boon, native Arkansan **Gina Wilkins** was introduced early to romance novels by her avid-reader mother. Gina loves sharing her own stories with readers who enjoy books celebrating families and romance. She is inspired daily by her husband of over thirty years, their two daughters and their son, their librarian son-in-law who fits perfectly into this fiction-loving family, and an adorable grandson who already loves books.

As always, for the family that gives me strength and my reason for living, my husband of more than thirty years and our amazing son, two daughters, son-in-law and precious grandson.

Chapter One

Tess Miller stood quietly nearby as her older sister, Nina Miller Wheatley, made a minute adjustment to an impeccably set Thanksgiving dinner table. Nina's formal dining room glowed not only with the light from a crystal chandelier but from multiple candles on the table and antique sideboard. Fall flowers spilled over crystal vases onto Pilgrim figurines and pumpkins nestled beside them. Calligraphy place cards rested in little turkey-shaped holders beside the brown-and-orange plaid place mats. Tess didn't know why they needed place cards when the entire dinner party consisted of Nina, her husband, their three kids and herself, but her overachieving sister never did anything halfway.

There was enough food for another six people, at a minimum. Turkey and dressing, several side dishes, salads and four choices of desserts crowded the serving tables. Tess had brought a casserole and a cake, both of which Nina had proclaimed "very nice" and had then set at the back of the buffet.

Nina wore a rust silk blouse and dark brown slacks that showed off her gym-toned body. Not a salon-tinted blond hair was out of place in her stylish do, and her makeup was perfect despite the hours she'd spent in the kitchen. She'd given a critical once-over to Tess's black wrap top and slim charcoal pants, but her only comment had been that maybe Tess should consider adding more red highlights to her hair, just to "spice up" her shoulder-length auburn bob. Tess was perfectly content for now with the color nature had given her, but she hadn't wasted breath arguing.

The sisters didn't look much alike. Tess's brown eyes had a more golden tint than Nina's, her face was more oval and she'd inherited their father's shallow chin cleft. At five-four, she was two inches shorter than her sister, though she'd always wondered if being taller would have made any difference in Nina's still treating her like a child.

"Everything looks beautiful, Nina," she said, knowing just what to say to make her sister happy. "I can tell you've worked very hard."

Nina heaved a long-suffering sigh. "You have no idea. All the chopping and mixing, cooking and baking, not to mention keeping up with all the kids' extracurricular activities and volunteering at two different schools. I'm utterly exhausted, but of course it's all worth it for my family."

Through her mental sigh, Tess heard a football game playing in the den. She knew her brother-in-law, Ken, and her nephews, thirteen-year-old Cameron and nine-year-old Austin, were parked in front of it, though both boys were probably engrossed in handheld video games. Almost fifteen-year-old Olivia was in her room, likely risking carpal tunnel syndrome with marathon texting to her bazillion friends. None of them had offered assistance to their mother, though Nina wouldn't have accepted if they had. She loved being a martyr to her overly indulged family.

Nina shook off her air of selfless weariness to replace it with a sympathetic smile toward her much younger sibling. "You wouldn't understand, of course, not having a husband and children of your own to take care of."

She didn't add the uniquely Southern, artfully patronizing "bless your heart," but Tess heard it anyway. Ever since Tess turned twenty-one eight years ago, Nina rarely missed an opportunity to voice her concern that her sister would remain single and childless. It didn't help that her only semiserious relationship during those years had crashed and burned.

While Tess wanted a family of her own, she was increasingly resentful of her sister's condescension, making every holiday gathering progressively more uncomfortable. That was a shame, because she and her sister were the only surviving members of their immediate family. Their parents, who'd been in their midforties when Tess was born thirteen years after Nina, had both died within the past six years. Now Nina always made a big show of including Tess at every holiday table because as she said, "Tess has no one else to share the special days with."

Tess drew a deep breath before asking, "Would you like me to call everyone to the table?"

"In a moment. First I want to ask if you'd allow me to

give your number to Cameron's orthodontist, Dr. Mike. He's really quite nice, if a bit socially awkward. He's been divorced for almost a year. He seemed interested when I showed him your photo on my phone, but after that little fit you threw last time, I knew better than to give him your number without asking." Nina rolled her eyes, as if making it clear she thought it unreasonable that Tess objected to Nina handing out her number to just any single stranger.

"Seriously, Nina, stop trying to fix me up," Tess said with a firm shake of her head. She didn't mind her friends arranging the occasional blind date, but she'd rather her meddlesome sister stay out of her love life, such as it was. The thought of her photo being shown to random men made her very uncomfortable. "I don't need you to arrange dates for me."

"Well, someone should. I don't see how you're going to find anyone sitting in that office working for your taskmaster of a boss. I mean, sure, you meet construction workers and architects and suppliers, but you're too professional to flirt with them on the job and you're never *not* on the job, so where does that leave you, hmm? Needing a little help meeting someone, that's where. And because I'm actually out in the community mingling with nice, successful people, who better to direct a lead or two your way?"

"If I want your help, I'll let you know, all right?"

Nina didn't quite growl her frustration, but she seemed to be making an effort to restrain herself. "You haven't forgotten about Dana's party the second Saturday in December, have you? You have to be there. Everyone's expecting you. You can come alone, of course, but you know how snooty some of our cousins would be if they think you can't find a date. Perhaps that would be a good time for you to spend an evening getting to know Dr. Mike?"

"I'll find my own date, thank you." Tess wasn't sure where or how, but she'd bring a date if she had to hire someone!

Maybe she shouldn't let Nina get to her this way. Maybe she should go to the family gathering alone as she usually did, with her head high and her shoulders squared. Confident, composed and contentedly independent. But then she'd have to endure everyone trying to set her up with their dentists, accountants and gynecologists.

Before her sister could demand details, Tess turned toward the dining room doorway, which was decorated with a garland of autumn leaves and just-too-cute little gourds. "I'll call everyone in to eat. It would be a shame to let this delicious food get cold."

It was probably the only threat that could have derailed Nina's attention from Tess's personal life. At least for now.

Tess must not have known anyone else was in the office at 6:00 p.m. on the Saturday after Thanksgiving. No other reason she'd be chatting on her cell phone with her office door open, so her words drifted out very clearly to Scott Prince in the lobby. He didn't mean to eavesdrop, really. It was simply that while he hesitated, trying to decide if it would be rude to interrupt her, he heard a bit more than he intended.

He'd just quietly entered the reception area of Prince Construction Company, Inc., the Little Rock enterprise into which he'd invested all his time, sweat, money and dreams for the past nine years. It had been a struggling little local-only construction company when he'd purchased it from the retiring owner, with whom Scott had interned while he'd obtained a master's degree in construction management. His family and friends had been concerned to see him take such a major financial risk, considering him too young and inexperienced at twenty-seven to successfully run a complicated business. It had taken almost a decade of personal sacrifice and unwavering determination to prove their doubts unfounded, but he was now owner and CEO of a successful, multistate enterprise specializing in small to medium commercial construction projects.

Tess had started working for him as a clerk over six years ago and had become his office manager and valued administrative assistant. No one got to him except through her. Some people said he was gifted when it came to surrounding himself with the right people. Tess was a prime example of that. He admitted freely that the whole operation would fall apart without her to oversee the office.

But this was Thanksgiving weekend, not an official workday. Shouldn't she be spending it with family or friends—at least unless he needed her for some crisis or another, as he confessed he so often did?

"It was the usual painful family meal," he heard her say from the other room, almost as if in answer to his silent question. "My sister tried to fix me up with every single male she's ever met, because she says I'm incapable of finding eligible men on my own. My brother-in-law finally told her to lay off because as he said, 'Some women are just meant to be single.'"

Scott grimaced, knowing now why Tess had chosen to work on the long weekend rather than to spend more time with family. He almost spoke up then to let her know he was there, but she started talking again.

"So, anyway, Nina nagged me about bringing her son's orthodontist to Dana's big Christmas bash, but I told her I'd find my own date, thank you very much. No, I don't know who it will be. You know my lousy luck with the online dating sites I've tried lately. Maybe I'll just take Glenn. Yes, I know you keep telling me he's boring, but maybe we've been too critical of him. He's a nice enough guy. Makes no secret that he's ready to settle down and start a family. Maybe I've just been too—"

Scott opened and closed the front door. More loudly this time. He'd suddenly realized that he'd been standing in one place for too long, hearing more than Tess would surely want him to know.

He heard her mutter something quickly, followed by the thud of her phone, then the squeak of her chair. Moments later she appeared in the open doorway looking slightly flustered, though she almost instantly assumed her usual calm and collected expression. She was dressed more casually than on weekdays in a blue-and-black patterned tunic with black leggings tucked into flat boots. She'd left her hair down rather than in the neat twist she usually wore for work. He'd seen her weekend look many times before, of course—but he thought she looked particularly pretty today. The slight flush that lingered on her cheeks was definitely becoming.

"Scott? What are you doing here? I thought you and your dad and brothers were driving to Missouri for the Razorbacks game today."

"We were. But Eli had to be on call because one of

his partners broke an arm in a Thanksgiving biking accident. Then Jake's son came down with a virus and our plans all fell apart. We gave our tickets to Mom and Dad's neighbors and their kids. They were happy to get them."

"I'm sorry your plans were canceled. You really needed a break from work."

He felt his mouth quirk into a half smile. "Are you saying I've been surly lately?"

"Not surly, just… Okay, maybe a little surly," she said with a quiet laugh.

He could count on Tess to be honest with him, sometimes brutally so. Somehow she always managed to do so without crossing boundaries of the employee-employer relationship, even when she was annoyed with him. And she had been annoyed with him on several occasions.

He cleared his throat. "Sorry about that. You have to admit, the past few months have been challenging." They'd dealt with a couple of big, complicated jobs, a burglary at a job site that had cost them several expensive tools, even a break-in here at the office earlier in the year. Speaking of which…

He frowned. "Why was the security system turned off? You shouldn't be here alone on a weekend, especially after dark, without that alarm activated. As I've just proved, anyone could have walked in."

She lifted an eyebrow. "Didn't you have to use your key?"

He was still surprised she hadn't heard him enter the first time, which only illustrated how focused she'd been on her conversation. "Well, yes, but still…"

Relenting, she smiled. "I've had the security system

on almost the whole time I've been here. I turned it off when I ran out to my car for something I'd forgotten and I was going to turn it back on after I finished a phone call in my office."

He kept his expression as unrevealing as he could manage. He knew she'd be embarrassed if she thought he'd overheard too much of that call. "I want you to be safe when you're here alone. Keep the blasted thing turned on."

Sending a salute toward him that was just short of impertinent, she said, "Yes, sir. I'll do that."

He sighed and shook his head. "Insubordination. Remind me again why I keep you around?"

She laughed easily, slipping back into the comfortable relationship they'd forged during their years of working side by side. "Because you know this entire enterprise would collapse without me."

He chuckled after she pretty much echoed his thoughts from earlier. He had to concede her point.

She'd made her mark on every aspect of his business, from the state of the reception area to the total of the bottom line.

Speaking of the reception area… He suddenly noticed decorations that hadn't been there a few days earlier. A Christmas tree sat in the front corner, decorated with gold-and-white ornaments and tiny white lights. A strand of garland wound with gold ribbon draped the front of the reception desk, matching the wreath on the door. On the tables sat frosted glass holders with fat white candles. All very subtle and tasteful—very Tess, he thought with a faint smile. She could have assigned one or two of the clerical workers she now supervised to decorate, but she'd no doubt taken care of it herself, as she had every Christmas since she'd started working for him.

"You came in today just to decorate?"

"I thought I'd get the decorations up while I had a quiet afternoon to work on them. I'm almost finished."

"Looks nice. Is there anything I can do to help?"

"I've got it, thanks. There are only a few more things I want to do."

Nodding, he moved toward the closed door of his own larger office to the right side of hers. "Let me know if you need anything. I'm going to review the paperwork for that Springdale job we start Monday, just to make sure everything is lined up."

"I left a couple of contracts on your desk for you to look over and sign. They could have waited until Monday, but since you're here…"

"I'm on it."

He glanced over his shoulder as he opened the door with his name engraved on a brass plaque. Tess stood half-turned away from him, frowning in concentration at the Christmas tree, which looked perfect already to him. She really did look pretty today. He thought fleetingly about telling her so, but something held him back.

He made a cup of coffee with the pod brewer on his credenza. "Would you like a hot drink?" he asked through the open doorway as the enticing aroma filled his office. The rack beside the pot always included a variety of herbal teas that he knew Tess liked. They often shared drinks at his desk as they discussed business.

"No, thank you," she called back without making an appearance. He told himself he wasn't disappointed that she was too busy for a cozy chat, which meant he had no excuse to procrastinate any longer with the work he'd come in to see to.

Taking a seat at his desk, he tried to concentrate on paperwork for the next twenty minutes. Despite his resistance, his thoughts kept returning to the one-sided conversation he'd accidentally overheard, and the glimpse of insight it had provided into Tess's personal life. Of course, he couldn't have worked so closely with her for six years without knowing some things about her.

Through night classes and online courses, she'd completed her business degree and had earned postgraduate hours since she'd started working with him. He knew she took pride in those accomplishments. During that same time, he'd seen her deal with the illness and loss of both her parents. He'd gotten the impression the majority of the caregiving had been on her shoulders because her sister had been so busy with her young children. Yet he'd never once heard Tess complain. Whatever she dealt with in her off-hours, she'd always reported to work with her usual serene efficiency.

Serene. He repeated the word in his head, thinking how well it suited his assistant. Throughout several major work upheavals, when he'd been edgy and bad-tempered amid the confusion and mayhem, Tess had remained…well, Tess. She came in every morning with a smile, an encouraging word and a roll-up-her-sleeves attitude that let her tackle each day's tasks with single-minded focus.

One would think someone so agreeable would be a bit of a doormat, easily intimidated, perhaps. Not Tess. He'd witnessed her hold her own with even the most belligerent, disgruntled employees and clients. One of his job foremen had confided to Scott that Tess reminded him of a nun who'd taught his junior high math classes. "Nice lady most of the time," he'd clarified. "But get out of line, and you'd get a ruler across the knuckles before you could spit."

Scott could imagine Tess wielding a mean ruler if necessary. But he'd never thought of her as a nun—had he?

He cleared his throat and reached hastily for his quickly cooling coffee, almost knocking over the cup in his clumsiness. He salvaged the papers on his desk at the last moment and with a muttered curse.

"Everything okay in there?" Tess called from the other room.

"Yes, fine, thanks."

Maybe he hadn't thought of Tess as a nun, but before that overheard conversation, he'd had no idea she'd tried online dating, or that she'd been actively looking for a match. Meeting strange men online was dangerous, he thought·in disapproval. Sure, people did it all the time these days, but it just didn't seem right for Tess.

He knew she'd been in a relationship about three years back that hadn't worked out. That was about the same time he'd been briefly engaged to a stunning but capricious woman who'd understandably—and angrily—chosen to pursue a career in modeling over marriage to an often-neglectful workaholic. He still winced when he remembered the scene Sharon had caused when she'd broken up with him in a crowded restaurant, and all because he'd been a few minutes late meeting her there. Okay, twenty minutes late, but he'd texted to let her know he'd been held up—again—by yet another work crisis. She'd known going into the relationship that his business required a great deal of his time, but like others he'd dated before her, she'd expected more from him than he'd been able to give. She'd stormed off furiously when she'd finally concluded that his construction company meant more to him than their relationship. The split hadn't been amicable, but then for some reason, his breakups never were.

He wondered if Tess had remained on good terms with her former flames. He wouldn't be surprised if she had. Unlike the volatile Sharon, Tess was the practical, pragmatic type. In the years she had worked for him, he'd never heard her carry on about romance and unrealistic fantasies.

Of course, he rarely allowed himself to think of Tess as a vibrant, available single woman. After all, she worked for him, and he'd never even considered overstepping their professional boundaries and risking their comfortable work relationship. She had just turned twenty-three when she'd applied for the clerical job with him. He'd been a couple months shy of thirty-one, and had already owned the business for over three years. Perhaps that was why he'd thought of her all this time as much too young for him, though the actual gap was only seven years. She would soon turn thirty, he mused, surprised by how quickly time had passed. He supposed it was only natural that she would now be considering marriage and children. After all, he'd given quite a lot of deliberation to those things lately, too.

She strolled in through his open doorway. "I thought I'd put this candle on your table. I know you don't like a lot of froufrou in your office, but this isn't too much, is it?" She held a hurricane glass candleholder with a little garland around the base. "You've got a few meetings scheduled in here during the next couple of weeks."

He often eschewed the main conference room in favor of the cherry table in his office. Everything he needed was available to him in here—a projector and screen, whiteboard and display easels and blackout shades to hide the distracting views of the Arkansas River and the distant rolling hills. He loved his office. It was exactly what he'd envisioned back when he'd first started building his own business.

"I don't mind a candle on the table," he assured Tess, making her smile.

"How was your Thanksgiving?" she asked as she fussed with the garland.

"Nice. Noisy. The kids were wound up from all the attention."

Both his brothers were happily married fathers. His older brother, Eli, a family practice physician, had twin girls, Madison and Miranda. Cute as little bunnies, they were almost five years old and full of energy. He was their "uncle Scotty," and he adored them, just as he did his little nephew, too. Six-month-old Henry was his younger brother, Jake's, kid. Both his brothers had been lucky enough to find their soul mates—Eli and Libby had started dating when both were in medical school, while Jake, an attorney, had met psychologist Christina at a cocktail party a couple years ago.

As much as he'd enjoyed the gathering, Scott had been painfully aware that he was no closer to having a family of his own than he'd been during the last solo holiday season. None of his relatives was actually nagging him to marry—after all, the next generation of Princes was already well established—but he couldn't help wondering if they thought something must be lacking in him. Increasingly, he wondered the same thing about himself.

Without arrogance, he could admit he'd accomplished a great deal in his almost thirty-seven years. Valedictorian in high school. Summa cum laude college graduate. A master's degree. His own business. He had a nice home he'd remodeled himself, with a couple of empty bedrooms he hoped to fill someday. All his life he'd heard about biological clocks, but he'd never quite understood the term until he found himself only a few years from forty without any immediate prospect of a wife and kids. During these past twelve months, he had attended cocktail parties and professional mixers— more than he would have liked, actually. He'd gone on blind dates, been to clubs and bars and charity fundraisers. He'd met a lot of nice women, had some good times, made a few friends…but he'd yet to find anyone he thought would be a lifelong partner.

After his brief engagement to Sharon had ended so disastrously, he'd wondered privately if he was destined to remain a workaholic bachelor. He was accustomed to success, to achieving the high-reaching goals he set for himself. His only experiences with failure had been in the romantic area of his life. He really hated failure.

Tess stepped back to critically study the centerpiece she'd created. Apparently deciding it would suffice, she turned to the door, asking over her shoulder on the way out, "Have you signed those contracts?"

He reached hastily for the stack he'd yet to touch. "On it."

He wondered half seriously what she'd have said if he shared that he'd been fretting about how to find a mate.

Knowing Tess, she'd set her mind to solving that issue for him. He'd probably come in on Monday to find a line of qualified applicants standing outside his office door. Having trouble in her own quest wouldn't stop her from setting to work on his if he asked.

His smile faded as it occurred to him that maybe he was on to something here. Oh, not the part about asking Tess to find candidates for him, but the idea that he'd been going about this all wrong. Perhaps he should approach this endeavor with the same attitude he'd used in establishing his successful business. Practicality and analysis were his strengths. Romance obviously was not. There had to be nice women out there who didn't require all the fancy trappings of courtship, but simply wanted to marry an upstanding, decent guy and start a family. Surely a union based on common goals and values, preferably even friendship, would appeal to someone besides himself. Maybe if he spelled out from the start what he had to offer—and what he didn't—there would be no artificial expectations that could only lead to another disappointing failure.

When he'd drawn up his original business plan, he'd made lots of lists. Where he needed to focus his efforts, how he wanted to solicit clients, specific steps for growing the business in a sensible, feasible manner and at a reasonable, sustainable pace. Perhaps he should approach his marriage plan in a similar vein.

He visualized a mental list of the type of woman he thought would suit him best. It should be someone organized and efficient, much like himself. Practical—the kind of woman who would understand he was never going to be a smooth-talking Romeo, but that he would be loyal, generous, committed, dependable. That was the type of husband and father his dad was, and that his brothers had become. Maybe they had married for more emotional reasons, but that didn't mean he couldn't make his own future partnership just as successful. Middle kid that he was, he'd always had his own way of doing things, as his mother had pointed out on many occasions. His way had turned out well for him in business, so why not in marriage?

His wife didn't have to be model beautiful, as his ex-fiancée had been, but it would be best, of course, if he was attracted to her. He'd always been drawn to kind eyes and a warm smile, and he had an admitted weakness for dimples...

He heard Tess moving around in the other room. She had nice eyes, he thought, along with a generous smile with occasional flashes of dimples in the corners. She never wore much makeup, but he'd noted some time ago—just in passing—that her skin was creamy and flawless without it. He supposed she would be considered girl-next-door attractive rather than strikingly beautiful—but then again, there was nothing he'd have changed about her appearance. On more than one occasion, especially during the past year or so, he'd found himself admiring her attributes in a manner that had made him immediately redirect his thoughts, chiding himself that it was inappropriate to even notice those things.

A muffled thud and a disgruntled mutter drifted in from the lobby. Curious, he stood and walked around his desk to stand in the open doorway. "What are you doing?"

Tess was on the floor beneath the big artificial tree, propped on one arm as she stretched to reach something he couldn't see. "I knocked off an ornament when I was trying to straighten a branch. Oh, here it is."

Holding a sparkling gold orb in her hand, she swiveled so that she was sitting cross-legged on the floor looking thoughtfully up at the tree. After a moment, she leaned forward and hooked the ornament to a branch, then leaned back on her hands to gaze upward. Tiny white lights glittered among the thick green branches, their reflection gleaming in the dark red highlights in her hair.

"How does that look?" she asked.

"Looks good," he murmured slowly, his eyes on her. "Really good."

She pushed herself to her feet and brushed absently at her slacks. "Do you think a candle in a snowflake-shaped holder on the reception desk would be too much?"

He cleared his throat. "I'm sorry. What?"

When she realized he was staring at her, she cocked her head to eye him with a frown. "Scott? Are you okay?"

"Yeah, fine. Just…absorbed with a dilemma."

"You'll figure it out," she said encouragingly. "You always do."

Her steadfast confidence in him had bolstered him through some of his most challenging periods during the past six years. Her absolute dedication to the company had been instrumental in its success. She understood why it was so important to him in a way that perhaps no one else did, because it seemed almost equally valuable to her. In some ways, he thought she knew him better than anyone outside his immediate family. Even some of his longtime friends were unable to read him as well as Tess. She was more than an employee, more than a professional associate. Not exactly a personal friend—but whose fault was that? His or hers? Both?

Tess had often teased him about being "blessed with strokes of inspiration," in her words. Solutions to thorny problems tended to occur to him in sudden, compelling flashes, and he had learned to respect his own instincts. They had let him down only on very rare occasions.

He had just been staggered by another one of those brilliant moments of insight. In a near-blinding flash of awareness, he'd realized suddenly that the woman he'd mentally described as his perfect mate had just been sitting under the Christmas tree.

Chapter Two

Tess wasn't particularly concerned about Scott's sudden distraction. This was an expression she knew very well, the way he always looked when he'd been struck with a possibly brilliant solution to a troublesome dilemma. She would wait patiently for him to share what he was thinking—or not. Sometimes he had to mull over details for days before he enlightened anyone else about his latest inspired idea.

Glancing around the reception area, she decided she'd finished decorating. The offices looked festive and welcoming but not over the top. "I'm calling it done," she said, more to herself than Scott, who probably wasn't listening anyway. "Any more would be too much."

He gave a little start in response to her voice—honestly, had he forgotten she was even there?—then cleared his throat. "Um, Tess?"

Picking up an empty ornament box to stow away in a supply closet, she responded absently, "Yes?"

When he didn't immediately reply, she glanced around to find him studying her with a frown. The way he was staring took her aback. Did she have something on her face? Glitter in her hair? She thought he might look just this way at finding a stranger in his reception room.

"Scott?"

He blinked, then glanced quickly around them. "Not here," he muttered, apparently to himself, then addressed her again. "Have you eaten?"

"I was going to stop for takeout on my way home."

"Want to share a pizza at Giulia's? There's something I'd like to discuss with you."

It wasn't unusual for them to share a meal after working late, and the nearby casual Italian place was one of their customary destinations. Because she had no other plans for the evening, she nodded. "Sure. I'll just grab a notebook."

"You won't need to take notes. We're just going to talk."

That was odd, too. They'd worked through shared meals but never just talked.

He was still acting peculiarly when they were seated in a back booth in the restaurant.

Sipping her soda while waiting for their pizza, Tess studied Scott over the rim of the glass. He was visibly preoccupied, but she knew occasionally it was possible to sidetrack him from his musings, at least briefly. She gave it a try. "Tell me a funny story about your nieces," she suggested, leaning back in her seat. "I could use a good laugh this evening."

He blinked a couple of times before focusing on her from across the table. Candlelight gleamed in his dark blue eyes. His hair, the color of strong, rich coffee and a bit mussed from the winter evening breeze, was brushed back casually from a shallow widow's peak. A few strands of premature silver glittered in the dark depths. There was no denying that her boss was a fine-looking man, trim and tanned with a firm, square jaw, nicely chiseled features and a smile that could melt glaciers when he turned on the charm.

Sometimes she still thought of the first time she'd met him. She'd been struck almost dumb by her first sight of the great-looking, intensely focused man sitting behind a cheap, cluttered desk in his first office. She still cringed a little when she thought of how incoherent she'd been during that awkward interview. She wasn't sure what he'd seen in her to take a chance on hiring her, but she was so glad he had. She loved her job and took great pride in the success of the business.

Scott thought for a moment before complying with her impulsive request. "During breakfast Thanksgiving morning, Madison reached for the butter and knocked over an entire glass of cold milk directly into Eli's lap. Eli jumped and knocked over his cereal bowl, which landed on their shih tzu. The dog went tearing through the house scattering milk and Cheerios all over the floors while the girls chased after it, smashing the cereal underfoot. Eli was laughing when he told us the story over Thanksgiving dinner, but his wife was not amused."

Tess laughed. "That sounds like a scene from a TV sitcom."

"Right? Eli said it's pretty much life as expected with energetic almost-five-year-old twins."

"I can imagine. It must be exhausting."

He smiled up at the server who set their pizza in front of them, then continued the conversation as Tess reached for a slice. "Eli and Libby put on the long-suffering act, but they love every minute with those girls."

She'd met all the members of Scott's family, most recently in September, at the annual PCCI picnic at sprawling Burns Park in North Little Rock.

She doubted he got the same kind of grief from his family that she did from hers just because he hadn't yet found his own life mate. From what she knew of them, she thought perhaps they'd tease him a little, but probably not in the insultingly patronizing tone her sister used toward her. With Thanksgiving behind them, the holiday season was now well under way. Parties, traditions, family gatherings loomed ahead. She wished she could feel a little more enthusiastic about what was to come in the next month.

"You like children, don't you, Tess?" Scott asked unexpectedly.

"I love children." She hoped her quick smile hid the wistfulness that underlaid her reply.

"Yeah, me, too."

Looking down at his plate, Scott toyed with his food, seemingly lost in his thoughts again. With silence reigning, she took another bite of her veggie pizza.

He cleared his throat and she glanced up. Her eyebrows rose in response to his expression. "What?"

"You remember when I had that unexpected appendectomy last year and you had to come to my house to work the next day because we had that big deadline?"

She was rather surprised he'd mentioned that incident. He'd seemed to try very hard to forget that day since. "Of course I remember."

Hypersensitive to the painkillers, Scott had spent a few hours rambling somewhat disjointedly until the effects wore off. He hadn't said anything too far out of line, but he'd been amusingly whimsical and had continually heaped praise on her, telling her how important she was to him and how he couldn't get by without her. Even knowing his effusiveness was fueled by medication, she'd taken the compliments to heart.

The only seriously awkward moment had come as she'd prepared to leave. Though Scott wasn't a "hugger," he'd hauled her into his arms for a somewhat clumsy embrace, thanking her too heartily for her help. She'd convinced herself afterward that he had surely intended to kiss her cheek, but he'd missed. His lips had landed squarely on her mouth.

It had lasted only seconds. Hardly long enough to be called a kiss. Even under the influence of the medicines, he'd been aware enough to jump back immediately, stammering apologies, flustered, his face uncharacteristically flushed. Tess had laughed it off, attempting to mask her own reactions behind indulgent humor. Despite her assurances the next day that he'd said nothing untoward, Scott had been embarrassed by his lack of control and obviously concerned that he'd crossed professional lines. They had implicitly agreed to put the incident behind them and never refer to it again. To be honest, though, there'd been times when she'd found herself reliving that almost kiss and wondering what it might have been like had it been real.

Scott cleared his throat, bringing her abruptly back

to the present. "So, the thing is, I'd like to handle this conversation the same way we did that incident. Though I am completely clearheaded and unaffected by any outside influences tonight, feel free to forget anything I'm about to say, if you want, and to pretend it never happened next time we see each other. That's why I wanted to talk here, away from the office."

Lifting her eyebrows in confusion, she looked at the tall, thin glass in his hand. "You've only had a few sips of your beer, so that's probably not the reason you aren't making any sense."

Setting the glass aside, he shook his head. "As I said, I'm not under the influence of anything. Just not quite sure how to begin this conversation."

Swallowing a bit nervously, she touched her napkin to her lips, then lowered her hands to her lap to toy with the checkered tablecloth. Since when had Scott ever had trouble talking with her? This couldn't be good. "Just say it, Scott."

He nodded. "Your job means a lot to you, right? I mean, it matters to you that the company is successful. Reputable."

Her chest tightened. A cold, hard knot formed in her throat, forcing her to clear it before she could ask, "Have I done something wrong? Have I messed up somehow? Is that what you're trying to tell me?"

He shook his head quickly. "Of course not. Just the opposite, in fact. You've gone above and beyond this past year. I'm not exaggerating when I say I don't know what I'd do without you."

Relief flooded her. Her hand felt just a little unsteady when she tucked a strand of hair behind her ear. "Then, what…?"

"I overheard some of a phone conversation you had earlier," he blurted. "You were talking about the upcoming holiday parties, and about problems you've been having with online dating."

She felt warmth spread across her face. He'd heard her conversation with her friend Stevie? How humiliating!

"So anyway," he continued before she could speak, "I've got a bunch of holiday events coming up, too, and no one to attend them with me. Which made me wonder why we couldn't go to some of those parties together."

Of all the things he could have said, this was the least expected. Surely he wasn't suggesting…

"You mean…as coworkers?" she asked in a tentative attempt at clarification.

"No, nothing to do with work. I guess you could say I'm asking you out."

She stared at him, her mind going completely blank with shock. "Oh. Ah."

"I've been thinking about how you and I get along so well and always have," he said, cutting into her stunned stammering. "About how much more comfortable it could be if we attend these things together rather than going alone or trying to deal with early-dating drama with other people during the holidays. So, what do you think?"

She moved his glass firmly to the other side of the table, symbolically out of his reach. "I think you had too much of this on an empty stomach. It must have gone straight to your head."

He made a sound that was half amusement, half exasperation. "I've had maybe three sips of the beer. I'm not intoxicated. I had this inspiration at the office and

I've been trying to figure out how to bring it up to you. I guess I'm not doing a very good job of it. I'm really bad at this sort of thing."

"After hearing me complain about online dating, you decided we should attend holiday parties together?" She still wasn't sure she entirely understood where he was going with this. "And you're not just talking about business-related events?"

"No. There are several events coming up very soon that I'll be expected to attend with a plus one. I'll admit I've been putting off thinking about them until the last minute because I didn't know who to ask, but I suddenly realized there's no one I'd rather go with than you. And wouldn't you rather attend your parties with me than with some guy you think is boring?"

So he'd heard her talk about Glenn. She resisted an impulse to hide her face in her hands as she understood exactly how much of her conversation he'd unintentionally overheard. She wasn't angry with him for his eavesdropping; after all, her door had been open and she'd made no effort to speak quietly. But that was because she'd thought herself alone in the office. Remembering the way he'd announced his arrival with excessive noise, she figured he must have been uncomfortable with what he'd overheard. But that hadn't stopped him from mulling it over afterward, had it?

After clearing her throat, she said, "The holidays can be difficult for singles. Trust me, I know. My older sister is a champ when it comes to dropping patronizing hints and comments, especially since one of my two best friends just got married and the other is in a steady relationship. Even though I'm mostly okay with going to parties and other events on my own, sometimes I think it would be nice to have someone to accompany me. Someone I like and enjoy spending time with. But—"

"You don't feel that way about me?"

"Of course I do. But—"

"You like me. You're certainly comfortable with me. You seem to enjoy spending time with me."

"Well, yes, but—"

"So what's the problem? You attend a few things with me. I'll go to your gigs. It'll take a lot of pressure off both of us."

He was on a roll now, a mode she'd seen him in many times. He'd had what he considered a brilliant idea and he was running with it. True, his "aha" moments had served him well in the past, earning him a reputation as a business genius. But he'd really gone off the rails this time.

"May I speak now?"

He grimaced. "Oh. Sorry. Go ahead."

"As I was trying to say, I understand what prompted your suggestion and it makes sense in some ways. But," she said quickly when he started to speak again, "I don't think you've considered all the ramifications. Showing up together for professional gatherings wouldn't raise eyebrows because we're usually together in that capacity. But in social functions, with families and friends… Everyone's going to wonder if there's something going on between us other than the construction business."

"Would that be such a bad thing?"

Maybe he'd misunderstood what she was trying to say. "To have people speculating about us? It's not that I care so much about gossip, personally—well, not too much—but I'm not sure how good it would be for the company."

He shook his head. "I wasn't talking about the gossip. I meant the part about our relationship being more than a professional one."

She stared at him across the table, trying to read his face. Was he joking? It wasn't his usual style of humor, but surely he wasn't suggesting that they should start... dating?

"Okay, maybe I'm getting a little ahead of myself," he said quickly, probably in response to her stunned expression. "But think about it, Tess. We make a hell of a team. Everyone says so. How many times have we been teased about being so in sync that we're accused of communicating telepathically?"

She could hardly count the number of times during meetings when she and Scott had exchanged thoughts with little more than a glance and a nod, to the bemusement of their associates. "Well, sure, but—"

"We both love children," he reminded her. "We want families of our own. We share many of the same values. I always respected the way you took care of your parents, even though it meant a great deal of sacrifice for yourself. That's the same kind of family loyalty my own parents instilled in me and my brothers."

Children? He was talking about kids now? "I've, um, always admired how close you are with your family. But—"

"I'm pretty sure we've both tried all the conventional dating methods. We've had relationships we hoped would lead somewhere, only to end up single again. It occurred to me that maybe we've both been going about the process all wrong, ignoring the obvious solution right in front of us. We've been successful partners for more than six years, longer than any other relationship I've ever had."

She bit her lip. He was doing it again. Enthusiastically barreling along without giving her much chance to respond. She knew how to break in, how to get his attention and make her point. Even if he didn't agree, he always listened and respected her opinion—but she didn't for the life of her know what she'd say if she stopped him just then. She was literally struck speechless.

After a moment, Scott grimaced and made a little sound that seemed self-chiding. "You're completely gobsmacked by all this, aren't you?"

"That's one way to phrase it," she managed to say fairly steadily, though her pulse rate was still fluttering like crazy.

He reached across the table to lay his hand over hers. "Sorry, Tess. You know how I get when I'm inspired by an idea."

She knew exactly how he got. Which was why she was suddenly so nervous.

He squeezed her fingers. "It's just something to think about. You have to admit it makes sense, but I won't take offense if you decide you don't want to try it. Nothing will change between us, if that's what you prefer."

Her attention was drawn to their joined hands. His was strong, tanned and very warm. She'd always admired his hands, secretly studying them as his capable fingers had flown over the keyboard or tablet screen. Her own felt suddenly small and soft beneath his, feminine to his masculine. She found herself mesmerized by the contrasts, the sensations, the intimacy of that contact.

What on earth was wrong with her? Though that

medicine-fueled embrace had been a definite glitch, it wasn't as if Scott never touched her. He was in the habit of patting her shoulder when he was particularly pleased with her or high-fiving her when a job was completed satisfactorily. But now, with just this casual hand-holding, she was suddenly transported back to inarticulate appreciation of just what an attractive and compelling man he was. The thought had always been present at the back of her mind, but she'd kept it firmly locked behind professional boundaries she had never expected to cross.

Maybe they had both lost their minds.

"Why don't you think about it for a couple of days?" Scott suggested after another moment of silence. "We could start slow, attend a party or two together, see how it feels. We'd figure out what to say to anyone who questions us. Whatever happens, nothing has to change at work. This would be a totally separate experiment."

Experiment. The word cut through the daze that had temporarily engulfed her. She drew her hand from beneath his and picked up her soda again, holding the cool glass in a firm grip to control a slight tremor. "I'll think about it," she said evenly, "but I'm not sure it's a good idea to mix business with personal pursuits. From my observances, it's rarely successful."

"Maybe for people like us it's exactly the right way to go about this. Thoughtfully, practically, logically. As adults who share common goals and common interests, not starry-eyed kids too caught up in fantasy to give serious consideration to the future."

People like us. This could be the least romantic discussion of dating and potential marriage she'd ever had, she thought, frowning down at the now unappetizing food that remained on her plate. Not that she'd ever expected romance from her prosaic employer. Okay, maybe she'd let herself daydream a time or two, especially in those early years, but she'd long since convinced herself she was completely happy with her comfortable friendship with Scott. Now he was suggesting changing the parameters of their relationship, carrying the success of their business collaboration into a personal partnership. And while she was utterly—well, gobsmacked by the proposition, she had to admit that a part of her recognized the unassailable logic of his idea.

She'd tried romance. She'd crashed and burned. Scott had been engaged. It hadn't ended well. So maybe he was right that a union based on common goals and interests was much more fitting for, as he'd said, people like them.

He gave her one of the quick, crooked smiles that almost always made her melt inside, even when she'd been annoyed with him. "Or you could always go to your parties with boring, no-chemistry Glenn."

She pointed a finger at him. "It's not wise to tease me about something you overheard while eavesdropping on a private conversation."

He held up both hands in a gesture of surrender. "You're right and I apologize. But will you think about what I suggested?"

"I'll think about it," she agreed after a moment.

Looking satisfied that she hadn't shot down the idea out of hand, he nodded and pushed away his plate. "Great. Just let me know what you decide."

As far as he was concerned, apparently, the new business at this impromptu meeting was concluded.

She had no doubt that if she presented good reasons

why she thought it best to decline, he would accept her answer graciously and they would go on with their professional lives exactly as they had before. But maybe she needed to give his suggestion a bit more thought before she reached that conclusion.

Declining dessert, she gave the excuse that she had things to do that evening. The silence wasn't quite as comfortable during the short drive back to the office in Scott's car. She suspected that was why he turned on the radio to a station already playing nonstop holiday music.

"I left my tablet inside," she said after he parked next to her car. "I'll just run in and get it."

"I need to collect a few things, too. I'll walk you in."

She'd left the Christmas lights on when they'd gone out, so they were greeted by the cheery glow of the tiny white bulbs on the tree and garlands, an unnecessary reminder of the upcoming festivities. She glanced at Scott. It was all too easy to imagine herself walking into her cousin's party with him at her side. Her sister, especially, would be stunned to see Tess with her handsome, socially prominent boss.

Was that really a good enough reason to risk upsetting the solid working relationship they'd built between them during the past six years?

Needing a distraction, she glanced around the reception area and noticed a strand of garland had slipped from the light fixture behind the desk. She rose on tiptoes to fix it, but Scott stepped up to help her, reaching over her head to secure the end into the cluster of greenery and glitter.

"Thanks," she said, smiling automatically up at him.

Her smile faded when their gazes met and she realized just how close he stood to her. So close she could almost feel the warmth and energy radiating from him. So close she could see the sudden heat reflected in his dark blue eyes. It was a look she'd never seen there before during all the times they'd been alone in the office together, all the late nights and long weekends and holidays when they'd given up personal time to work toward the mutual goal of making the business successful and profitable.

He took a half step nearer, so that they were almost but not quite touching. His voice sounded deeper than usual when he said, "We've agreed that come Monday this conversation never happened, if that's the way you want to play it. With that caveat in mind, there's one more experiment I think we should try to help you make up your mind."

That was the only warning of his intention as he dipped his head down to hers. He stopped with his lips only a whisper away from hers. "Say the word and I'll back away now," he murmured, his warm breath brushing her skin. "Or we can satisfy our curiosity and give you just a little more to think about while you make your decision about my proposition."

She couldn't even argue about that "our curiosity" comment. He'd know she was fibbing if she denied that she'd ever wondered what it might be like to kiss him—a real kiss, this time, not an accidental brush of lips.

"This never happened?" she asked in a husky whisper, letting her hands rest against his broad chest.

His lips curved into a smile. "Totally your call."

The temptation was too great. A chance to find out what it would be like to share a kiss with Scott without worrying about the consequences? Maybe it wouldn't be quite as easy as he made it sound, but for once in her safe, responsible life, she gave in to a reckless impulse. It took only a shift of her weight to bring their lips together.

Chapter Three

Maybe Scott had intended for it to be a quick meeting of lips, merely a sample taste of what could be—but it turned quickly into a kiss that made her knees go weak. He wrapped his arms around her and drew her more firmly into his embrace. Gripping his shirt, Tess tilted her head to provide better access for both of them, her lips parting and softening beneath his. Heat coursed between them, surging through her veins to sizzle in her pounding heart. She felt her toes curl in her shoes, the kiss affecting her literally from head to heel.

Her pulse raced frantically by the time they broke apart. For a moment Scott looked as disoriented as she felt, blinking as if to bring their surroundings into focus. It seemed that he, too, had been surprised by just how good the kiss had been.

Maybe they shouldn't have conducted that particular

experiment here at the office, she thought with belated qualms. She might never again stand in this particular spot without remembering how it felt to be held against that hard, strong body, their mouths fused, their hearts pounding together.

Maybe once all the Christmas decorations were put away, once the place looked normal and completely businesslike again, it would be easier to wave this off as a holiday anomaly.

Maybe.

Scott tugged at the unbuttoned collar of his shirt as if to loosen it, then glanced up at the garland they'd just straightened. With a slightly lopsided smile, he asked, "Did you tuck a sprig of mistletoe into that thing, by any chance?"

Clearing her throat, she tried to speak in the same light tone he'd used. "No mistletoe. Just a little fake balsam and holly."

"The whole place looks great. You did a nice job decorating." He scooted backward as he spoke, looking around the office as if suddenly fascinated by the holiday touches. Did he regret the kiss, or was he giving them both time to mentally process what had just happened between them? She couldn't tell from his profile, and he wasn't meeting her eyes.

She pushed back her hair and took a steadying breath. "I'd better go now. I have some things to do at home."

After a moment, he turned to face her, his expression still inscrutable. "We're okay?"

"We're okay," she assured him, touched by the hint of anxiety she thought she detected in his voice, though it didn't show on his face.

"And you'll think about the things I said?"

"Of course I will." As if she'd have any other choice.

"You have to admit, we make a hell of a team, Tess. We always have."

She couldn't argue with that. There'd been a connection between them from that very first day. But was their professional bond strong enough to sustain a more personal relationship?

Making a hasty escape from the office that was as much her home as her own apartment, she decided to call an emergency meeting of her two best friends. She very much needed Stevie and Jenny to let her know if she was insane. Because she was suddenly thinking that maybe Scott's surprising proposition wasn't completely crazy.

"Wow."

Tess nodded ruefully in response to her friend Stevie's succinct response to being told about Scott's out-of-the-blue proposition. "I know. I'm still trying to wrap my head around it myself."

Sitting in the living room of Tess's place Sunday afternoon with cups of tea in hand, her friends Stevie McLane and Jenny Baer Locke stared at her with almost identical thunderstruck expressions. Tess figured her own face must have looked much like that when Scott had sprung his suggestion on her that they should try dating. Especially when he'd made it clear that he was looking beyond merely attending events together to potentially building a future as a couple.

"He really hinted you could have children together?" Jenny asked, her dark eyes wide.

"Indirectly. At least, I think he did." Tess held up

her free hand in a gesture of bewilderment. "The whole conversation was a little hard to follow."

"What did you say?" Stevie demanded with avid curiosity.

"I told him I'd think about it."

"Wow." This time it was Jenny who expressed the sentiment. "You must have been stunned."

"That's an understatement." *Gobsmacked* still seemed a more accurate description.

Stevie set down her teacup to study Tess intently. "This could make things awkward, to say the least, when you report to work on Monday."

"Scott assured me there would be no awkwardness. He said when we're at work, we can pretend the conversation never took place."

"Can you do that?" Stevie sounded skeptical. "Really?"

After only a momentary hesitation, Tess nodded. "I think so. Scott and I have never had trouble being completely professional on the job, no matter what was going on in our personal lives. We just focus on business."

Which didn't mean there wouldn't be complicated emotions swirling inside her next time she was with her employer, she acknowledged privately. She only hoped she would do as good a job of hiding them as she had in the past.

Stevie shook her head, making her blond curls bob around her pretty face. "I have to admit I wasn't expecting to hear this when you invited us here this afternoon. I thought you'd tell us about the latest aggravating thing your sister did to you. Hey, you don't suppose she somehow put Scott up to this, do you? She is determined to marry you off after all."

With a wry smile, Tess said confidently, "No, Nina wasn't involved. This was totally one of Scott's brain flashes. Apparently, something he overheard me say to you triggered it."

Jenny nodded thoughtfully. "That sort of makes sense. You said you were complaining about your bad experiences with online dating and wishing you had a companion for some upcoming events. If he's been thinking along the same lines lately for himself, I can see how he might make this leap."

Successful business owner Jenny always looked at all the angles. Until six months ago, Tess had thought Jenny the most practical of all her friends. It had turned out, however, that Jenny had a romantic and slightly reckless side she'd been suppressing for quite a long time, a side that had emerged when she'd been reunited unexpectedly with her college boyfriend after a decade apart. Jenny had been considering an offer of marriage from a wealthy, socially connected attorney most people had considered a perfect match for her. Yet only a couple weeks after a chance reunion with Gavin Locke, she'd surprised everyone by breaking off her relationship with Thad. Barely two months later, she'd married her police officer first love in a sweet, simple little ceremony that had been a far cry from the lavish, very public wedding she would surely have had with Thad.

Stevie swiveled in her seat to frown at Jenny. Both daughters of single mothers, Stevie and Jenny had become friends in high school. They'd attended the same college and had remained close since. Tess had met them two years ago in a yoga class, and she'd fit right in with them, so that they were now a tight trio. Each brought her own strengths to the alliance. Jenny was the friend who offered shrewd advice and blunt candor. Stevie was the embodiment of generosity and thoughtfulness, the one who'd do anything for a pal—to her own detriment, at times. As for Tess… Well, she'd been told she was the encourager, the one who always supported and bolstered the confidence of her friends. She could use a little of that encouragement herself as she faced this potentially life-changing decision.

"Surely you of all people aren't suggesting Tess should actually consider marrying His Highness?" Stevie demanded of Jenny, employing the nickname she often used when referring to Scott. Tess was actually surprised Stevie seemed so perturbed. Perpetually upbeat and positive, Stevie was an unapologetic romantic, and Tess would have thought her friend would be more intrigued than troubled by this development.

"I'm not saying she should start booking bands or ordering flowers," Jenny shot back with a shake of her head. "Just that maybe it's not such a crazy idea. I can understand why Scott thinks it's worth examining more closely. Assuming he and Tess really are able to compartmentalize their work and personal lives so it wouldn't affect their professional relationship, what could it hurt to go to a few parties together?"

"I don't think anyone's that good at compartmentalizing. I mean, seriously, could you work with Thad now after dumping him for Gavin? You don't think that would be awkward?"

While Tess swallowed hard at the images Stevie's question invoked, Jenny squirmed a bit in her chair. "I didn't dump Thad," she muttered, obviously uncomfortable with the blunt term. "When I told him Gavin and I had found each other again and realized we were still in love, Thad graciously bowed out."

"Okay, that's not dumping at all," Stevie said, her tone fondly mocking.

Jenny sighed. "Still, point taken. I've crossed paths with Thad a couple times in the past six months and we've been perfectly civil, but I can't deny it was awkward. I can't imagine spending eight hours a day with him now that I'm happily married to Gavin."

Jenny wasn't just happily married, she was blissfully married, Tess thought with a touch of wistfulness. Jenny would always fret about the dangers in Gavin's job, just as he occasionally became frustrated with the long hours her popular fashion boutiques required of her, but they were crazy in love.

"So even though you turned down a practical business-based marriage in favor of true love for yourself, you think this would be a good idea for Tess?" Stevie challenged.

Jenny tossed back her layered dark hair and lifted her chin in a familiar pose of obstinacy. "All I said was that maybe she should at least consider the possibility. And it wouldn't be such a bad idea for Tess to examine her feelings for Scott. It's not as if you and I haven't wondered—"

Stevie cleared her throat loudly, but not before Tess figured out exactly where that statement had been headed. "The two of you have talked about my feelings for Scott?"

With a chiding look at Jenny, Stevie sighed. "Okay, maybe it's crossed our minds that your total devotion to Scott isn't entirely due to employee loyalty. But we both know you'd never overstep any professional lines," she said hastily. "You've risen in the ranks of his company because you're damned good at your job—irreplaceable, really—and everyone knows it. You've always insisted you had no romantic feelings for Scott, but I couldn't help thinking sometimes you were denying those feelings even to yourself.

"It's not like I've made a secret of my suspicions," she added with a touch of defensiveness. "I've asked you several times if you've been so picky about the men you've dated lately because you've compared them to His Highness and they've all come up short. I just don't want you to get hurt if it should turn out his feelings aren't the same as yours."

Tess felt her cheeks warm. She had to concede Stevie had quizzed her about Scott on more than one occasion, and each time she'd laughed and brushed off the questions. "I wasn't comparing other men to Scott."

"Not consciously, maybe, but subconsciously?"

"We are not getting into amateur psychoanalysis hour," Tess grumbled into her teacup.

Jenny crossed her ankles and settled more comfortably into her chair. "You have to admit Scott has quite a few qualities you would naturally look for in a mate. Let's face it, if you didn't work for him and you met him online, you'd think he was exactly what you're looking for."

Tess looped a strand of her hair idly around one finger. "A workaholic confirmed bachelor with a noted weakness for busty blondes? Really?"

Jenny shrugged. "Obviously he's not that confirmed a bachelor if he's actively contemplating marriage and children. And he's never married any of the busty blondes he dated, so maybe it's not such a weakness after all."

"He did propose to one." With a slight scowl, Tess pictured the stunningly beautiful almost Mrs. Prince. Sharon had always been perfectly civil to Tess, though she'd had a subtle way of making it clear that as valuable as Tess might be to Scott in the office, he belonged to her after hours. Tess had never wanted to believe she'd thrown herself into an ill-fated romance of her own at about that same time as a reaction to Scott's engagement—but there had been times in the past couple years when she'd wondered...

Jenny made a face. "And his engagement lasted all of—what?—five months?"

"Four." Her own failed romance hadn't even made it that long before it crashed and burned, a year or so before she'd met Jenny and Stevie. James had accused her of always putting her job ahead of him, and he'd been jealous of her relationship with Scott, though she'd assured him repeatedly that there had never been anything personal between her and her employer.

Jenny gave a hint of a righteous smile. "So there you go. After realizing said busty blonde was the wrong match for him, he started thinking about a right match... and maybe he finally realized she'd been right in front of him for a long time. Is that so hard to believe?"

"What is easier to believe is that my newlywed friend is seeing everything through romance-tinted filters these days," Tess replied indulgently to Jenny. "It's very sweet, but..."

"*Was* there any romance to Scott's proposition?" Stevie cut in to ask.

"Not an iota," Tess answered, and though she'd tried

for wry humor, she was aware her tone came across more as grumpy. "Unless you consider 'we make a hell of a team' a passionate declaration."

"Not so much," Stevie said with a sigh. "Not even a kiss, huh?"

Tess took a too-hasty sip of her tea that made her cough. By the time she caught her breath again, both her friends were studying her much too closely.

Stevie leaned forward. "There *was* a kiss?"

"Well, yes. Sort of…coincidentally."

Jenny's cup hit the side table with an eager little *thump.* "Oh, this I have to hear. How did he coincidentally kiss you?"

"He, um, thought I'd hung some mistletoe in the office."

Neither of her friends bought that explanation for a moment, as their expressions clearly informed her.

She sighed. "Okay, we knew what we were doing. I guess it was an impulse. Curiosity. Scott called it an experiment. I'm not sure I can explain it completely."

Stevie waved a hand dismissively. "Forget explanations. We want details. How was it?"

"It was nice."

Her friends groaned in unison at the guarded reply.

Stevie cocked her head skeptically. "You're telling me that after six years of being pretty much joined at the hip with that undeniably great-looking guy, you finally kiss him and it's just…nice?"

Jenny tsked her tongue. "I don't believe it. Scott hasn't spent time with all those busty blondes without picking up a few tricks."

The image of Scott picking up kissing tricks from a series of blondes made Tess scowl when she realized just how intensely she disliked the idea. It was difficult to keep believing she wasn't harboring secret feelings for Scott when just the thought of him kissing another woman caused a knot to form in her stomach.

"Well?" Jenny teased. "Was it good?"

"It was better than good," she conceded with a sigh. "The man knows how to kiss. No surprise, I guess, since he's so successful at everything he does."

"Except finding a bride," Stevie added pointedly.

"That remains to be seen," Jenny murmured.

Tess made a sound like a strangled growl. "Can someone remind me why I thought it was a good idea to consult with you two about this?"

"Because we're your best friends and we love you," Stevie replied immediately. "Even if Jen and I don't necessarily agree on everything, we absolutely want what's best for you."

Tess could hardly continue to pout after that. "That is why I called you. I just needed to talk this through while I decide how to answer him."

"You didn't mention any of this to your sister?" Jenny looked as though she already knew the answer, but asked just for confirmation.

"I wish Nina and I had the kind of relationship that would make me feel comfortable discussing this sort of thing with her, but we just don't. I don't know if it's because of the age gap or her preoccupation with her family and her schedule, or maybe we're just too different to fully understand each other, but I don't think she'd be of any help at all with this."

Nina would probably tell her to stop waffling and latch on to this eligible bachelor before he got away, perhaps adding that it wasn't as if Tess could count on any other offers. Tess bit her lip as she could almost hear the words in her sister's blunt voice—or was that her own insecurity whispering at the back of her mind?

"It really is a shame you and Nina aren't closer. I always wanted a sister, myself," Jenny mused with regret. "I thought I'd missed out on something, being an only child. I was lucky enough to meet Stevie in high school, and she filled a big gap for me."

"That goes both ways," Stevie assured her. "I love my brother, but I certainly can't talk to him about relationship issues."

"And I'm lucky to have you both in my life now," Tess assured them, then quickly waved a hand. "That's enough of the sappy talk or we'll all end up sniffling. So I'm ready for advice. Stevie?"

Uncharacteristically somber, Stevie took her time deliberating her response. "I'd be wary," she said after a moment. "You and Scott work together so well, and you love your job so much. I'd hate for what could turn out to be an impulsive mistake to change everything for you."

"Jenny?"

Jenny shrugged. "As I've already said, I think it could be worth considering. You and Scott are mature adults with a great deal in common. You both know the personal and professional risks you'd be taking, so maybe you could take steps to minimize repercussions if it doesn't work out. Yes, it's a gamble, but isn't every relationship, in some way?"

Any other time, Tess might have been amused at the role reversal from her friends. Reckless Stevie advising prudence, practical Jenny encouraging a romantic gamble. Tess couldn't help wondering if the turnaround could be attributed to the state of her friends' own relationships—Jenny was so happy in her new marriage, whereas Stevie had been involved for some time with a moody musician who'd been spending increasingly more time with his moderately successful local band than with her. Tess and Jenny had worried lately that Joe was growing restless, perhaps even beginning to stray. Both suspected Stevie secretly echoed their concerns. Tess had never truly believed Stevie and Joe shared the kind of commitment that would last a lifetime, but Stevie always gave everything she had to making her relationships work, even when it became obvious to others that her efforts would ultimately fail. She was always so optimistic—which made Tess even more nervous that Stevie was the one urging caution.

"So what are you going to tell Scott?" Stevie asked.

Tess spread her hands in confusion. "I have no idea."

"And we haven't helped much, have we?" Jenny asked ruefully. "With our completely opposite advice."

"You've helped tremendously. You've listened without judgment while I expressed my concerns. I'll think about everything you've both said while I make up my mind."

"If you need to talk any more, you know where to find us," Stevie offered.

"I know. Thanks. And now, how about if we table this topic for a while and maybe order take-out?"

"I'd love to, but I can't stay," Jenny said with a glance at her watch. "Gavin has the night off and we're having a date night. We might even see a movie. In a theater. With popcorn and everything."

Knowing how rare a free evening was for them, Tess smiled. "Good for you. Stevie?"

"Sorry. I'm out, too. I promised Joe I'd drive him and his band mates to the airport this evening. They're catching a late flight to Austin for a gig there."

Tess and Jenny exchanged quick glances. Stevie spent a lot of time as an unpaid assistant for her boyfriend's alternative rock band, Eleven Twenty-Five. As busy as she was with her own kitchen design business, she still spent hours making calls for the band, dealing with printers and club owners, hauling supplies in her SUV, making flight arrangements. Tess wasn't entirely sure what Stevie received in return. But because it was none of her business and Stevie hadn't asked for advice, she kept her mouth shut. "Another time, then."

"Soon," Stevie promised. She jumped to her feet, tossed back her curls and carried her teacup toward the kitchen, looking suddenly restless. "I'd better get going. I promised Cole I'd feed his cat while he's out of town."

Cole McKellar was Stevie's next-door neighbor, a quiet widower who sometimes helped Stevie with home maintenance in exchange for occasional cat-sitting. Tess hadn't met him, but Stevie always spoke fondly of him. It was part of Stevie's charm, as well as her weakness, that she liked almost everyone, and she had a near compulsive desire to take care of her friends. She stopped to give Tess a quick hug on her way out. "Seriously, call if you want to talk more. I'm always available as a sounding board."

"Same here," Jenny seconded as she prepared to follow Stevie out. "We're here for you, pal."

Smiling broadly, Tess locked the door behind them. Her smile faded as it occurred to her that an entire Sunday evening of solitude stretched in front of her now that her friends had rushed off to be with their significant others. Maybe she'd do a little Christmas decorating of her own place.

Not much was going on this last day of the long holiday weekend. Her sister had invited her for dinner, but she'd begged off, having endured enough nagging this week. Usually Tess enjoyed an evening to herself with nothing to do but lose herself in a good book or catch up on TV shows she'd recorded. Tonight she felt too antsy to relax, too aware of the silence in her condo. There were too few distractions from her convoluted thoughts, and she was no closer to a decision now than she'd been before her friends had arrived.

As she retrieved her small artificial Christmas tree from the storage room attached to her condo's little balcony, she had to face the fact that neither Jenny nor Stevie could really help her with her personal problem. Sure, they could offer suggestions, advice—even differing opinions, as it turned out. Yet she was the one who was going to have to decide whether to take Scott up on his offer to explore new possibilities in their relationship or remain on the same safe, comfortable path they'd walked for the past six-plus years.

She'd never been a risk taker. The dutiful, responsible younger daughter—she'd always been so cautious, so careful. How could she possibly foresee all the potential pitfalls this time, when it affected every aspect of her future—her social life, her career…and maybe even her so-far-unbroken heart?

After the long weekend, the Monday workday hit the floor running. Phones were already ringing when Tess walked into the office, and the buzzing, beeping and bustling continued for hours. Before two o'clock she'd dealt with one panicky client, two surly vendors, three frantic contractors and a clerical job applicant who could barely articulate around the wad of gum in her mouth. Mentally marking that name off the list of potential employees, she sat back and drew a long breath. It felt almost like the first chance she'd had to breathe since she'd arrived almost six hours earlier.

At least she hadn't had to worry about what to say to Scott. He'd been in meetings and phone conferences all day, and she'd seen him only for a brief consultation about a business issue. There'd been no time for personal conversation, nor even for awkward pauses. Today had been all about work, catching up and looking ahead. As she'd assured her friends, compartmentalizing wasn't really that difficult for her and Scott. When they were in the office, nothing was more important to them than taking care of business.

As if in response to her thoughts, he stuck his head in the open doorway to her office. "What's Art Connolly's wife's name?"

"Debbie. And their son is Art Jr., but they call him Buzz."

"Debbie. Buzz. Got it. Heading out for the meeting. Shoot me a text if you need anything."

"Okay. Have a good—" But he was gone before she could finish the sentiment.

Her mouth twisted in a wry smile. If nothing else had demonstrated how efficiently Scott could put their Saturday-evening conversation out of his mind, that little exchange would have done the trick. There had been nothing at all personal in his tone or expression, no meeting of eyes, no more warmth in his voice than she heard when he spoke with the receptionist on his way out. She couldn't imagine any observer would even suspect that less than forty-eight hours earlier, Scott had all but asked her outright to consider having his children.

Had their conversation even crossed his mind this morning? Despite how busy she'd been, it had hovered constantly at the back of hers. Did that mean they were already unevenly invested in this looming decision? Was it really of little import to him if she accepted his offer or politely declined? Was he less concerned about the repercussions—maybe because he didn't believe he would be as deeply affected in the long run? Had he changed his mind, had later misgivings about his impulsive suggestions, or was he really too wrapped up in business today to give anything else a second thought?

"Um, Tess?"

Blinking, she glanced toward the doorway to find a heavily pregnant young woman standing there studying her with a slight frown. She got the distinct impression it wasn't the first time her name had been spoken. "I'm sorry, Heather, I was distracted. What can I do for you?"

"The next applicant for my job is here for her interview. And I wanted to remind you I'm leaving a little early today for a doctor's appointment."

Tess nodded. "I remember. I hope it goes well."

At almost eight months along, Heather had recently given notice that she would not be returning after her delivery. Now Tess was hiring a replacement.

"The applicant's name is Sofia Vasquez. She seems very nice—and she's not chewing gum," Heather added with a wink.

Tess laughed. "Good to hear."

"I'll send her in. And unless you need anything more from me, I'll see you tomorrow."

Tess couldn't help smiling as she watched Heather retreat in her pregnancy waddle. Which reminded her, she needed to pick up a gift for the office baby shower scheduled for tomorrow afternoon. She should have taken care of that already, but she'd been so busy lately.

Putting thoughts of tiny sleepers and pastel blankets out of her mind, she stood with a professional smile to greet the job applicant entering her doorway.

As was so often the case, Tess was the last person remaining in the offices that evening, well after darkness had fallen. She'd just completed the hiring of Sofia Vasquez, and sat back in her chair with a weary sigh. It had been a long day, with only a twenty-minute respite for a quick salad in the break room, and she was tired to her toes.

She cleared her desk and pulled out her phone, doing a quick check of her personal email before calling it a day. She frowned when she saw an evite to her cousin's holiday party. It was addressed to "Tess and guest," and she was expected to RSVP. She would deal with that later, she decided. It was after six, and she was ready to hole up at home with pj's and tea. Slinging the strap of her bag over her shoulder, she grabbed her coat and headed for the break room to retrieve her salad container.

Now, of course, she was reminded again about Scott's offer to accompany her to her holiday affairs. There certainly hadn't been time during the past couple of hours to think about his proposition—not much anyway. Scott wasn't the only one who could compartmentalize, she thought in satisfaction. And if he'd changed his mind, fine. They could agree to pretend the conversation had never taken place. After a few days, she probably wouldn't give it another thought.

"Yeah, right," she muttered, thinking she'd never convince her concerned friends if she couldn't even believe it herself.

Impatient with her own dithering, she collected her plastic salad container from the drying rack next to the sink. With big windows looking out over the now-dark river, the break room had been decorated by the office staff. Normally, Tess's spirits would have been lifted by the sight of the silly stuffed reindeer grinning from the top of the microwave, but she had too much on her mind this evening. Gripping her salad dish, she turned toward the door. She jerked to a stop when she saw someone standing there.

"Scott," she said when she caught her breath again. "I didn't hear you come in."

Leaning casually against the doorway, he smiled. "Seems as if that's becoming a pattern. And do I have to point out again that the security system isn't on?"

"Give me a break, everyone just left. I'm on the way out myself."

"Crazy day, huh?"

"Very." She filled him in on the new hire.

Scott nodded. For the past couple of years he'd given her free rein for hiring and supervising the office staff. She often joked that her official title should have several "slashes" in it—office manager/human resources director/customer service representative/personal assistant to the boss. While she enjoyed the variety of her duties, the challenge was doing them all well, a feat she thought she managed most days.

"I'm sure you made the right choice," he said. "Oh, and we got the Kilgo job today."

"Congratulations. I know you and Andy put a lot of hours into that bid." Andy Staples was one of the project managers, an architect who'd been with the firm from the beginning. If Tess thought of herself as Scott's right-hand woman within the home office, Andy was definitely Scott's second in command everywhere else.

"Yeah. We're both excited about the project. So you were about to leave for the day?"

Because she was wearing her coat and holding her purse and empty lunch dish, the answer seemed obvious, but she nodded. "Yes. Do you need anything before I go?"

"Want to have an early dinner somewhere? Talk awhile?"

His smile and the gleam in his navy eyes took her aback. That quickly, he'd transformed from work associate to would-be suitor. Was he really able to separate the professional from the personal that easily, or was he just that much better at masking his thoughts and feelings when he was in work mode?

"I, um—" It took her a bit longer to make the switch. "I have to stop by a baby-supplies store. We're having Heather's shower tomorrow afternoon and I haven't had a chance to get anything for her. So maybe we should—"

"Stop by there together," he finished for her. "I haven't gotten anything for her, either."

She blinked. "You want to go baby shower shopping together?"

"Well, there are things I'd rather do," he replied candidly. "But you need a gift and so do I, so it makes sense for us to go together, right?"

She bit her lip. She wasn't sure she knew what made sense anymore.

The phone in her hand beeped and she glanced down at the screen. Her sister had sent a text unnecessarily alerting her that cousin Dana's party invitations had gone out. Nina had also felt the need to remind her that Awkward Orthodontist was still available as a potential escort—though not in those exact words, of course.

Tess sighed, then glanced up at the doorway where her good-looking employer stood smiling at her. "Okay, fine. Let's go buy something cute and fuzzy," she said more gruffly than she'd intended.

His eyebrows rose and his smile turned a bit quizzical, but he merely nodded and moved out of the doorway, motioning for her to precede him.

Chapter Four

Had they done this even a week earlier, Tess thought it wouldn't have felt at all odd to walk into the baby store with Scott to find gifts for their coworker. Well, not very odd anyway. But now the comfortably established camaraderie that had previous existed between them had changed. Permanently? That remained to be seen.

She and Scott paused in the baby furniture aisle, their heads close together as she scrolled through the baby registry on her smartphone, showing him the check marks that indicated items already purchased by others.

"There's not a lot left," she said with a self-censuring frown. "I should have taken care of this sooner."

Scott glanced up from the phone screen to study her face. "That's not like you. You're usually ahead of schedule on stuff like this."

She gave a little shrug. "I guess it was Freudian," she

said lightly. "As happy as I am for Heather, I hate the thought of her leaving us. I'll miss her."

She didn't want to think there'd been an even deeper emotional reason she had been reluctant to peruse catalogs of baby supplies.

Before Scott could respond, a young man in a store uniform paused near them. "Can I help you find anything?" he asked cheerily. "Do you need help setting up a registry?"

"Oh, no, we're not—" Tess stopped her automatic and completely unnecessarily explanation with a slight grimace. "I mean, we don't need help right now. Thank you."

The young man moved on and Tess focused more intently on the list, avoiding Scott's eyes. "There are still a few nice things left. I'm sure we can each find something."

"Maybe we could go in together on a gift?"

Picturing someone reading aloud a card that said, "From Tess and Scott," she cleared her throat. "Maybe we'll just each buy our own."

She heard the amusement in Scott's voice when he said, "Or that. What should I get?"

She pointed to the screen. "No one's bought this fancy baby monitor set yet. That's about what you usually spend for this sort of thing."

"And no one would know that better than you," he murmured with a smile. "Okay, so I'll get the monitor. That was easy enough. What are you getting?"

"I don't know yet." She scooted past a giddy young couple who appeared to be choosing items for their own registry, so absorbed in the colorful displays that they didn't realize they were blocking an aisle. Tess couldn't really be annoyed with them; they looked so excited and eager, and they apologized sheepishly when they realized they were in her way.

She moved down an aisle, idly touching one cute little item after another, looking for something that spoke to her of Heather. Heather and her husband had chosen a nautical theme in navy, red and taupe. According to the registry, the bedding items had all been purchased, but the coordinating laundry hamper and changing table cover were still available. She chewed her lower lip as she debated between the two.

"Not exactly an exciting choice, is it?" Scott asked as he eyed the options. "A laundry hamper?"

"They're things Heather wants. That's all that matters. I'll get the hamper. But I'm going to get a nice little outfit to go with it," she added with a decisive nod. "Something not on the list for a surprise."

"Excuse me?"

In response to the voice, Tess glanced around to find an older, silver-haired woman eying Scott with an oddly assessing expression.

Scott smiled at the woman. "Yes, ma'am?" he asked, instinctively displaying the manners his Southern mother had drilled into him.

"Do you mind if I ask how tall you are?"

With a quick, amused glance toward Tess, Scott replied politely to the diminutive senior citizen. "I'm six-one. Do you need help reaching something?"

"No. I need you to stand right here by these strollers and tell me which one would be more comfortable for you to push. My grandson is about your height, and his wife's expecting. I'm here to buy them a stroller, but

I want to make sure the handle is high enough for my grandson to push comfortably."

"I think most of them are adjustable," he explained, reminding Tess of his familiarity with his young nieces and nephew. "There's usually a button to push to raise or lower the handle."

The woman still wanted him to pose with a couple of strollers, just so she could "get a mental picture" of her grandson with her ultimate choice. Obliging, Scott took down the display models the woman indicated, then stood behind each one. His mouth quirked into a wry smile, he waited patiently while she studied him from all angles. She narrowed her choices down to two, had him stand behind each for another look, then pointed. "I think I like that one best."

"That's the one I'd have picked, too," Scott assured her as he hoisted the display model back onto its shelf. Having enjoyed the entire encounter from close by, Tess couldn't help but admire his gracefully strong movements.

"Really?" His new friend beamed in pleasure. "Is that the same stroller you two are buying for your little one?"

Tess's smile faded. "We're shopping for a friend's baby shower," she blurted.

"Oh. Well, I'm sure you'll choose something nice. Thank you, young man," she said over her shoulder as she bustled toward the customer service desk. "I appreciate your help."

"You're very welcome," Scott called after her before turning back to Tess. "Well, that was interesting."

Ready to get out of this baby-obsessed place, Tess grabbed the hamper, then marched over to the clothing section with Scott behind her. Flipping through the outfits, she selected a three-piece set consisting of a red snap-bottom shirt, navy pull-on knit pants and a navy-and-white-striped hoodie with an embroidered sailboat. It was cute and looked comfortable, and it worked well with the nautical theme. "This will do. I'm ready to check out now."

They paid at separate registers for their purchases, then headed for the door almost at the same time. Still, she was a good three steps ahead of Scott when they reached their cars, which were parked side by side in the lot.

"Were we racing?" he asked ironically when he caught up. "If so, you win."

"Sorry," she muttered. A night breeze blew steadily against her face, but didn't seem to cool her overly warm cheeks. She couldn't have explained why she felt so uncharacteristically awkward and foolish all of a sudden. She hated this feeling of being not quite in control.

He took a step closer to her. The parking lot was well lit with tall security lamps decorated with holiday wreaths, but his eyes were shadowed from the light behind him. She couldn't quite read his expression. Still, she could see he wasn't smiling now.

He touched her arm. Even through the fabric of her coat and clothing she was intensely aware of that point of contact between them. She hoped he attributed her shiver to the weather.

"Tess, you've been tense and jumpy ever since I came back to the office. I'm guessing you're trying to figure out how to tell me you aren't interested in the suggestion I made the other night. I don't know if you're afraid of hurting my feelings or worried that I'll be upset with you or what, but really, you can relax. I promised I wouldn't let your answer affect our working relationship—or our friendship—and I'm standing by that promise."

A brisk gust of cold wind whipped a strand of hair out of her loose updo and into her eyes. She reached up to push it back. Were they truly going to have this conversation in a parking lot?

"We can get past this, right?" he asked quietly, the question barely audible over the drone of passing cars and the voices of shoppers milling in the lot around them. "We'll be okay?"

She moistened her chilled, dry lips. "Actually, you've completed misinterpreted why I'm so nervous tonight," she said. "I'm not trying to figure out how to turn you down, Scott. I'm trying to find the courage to tell you I'm willing to give it a try."

It wasn't often she saw Scott startled into immobility. She thought maybe she was viewing it now, as he went very still, his hand unmoving on her arm. After a moment, he said, "So it's a yes?"

She took a leap of faith and nodded. "Yes."

A car cruised past them in search of a parking space, bone-vibrating bass booming from the interior as the passengers gambled deafness in favor of volume. Roused into recognition of their surroundings, Scott glanced around with a grimace. "So…dinner?"

She nodded again. It was too late to bolt in panic now, she reminded herself, though she had to admit the thought occurred to her.

They dined at a barbecue restaurant within view of the baby store. First pizza and then barbecue, Scott thought after they were seated in the casual, noisy dining room. He made a mental note to take her someplace nice soon, now that they were dating…or whatever it was they were doing. For now he was aware of a deep sense of satisfaction that she'd decided his brainstorm wasn't so crazy after all.

Because it seemed to calm her, he kept the dinner conversation light and primarily centered on work. They discussed the new employee she'd hired, and he shared his enthusiasm for the apartment complex project he'd contracted that day. Though a bit quiet at first, Tess was soon chatting easily enough, helping him plan ahead for the holidays that always played havoc with schedules. Every year it seemed they ran into delays and shortages between the first of December and New Year's Day, whether because of vacations or weather or a half dozen other seasonal issues.

This was their strength, he reminded himself. Their common ground. He didn't have to try to woo her or put on a calculatedly romantic facade for her. He could simply be himself, which only confirmed his belief that they were uniquely suited as a match. Pushing his luck a bit, he took advantage of her more relaxed mood to say, "There's that thing Thursday night. The Holiday Open Home party."

He knew he didn't have to be more specific. His company had participated in the Holiday Open Home fund-raiser for the past five years. Each year, one of the area's most luxurious homes was lavishly outfitted for the holidays with donations from local builders and decorators. Tours were conducted during the first three weekends of December, with all the receipts given to a local women's shelter. In return for a monetary donation, Scott's company was listed in the publicity material. The event's organizers always hosted a cocktail party for donors on Thursday evening before the tours began on the first Friday. The gathering was covered by the media and attended by the professionals who considered the event part of their annual advertising and charitable budget.

The parties were usually rather dull, but Scott figured it was good to be seen at them, so he tried to make a regular appearance. Because Tess was in charge of the firm's charitable donations, she was always invited to the cocktail party by the organizers. It occurred to him only then that though she'd probably been invited to bring a guest, as he was, she'd always attended on her own. He wasn't sure why, unless she'd considered the event strictly business.

She toyed with a forkful of coleslaw. "Yes, I remember."

"Why don't I pick you up and we can go together?" It seemed like a good opportunity to make their debut as a couple. Their business associates could become accustomed to seeing them together outside the office so that it wouldn't cause quite such a stir when they made it clear their relationship had moved beyond professional.

"We won't be making any announcements about our personal plans or anything like that," he assured her when she didn't immediately respond. "Just attending together. You know, sort of kicking off the season."

She nodded. "All right. We'll go together."

He chuckled drily. "It's a party, Tess, not a tax audit."

A quick, rueful laugh lit her eyes and curved her lips. She had such a very nice mouth. Full and soft, perfectly shaped. He found himself transfixed by her lips now, remembering the feel of them against his. The taste of them.

"I was somewhat less than gracious, wasn't I?" she acknowledged apologetically. "I'm sorry, it isn't that I don't want to go with you. I'm probably just overthinking things. You know how I get."

"Having second thoughts?"

"No." Her answer was immediate and steady. "I've considered everything you said and it makes sense to me. We do make a good team."

"We always have," he agreed with a surge of satisfaction.

"And it will be nice to have you with me at some of the events I have to attend in the next few weeks. I can't wait to see my sister's face when she sees you at the parties with me," she added, almost as if to herself. "I dare her to find anything to criticize about you."

He was a bit taken aback by the glint in her amber eyes. Maybe she'd intended that as a compliment? But he wasn't sure he wanted to be used as a pawn in some sort of battle of wills between Tess and her sister. He was trying to decide how to broach the subject when someone called his name from nearby. "Hey, Scott, thought that was you. How's it going?"

He glanced up to nod warmly at the couple who paused beside him. An old friend of Eli's, Bryan Crawford, held a towheaded toddler on one hip while his wife, Jessica, held the little boy's golden-blond older sister by one hand. "Hi, Bryan. Jessica. Nice to see you both."

"This is a coincidence," Bryan said with a broad grin spread over his ruddy face. "We just saw Eli and Libby an hour ago. We were all attending an open house at the girls' preschool. Your nieces are growing fast, aren't they?"

"They are. It's been a while since I've seen you, Bryan."

The other man chuckled and ruffled the hair of the drowsy boy he held. "Yeah, I haven't had much time for pickup basketball games lately. You know how it is once you have kids, always something on their schedule."

Jessica rolled her eyes with a weary bark of a laugh. "Now, how would Scott know about that, honey? He's the carefree bachelor in the Prince family, remember? Libby says he's too busy running that company of his to settle down and chase after a couple of kids." As if on cue, their daughter, who was the same age as Scott's nieces, whined and tugged impatiently at her mother's hand.

"Yeah, lucky guy," Bryan said with a grin, but the way he patted his son's back made it clear he wouldn't change places with the "carefree bachelor."

His smile feeling a bit strained, Scott motioned toward Tess, who was sitting very quietly watching the exchange. "Bryan and Jessica Crawford, this is my friend, Tess Miller."

He very deliberately neglected to mention their work relationship. This was the start of their new phase. Step one of what he was beginning to think of as his marriage plan was successfully under way. Tess was willing to give it a try. Which meant this evening was officially a date, not a business dinner.

Neither looking surprised to have found him dining with an attractive woman, the Crawfords murmured their polite "nice to meet yous," then gave in to their daughter's increasingly insistent urgings and made their exit. The toddler waved bye-bye over his dad's shoulder, making Scott chuckle and wave back.

"Cute kids," Tess said, drawing his attention back to her.

"Bryan's an old friend of Eli's. His daughter's in school with the twins, at Miss Bitty's. I think Libby had the girls on a waiting list for the place while she was still pregnant with them."

"I've heard of it. It's supposed to be one of the best. I know my sister looked into it when her oldest was a toddler, but it was too expensive for them then. She didn't want to admit that, so she just told everyone it wasn't her favorite option."

Was that another little dig at her sister? As close as he was with his own clan, it bothered him to think about Tess being estranged from the only immediate family she had left. From what he'd heard her say on the phone, it sounded as though Nina's nagging was most of the problem. So if his presence at the parties helped alleviate that problem, then maybe he didn't mind so much after all. Wasn't mutual benefit the whole point of this dating experiment?

"So," he said, "we're on for Thursday night, right?"

She gave him a too-bright smile. "Yes. We're on."

"Great." Personal business out of the way, he turned his attention back to business. "Now, about those meetings tomorrow…"

Twenty minutes later, he walked her to her car. Their breath hung in the air as they continued the work-related conversation they'd started inside, finishing up with a list of tasks he wanted completed the next day.

"I'll have Heather and Lynne start on those things in the morning," Tess agreed with a brisk nod, drawing her coat more closely around her against the chilly night air. "They should be able to finish most of it before the baby shower at four. I'll make sure your office is set up for the ten o'clock meeting, and the conference room upstairs for the one thirty. You should have plenty of time between meetings for that lunch with Garvey and Hannity."

It occurred to him that she was so confident, so at ease with him when they spoke of work, in marked contrast to the hesitation she showed when they veered into their new personal arrangement. Of course, she'd had several years to grow comfortable with him in the business setting; he supposed it would take a little practice in this new arena. And because there was no time like the present to begin…

He caught her arm as she reached for her car door. When she looked up at him, he lowered his head to brush his mouth against hers. "Your lips are cold," he said, smiling against them. "Maybe I should warm them up for you before you leave."

"That would be considerate of you," she murmured, and tilted her head into a more accessible position.

With a muffled chuckle, he kissed her. After only a heartbeat's hesitation, she was a willing and eager participant in the embrace.

His powerful reaction to their kiss in the office Saturday evening had caught him by surprise. He'd tried shrugging it off as first-time novelty, though technically it hadn't been a first kiss between them, if he counted that embarrassing, medication-fueled buss after his surgery. He decided not to count that one.

He'd tried blaming mistletoe, even though Tess had assured him there hadn't actually been any in the office. He'd even wondered if maybe he'd exaggerated the kiss in his memories, that maybe it hadn't been quite as spectacular as he remembered. He knew now that he had not. Kissing Tess felt so damned good that he had to ask himself now what had taken them so long.

Only his awareness of their very public surroundings made him draw back reluctantly when he would have liked very much to deepen the kiss. He opened her car door for her and then moved back to watch her slide in. Even as they said their good-nights, he was tempted to ask her to come home with him for coffee—but maybe it was a bit too soon for that.

Step one, he reminded himself while he watched her drive away. He climbed into his own car with a mixture of frustration and satisfaction with the way the evening had gone. They'd get to step two when the time was right.

"I don't know." Tess craned her neck to study her back view in the full-length mirror. "Does it seem a little tight to you?"

Jenny and Stevie answered in unison. "No."

A bold red sheath, the dress was closely fitted to her body, ending in a flirty double kick pleat just behind her knees. It wasn't overtly revealing, just brighter and snugger than her typical outfits.

"Your butt looks amazing in that," Stevie said bluntly. "I wish I could wear it, but that bateau neckline would never work with my boobs."

Tess's gaze was drawn to the reflection of her bust. The dress was definitely flattering there. As the least endowed of the trio, she couldn't help but push her shoulders back and pose a bit, making her friends laugh.

It was Wednesday evening and they had gathered in Jenny's fashion and accessories boutique, Complements. The store closed at seven on weeknights, staying open until nine Fridays and Saturdays, so Tess and Stevie often met there after-hours on Wednesdays to play in Jenny's new deliveries. They'd even been known to pitch in hanging up garments and setting up displays, mostly because they had fun doing so.

Tonight both Tess and Stevie were looking for outfits to wear to the Holiday Open Home cocktail party the next night. Stevie was attending as one of the donors; she'd been selected this year to design and oversee the kitchen update. It was for a good cause, not to mention she'd make the most of the professional exposure.

They stood in the dressing room area where several cushy benches were grouped around a large, full-length, three-way mirror. Six stalls with floral curtains for privacy surrounded them, but since they were the only ones in the store, they weren't overly concerned with modesty.

"The color is amazing on you, Tess," Jenny assured her. "I told you it would be."

Tess had worried that the red wouldn't go well with her auburn hair, but she should have known to trust Jenny's eye. "It does look festive without being too Christmassy. Not too splashy for the event?"

"You know what those things are like." Jenny waved a dismissive hand. "There will be people there in designer silks and others in jeans. If Sandy's there she'll have on a few strips of cloth and a boatload of diamonds. Trust me, this dress is exactly right for a charity holiday cocktail party."

Tess bit her lip against a grin at the description of their mutual acquaintance's fashion tastes. A notorious man-eater, Sandy had once made a fairly blatant play for Gavin. Not that he'd had eyes for anyone but Jenny.

"I'll give you the usual bestie discount," Jenny added persuasively.

"Okay, I'll take it."

Jenny smiled. "Great. And since you're in a buying mood, there's another dress I want you to try on. I think it's perfect for you, maybe for your cousin's party."

"I'm sure I already have something that will work for that."

But Jenny was already headed out to the showroom, saying over her shoulder, "Just try it, okay?"

"And that," Stevie said with a giggle, "is why Jenny now has two successful stores in the state and is considering a third."

"She is good," Tess admitted with a shake of her head. Twisting to admire the red dress once more in the mirror—her butt really did look good—she asked absently, "Aren't you going to try things on?"

"Oh, yeah, sure." Stevie turned toward one of the stalls. "Jenny hung some things in here that she thought I'd like. I just wanted to see that red dress on you first. I knew it would be amazing."

"It is pretty, isn't it?"

"You'll knock Scott off his feet," Stevie remarked through the open doorway to the stall, her voice muffled as if she were pulling her shirt over her head.

Tess's hand froze on the side zipper of the dress. She moistened her lips. Yes, she'd wanted something nice to wear to the event, and she'd been pleased that the dress had suited her so well, but she didn't want to look

as though she was making any special effort to knock
Scott off his feet. She turned when Jenny returned with
a green garment draped over her arm. "Does this look
like I'm trying too hard?"

Jenny sighed gustily. They were close enough friends
that she understood the question immediately. "No,"
she said firmly. "Looking nice and appropriate for an
event—even looking as beautiful as you do in that
dress—is not trying too hard. It's simply putting your
best foot forward."

Stevie stepped out of the stall wearing a filmy black
dress shot through with silver threads. The skirt fit
snugly at her hips, then flared out around her knees.
She did a little spin and the hem swirled around her.

Tess nodded. "Pretty."

Shorter and curvier than her friends, Stevie's blond
curls and large blue eyes made her look younger than
her thirty-one years. She tended to be a more bohemian
dresser, so Tess wasn't particularly surprised when her
friend looked in the mirror, then made a little face at
the reflection. "I don't know. Maybe."

"No." Jenny thrust the green dress at Tess. "Try this on
while I help Stevie find something that suits her better."

"Yes, ma'am."

Stepping into the stall, Tess changed into the dress
Jenny had brought her. A rich, dark green, it was another body skimmer, ending well above her knees to
make the most of her legs without being too short for
comfort. The neckline was a deep scoop outlined with
a thin line of gold fish-scale sequins, just enough to add
a little holiday sparkle.

It was a wholly impractical purchase, of course. Like
the red cocktail dress, it would be something she'd wear

only a few times. It was kind of hard to justify buying two party dresses at one time, but she loved them both.

"Gold earrings," Jenny said appraisingly from the open doorway. "Thin black tights and those high-heeled booties I sold you in the fall."

"You're killing me."

Her friend laughed without compunction. "Every girl needs to splurge occasionally. Especially when she's seeing a new guy."

Tess groaned. "Come on, Jen. Scott is hardly a new guy."

"He is when it comes to your social life." Jenny winked. "And I'm going to help you make sure he sees you as more than his trusty office sidekick."

Warmth flooded Tess's face, but she couldn't help glancing once again at the mirror. She did look different dressed this way.

"Okay, I like this one." Stevie danced into view in a short rose silk dress with a filmy mesh overlay. Gray beads and sequins were worked into an overall art deco–inspired pattern on the mesh, which ended in a beaded, scalloped hem. "I feel like a flapper. Makes me want to do the Charleston."

"T-strap shoes. Silver bracelets." Jenny nodded as if it was all decided. "Do your hair in that little twist off the face I like so much."

"Do you know how to Charleston?" Tess asked curiously.

Stevie laughed. "Not a clue. But it would be fun to learn, wouldn't it?" She glanced in the mirror again. "Sold."

Tess laughed. "Hooray for bestie discounts!" she

cheered as she went in to change out of the green dress that would be accompanying her home.

When she carried her purchases into the glittering, holiday-decorated showroom, Stevie was already paying for her choice and looking forward to wearing it at the charity event.

"I hope I'll get some new business," she added. "I can't wait to show you the kitchen. The updates are gorgeous, if I do say so myself."

"Will Joe be back from Austin in time to attend the party with you?"

Stevie's smile dimmed noticeably. "No, they're staying a little longer, making some good contacts in the Austin music scene. Joe thinks they have a nice gig lined up for next weekend."

"Good for them." Tess resisted an impulse to glance at Jenny, though she suspected they were both thinking the same thing—that this was the beginning of the end of Stevie's relationship with Joe.

Tess had heard all about Stevie's romantic history during late-night girls-only wine and confidences sessions. She knew her friend had a weakness for musicians, several of whom had broken her tender heart over the years. Would her heart be broken again, or was Stevie more prepared this time, more guarded?

At least she didn't have to worry about having her own heart shattered if this experiment with Scott didn't work out, she told herself. By approaching their relationship logically and cautiously, based on friendship and mutual goals rather than capricious emotions, they were protecting themselves against the sort of pain Stevie seemed to continually court with her impetuous infatuations.

"Well," Jenny said brusquely, breaking into Tess's somber thoughts, "it's Joe's loss that he won't get to see you in this dress, at least not this time."

"That's okay." Stevie's usual glint of mischief lit her eyes as she grinned at Tess. "That'll free me up to spy on Tess and His Highness all evening. After all, Jen, I promised you all the juicy details."

Tess rolled her eyes as Jenny laughed. "There will be nothing to report. We're just going to make an appearance at this thing, do a little networking and schmoozing for the business, then get out of there."

"To go where and do what?" Jenny teased lightly. "Do you and Scott have plans for after the party?"

"We haven't talked about it."

They hadn't actually had an opportunity to talk about anything but business since they'd parted in the parking lot Monday night. The past two days had been one pressing situation after another. Scott hadn't even had a chance to attend the office baby shower yesterday.

Only once had she suspected Scott's thoughts had wandered into personal territory. She'd caught him looking at her lips as she'd stood beside his desk waiting for instructions while he'd listened to a long-winded caller on his phone. Something had told her he was remembering their kisses—which, of course, had sent her thoughts, too, in that direction. Her lips had tingled as she'd instinctively moistened them. His eyes had narrowed and darkened, his expression making her pulse rate jump. She hadn't quite known whether to be relieved or a little disappointed when Andy had rushed into the room with another decision to be made, pushing all private issues aside.

"Has he said anything more about, you know, wanting to have your babies and stuff?" Stevie inquired, a little too artlessly.

Tess gave her friend a chiding look. "It's been a very busy week at work. And honestly, Stevie…"

Stevie shrugged. "You know I'm still concerned that you'll settle for Scott because of all the pressure your sister has been putting on you, and maybe the biological clock thing. I remember that silly, panicky feeling just before I turned thirty. I met Joe not long after that," she added quietly.

Was Stevie acknowledging that Joe had been a "Mr. Right Now" who'd shown up at a time when she was vulnerable? It was what Tess had always believed, but she hadn't thought Stevie was aware of it.

"A lot of people might be surprised to hear you suggest Tess would be 'settling' for Scott Prince," Jenny commented. "You are aware that he's one of this city's most eligible bachelors?"

Waving a hand dismissively, Stevie said shortly, "I'm not denying that Scott's a great catch. I'm just saying Tess deserves more than being a means to an end for a guy who's already accomplished many of his life goals and now wants to check marriage and kids off his list of aspirations."

Both Tess and Jenny stared at Stevie in response to that rather astringent assessment. Tess swallowed past a hard knot in her throat, while Jenny frowned in disapproval. "That was kind of harsh. I can't imagine Scott sees Tess as just a means to an end. I think it's more likely he's realized how lucky he is to have her in his life."

After a moment, Stevie held up both hands in apologetic surrender. "You're right. That was a tacky comment. Sorry, Tess, I certainly didn't mean to imply that Scott wouldn't be damned lucky to have you. I just hope he knows it, that's all."

Tess cleared her throat. "We're just exploring possibilities, Stevie. I haven't even decided what I'm going to do yet."

"Don't listen to me, okay?" Stevie's eyes were suddenly a glittering bright blue, glossed over by unshed tears. "Just have fun and make up your own mind what you want, with or without Scott. I just want you to be happy. I want all my friends to be happy."

Visibly concerned, Jenny moved around the counter to catch Stevie's fluttering hands. "What's going on, Stevie? Is this about Joe?"

Pasting on a semblance of her usual sunny smile, Stevie freed one hand to dash at her eyes and shook her head. "No. I'm fine, really. Just… I don't know, I'm kind of out of it today. I didn't sleep very well last night and I had to get up early this morning to feed Dusty before I left for work. Sorry."

Jenny patted her shoulder. "Of course. Do you need chocolate? I think I have some in my office. PMS is a bitch, am I right?"

Stevie's smile flickered momentarily, but she nodded and laughed cheerily. "You're so right."

Stevie was smiling again, but Tess still had some doubts about her friend's state of mind. Still, she went along with the change of subject. "You're still feeding your neighbor's cat? When is he supposed to be back from his business trip?"

"Tomorrow, thank goodness. Dusty's a sweetheart, and I don't mind sitting with her to keep her company when I have extra time, but I know she misses Cole."

To avoid any further potential pitfalls, they kept the conversation breezy for the short remainder of their visit. They parted on their usual affable terms, agreeing to get together again soon, with Tess and Stevie saying they'd see each other at the Holiday Open Home. Just to make it clear there were no hard feelings, Tess added a little extra warmth to her smile when they waved goodbye in the parking lot.

Still, Stevie's words echoed in her thoughts as she drove home. *Tess deserves more than being a means to an end for a guy who's already accomplished many of his life goals and now wants to check marriage and kids off his list of aspirations.*

She had a few life goals of her own, which just happened to be aligned quite closely with Scott's. Yet she didn't actually see him as just a means to an end, did she? Which brought up the question—what, exactly, did she want from Scott?

She almost chose not to wear the new red dress after all. For some reason, only minutes before Scott was due to arrive at her door, she glanced in the mirror and was taken aback by the reflection of the polished woman in the bright red dress with a glitter of diamonds at her ears. It wasn't that she hadn't dressed up for an event before, or worn bold colors. But something about that woman in the mirror looked different tonight, and she couldn't quite define what it was. Telling herself she was being silly, and that Stevie would certainly report to Jenny if she didn't wear the red dress, she turned away from the mirror and carried her tiny purse into the living room to wait for Scott.

She tried to remember if he'd ever actually been inside the condo she'd purchased two years ago. Had he come in the time he'd stopped by in his four-wheel-drive truck to pick her up for work after a late-January ice storm? No, she recalled, she'd met him downstairs.

She cast a quick glance around her place, trying to see it through his eyes. Stevie had helped her decorate in a warm, cozy style built around classic pieces with unexpectedly whimsical accents. The colors were greens, grays and off-white, her favorite combination. It was so well suited to her.

She sat down on the cushy sofa and sighed, trying to release some of her nervous tension about tonight. When her doorbell rang, she found herself wishing she could exchange the snug red dress for comfy pj's and spend the evening at home with popcorn and hot cocoa. Alone? Maybe.

Or maybe not, she thought, opening the door to find Scott standing there looking like sex in a suit.

"You look very nice," he said. "Are you ready to go?"

Maybe it wasn't quite the reaction she'd hoped for from all the effort she'd put into her appearance tonight. Still, she told herself it would have been foolish to expect Scott to be knocked off his feet, as Stevie had predicted, by a snug red dress. Whatever she wore, she was still just Tess. She supposed he knew her too well by now to see her any other way.

Chapter Five

Maybe it was the dress. It looked amazing on her. It was all he could do to keep his gaze focused on her face, especially when she happened to turn her back to him. She did so again, to reach for a glass of champagne from a passing server, and he couldn't resist noticing how the snug dress cupped her shapely bottom. He was only human after all.

"Scott. Good to see you. How's it going?"

Drawing his attention back to the networking he was here to do, he shook a couple of hands and exchanged meaningless small talk before his gaze was drawn inexorably back to Tess mingling on the other side of the crowded room. Even among the other guests crammed in the almost overly decorated large living area of the Holiday Open Home, she stood out—at least to his eyes.

There was something different about her tonight. He

couldn't quite decide what it was. She'd chatted easily enough with him during the drive. She worked the room like the pro she was, making nice with people who were either potential clients or referrals for PCCI. He was quite sure she worked his name into every conversation, subtly extolling his business acumen. She'd always been his most loyal cheerleader—and his most bluntly honest critic. His most valuable asset. But there was something different about her tonight.

Maybe it *was* the dress.

Or maybe it was the knowledge that tonight he'd be taking her home when the party ended.

As if in confirmation, she glanced his way, saw him looking at her and smiled. He lifted his champagne flute in acknowledgment. He took a sip, but what he really wanted was to taste her lips again.

A surge of hunger swept through him, and for a moment, he was unnerved by the strength of it. He reassured himself with the reminder that sexual appeal was a plus when it came to choosing a compatible mate. He wouldn't examine too closely how long he'd been aware of his attraction to Tess, but now that they were dating there was no real reason to continue to suppress it. He could handle, even welcome, a mutually gratifying physical relationship. It was romance he simply couldn't seem to comprehend, and at which he'd proved so incompetent.

He didn't want to mess this up. There was too much at stake to take unnecessary risks. But fortunately he and Tess seemed to be on the same page in both their business and personal agendas. Her sexy red dress hadn't changed anything. But she did look damned good in it.

For the first time since they'd arrived an hour earlier,

he'd found a moment to himself, sipping champagne in a relatively quiet corner of the two-story living room. Between the Christmas music playing from cleverly hidden speakers and the chatter of milling guests, not to mention that he'd been too busy to eat more than a few bites all day, his head was beginning to ache dully. He hoped he'd hidden his discomfort behind his best social smile as he'd worked the event. They'd already been given the official tour through the impeccably styled and glitteringly festive six-thousand-square-foot house, and now it was just a matter of making sure his company was represented to maximum effect before they could make a graceful escape. No one had seemed surprised to see him enter with Tess at his side; everyone who knew them probably assumed they were simply attending in a business capacity. It would take a few more appearances to get the message across that their relationship had changed.

A movement next to him made him glance around to find a petite blonde in a sparkly dress frowning at him. She smoothed her expression quickly, but not before he'd seen the disapproval on her pretty face. "Is something wrong, Stevie?"

"I was just looking for Tess."

"She's over there, by the Christmas tree, chatting with the mayor and his wife. Apparently Tess and the mayor's wife are on some sort of civic committee together."

"I'm sure she's worked you and your company into the conversation a few times," Tess's friend murmured, echoing Scott's thoughts from only moments earlier. "You have to admit she's your most dedicated ally."

"No argument here. I owe a great deal to her. She's

a big fan of yours, too. I've heard her directing several people to look at your kitchen this evening."

Stevie nodded. "She's the most loyal and supportive person I've ever known. Always the one in the background quietly doing all the work and getting too little of the credit."

Okay, there was definitely a message here. He just wasn't entirely sure what it was. Was Stevie implying that he hadn't given Tess enough credit at work in the way of salary, title, promotions? Or was there a more personal implication to her comments? How much had Tess told her?

"Tess has certainly been instrumental in the success of my business," he said to reassure Stevie that he was fully mindful of that fact. "I've told her many times, both publicly and privately, that I don't know what I'd do without her."

"You're lucky to have her. She has plenty of options, you know."

He was well aware that Tess had been approached by other employers, some who'd met her through his business and coveted her organizational skills for their own enterprises. One of his own friends had recently offered her a position as human resources director for his trucking company, promising he'd add 20 percent to whatever Scott was paying her. Lane hadn't even bothered to be subtle about trying to hire her away; he'd made his move in Scott's own office. Scott had been gratified when Tess had made it clear she wasn't looking for a new job, and he'd tried to be good-natured about it with Lane. But come to think about it, they hadn't really spoken since, though Scott wasn't carrying a grudge. Still, if the truth were told, he'd been annoyed. Maybe even territorial in a way that hadn't been entirely business related. Had it been about that time that the seed of this marriage plan had been planted unknowingly in the back of his mind?

"Anyway," Stevie said when he sipped his champagne to avoid having to figure out a way to respond to her, "I'm just saying I wouldn't want Tess to be taken for granted. I would hate for her to be hurt. By anyone."

He lowered his glass and met her eyes. "So would I."

"Good."

"Hey, you two. Sorry I got detained for so long, I got caught up in a conversation about the chances of my nephew's basketball team making the state playoffs," Tess explained as she rushed up to join them. "Stevie, the mayor's wife wants to remodel her kitchen within the next few months. I told her she should be sure to talk with you before she leaves. Be ready to make a pitch," she added with a smile.

"I'll be ready. Thanks, Tess."

Only moments later they were interrupted by someone who wanted to question Stevie about a function of a trendy new feature in the impressive chef's kitchen.

Scott turned to Tess after Stevie had moved away. "What's with your friend?" he asked quietly. "She seems unusually subdued this evening."

On the few occasions when he'd met Stevie before, she'd always been laughing, animated, a bundle of barely suppressed energy in a compact package. Tonight she'd seemed more serious than he'd ever seen her, and he didn't know if it was only due to her doubts about Tess and him.

He saw concern flit across Tess's face as she glanced in the direction in which Stevie had just disappeared.

"I think she's going through some issues with her boy-friend," she murmured. "But I don't really know, so I'm only speculating."

That seemed to be all she was willing to say about Stevie's problems, so he changed the subject. "I think we've put in our time, don't you? How about if we duck out now?"

"Sounds good to me."

"Do you want to say good-night to your friend?"

She shook her head. "Stevie's busy. I'll send her a text later. Let's go before someone else corners us."

Smiling at her eagerness to escape, he moved across the room with her, exchanging nods and quick hand-shakes on the way out. Tess shivered as she slid into the passenger seat of his car. She grabbed her coat from the backseat and wrapped it snugly around her over the seat belt. "I think the temperature has dropped a few degrees since we went inside."

He started the car. "Some people know better than to wear sleeveless dresses in December without a coat."

She laughed. "I brought a coat."

"And left it in the car."

"I didn't want to bother with having to check it and then wait to reclaim it. It was worth a few minutes of freezing to make a faster getaway."

"That was a bore, wasn't it? I was expecting live music or some sort of entertainment other than just walking through the rooms, then standing around with cheap wine and dry canapés."

"I have a feeling there will be a new chairperson for the Holiday Open Home committee next year," she agreed wryly. "It's been so much better planned in the past."

"Oh, well, as long as they met their fund-raising goals, I guess that's all that matters."

"True. And I'm sure Stevie will get some new business from it. Her kitchen was gorgeous, wasn't it?"

"It was very nice." It still bothered him a bit to remember the way Stevie had frowned at him, as if she had some valid reason to worry that he would hurt her friend, but he shook off the concern. Maybe it was only that Stevie was having relationship troubles of her own, as Tess had implied, and was subsequently pessimistic about any new relationship. Maybe if they'd been in a place where they could have had a private conversation, he would have assured Stevie more forcefully that he had no intention of hurting Tess. Considering his belief that broken hearts were the result of unrealistic expectations, his plan was much healthier and saner than Stevie's idealistic and deliberately naive approach to the search for a life partner. Would Tess's friend see his point if he explained, or would she still disapprove of his prosaic tactics?

Not that it mattered. The only concern to him was that Tess approved.

Feeling a bit more cheerful now that their first official outing had been generally successful, he said, "I'm starving. I've hardly had time to eat anything today and those little nibbles at the party didn't fill me up. Want to stop for something to eat?"

"I ate before the party. But if you'd like to come in to my place, I'll make you an omelet or something."

His fingers tightened a bit on the wheel, but he made sure to keep any hint of surprise from his voice. "Sounds good, thanks."

Oh, yeah, he thought. This was all working out just fine.

* * *

"And this," Scott said, his head close to hers as they peered down at the phone in his hand, "is Miranda holding Henry after Thanksgiving dinner. She and Madison love being the older cousins and taking care of the baby."

"Do you just remember who this is, or can you really tell those girls apart?" Tess asked with a laugh and a shake of her head. It always amazed her that Scott's family seemed to so easily identify each twin, though they looked exactly alike to her.

"I can usually tell. Their personalities are different enough that their expressions sort of give them away, even when they're dressed alike, which isn't very often. Eli and Libby think it's important that the girls develop their own identities, so that they aren't just known as 'the twins.' Still, every so often I mix them up, and they call me on my mistake pretty quickly."

They sat side by side on the deep-cushioned sage-green couch in her living room, flipping through family photos stored in Scott's phone. He'd already eaten and effusively complimented the generous omelet she'd made for him, and he'd quickly accepted her offer of herbal tea afterward. He seemed to be in no hurry to leave, and Tess was enjoying this relaxed, private time with him.

"Your nieces are really cute. And Henry's a little doll. Thanks for showing me the pictures. It looks as though you had a great Thanksgiving."

"We did." Setting his phone to one side, Scott touched her hand. "I'm sorry you didn't have a good Thanksgiving with your family."

Her first instinct was to deflect the sympathy with a

shrug and an assurance that her gathering with her sister's family had been fine and she'd had a lovely time. It was a bit embarrassing to compare her strained situation with his close clan. But if Scott was going to become a part of her life, he might as well know everything he was getting into. "I guess you know that Nina and I aren't close. I can never seem to live up to her standards, and I think it annoys her that I'm not jealous of her. Does that make sense?"

"It does, actually. You being jealous of her would be a validation that she's important. Impressive. If you don't want to be her, she probably wonders what you find lacking. Needing to be envied is a common weakness for people whose sense of self-worth comes only from the amount of admiration they receive from others."

He sounded like an amateur psychologist, but he was right. "That does sound like Nina," she agreed slowly. "It sometimes seems as though everything she does is slanted toward impressing others. She pores over fashion magazines and trend blogs trying desperately to stay current. She's raising her kids the same way. Nina would pretty much pawn her soul to buy them the 'right' label. She and Ken aren't wealthy, but they try so hard to keep up with the Joneses that it exhausts me just watching them."

"I've had friends fall into that trap before they realize it's a game they just can't win. There's always someone with more money, more toys, more admirers. I like nice things as much as anyone, but I buy what I like, not because someone else would be impressed by it."

She knew that about him, of course. She couldn't have worked side by side with him for six years without learning something about his core values. It was another point in their favor as a budding couple that they shared so many of those principles. Smiling, she waved a hand around her living room. "Same here, obviously."

"I've always admired your sense of style."

The compliment pleased her. She smiled. "Thanks. But I have to give credit to my friends—Stevie with her flair for design and Jenny for keeping my wardrobe reasonably up-to-date."

Draping an arm casually across the couch behind her, he ran a fingertip along the bateau neckline of her red dress. "If this dress is an example of Jenny's contribution, then I applaud her advice. You look spectacular tonight. I could hardly take my eyes off you at the party."

The brush of his hand against her throat made her pulse flutter there. She wasn't sure he'd even noticed her appearance this evening other than the perfunctory compliment when he'd greeted her. "Thank you. And yes, I bought the dress at Jenny's boutique for the party."

"Then, I can see why her business is doing well."

"She deserves every bit of her success. And her happiness." Tess thought of her best friend. "You know, Jenny got caught up in that game we were just discussing when she dated a man before she met Gavin. Thad Simonson runs in an exclusive crowd, and with his political aspirations, everything he says, does, wears or eats is shrewdly calculated. Jenny said she felt as if she was losing herself in that life. She spent so much time trying to please Thad and his followers—not to mention her overbearing grandmother—that she wasn't even sure what she wanted anymore. Since she married Gavin, she's happier than I've ever seen her. She says she feels as if she's just getting to know the real her, pursuing her own dreams. She and Gavin are planning a camping trip in the Smoky Mountains next summer. It's something she always secretly wanted to do, but Thad wasn't interested in sleeping in a tent and her grandmother would have called it a waste of valuable time."

"Sounds like fun to me. My brothers and I have been on several camping hikes."

"I know," she reminded him with a smile. "I was the one keeping the offices running while you were gone, remember?"

He tapped the shallow cleft in her chin in a teasing gesture. "You've taken a few vacations, yourself. We struggled to stay in business while you were gone, but somehow we managed."

She laughed, though she was increasingly aware of his proximity on the couch, the way his thigh brushed hers when he shifted his weight, the air of intimacy surrounding them in the quiet room.

"How about you?" he asked. "Do you like camping?"

"I don't know. I've never been."

He looked surprised. "You've never camped?"

"No. You have to understand, my dad was almost fifty when I was born. He had his first heart attack when I was only nine. My mom was forty-five when they were shocked by her pregnancy with me. She was diagnosed with lupus when I was still in junior high and her health was never good after that. Neither of them was interested in outdoor pursuits. Usually we just went out to eat or to watch Nina perform in pageants or at college. She majored in music, though she only attended for two years before she left school to marry Ken. She has a beautiful voice, but she sings only in her church choir now."

"What were your extracurricular activities in high school and college? Do you sing, too?"

"Oh, no, not really. I can carry a tune, but I don't have Nina's talent. By the time I was in high school my parents were both in such poor health that I had to help out at home a lot. I was on the school newspaper and yearbook staffs, because those were activities I could do during the schoolday. Nina was a young bride with small children, so she couldn't help much at our house. I contributed as much as I could preparing meals and doing housework."

Realizing she might sound as if she was whining, she shook her head and spoke more brightly. "Don't get me wrong, I've had a good life. My parents made sure I had everything I needed. They paid for my tuition and made sure I had a little nest egg to set me up in this condo when they were gone. I have good friends. I have a job I love, thank you very much. My relationship with my sister isn't really close, but it's not as if we're actually estranged. Considering the age difference and the lack of anything in common, we get by okay."

He covered her hand with his and gave her fingers a warm squeeze. "I'm glad you feel free to speak candidly with me. I don't think you'd have said those things to just anyone—not even to me had we had this discussion just a couple weeks ago. Right?"

"No, probably not," she conceded. "I'd have just said everything was fine. But if you come to my cousin's party with me, I'm sure you'll see how it is with my sister and me, so I wanted you to be prepared."

"*When* I come with you to your cousin's party," he murmured, emphasizing the first word, "I'm sure we'll get along fine with your family."

"Oh, undoubtedly. We're all very civil when we get together." Mostly because she bit her tongue until it almost bled to keep from snapping when they criticized her, she added silently, choosing to keep that comment to herself.

He laced his fingers with hers. "Maybe you and I could go camping sometime. I think you'd like it."

Her heart gave a quick thump at the thought of spending a night in a tent—or anywhere else—with him, but she managed to smile. "Both of us out of the office at the same time? Sounds like a recipe for disaster."

"I suppose we'll have to figure out how to handle that situation in the future," he said with a slight shrug and a smile that almost made her sigh aloud. "We've both been working damned hard for a lot of years. Now our company is well established, we have good people on our payroll that we can trust to take care of things occasionally, and we can be reached in a multitude of ways if we're needed. I think we both deserve to take some time away from work occasionally, don't you?"

Several things about that little speech stood out to her, but his use of the plural possessive was particularly startling. *Our company. Our payroll.*

"I've been giving it a lot of thought lately," he continued before she could answer what must have been a rhetorical question. "I'm closer to forty than thirty now, and all my energy thus far has gone into the company. Buying it, growing it, securing its future. As you know, I pretty much ignored my personal life. I made the one attempt at getting engaged, but that would have been a mistake even if it hadn't fallen apart due to my own negligence. Now I'm ready for more. Commitment. Marriage. Kids. Soccer games and teacher meetings and dance recitals. Eventually cutting back on work to travel and see the world with my wife."

"That sounds very nice." She almost sighed in response to the lovely images he'd invoked.

"But first," he said briskly, "we have to get through the holidays. What's next on our social agenda?"

There was that word again. *Our.*

She moistened her lips and drew her attention back to the topic. "I'm sure you remember that tomorrow afternoon is the reception at the Best Burger home office to celebrate the holidays and the opening of their twentieth restaurant." The relatively new, locally based fast-food chain was rapidly expanding throughout Arkansas and two neighboring states and had contracted with Scott to handle its new construction. It was one of the more lucrative deals Scott had signed during the past few years. He spent a lot of time making sure the owner of the chain was happy with the construction, including one currently under way in Little Rock. The three-to-five drop-in reception was for store managers, vendors and other professional associates, and Scott was expected to make an appearance. "I don't know if you want me to attend that with you…?"

"Absolutely. This was the deal, remember? We're doing all the holiday stuff together."

The deal. Was that the way he viewed their dating agreement? She supposed it summed it up well enough. She cleared her throat silently and nodded to indicate she was on board.

"So we'll stop by the Best Burger thing tomorrow afternoon. Do you have plans for tomorrow evening?"

This felt so familiar, she thought with wry amusement. How many hours had they spent coordinating their office calendars, planning business commitments for weeks or months at a time? She supposed it was only natural that they'd handle their personal plans in much the same way. "No, I don't have anything specific planned for tomorrow night."

"I have tickets for the symphony's holiday performance. I know it's short notice, but would you like to go with me? You know—a real date?" he added with a crooked smile that was too charming to resist. "Just the two of us."

"I would like that. I love the symphony."

Looking pleased, he nodded. "We'll pop back in to the office after the reception, then leave from there to have dinner and go to the concert, if it's okay with you."

She made a quick mental note to choose a day-into-evening outfit for the next day, and to take a sparkly jacket to slip on for the concert. "That'll work."

"What about the rest of the weekend? Do you have personal plans?"

"Saturday is my niece's birthday, and Nina has made reservations at that popular new Japanese restaurant."

Should she ask him to accompany her? She supposed the reservation could be changed to add one more, but was it too soon for Scott to join her at a family celebration? Would it make the evening better or even more awkward to have him there with her?

The possibility of joining her didn't even seem to occur to him. "I've got family stuff Saturday night, too. I told Jake I'd go to his house to watch the SEC West playoff game with him tomorrow night. Have fun at the party."

She nodded. It seemed that she and Scott were already beginning to define their future together: they would be free to pursue their own interests as individuals even as they attended some events as a couple. Practical and independent. The two adjectives had always been applied to her, so it made sense that they defined her budding relationship, as well. "Have fun with your brother."

It occurred to her that he was still holding her hand. It felt nice. His fingers moved on hers again, giving another little squeeze as he said, "Next weekend is fairly busy, too. We have our office Christmas party Saturday night. But before that, on Friday night, I have a dinner thing. Would you be free to go with me to that?"

"A dinner thing?"

He waved his free hand. "It's an engagement party. The couple sent out invitations a couple of months ago, I think, and to be honest, I'd forgotten about it until I got a reminder by email today. You know how hectic everything has been the past few weeks. This dinner totally slipped my mind."

This was the first she'd heard of an engagement party. She didn't handle his personal social calendar, but usually he mentioned upcoming events at least in passing. It did speak to his state of mind lately that he'd forgotten a commitment. "Did you tell them you'd be bringing a date?"

"Oh, sure. I figured I'd ask someone. I can't think of anyone I'd rather go with than you."

She swallowed. Accompanying him to the Holiday Open Home had been a relatively innocuous first social outing together. If anyone had been surprised to see them enter side by side, Tess hadn't noticed. She figured the Best Burger open house would be similarly easy. It was possible they'd see people they knew at the symphony performance, but then again, perhaps they wouldn't, nor would they likely be expected to explain why they attended together. But an engagement party... Well, that was very different. This would most definitely be interpreted as a date. "Are these close friends?"

He shrugged. "Bethany, the bride-to-be, is the youngest daughter of my mom's college roommate. I've known her all her life, but I wouldn't call us close friends. The groom just finished dental school in Louisiana and Bethany's mom talked Dad into interviewing him as a potential associate."

"So is he going to join your dad's practice?"

"Yeah, I think so. Dad's been wanting to add someone who specializes in pediatric dentistry, which apparently this guy does."

So the daughter of an old friend and his dad's new business associate. Which meant the entire Prince clan would probably be in attendance at this party. "You haven't, um, mentioned to your family that you and I are..."

"I haven't talked about us with anyone," he assured her. "But they'll probably get the picture when we show up at the party."

She nodded.

"Haven't changed your mind, have you?" He spoke lightly, but she sensed he was serious.

"No." In fact, now that he'd laid out such an enticing future for them, she was even more committed to their tentative plan. "I have to admit I'm a little nervous, but I'll go with you."

"Why are you nervous?" he asked with a little smile, holding her hand between both of his now.

"Well, it's your family and friends."

"Many of whom you've met several times. They already know you and like you."

"As your office manager."

"As a person," he corrected firmly. "My family doesn't tend to label people by their professions. The dinner's at Trapnall Hall and it shouldn't last overly long."

"I always enjoy events there this time of year. I'm sure the Christmas decorations are beautiful."

He lifted one hand to her face, running a fingertip lightly over her lower lip. "I'm glad you'll be going with me. It'll make the event much more tolerable."

Warmth seeped through her in response to his nearness, his touch. In some ways it still felt odd to be snuggled with Scott on her sofa, yet beneath the novelty was a growing certainty that it was exactly where they were meant to be. He'd simply realized it before she'd acknowledged it herself.

She rested a hand on his chest, allowing her fingers to curl a bit against his shirt to savor the warm strength beneath. He'd removed his jacket and tie and opened his collar, so he looked casually at ease, gazing at her in a way that made her heart beat a little faster. His eyes had darkened to a gleaming navy and his lips were curved into a faint sexy smile that made her ache to taste him.

"I'll try my best to make the party tolerable for you," she said, smiling.

His gaze was focused intently on her mouth. A low rumble of laughter escaped him. "I appreciate that," he murmured.

Silence fell between them then. Looking into his eyes, she realized that the time for conversation had ended. It was time for him to go…or not. Which didn't mean they had to rush to a decision about those options. She slid her hand up his chest to the back of his neck, her lips parting in an invitation he accepted instantly, eagerly.

Gathering her against him, he kissed her with a thoroughness and urgency he'd reined in previously. His mouth was hot, hungry on hers, his tongue sweeping deep to explore and challenge. She gave a little moan of surprise and pleasure, her arms closing around his neck to bring them even closer. His hand moved on her leg, toying with the hem of the dress and then sliding under to caress her thigh. She shivered in response to an image of his hands moving higher. Her breasts swelled against his chest, and a restless ache settled there. Just the thought of his hands closing over them made her tremble.

Slowly breaking the kiss, he lifted his head only a couple inches, his gaze sweeping her flushed face. Still nestled snugly in his arms, she was aware that he was breathing rapidly, that his eyes were dilated, his heart beating hard against hers. He was as aroused as she was, in control but reluctantly so.

She touched her fingertips to his jaw almost wonderingly. "Does this feel weird to you? Shouldn't it feel strange?"

His lips curved upward. "Maybe it should. But it doesn't. It feels…good. Right."

"To me, too," she confessed. "Maybe the strange part is that it *doesn't* feel weird."

He chuckled and set her a couple inches away from him. "I'm not quite sure how to unravel that statement, but I think I'd better go."

She blinked. "You're leaving?"

His voice was just a little rough when he nodded and said, "It's either that or I'm going to start trying to get you out of that pretty red dress. I'm not sure we're quite ready for that step yet."

Though a surprisingly insistent part of her wanted to argue, rational discretion prevailed. She scooted back another couple inches and reached up with unsteady hands to smooth her hair. "You should go," she agreed, pleased that her voice was reasonably normal. "We do have to work in the morning."

She walked him to the door to lock up behind him. With a hand on the doorknob, she smiled up at him, giving in to an impertinent impulse. "Scott? For the record—you wouldn't have to try very hard. With the dress, I mean."

His eyes widened, then narrowed. "You're determined to make me suffer tonight, aren't you?"

She patted his cheek. "Just saying."

His smile was decidedly lopsided. "So this is how it's going to go, huh? You're going to make me jump through a few hoops to prove myself worthy?"

Even though his amusement was obvious, she grew serious. "I know you're teasing—as I was—but let me make this clear. I don't play games. I don't expect you to prove anything to me. Outside the office, we're not boss and employee, but equals. Full partners. Yes?"

He matched her serious tone when he replied, "Absolutely. I've said from the start this has nothing to do with business. I expect you to speak your mind, state your wishes, read me the riot act when I deserve it, without fear of any professional repercussions." And then he looked thoughtful. "Actually, that's pretty much the way you act in the office, too. You've never been intimidated by me, have you?"

She thought fleetingly of that first interview so long ago, but merely smiled. "Not that I'd let you see."

He chuckled, then leaned over to brush his lips lightly across hers. "And now you know why I'm convinced we make such a great team, inside the office and out. Thanks for the omelet, Tess. It was delicious."

"You're welcome. Good night, Scott."

He hesitated for just a few moments longer and then gave a decisive nod and let himself out. Tess released a long breath and listened through the door as he walked away. Only when she could no longer hear him did she head for her bedroom to change out of the red dress and into her nightclothes. For the sake of her peace of mind, she made a deliberate effort not to imagine what it would have been like if Scott had been the one to remove the dress.

Chapter Six

As Tess had expected, no one seemed to find it newsworthy that she accompanied Scott to the Best Burger reception. It was their biggest regular client, and everyone knew she'd interacted frequently with representatives from the chain. Andy and Lana, their architect and cost estimator, had already left for the reception, so PCCI would be well represented.

The reception was drop-in and very informal. Tess had met most of the higher-ups in the fast food chain's echelon at one time or another. Aware of her function as valued assistant to Scott, they welcomed her warmly to their base of operations. The owner of the chain even introduced her to a district manager as "the glue that held PCCI together." Grinning, Scott said he couldn't dispute that assessment. He stayed by her side during the hour they mingled, but she doubted anyone thought they were actually there as a couple rather than a work team. Still, as Scott had said, it was good for people to get accustomed to seeing them together in a variety of settings. They stood by the food table—laden, of course, with snacks available at any local Best Burger restaurant—chatting with a variety of local business-people, and when they thought they'd accomplished their purpose in coming, they made a gracious escape.

"That went well," Scott proclaimed in his car on the way back to the office, sounding almost smug about it. "This whole dating thing is turning out just fine, wouldn't you say?"

Tess laughed. "Scott, I refuse to acknowledge that as a date."

He slanted a grin her way. "Was the Holiday Open Home a date?"

"More so."

"How about the baby shopping trip followed by the barbecue dinner?"

"Less so."

He chuckled. "So by your definition, we're just barely in the honeymoon part of this relationship."

Her heart gave a little jerk, though she didn't know whether it was in response to the word *honeymoon* or *relationship*. Maybe it was something about the words used in combination. But because he was kidding, she chuckled and said, "Yes, I suppose."

"But tonight definitely counts as a date. Just the two of us at the symphony, no professional obligations, nothing to do but enjoy each other's company and the music."

"That sounds nice," she agreed, relaxing again. She really was looking forward to the concert. As much as she loved music, she was sure she would enjoy it even more with Scott by her side.

By the time they'd finished returning calls, answering emails, signing paperwork and placing orders, Tess and Scott barely got away from work in time. They acknowledged wryly that they should have known better than to stop by the office. "A couple of hopeless workaholics," Scott said with a laugh as he locked up behind them. "That's why we get along so well. You understand me because you're just like me."

Straightening the short sequined jacket she'd donned over her day-to-evening black jersey dress, Tess smiled in return. "Was that supposed to be a compliment?" she teased.

"Just an observation." He placed a hand on her back as they walked side by side toward their cars. "I can count on you to understand that sometimes I get distracted or held up by obligations to the company. You won't expect me to apologize when unexpected problems crop up or when I have to cancel social plans rather than risk losing a valuable contract."

"Well, of course not." She suspected he was thinking of his ex-fiancée. Sharon had made her displeasure clear to everyone when she didn't think Scott was paying her enough attention. She'd even snapped at Tess a few times when Tess had answered the office phone and had to explain that Scott was in an emergency meeting and couldn't be disturbed. Even though she knew he was comparing her positively to his high-maintenance ex, she would just as soon not be compared at all. She deliberately changed the subject. "So you're following me home to drop off my car and then we'll have dinner before the concert, right? We'll have to choose someplace with fast service in order to make the start of the concert."

They did make it to the concert hall in time, but just barely. The lights were already dimming when they slid into their seats. Tess wasn't displeased by that. This way they didn't have to wait very long for the music to start, nor had they risked running into mutual acquaintances on the way in. The concert was wonderful, a charming mixture of classical pieces and Christmas favorites. She relaxed into her seat, letting the music wash over her, not worrying about work or family or the future, just enjoying the evening. After one particularly rousing number, she glanced at Scott to find him gazing back at her. Though the lights were very low, she could see well enough to tell that he was smiling at her, apparently enjoying her pleasure.

He reached over to take her hand, squeezing her fingers. "Glad we came?"

"Very much."

They'd both needed a couple hours away from work and expectations, she decided. True, they were on a date, and there was still the novelty of that—but it was Scott. With their demanding work schedule, they'd spent more time together over the past six years than most married couples. They communicated so well silently that she could even tell which musical numbers he enjoyed most without looking at him—which was probably also true in reverse. They were comfortable together…and yet underlying that familiarity was a new awareness that gave her a delicious buzz when he touched her. Knowing there would be more kisses later caused little ripples of anticipation to run through her.

Thinking of where those kisses would eventually lead made her breath catch in her throat.

But no. She wasn't thinking ahead now, she reminded herself. She wanted to enjoy every moment of this evening, just sitting beside him and listening to the music.

They each saw a few familiar faces on their way out, but the crowded rush to the exits prevented more than nods and waves. If there were any mutual acquaintances in the audience, she didn't see them, but then she wasn't really looking. She and Scott didn't linger in the hall, but made their way to his car as quickly as possible. They'd accomplished their mission. They'd enjoyed a concert while growing more accustomed to being out in public as a couple. Maybe by the time next weekend rolled around, she would be a little less anxious about attending the party with his family and friends. Had that been part of his reason for bringing her to this concert tonight?

They talked about the concert during the drive home, comparing notes on their favorite numbers, expressing their admiration for both the musicians and the vocal performers. Arriving at her place, he parked next to her little blue sedan. Each unit came with two designated covered parking spaces, leaving her with an extra for her guests. He walked her inside, and her heart beat more quickly with each step they took toward her door. Should she ask him in? Of course she should. Were they ready for that next step they'd alluded to when he'd left her here last time? Part of her was most definitely ready.

He started to automatically follow her inside, then seemed to realize he hadn't technically been invited yet. He hesitated. It briefly crossed her mind to send him on his way with weariness as her excuse, but she decided she didn't really want to say good-night just yet. "Would you like some tea?"

"Sounds good." His flash of a smile made her hands tremble. He closed the door behind them with a firm snap.

She set her bag on a table and draped her coat over the back of a chair. "Would you prefer tea or decaf coffee?"

"Actually, I'm not very thirsty."

She turned toward him. "Neither am I."

Scott stepped up to her and cupped her face gently in his hands. His palms were still cool from being outside, but her cheeks felt very warm against them. His eyes locked with hers, and she could almost imagine he could see her thoughts, her doubts as he gazed somberly down at her. "You can kick me out at any time," he reminded her gently.

"I know. The problem is…I don't want to kick you out," she replied, resting her hands on his chest.

His eyes heated, but still he kept his tone even. "Is that really such a problem?"

"I'm still trying to decide."

He moved his thumb against her lower lip, tracing the shape of it. His gaze following the movement, he murmured, "I've been trying to take it slow. Give you time to adjust."

Take it slow? It had been only a week since he'd sprung this proposition on her. She felt a slight frown crease her brows. "How are *you* adjusting so easily?"

His smile was warm, understanding. "You know me. Once I make up my mind about something, I rarely second-guess myself. Now that we've acknowledged how great we are together, it just seems as if it was inevitable all along."

Inevitable. Was that enough? She doubted Stevie would think so.

"And now that we've spent this time together," he added, his mouth so close to hers that his breath was a warm caress on her lips, "I can't believe it took me so long to see what was right in front of me."

Okay, that sounded a little more intimate. A little less deliberate. Not exactly a declaration of devotion, but that wasn't what she was looking for from Scott. She'd heard flowery speeches and passionate promises before, and those relationships had ended in disappointment if not actual heartbreak. Maybe this time she should put her faith in actions, not words. And speaking of action…

She wrapped her arms around Scott's neck when he gathered her closer, capturing her lips with his. Despite the five inch or so difference in their heights, their bodies fit very nicely together. Each time they kissed, the sensations grew more familiar—and yet more urgent. He'd said he'd been taking things slowly, so perhaps he'd held back in those previous embraces. He wasn't holding back now. He drew her closer, letting her feel his body's response, making her intensely aware of his growing arousal. His mouth was avid, his tongue insistent. Faced with a choice between pushing him away and doing what she really wanted, she gave in to temptation. She crowded closer to him, returning the kiss with an answering demand.

Take it slow? Hardly. This had been building in her for six years.

He was quick to recognize the silent invitation and

he accepted it with an enthusiasm that soon had them both breathing heavily, shoving impatiently at clothing to access the warm skin beneath. Scott's jacket and tie fell onto the couch. She left her shoes behind when she led him to her bedroom. He had his shirt untucked and partially unbuttoned by the time they reached the bed. She reached for the zipper at the back of her dress, but Scott's hands were already there as he gathered her into his arms for another hungry kiss. By the time the black dress fell to the floor, she was too deeply lost in the embrace, too eager for more, to be at all self-conscious.

She'd seen him without a shirt only once before. It had been the day they'd worked at his house after his surgery. Still loopy from the meds, he'd accidentally tugged off a corner of his bandage. She'd smoothed it back into place and then helped him don a fresh T-shirt. Other than the necessary touching, she'd kept her hands to herself that day, resisting the then inappropriate urge to run her palms over the firm planes and hard muscles of his chest, to follow a thin trail of hair down his ridged stomach to his shallow belly button and below.

She'd never forgotten how appealing he'd looked that day, all rumpled and drowsy and half-nude. Unbidden memories had haunted her more than once during lonely nights since, though she'd quickly and firmly suppressed them each time. She didn't have to restrain herself now. She gave her curious hands free rein to explore and savor every inch of him, even as he pushed her beyond coherence with his own bold forays of discovery.

They communicated with soft moans and approving gasps, with kisses and strokes and urgent movements. His mouth on her breasts made her arch with a choked cry of pleasure. Her hands closing around him tore a low groan from him. They rolled and writhed, shoving pillows to the floor, covers to the side. He dealt with protection swiftly and deftly before returning his attention to pleasuring her, which he did with even more practiced skill. Their hands were interlocked when he finally, finally thrust into her, filling an emptiness that seemed to have been waiting for him all her life.

For only a raw heartbeat of an instant, she was aware of a sense of panic, an overwhelming fear that this was too perfect, too powerful. The knowledge that everything would change after this night swept through her, and for just that second she fought to cling to the safe, cautious status quo. The comfortable camaraderie that had carried no risk of disappointment or heartbreak, no fear of losing what they'd found...of losing herself. But then he began to move, and any hesitation was replaced by an almost desperate need for release. Her mind emptied of any thought except that very moment, that very place, the two of them entangled in the cozy cocoon of her bed, their bodies joined, hearts pounding in unison. Her climax hit with a force that shattered any illusion that anything would ever be the same for them again.

He didn't stay the night. Referencing an early breakfast meeting with a couple of job foremen, he slipped from the bed and dressed to leave while she wrapped herself in a robe to lock up behind him. He paused before opening the door, and she got the distinct impression that he was trying to come up with the right thing to say. It wasn't like him to be at a loss for words.

To help him out, she said simply, "Good night, Scott. Drive carefully."

He kissed her lingeringly. "Sleep well, Tess. I'll call you tomorrow."

She nodded and reached around him to open the door.

His jacket over his shoulder, tie hanging from his pocket, his finger-combed dark hair tumbling onto his forehead, Scott turned just on the other side of the door to smile at her. "I knew we made a great team," he said in visible satisfaction. "I really am a genius."

That made her laugh, as he'd surely intended. "Yes, you are," she said.

Because she didn't want him to leave feeling too sanctimonious, she reached out to grab his shirt, tugged his mouth down to hers and gave him a kiss that turned his laughter into a groan.

"Okay, maybe I could stay a little while longer," he said rather hoarsely when the kiss ended.

She tossed back her tumbled hair and took a step backward. "Good night, Scott."

She closed the door almost in his face. Through the wood, she heard him sputter a rough laugh, then listened as his footsteps faded away. Only then did she allow herself to release a long, slow exhale.

After fastening the door locks, she turned toward her bedroom, then realized she was biting her kiss-swollen lower lip. She released it with a reassurance to herself that things really were going well between them. It was probably only weariness and lingering disorientation causing the heavy feeling deep in her chest. The sensation felt much like apprehension, but she couldn't fully explain it and didn't want to examine it too closely tonight.

* * *

The positive side of the showy dinner party Nina threw in celebration of Olivia's fifteenth birthday was that she was too busy being the hostess and mistress of ceremonies to have much time to focus on Tess. She'd reserved a private dining room in the restaurant for some thirty guests. Most of the guests were related to Nina's husband, Ken—his parents and two siblings and a few of their progeny—in addition to a few church, social and business acquaintances. More to Olivia's taste, there'd been a teen party the night before at the indoor pool of a country club. Though she visibly relished being the center of attention again, Olivia made it clear she'd enjoyed last night's bash much more than this dinner party. She huddled with her boyfriend and the few other friends she'd been allowed to invite while her brothers played handheld video games and Ken quietly did his part by standing at his wife's side, following her directions and bankrolling the event.

Tess would rather be just about anywhere else, herself. She loved her niece, spoiled little princess that she was, but this was not her idea of a fun evening. All in all, she'd rather have been watching the football game. Either alone...or not.

She wondered if Scott was having a good time. If he'd thought of her at all this evening. She'd never been one of "those" girlfriends, she mused. Though she both practiced and expected monogamy during her relationships, she'd never expected to know where her significant other was or what he was doing at all times, nor did she report her movements to him. But it would be nice to know that she'd crossed Scott's mind today as often as he'd hovered in hers. That he'd mentally replayed their lovemaking and relived the excitement, that he felt the same anticipation she did about the next time they'd be alone together.

She wanted to be confident that when he thought of her now, it wasn't only with a list of tasks he needed her to oversee at the office.

It was a relief when the dinner was over. She exchanged farewells with the other guests, most of whom she'd met previously, then lingered to say good-night to her family.

Holding her boyfriend's hand, Olivia sauntered up to her. "Thank you for the bag, Aunt Tess. It's really cool. I love it."

Pleased by the girlish delight in her niece's voice, Tess smiled. "I'm glad. Jenny helped me find it for you. She thought you'd like it."

They hugged quickly, and then Olivia and her lanky boyfriend hurried off to rejoin their friends. Satisfied that she could make her escape now, Tess looked around for Nina, finding her on the other side of the room saying goodbye to some departing guests. She made her way to her sister's side. "I'm leaving now, Nina. It was a great dinner. Thanks for inviting me."

"Of course you'd be invited," Nina replied with an impatient roll of her eyes. "We invited all Olivia's aunts and uncles."

Resisting an impulse to snap that she'd just been trying to be polite, Tess drew a deep breath and held on to her smile with an effort. "It was good to see everyone again."

"Don't forget next week is—"

"Dana's party," Tess finished in unison. "I haven't forgotten, Nina."

"You've responded to the evite?"

Nina was very much in "mama mode" this evening, treating Tess exactly the way she would one of her children. Again, Tess had to cling to patience. "I have responded."

"Did you tell her you'd bring a guest? Because if you haven't invited anyone—"

"I'm bringing a guest. It's already arranged, Nina."

Her sister's eyes widened in curiosity. "Who are you bringing?"

"Hon, we need to help Olivia carry out her gifts," Ken interrupted the conversation to say. "The room's booked for another party so they're ready for us to clear out."

Nina lifted her chin. "We have it reserved for another ten minutes. I will not be hustled out."

"It'll take us that long to gather everything up and get the kids out to the van. Come on, Nina, grab a couple bags, will you?"

Tess moved a step forward. "Can I help?"

Her brother-in-law gave her a quick wink. "We've got it, thanks. Get out of here while you can."

She took grateful advantage of his suggestion.

A particularly boneheaded play in the football game would have made Scott curse in exasperation had a baby not been asleep on his chest. As it was, he grumbled beneath his breath, making little Henry squirm and nestle his nose into Scott's shoulder. Scott hoped fleetingly that it wasn't a snotty little nose, but it wouldn't be the first time he'd been used as a tissue by one of his brothers' offspring. He patted the kid's diapered bottom and Henry settled back into a limp slumber. Sprawled on Jake's couch with his stocking feet crossed on the coffee table, Scott glanced at the canned soda on the table and wondered if he could reach it without waking his nephew.

As if he'd recently mastered the art of mind reading, but more likely correctly interpreting Scott's expression, Jake snagged the can and handed it over. "Game sucks, huh?"

With a nod of thanks, Scott took a sip of the beverage, which had gone rather flat in the past hour since he'd opened it. "Yeah. I thought the score would be closer than this."

"You okay there? Want me to take the rug rat?"

"He's okay. We wake him up, he's just going to want to eat again, and we promised Christina we'd give her a little more time to herself. Might as well stretch it out as much as we can after the week she's had."

The virus Henry had picked up at Thanksgiving had held on for several days. He was recovered now, but his parents were tired and frazzled. Scott's mom had helped out when she could, but as a full-time accountant, she'd been busy with end-of-the-year work for her clients. Today had been a day for Christina to get some rest, with Jake and Scott taking care of the baby.

His eyes on the big-screen TV on the opposite wall, Jake munched a handful of popcorn, then asked idly, "You going to Bethany's engagement party next Friday?"

"Looks like. You know Mom would pout if any of us skipped out without a damned good reason, and unfortunately I couldn't come up with one."

Jake chuckled wryly. "Yeah, us, either. We've got a

babysitter lined up, so I guess we'll make an appearance."

"Lousy time for an engagement party, if you ask me. This time of year, seems like I'm running from one party or fund-raiser or holiday reception to the next one. Bethany and what's-his-name aren't even getting married until spring, so I can't imagine why they thought they needed an engagement party now."

"Mom said Jeremy—that's the groom's name, by the way—has an aunt in poor health. They aren't sure she'll still be around for the wedding, but they wanted to have her at the engagement party."

"Oh, well, now I feel like a jerk." With a grimace, Scott set the soda aside and patted the sleeping baby again. "I'll be there. With a smile."

"Are you bringing someone?"

"Yeah. Tess is coming with me."

He wasn't sure how he'd expected his younger brother to react to that, but it hadn't been with a laugh. "Tess? Man, she really is on call 24/7 for you, isn't she? Do you pay her overtime for keeping you company at parties you don't want to attend alone?"

Scott shook his head. "She isn't coming as my employee. Tess has agreed to be my date for the party."

"Your date?"

"Yes."

"Like…a *date* date?"

Scott scowled, hardly pleased by the disbelief in his brother's expression. "So we're back to high school now? Really?"

Jake shrugged. "I'm just surprised, that's all. I didn't know you and Tess ever hung out outside the office."

"It's a recent development."

"You and Tess, huh? Wow."

Wow pretty much summed up the last few hours he'd spent with Tess, Scott mused, though of course he wouldn't say that to his brother. Henry wiggled and made a mewing sound. Scott bounced him gently while saying, "Yeah."

"Since when?"

"We've been out a few times." He smiled as he remembered the teasing conversation he and Tess had about how many real dates there had actually been.

"So is it, you know, serious?"

An erotic memory of deep-throated cries of satisfaction whispered in the back of his mind. Scott cleared his throat. "Getting there."

"Well, that's great," Jake said, still sounding surprised.

Henry squirmed again, then lifted his head from Scott's now-damp shoulder to blink up at him. He looked a bit surprised to find himself in his uncle's arms, but with his usual happy nature, he grinned broadly, displaying two shiny new teeth. Scott couldn't resist smiling goofily in response.

"What's great?" Christina entered the room looking considerably more refreshed than she had when Scott arrived. Short and somewhat square in stature, she had red hair, numerous freckles, warm green eyes and a smile that could melt glaciers. Henry had inherited her coloring. His wispy hair was already a bright ginger rather than Jake's dark brown.

"Scott's dating Tess," Jake blurted.

Christina blinked a few times, then nodded. "Good choice."

"You're not surprised?" her husband challenged.

"Not very much." She crossed the room to take her son, who'd reached out in response to her voice. She smiled at Scott as she relieved him of his charge. "I think you and Tess fit very well together."

Oh, yeah. He and Tess fit very well together indeed, he thought, shifting restlessly on the couch.

"I guess it makes sense," Jake said after a moment. "Tess is great, and everyone likes her. Not sure what she sees in you, bro, but you'd be lucky to keep her."

"Thanks a lot." Scott laughed as he carefully straightened his left arm. The pins-and-needles tingling of returning circulation told him he'd sat in one position too long holding the baby, but he wasn't complaining. He'd enjoyed bonding with his nephew.

"So, Scott, when did you realize you had feelings for Tess?" Christina asked while trying to extricate her eyeglasses from her son's grasp.

He wasn't quite sure how to answer. He remembered clearly that moment of recognition when he'd found Tess under the office tree and had suddenly realized how perfect she was for him. It had just made sense to him. Was that what Christina meant by "having feelings"— or was she imagining some sort of epic Hollywood romantic epiphany that hardly applied to two generally levelheaded adults with common goals and wishes?

Okay, so maybe last night had gotten pretty hot. Maybe he'd tossed and turned as he'd tried to sleep alone afterward, regretting that he'd made himself leave her bed. Maybe he was counting the minutes until he had her in his arms again. Physical chemistry was a good thing between a couple, especially when they'd agreed they wanted children, he considered as his gaze lingered on his giggling nephew.

Maybe the attraction had simmered beneath the surface for quite a bit longer than he'd realized, judging by how swiftly it had come to a boil when he'd finally been free to express it. Her heated responses reassured him that the attraction went both ways, though knowing Tess, she'd probably suppressed any such awareness in the past for fear that it would be unprofessional.

"Scott?" Christina looked at him quizzically over Henry's head, and he suspected the trained psychologist was trying to analyze his facial expressions. "You and Tess?"

"We've just started seeing each other," he said, choosing his words carefully. "It's occurred to us both how well we get along and how much we have in common, so we figured it was worth exploring on a more personal basis."

The couple looked at each other and then back at him. Jake broke the momentary silence. "Wow. What a romantic story. Almost brought a tear to my eye."

Frowning at his kid brother, Scott grumbled, "Bite me, Jake. We all know I'm no good at the romantic stuff. I don't have to put on an act for Tess. She already knows me better than anyone outside of the family. Anything that develops between us will be based on honesty and mutual goals."

Jake raised both hands in surrender. "Whatever works for you both. I just want you to be happy, bro. You know that."

"Yeah, I do. Thanks."

Henry was beginning to fuss. Christina bounced him in her arms to momentarily soothe him as she carried him toward the couch. "I need to feed him and give him his bath, then put him to bed. Say good-night, guys."

Both Scott and Jake rose to bestow hugs and kisses on the youngest Prince. He gave slobbery smacks in return, then waved bye-bye over his mother's shoulder as she carried him from the room. She paused in the doorway to look back at Scott. "I like Tess a lot," she said. "I always have."

"I'm glad to hear that."

She looked uncharacteristically fierce when she added, "Don't hurt her."

"I won't."

Nodding decisively, Christina swept out of the room with Henry.

While he appreciated the sentiment, Christina should know that hurting Tess was the furthest thing from his mind. Wasn't that the whole point of approaching her the way he had with his proposition?

"So when *did* you—"

"Halftime's over, Jake," he cut in flatly. "Let's watch the game, okay?"

"In other words, you don't want to talk about you and Tess any more this evening."

"Exactly."

Jake directed his attention to the television screen, obligingly bringing the conversation to an end. But even though they weren't talking about it, Scott figured his brother was still mulling over this new development. He knew thoughts of Tess would hover in his own mind until he saw her again.

Although rather hectic and borderline chaotic, that second week in December was nevertheless enjoyable, as far as Tess was concerned. The business problems that cropped up were no more than expected and fairly easily resolved. Sofia started training with Heather and was obviously going to fit in well with the staff. People seemed to be in a generally good mood during the week, because of the approaching holidays or perhaps because the weather had taken a nice turn.

As for her personal life—that was going nicely, too. Though both busy with previously arranged after-work obligations, she and Scott managed to find time together during the week. Scott had business plans Monday evening and she had a civic club meeting. He called her just as she was getting ready for bed and they talked about their respective meetings, sharing a couple of amusing anecdotes. Something else that was new for them, she thought with a smile as she climbed beneath her covers afterward. A chatty personal phone call made for no other reason than to hear each other's voices, to stay in contact despite their individual pursuits. It was nice that his was the last voice she heard before ending the day.

They dined at a restaurant following a long day at work Tuesday, slipping out after the rest of the staff left. Tess had rather hoped the evening would end back at her place, but the muted beep of Scott's phone just as they finished dessert dashed that fantasy. Scott looked at her in apology after disconnecting the call. "I'm sorry."

"Something has come up," she said, easily reading his expression.

He nodded. "Apparently a bunch of punks climbed the fence around the rental units we're building in Sheridan and had a little vandalism party before the cops rounded them up. Andy and I are going to look around and see if they've done any permanent damage. I guess Andy could go without me, but…"

"But you need to go check it out yourself," she said

matter-of-factly, knowing him too well to imagine otherwise.

He grimaced and nodded. "We were so close to finished with that project. I'm hoping there's nothing that'll hold us up too long. I need to put the crew on the fabric store job after the holidays, and I'm sure we'll have weather delays in January and February. We always do."

"You don't have to explain. Just go. Let me know if there's anything I need to do."

"You're the best, Tess," he told her warmly.

He might as well have given her a cheery knuckle-chuck to the chin. Even though he gave her a fairly heated good-night kiss when he dropped her off at her condo, his attention was obviously focused already on what he would find at the job site. Tess let herself in her door with a wry smile. She honestly didn't resent him at all for rushing off to work. How many times had she walked out on plans with her friends because something had come up at work and Scott had requested her assistance? Her ex-boyfriend James had accused her of being at Scott's "beck and call" 24/7…and worse, liking it that way.

Still, she thought as she prepared for bed in her quiet home, it would have been nice if the evening had gone the way she'd hoped.

Fortunately the damages to the Sheridan job hadn't been too extensive, so Scott was able to make arrangements for fairly swift repairs. They got a great deal accomplished in the office on Wednesday, to everyone's satisfaction. She didn't see a lot of Scott that day, only when he dashed in with barked instructions and scribbled his signature on whatever she slapped in front of him.

Though she had to silently chide herself a couple of

times when she found herself watching his sexy mouth instead of listening closely to his words, Scott seemed to have no trouble at all seeing her as the same efficient assistant she'd always been to him. She was fairly confident the staff saw nothing different in their professional behavior, which was a relief to her even though she was aware it wouldn't be much longer before the news got out. She wasn't looking forward to that part, mostly because she suspected everyone would watch them surreptitiously when they were together, at least until they got used to the idea that the boss and the office manager were more than business associates. Considering that it had taken her more than a week to wrap her head around the idea, she expected the transition to be a bit awkward.

It would have been nice to think Scott was having just a little trouble keeping his personal feelings for her, whatever they might be, so well hidden. She'd hate to think she was the only one having to work at that.

Scott was scheduled for an overnight trip Thursday to a job site in Joplin, Missouri, planning to be back just in time to make it to the engagement party dinner on Friday night, and there was a long list of things to do to prepare for his meetings there. The sun had long set by the time Tess and Scott wrapped up their work. Predicting it would be a wearing day, she'd left a beef-and-vegetable stew in the slow cooker that morning, and Scott eagerly accepted her invitation to share it with her.

At his suggestion, they didn't discuss work during the meal. Instead, they talked about their families and friends outside the office. He shared stories about babysitting little Henry last Saturday, making her laugh at his description of changing a soaked-through diaper and onesie. "Jake just stood there and laughed at me," he added with mock indignation. "Didn't even offer to help."

She laughed again. "Did he take video?"

"No."

"Then, consider yourself lucky. The whole episode could have ended up on YouTube, you know."

He chuckled. "There is that."

"You enjoy being an uncle."

It hadn't been a question, but he smiled and nodded. "Very much."

He'd be a wonderful father, she thought with a little ripple of wistfulness. He was already comfortable with kids and experienced enough through his brothers that he was prepared for the reality of parenthood.

"I told Jake and Christina that you'd be coming with me to Bethany's party," he said, somewhat abruptly changing the subject.

They'd been clearing away the dishes when he spoke, and she paused in the act of loading the dishwasher. "Did you?"

"Yeah." He closed the refrigerator door after stashing away leftovers. "Christina said she likes you very much."

It was nice to hear. "I like her, too. All your family seems nice. Have you told them that we're…um…"

"Seeing each other?" he supplied with a smile. "By Sunday morning the whole family knew. They're cool with it."

She wondered what, exactly, his family had said, but she assumed he would tell her when or if he was ready. For now, he seemed to consider the question of his family's reaction settled. "What did your sister say when you told her I'm coming to your cousin's party with you?" he asked.

"I haven't actually told her," she admitted. "She knows I'm bringing someone but there hasn't been a chance to tell her it's you."

That wasn't entirely true, of course. She could have made time to talk to Nina. She couldn't even explain why she'd hadn't.

Scott studied her face a bit too closely. "Will you mention it before we show up?"

"If I speak with her. Hand me that ladle, will you?"

He let the topic go, but she knew he didn't fully understand her relationship with her sister. How could he, when she didn't herself? He would simply have to see for himself when they spent time with her family. As close as his clan was, he would surely be aware of the difference in hers.

He wiped his hands on a kitchen towel. "So what had you planned for the remainder of the evening, if I hadn't come to eat your food?"

"Promise not to laugh?"

He grinned. "No."

She wrinkled her nose at him. "Okay, fine. *Rudolph the Red-Nosed Reindeer* and *Frosty the Snowman* are on tonight. I've watched them every year since I was a little girl. Usually I make hot chocolate and curl up on the sofa for an hour of Christmas nostalgia before I take care of anything else that needs to be done, like laundry or paperwork or laying out clothes for tomorrow."

He didn't laugh. Instead, she thought he looked almost charmed by her admission—which, of course, endeared him even more to her. He reached out to smooth her hair in a casually affectionate gesture. "Do you have any marshmallows for that hot chocolate?"

"Of course."

"Then, may I hang around and watch the elf become a dentist with you?"

"I'd like that."

He brushed a kiss over her lips. "So would I."

They made it halfway through the first show before teasing chocolate-flavored kisses turned to aching, impatient need. Tess tugged at his shirt, needing to touch him, all of him, and his hands were busy beneath her soft sweater, stroking and circling and tugging lightly until her breathing was fast and ragged.

"What about your Christmas specials?" he asked when she jumped to her feet and held out a hand to him, making sure he couldn't mistake the invitation.

"I know how they end." She smiled. "I can always watch the DVDs if I want."

Taking her hand, he turned with her toward the bedroom. "I'll buy them for you," he promised with a low laugh.

"I'll buy them for myself. There are other things I want from you, Scott Prince."

Grinning, he swept her against him. "Happy to oblige, Tess Miller."

They proved without doubt that the first time hadn't been a fluke. Their lovemaking this time was just as spectacular, just as breathtaking. As much as Tess hated clichés, she had to admit if only to herself that she'd honestly never felt anything like that before.

Because he'd be making an early start the next morning, Scott didn't stay long. He left her with smiles and kisses at the door.

"Be careful during your drive," she urged him.

"I will. You know how to reach me for whatever."

"Yes. See you Friday."

"Friday," he repeated, stepping out her door. He glanced over his shoulder with a rather odd expression. "I'll miss you."

Why did he sound almost surprised? "I'll see you Friday," she repeated and gently closed the door.

Was it really such a surprise to him to think he might miss her? True, they hadn't really talked about their feelings for each other—they'd talked about common dreams and goals and values, about families and children and other interests, but they hadn't said anything about love. They'd shared fiery kisses and mind-blowing lovemaking, but even in the throes of passion they'd whispered only encouragement and pleasure. She didn't expect flowery declarations from him; she knew him too well. But "I'll miss you" sounded innocuous enough. Why had it seemed so hard for him to admit?

And why hadn't she told him she would miss him in return? Because she realized now, as she climbed into the sheets still warm from his body, that she would miss him very much, even though she would see him again in only two days. And that was a bit daunting, indicating that she was investing a great deal in this budding relationship.

Apparently he wasn't the only one getting a little nervous with the speed and intensity with which this momentous development was taking place between them.

Chapter Seven

With Scott out of town and it being Heather's last day, Friday was particularly busy at work. By the time Tess arrived home, she was already tired, though she still had a party to get through that evening. A fairly momentous party, actually. She would be spending the evening with all of Scott's family for the first time since they'd become lovers. She doubted he'd shared such details with his relatives, but would they be able to sense the differences between her and Scott?

Scott arranged to pick her up at seven thirty, giving her just enough time to freshen up and change into the green dress she'd bought at Complements. He'd texted that he would be on time, but she knew he was rushing to make it after driving all afternoon from Joplin. She turned in front of her mirror. She'd followed Jenny's advice of thin black tights and heeled booties, and was glad she had. The dress was a bit shorter than usual for her, though perfectly appropriate for a party this time of year.

"Let me guess," Scott said when she opened the door to him a few minutes later. "Another purchase from your friend Jenny?"

Her coat draped over one arm, a small gold clutch in her hand, she smiled. "Yes. I bought it the same day as the red one. My holiday splurge for the year."

"And worth every penny," he assured her. "You look great. I suppose it would ruin your lipstick if I were to kiss you right now?"

She tilted her face up to him with a smile. "I can reapply it."

Grinning, he swooped in. "Always resourceful," he murmured just before his lips covered hers.

It was so good to kiss him again. Just to be with him again. Though they'd spoken by phone several times for business and once just for themselves, it still seemed as though the past two days had passed much too slowly. She'd had dinner with Jenny and Stevie last night and both had commented that she'd been unnaturally distracted.

"You're thinking about Scott, aren't you?" Jenny had accused her.

Feeling her cheeks warm, Tess had shrugged sheepishly. "A little."

"This courtship is moving fast, wouldn't you say?" Jenny had asked with raised eyebrows. Both she and Stevie had studied Tess's face closely when they'd gotten together, and Tess wouldn't be at all surprised to know that her friends could tell she and Scott had taken the next natural step in their relationship.

"It's not as though he's someone I just met," Tess had replied logically.

"True. It's just a big change, and it's happened almost overnight."

Tess could have responded that once Scott got a plan in mind, he rarely saw a reason to delay implementing it. She was his new plan, she'd thought a bit wistfully. And he seemed quite satisfied with how it was coming along.

Stevie, who'd been so perky and bubbly that Tess had wondered if there was some overcompensation involved in the cheeriness, grew a bit quieter when Scott's name came up. "I talked with him a little at the Holiday Open Home," she'd confessed. "I have to admit I was trying to read his feelings about you, just for my own curiosity."

Lifting her eyebrows, Tess had asked, "And...?"

"And I still don't know," Stevie had said. "He's a hard guy to read. He told me he values you highly. When I told him I'd hate to see you hurt, he assured me he would hate that, too."

Tess didn't know how she felt about Stevie issuing warnings on her behalf. She was certainly capable of taking care of herself, of course. Still, it was so characteristic of Stevie to feel protective of her friend. Hiding her annoyance, she'd let it go.

It was the same tonight, though as she entered the engagement party, it was nervousness she hid, this time behind a forced smile. Scott's hand at the small of her back was reassuring, reminding her she wasn't in this alone. They'd passed the test of whether they could continue to work efficiently despite their personal relationship. Tonight it was important they not be seen as boss and office manager, but as equals. To that end, she held her head high and her shoulders back as she and Scott entered Trapnall Hall, the historic antebellum home that had been rented for tonight's event.

Built in 1843, the Greek Revival–style brick house had been meticulously restored, and served as the Arkansas governor's official receiving hall. Tess had been here a few times in the past for various events—business gatherings, a couple of weddings, a charity fashion luncheon, among others—but it had been a while and she was struck again by the beauty of the place. Decorated for the holidays and the reception, it was undeniably the perfect setting for a momentous celebration. The guests mingled around impeccably set round tables with white cloths and glittering tableware, and Tess was secretly relieved to note that her green dress with its touch of glitter had been just the right choice for the evening.

She suspected that Scott's family had been waiting for them to arrive. The whole clan descended on them almost immediately, greeting them both with warm smiles and cheek kisses.

Short and plump, Holly Prince was towered over by her husband and three sons, adored and healthily feared by all of them. Tess had always liked the cheerful, gregarious woman, but suspected no one had better hurt anyone in Holly's family lest they feel her wrath. Her husband, Barry, like their sons, was tall and naturally slender. His thinning silver hair topped a face that Tess had always thought looked like Scott in one of those age-progression drawings. Eli and Jake bore a resemblance to their dad, but Scott was his younger duplicate.

"We're so happy to have you here with us this evening, Tess," Holly assured her. "You look lovely. What a pretty dress."

Scott's sister-in-law Libby studied the green dress with envious dark eyes. "I've been looking for something similar for a Christmas party next week. Do you mind if I ask where you got it?"

Tess was always happy to plug her friend's boutique. She chatted for a few minutes with the Prince women until Holly towed her into the room to present her to other guests, including the happy young couple. No one seemed surprised Scott was there with a date, reminding her that he'd never had trouble finding female companionship, an uncomfortable thought she immediately pushed away.

Tess and Scott dined at a table for eight with his parents, two brothers and their wives. Because she already knew everyone, Tess was able to join in the lively conversation easily enough, though it once again amused her that the Prince clan tended to talk over one another when they got deeply involved in a topic. They were so obviously close-knit, sharing quick grins and private jokes and good-natured insults, yet making Tess feel welcome among them.

She could see both Libby and Christina felt close to their in-laws, as comfortable in the circle as if they'd been born into the family. Tess suspected the ease was partially a result of Holly and Barry Prince's warm, laid-back parenting style. Scott had informed her his parents had been fairly strict when their sons were in their formative years, but they made it a practice not to get overly involved in their adult lives. They were always there for their sons and grandchildren, but they kept their advice and opinions to themselves unless asked—a policy that served them well with their daughters-in-law, Scott had added with a smile.

Dinner was followed by half a dozen heartfelt toasts from family and friends of the bride- and groom-to-be and then a twenty-minute performance by a smooth-voiced, Arkansas-born pop singer who'd performed well on a nationally televised talent show. The party pretty much ended with the resulting applause.

Scott gave her a sign that he was ready to slip out as soon as possible. She thought he was probably tired after being in meetings for two days, then on the road for four hours that afternoon. He got delayed for a few minutes of conversation with his father, and Tess hovered patiently nearby, watching in amusement as various starstruck party guests posed for snapshots with the singer.

Her attention lingered for a moment on the engaged couple, who were saying goodbyes to departing guests at the door. They were holding hands, she noted, their fingers interlocked at their sides. Every few minutes their gazes held and they smiled just for each other. They looked young and happy and visibly in love, she thought with a funny little pang she couldn't quite define.

"Tess, it was lovely to see you this evening," Holly said warmly as she, too, prepared to leave.

"You, too, Mrs. Prince."

The older woman patted her arm. "Please, call me Holly. There's no need to be so formal now that you and my son are seeing each other."

Was that Scott's mother's way of giving her blessing? Tess smiled but had no chance to respond before Scott returned to take her arm. "Okay, now we can leave. We've done our duty, right, Mom?"

Holly rolled her eyes comically. "Yes, Scott. You may go now. Thank you for coming. I know Bethany and her family were happy to have you here."

"As if I'd have had the nerve to skip it," he muttered, kissing his mother's soft cheek with a fond impertinence that displayed absolutely no wariness of her. "G'night, Mom."

She stroked his cheek. "Good night, sweetie. Drive carefully."

Tess bit her lip as another twinge rippled through her. Maybe she was just weary from a long, busy week, but she was feeling a bit more sentimental than usual tonight.

"You've been quiet since we left the party," Scott observed as he walked her to her door a short while later. "Is everything okay?"

"Of course." She tucked a strand of hair behind her ear and smiled faintly up at him as she unlocked her door. "Just tired, I guess. Probably not as much as you, though. You've had a very long day, haven't you?"

He didn't look entirely reassured. "No one said anything to you? Upset you in any way?"

"Of course not, Scott. Everyone was very nice. Frankly, I was expecting some personal questions or comments, but between dinner, speeches and the musical performance, there wasn't a lot of time for personal conversations."

"Yeah, that worked out pretty well, huh? Folks could get used to seeing us together without getting nosy about the details." He looked rather pleased with himself, as if he'd arranged that in advance.

She stepped inside her living room and looked over her shoulder. "Are you coming in?" she asked when he seemed to hesitate.

He took a couple steps forward, his smile faint. "Sorry. I'm a little slow this evening."

"You're tired." She studied his face, seeing dim shadows beneath his eyes, slightly deeper than usual lines around the corners of his mouth. To what lengths had he gone in order to get back in time for the party? "Go home, Scott. Get some sleep. I know you have that project manager meeting in the morning. Are you sure you don't need me to be there?"

"No, I'll text you if we have any questions for you. I'm sure you have things to do."

She nodded. "I do have shopping to finish and errands to run before Dana's party. Um, you're sure you still want to—"

"I'm going to the party with you," he said flatly, brooking no argument. "I keep my word."

She offered to drive the next evening, but he insisted that would be out of her way. "The party starts at seven, right? So I'll be here around six thirty."

"No rush," she assured him with a wrinkle of her nose. "It's not as if I care if we're the first ones there."

He chuckled and shook his head. "I'm not having your sister blame me for making you late. I'll be here on time."

He continued to stand in the center of the room, one hand squeezing the back of his neck. She got the distinct impression that he was torn between staying and leaving. But just as she hated sending him away, she knew it was best tonight.

"Go get some rest," she repeated quietly. "I'll see you tomorrow."

He reached out to pull her into his arms. "I am tired," he admitted. "I'm afraid once I get horizontal I'll be out for a while, and I do have that early meeting. So maybe it's best if I head home."

Nestling her cheek into his shoulder, she gave him a hug, savoring the feel of him before she had to let him go. "We'll see each other tomorrow."

He kissed her lingeringly, then took a step back. "Maybe we should start thinking about having only one place to go to when we're not at the office."

Was he really talking about moving in together? They'd been moving fast to this point, but that was kicking the relationship into hyperdrive!

He laughed wryly in response to whatever he saw on her face. "You don't have to respond to that tonight. Just leaving you with something to think about."

"As if you haven't given me enough to think about lately," she muttered with a shake of her head. "Go get some sleep, Scott."

"Yes, ma'am."

She moved to lock the door behind him. "Scott?"

He turned just on the other side of the doorway to look at her. "Yes?"

"I'm glad you're back. I missed you."

This time he was the one who seemed caught unprepared. After a moment, he said simply, "Good night, Tess."

He turned and walked away before she closed the door.

He'd been in an odd mood this evening, she thought

as she secured the locks. Maybe it was simply that he was exhausted.

It would have been nice if he'd said he missed her, too.

Tess's phone rang late the next morning just as she was loading a few bags of groceries into the backseat of her car. Slamming the door, she lifted the phone to her ear as she slid into the driver's seat. "Hi, Jenny," she said, having checked the caller ID screen before answering.

"I'm just calling to let you know that Scott's sister-in-law came into the shop this morning looking for a party dress. She ended up buying two outfits and some accessories, even a couple of Christmas presents. She said to tell you thanks for sending her to me, so thank you from both of us."

"You're both welcome."

"We were very discreet and didn't gossip about you and Scott."

Tess chuckled. "I appreciate that."

"She did, however, make it clear that the family approves of you and Scott dating."

"They seemed okay with it at the party."

"More than okay, I think. They think you and Scott are a good match."

A good match. A great team. Inevitable. The labels echoed through her mind.

Their relationship sounded so ordinary when described that way. Unexciting. Even calculated. Was that how their friends and families saw them? The way Scott saw them?

"I'm glad to hear they approve," she said, keeping her tone steady.

"You're okay? You sound a little funny."

"I'm in my car in a parking space. Just finished running some errands and buying groceries."

"Oh, sorry, I didn't mean to catch you at a bad time. We're going to have to get together soon, right? I want to hear details of how things are going with you and Scott, of course. And we need to talk about Stevie. I'm getting a little worried about her."

So Tess wasn't the only one who'd noticed that Stevie hadn't quite been herself lately. "I'll call you to set something up," she promised.

"Great. Gavin has three days off, so I'm planning to work here until three or so this afternoon and then he and I are heading up to the cabin until Monday evening. We're looking forward to a few days away. But as soon as I get back, you and I are making plans, okay?"

"Absolutely."

She put her phone in the console after disconnecting the call and backed out of the parking space. Her errands were done, so her intention was to head straight home and rest awhile before the party. Tonight was going to be a more emotionally stressful event than the previous ones. She expected her family to be much more nosy and critical than Scott's had been. Would her sister be able to tell by looking at them exactly how much had changed in the past couple of weeks?

Her concerns about the evening were driven from her mind a few minutes later when a car ran a stop sign in an intersection near her condo and crashed into the back-passenger side of her car. Her seat belt tightened, holding her in her seat, and she gripped the wheel with white-knuckled fists as she brought the car to a stop. The jarring, sickening sound of the impact rang in her ears, her heart pounded and her knees shook beneath the steering wheel. After a quick visual self-exam that told her she was still in one piece, she opened the door with trembling hands to assess the damage to her car and the other driver. To her relief, she could see that he was already out of his car and seemed unharmed.

She was grateful no one was hurt, but really she hadn't needed this today, she thought with a groan. As she leaned back against her dented car, one thought rang through her mind: Was this an omen for how things would go tonight?

"So meeting her family tonight, huh? The big audition."

Standing on a ladder outside his parents' home, Scott looked down at his older brother, who stood below him, steadying the ladder. "I've met Tess's sister before. They don't have much family left except for a cousin I'll meet tonight."

"You've met the sister as Tess's boss, not her boyfriend," Eli pointed out. "That's different."

"True." It was still a bit odd to hear himself referred to as Tess's boyfriend, but he supposed that was a close-enough description outside the office. For now. "Okay, the bulb's replaced. Mom can quit fussing now."

He and Eli had both just happened to drop by that afternoon. Taking advantage of their presence, their mother had talked them into replacing a burned-out bulb on the strand of Christmas lights strung over the portico entrance. That dark bulb had been driving her crazy for the past week since they'd paid a neighborhood teen to hang the strand. Scott's dad had wanted to take care of it, but only three months past knee-replacement surgery, he'd been forbidden by his wife and sons to climb the ladder.

Scott descended the rungs, then jumped the last couple of feet to the ground. He brushed off his hands on his jeans and reached for the ladder. "Grab the other end and help me carry this around to the shed," he ordered his brother. "Then I have to get out of here and get changed into my party clothes."

Eli chuckled and gripped his end of the ladder. "If you're anything like me, you're already tired of Christmas parties. I've lost track of the number of invitations Libby has accepted on our behalf. And that doesn't even count the open house we're hosting at the clinic next weekend."

"Know the feeling. Tess and I have already been to several."

"So the family's still trying to figure when and how you and Tess got together. It's as though one day you were business associates and the next day you're a couple. Unless it's been going on awhile and you've been keeping it quiet for some reason?"

"No. It's a recent development." He'd found himself using those words a lot lately. Maybe he should think of a new phrasing.

"Mom's a little worried."

Frowning, Scott stopped walking, causing his brother to stumble at his end of the ladder. "Why is she worried? I thought Mom liked Tess."

"Dude, give me a heads-up when you're going to stop like that, will you? Almost gave me whiplash. And Mom likes Tess very much. Which is why she's concerned."

"Because…?"

"She said you aren't acting like a man at the early

stages of a romance. She said she remembers how I was when I fell for Libby. Goofy. Distracted. Kind of hyper."

"Young," Scott added with a shrug. "You were just a kid when you met Libby."

"I was in med school. Not that young."

"A decade younger than I am now. I'm a little past the goofy, hyper stage."

"You and Tess are hardly a couple of senior citizens," Eli scoffed. "You're both younger than I am—and trust me, Libby still knows how to make me go all goofy."

Scott opened the door to their dad's backyard garden shed. "You can spare me the details, thanks."

Now that he thought about it, he was a little distracted today. He'd had to focus a bit more than usual on conversations because his mind kept wandering to a condo on the other side of town. He could hardly remember what he'd eaten at his breakfast meeting, but he still vividly recalled every touch, every taste, every sensation of making love to Tess. But that was only to be expected, right? He was a red-blooded guy with a healthy appreciation for great sex—and sex with her had most definitely been great. He wasn't the type to kiss and tell—or bag and brag, as a few of his buddies termed it—so he wouldn't discuss his intimate relationship with Tess even with his brother, but it had reinforced his certainty that he and Tess were well-matched in every way.

They stored the ladder, then brushed off their hands as they stepped back. "Anyway," Eli continued, seemingly determined to make his point, "Mom is worried that you aren't fully emotionally invested in this courtship, or whatever you're calling it. She thinks you're following your usual pattern of getting involved more because you think you should than because you've lost your heart."

Taking after their dad in personality more than appearance, Eli had always been the most sentimental of the Prince brothers. He'd had his heart broken, or at least painfully bruised, a couple of times before he'd found his Libby. So was he expressing their mother's concerns—or his own?

"You can tell Mom to stop fretting. My heart is exactly where it's supposed to be," Scott replied lightly. Losing one's heart—what a weird saying, he mused. His beat steadily in his chest. It had most definitely raced when he'd made love with Tess, but he'd never felt in danger of "losing" it. He knew what the metaphor meant, of course, but it had just never seemed to apply to him.

"She's afraid you're going to hurt Tess."

Scott heaved an impatient sigh. "Everyone keeps saying that. Isn't anyone concerned that maybe the opposite could happen?"

"No, not really."

"Thanks a lot. But you can all quit worrying. As I have said to anyone who's expressed concern, I'm not going to hurt Tess. I would never hurt Tess. She and I have talked extensively and we both know exactly what we want, what we're doing."

"So you are thinking long-term?"

"Yes," Scott replied simply.

"Okay, then." Eli nodded and locked the storage shed. "I'm happy for you, bro. Tess is a fine woman who'll fit right in with our family. You're damned lucky she's interested in you. Don't screw it up."

It might have been nice for his brother to have a little more faith in him, but still Scott was satisfied that his family approved of his choice. As Eli had said, Tess fit in well with the independent, capable women in the Prince family. Everything was falling into place very nicely. As he knew it would. When he had one of his brilliant ideas, he was very rarely wrong.

Which didn't explain the odd feeling that had hovered in his belly since he'd left her place after making love with her Wednesday night. He still remembered that moment when the words "I'll miss you" had left his mouth, before he'd even realized he was going to say them. When it had hit him that he would, indeed, miss her, even though he would be gone only one night.

He'd made trips before, several considerably longer than one night, and yet it seemed different now. Like an inconvenient necessity from which he couldn't wait to return. What the heck was that?

He'd done it again last night. Blurted out a thought he hadn't taken time to consider. He'd come close to suggesting that Tess move in with him. Granted, it was the logical progression of this courtship, but were they really ready for that just yet? He hadn't been flattered by the way she'd all but jerked back from him in response to his hint. She kept assuring him she was on board with his long-term plan—and she certainly seemed more than amenable to exploring all the possibilities—but there had definitely been doubts in her eyes when he'd even hinted that they give up their separate homes.

He and Eli walked into the kitchen to say goodbye to their parents—then both recoiled in exaggerated horror at finding their mother bent back over their dad's arm being soundly kissed.

"Jeez, I didn't need to see that," Eli grumbled, waving a hand in front of his eyes as if he'd gone blind.

"Get a room, people," Scott muttered, copying his brother's gesture.

Laughing, their parents straightened, though their dad kept his arm around his wife's soft waist. "Holly just said she'll make fettuccine Alfredo for dinner. I've had a hankering for that for weeks, and I've finally worn her down."

Shaking her head in exasperation, his wife muttered about all the rich foods they'd be eating during the holidays, but she was already pulling supplies out of the pantry.

"And garlic toast on the side?" their dad asked hopefully. "With plenty of butter? Maybe a chocolate cake for dessert. I'll make the cake."

"Don't push your luck." Their mom looked at her sons with a roll of her eyes. "You see what I have to put up with? Tomorrow I'll have to nag him onto the treadmill to make up for this meal and he'll pout like a toddler. Mark my words."

"She takes good care of me because she's crazy about me," their dad boasted, winking at his smiling bride. "I'm a lucky man."

His sons heartily agreed.

Dressed for the party in a sport coat and slacks, Scott drove into Tess's parking lot, eager to see her again. He frowned as he turned toward her unit and saw a dark compact parked in her slot. Frowning, he checked to make sure he hadn't made a wrong turn, but the painted numbers assured him he was in the right place. Noting a rental car sticker on the back bumper of the compact, he parked beside it. Was Tess's car in the shop?

She opened the door to him with a smile that showed no evidence of awkwardness. He kissed her in greeting.

"You look nice," he said with a glance at the boxy black jacket she wore with a silver tank, subtly striped black and charcoal pants and chunky jewelry. Another outfit from her friend's store? Wherever it had come from, it looked great on her. But then, everything did.

"Thanks. So do you," she returned with a cheeky pat on his jaw.

He chuckled, then asked, "So what's with the rental car downstairs? Where's your car?"

She groaned and rolled her eyes as she collected her bag and coat. "I was in an accident this morning. My car had to be towed to a body shop. I'm waiting to hear about the damage."

Scott froze, trying to process her words. "Wait. What? You were in a wreck?"

"Yes. Obviously I was unhurt, and so was the guy who ran a stop sign and hit me, but it was a nuisance to have to deal with it. I had groceries in the car that had to be salvaged and a few other things I had to take out before it was towed off. Now I'm sure I'll have to fight the guy's insurance company to get everything I should—you know how they try to pay as little as they can get away with. I hate that part."

He was still trying to wrap his mind around this. "How did you get the rental? Was it delivered to you at the scene?"

"No, I called Stevie. She came to pick me up and drove me to the rental lot."

His jaw going tight, Scott made a show of pulling his phone from his pocket and checking the log.

Tess raised her eyebrows. "What are you doing?"

"Just checking my missed calls. I thought maybe I hadn't heard you trying to reach me."

Something in his tone must have warned her he was annoyed. She eyed him guardedly when she said, "I didn't try to call you."

He stashed the phone again. "You had a car accident and you needed help. Why didn't you let me know?"

"I guess I didn't even think about it. I knew you had that meeting this morning and Stevie was—"

"You didn't even think about it," he cut in to repeat slowly.

"As I said, I knew Stevie was available and she wouldn't mind helping me out. She was just the first one I thought of."

He told himself he had no reason to be angry with her. No right, to be honest. But still it irked him that she'd turned to someone else for help. He drew a deep breath and touched her arm, searching her face. "You're sure you're okay? Any pain or discomfort?"

"I'm fine. Really, I wasn't hurt at all, just shaken up."

"So you still feel up to the party?"

"Of course."

"If you get a headache or anything…"

"Scott." She patted his hand on her arm. "I'm fine."

He nodded, trying to lighten his expression, though he wasn't sure he succeeded. "We should go, then."

She moved toward the door and he followed, still trying to decide why it bothered him so much that she hadn't even thought to call him after her accident.

Chapter Eight

Tess had always been able to read Scott's moods fairly accurately. Some of their coworkers claimed to have a hard time telling what he was thinking when he got quiet or preoccupied, but it had always been easier for her. She couldn't read his mind, of course, but she could usually tell when he was working out a problem in his head, when he was making mental lists or plans, even when he just wasn't feeling well. Tonight she could see he was annoyed—and his irritation was directed right at her.

It had never occurred to her that he'd be upset with her for not calling him after the accident. Stevie was almost always the one she called when she needed a hand, and Stevie knew, of course, that Tess would gladly return the favors. That was what one did in a personal predicament such as a fender bender—call a friend, a family member, a significant other.

Not the boss.

Apparently she was still in the process of adjusting to the major change in her relationship with Scott. Was that why he was so cross with her? He'd taken her unintentional slight as an indication that she wasn't invested in their relationship. But seriously, shouldn't the past week have convinced him otherwise?

She turned to ask him, but they'd arrived at their destination. Dana's party was being held in her west Little Rock home, a sprawling Mediterranean modern–style house built beside a golf course in a gated community. Dana had married into money, becoming the second wife of a considerably older investment banker who indulged her shamelessly. Though she considered her cousin rather materialistic and showy, Tess still liked her well enough. In small doses.

"Nice house," Scott commented as he parked among the other cars in the big circular drive. Knowing Scott as she did, Tess was sure he thought the place was overdone, particularly when it came to the holiday lights and decorations that covered nearly every square inch of the house and grounds.

"Dana does like her flash."

"I see that. I'm sure your sister approves."

"My sister is so jealous her brown eyes turn green here," Tess corrected him wryly.

He looked a bit puzzled. "So Nina won't be here this evening?"

"Oh, Nina will be here to spend time with her dear cousin Dana. Snuggly selfies will be taken and posted to Facebook before the evening is over. Probably in front of a sixteen-foot Christmas tree done up in real gold and crystal."

Scott laughed. "Okay."

"Trust me. My sister will bask in our cousin's social glory all evening, even as she secretly hopes every bite Dana nibbles goes straight to her thighs."

He laughed again. "Sounds like a fun party."

"Well, I can assure you the food will be amazing. Dana always puts out a great spread."

"That sounds promising anyway." He unfastened his seat belt and reached for his door handle. "Tell me again how she's related. Your mom's side or your dad's?"

"Her mother and my mother were first cousins. But they were very close, almost like sisters, so we saw Dana quite a bit growing up. She's five years older than I am."

"Got it." He opened the door and climbed out.

At least he'd seemed to have put her car wreck out of his mind for now, she thought. She needed to do the same. She'd worry about insurance and repairs and a man's prickly ego after the party.

She had to admit it felt good to walk into the soaring foyer with Scott at her side. The two-story entryway was anchored by a curving staircase laden with garland and lights leading up to a balcony-railed second floor. Beyond the staircase was the ballroom-size great room, from which guests could see into the formal dining room and elegant music room. The whole place looked as if Christmas had exploded inside, coating every surface with glitter and garland.

She couldn't help noticing the women whose eyes widened in appreciation at seeing Scott, then in surprise at recognizing her with him. It occurred to her that she'd attended the last social gathering here solo, and she'd been perfectly comfortable doing so—but she didn't mind having a polished, handsome escort, either. Was that shallow? Probably. She'd do some sort of penance tomorrow to make up for it.

Nina spotted them almost immediately, most likely because she'd been watching the door. Tess saw the startled expression on her sister's face when she recognized Scott. And then Nina shook her head. Tess knew her well enough to recognize the expression. Why was Nina exasperated with her now? Seriously, what could she possibly find to criticize about Scott?

Towing Ken in her wake, Nina made a beeline straight for them. "I'm glad you could finally make it, Tess."

It was all of five minutes past seven, Tess thought with a stifled sigh.

"And Scott. It's so nice to see you again." Nina offered her right hand with its gaudy profusion of diamonds. "Such a nice surprise."

He shook her hand lightly. "It's good to see you, too, Nina. It's been a while, hasn't it?" He'd met her a few times during the past six years when she'd dropped by the office.

"Yes, it has. Tess doesn't invite me to join her for lunch very often these days."

"Actually, I've invited you to lunch several times in the past few months," Tess refuted evenly. "You're the one who always has something else to do."

Nina heaved a sigh. "Oh, hon, I know. When you're the mother of three popular and active students, it seems as if there's always a demand on your time." She turned to Scott.

She turned then to Ken. "Scott, I don't believe you've met my husband, Ken Wheatley. Ken, this is Tess's boss,

Scott Prince. Wasn't it nice of him to do her a favor and accompany her this evening?"

Nina was really in a mood this evening. Tess didn't know what had gone wrong that day for her sister, but she was getting the sharp edge of it.

She glanced at Scott. He was still smiling, smoothly civil. Probably only she could tell that he was irked when he said lightly, "Actually, this party was just an excuse for me to spend an evening with Tess away from work."

Ken gave Tess a perfunctory kiss on the cheek. "You look nice tonight, Tess."

That drew Nina's gaze to Tess's clothes. "Pants? Oh, well, I suppose you're comfortable. Come in and say hello to Dana and Lloyd. Jolie and Cam are here, and Mary and Bill. Oh, and Glenn's here. He came stag. He asked about you."

She was not the only woman at the party in pants, Tess fumed with a quick glance around that showed her a wide variety of outfits. Hers fit in just fine.

"Glenn?" Scott murmured into Tess's ear when her sister turned away. "The guy you dated? Mr. Boring?"

She gave him a look. "I thought we'd agreed you weren't to mention anything you overheard during that phone call," she said, keeping her voice as low as his.

His smile was unrepentant. "I don't think I agreed to that at all."

She looked past him to smile and return a wave from an acquaintance just inside the doorway of the grand room. "I think I feel a headache coming on," she said to Scott through a forced smile. "It would be such a shame if we have to leave early."

He laughed softly and put a hand at her back as they

followed her sister and brother-in-law into the gathering. "Introduce me to our hosts, Tess. I need to compliment them on their very tasteful decorations."

This time a sputter of laughter did escape her. Perhaps the party wouldn't be so bad after all, not with Scott at her side.

The gleam of amusement in Tess's eyes was reward enough for the effort he'd made to come to this thing with her, Scott decided. No wonder she'd been so stressed at the thought of attending. Her sister treated her like a recalcitrant child, while their cousin was too busy showing off to make a real connection with anyone at the party. Tess seemed to know quite a few of the other guests, but not in a close way. Most of them mentioned how they rarely got to see her. When Nina made a point to introduce him as Tess's boss, they nodded knowingly.

He got the distinct impression that he was known among Tess's friends and family as a somewhat demanding employer. Totally unfair. He never required Tess to be at work all the time. She just happened to be as committed to the company as he was, as conscientious about her responsibilities there. Had Tess used him as an excuse to escape to the refuge of the work she loved rather than tolerate the condescension of her sister and cousin? Okay, he could live with that. He couldn't even blame her for latching on to any excuse she could find.

He did wish Nina would back off the "Tess's boss" introduction, though. His family had accepted that he and Tess were a couple now. Hers seemed to think she'd brought her employer as an escort for lack of another option. He was doing his best to change that impression. He stayed right by her side all evening. He deflected conversation away from work as much as possible. He mentioned other functions they'd attended together. He did everything but plant a kiss on her mouth to demonstrate that his presence at her side was anything but business related.

At least Tess didn't refer to him as her boss, but tended to say simply, "This is my friend, Scott Prince."

Friend. Better than *boss*, he supposed, but still he found himself vaguely dissatisfied by the introduction. But really, what else could she say, he asked himself as he shook the hands of yet another couple whose names he would surely forget. *Boyfriend* seemed juvenile. He supposed *friend* would have to do. For now.

Tess hadn't been wrong about the food, he thought as he popped a lobster puff into his mouth, followed by a spinach-and-goat-cheese mini quiche. Both were delicious, as was everything he'd sampled on the bountiful buffet. He already had his eye on the desserts table, his sweet tooth kicking into high gear at the sight of all the delicacies available there.

"You were right about the food," he said to Tess as they took a seat at one of the little tables artfully scattered about the great room. "Good stuff."

She smiled and picked up a wild-mushroom toast square from her own plate. "Dana would love hearing you say that. She takes great pride in her parties."

He could tell she was fond of her cousin despite their dissimilarity. "I'll be sure to compliment her when we take our leave."

"There you are, Tess. I saw you earlier but couldn't make my way to you."

Scott felt her stiffen a bit, though she turned in her seat with a smile in response to the male voice. "Hi, Glenn. How have you been?"

The portly, broad-faced man who appeared to be in his midthirties, perhaps a couple years younger than Scott, took Tess's outstretched hand and pumped it a bit too enthusiastically. "You look great tonight," he said, seemingly unable to look away from her. "It's been too long since we've seen each other."

"Oh, you know how it is," Tess replied, skillfully extracting her hand. "Work responsibilities get pretty crazy this time of year."

She turned to Scott, who rose to offer a hand to the other man. "Glenn Stowe, this is my friend, Scott Prince."

Glenn shook Scott's hand with an expression that made it clear he wished he was the one with Tess, instead. "Prince," he repeated, glancing from Scott to Tess and back again. "You own the company Tess works for?"

"Yes, I do."

He could almost see the change in Glenn's posture. It couldn't be more obvious that Glenn took encouragement from learning Scott's identity. "It's nice to meet you. Tess has spoken of you often."

In a business context, Scott silently finished.

Glenn had already turned back to Tess. "I'm so glad you weren't injured in that car accident this morning. You're sure you're all right? I can't help worrying that you should have had a doctor check you, just in case."

"I'm fine, Glenn, really. No sore neck or anything, just impatient to get my car back."

"So you knew about Tess's wreck?" Scott asked, working hard to keep his tone politely neutral.

Tess explained quickly, "Didn't I mention it? Glenn is my insurance agent."

"Yes, I see why you had to call him."

She cleared her throat, then glanced around. "Excuse me, guys, my cousin is motioning for me," she murmured, taking a few steps away. "I'll catch up with you later, okay, Glenn? Scott, I'll be right back."

"I'll guard your food," he assured her with a somewhat strained smile.

She gave a quick laugh. "That's leaving the fox in the henhouse. My crab Rangoon better still be on my plate when I get back."

Though it was hard to take his gaze from her as she moved so gracefully away, he turned back to the table. He was almost surprised to see Glenn still standing there.

"There are more of the crab things on the buffet table if you want your own," the other man offered helpfully.

"Thanks, Glenn, but she was teasing."

Glenn nodded. "It's hard to tell sometimes with Tess. She has a very subtle sense of humor."

Scott didn't think the reference to a fox in a henhouse had been all that subtle, but maybe Glenn just had a different sense of humor. "Yeah, I guess she does."

"Working so closely with her for so long, I suppose you've gotten to know her pretty well."

"Yes, I think I know Tess quite well." Was he being too subtle for Glenn, or had the other man picked up on the hint? He didn't consider himself the possessive type usually, but occasionally deeply ingrained male instinct just took over.

"She and I have been out a couple times," Glenn confided. "I'd hoped to attend this party with her tonight, but I guess I waited too long to ask. I sent her a text last week but she said she had already made plans. With you, I suppose."

Obviously, Scott almost said, but he merely nodded.

"Maybe I'll see if she's free for New Year's Eve. I should ask earlier this time. But it's nice that Tess wanted her family and friends to meet her boss this evening. We all know how much her career means to her."

Scott didn't know if this guy was doing some clumsy fishing or if he really was as socially clueless as he acted. But Scott was getting fed up with this "boss" crap. "Tess won't be available on New Year's Eve," he said bluntly. "She'll be with me."

"Oh?" Glenn blinked, finally catching on. "Ah. So you and Tess are…"

"I'm going to marry her," Scott replied clearly, succinctly.

He heard a gasp behind him. Maybe a couple of gasps. With a slight wince, he looked around to find Tess a few feet away, staring at him in disbelief. She stood between her sister and her cousin, with her brother-in-law only a few steps behind them. All of them were looking openmouthed at him.

"Oh, my gosh, Tess, why didn't you tell us?" Dana squealed, clapping her brightly manicured and bejeweled hands together. "You're engaged!"

Her head spinning, Tess stammered, "I, um—"

"Yes, Tess, why *didn't* you tell us?" Nina demanded, still looking as though someone had knocked the breath clean out of her. "How long has this been going on?"

"I want to see the ring," Dana insisted, snatching at Tess's bare left hand. "Oh…no ring?"

"Not yet," Scott supplied, giving Tess a look that was a mixture of sympathy, apology and…defiance? Daring her to dispute him, perhaps? "Maybe Santa will bring her one for Christmas."

"Oh, how exciting!" Dana giggled. "Bet it'll be a good one."

"Congratulations, Tessie." Ken kissed her cheek. "I hope you're both very happy," he added, reaching out to shake Scott's hand. "Welcome to the family, Scott. You've got yourself a treasure here."

Scott looked at Tess again when he responded, "Yes, I'm aware of that."

They were suddenly surrounded by well-wishers, hugged and congratulated and barraged with questions neither was prepared to answer. She noted that Glenn had disappeared into the crowd after unwittingly initiating this excitement. Standing at Scott's side, she gritted her teeth behind a bright smile and settled for a couple of stock answers. "It's a recent development" and, "No, we haven't set a date yet." She appeased her sister somewhat by promising to visit the next afternoon with all the details.

"We weren't planning to announce it just yet," she added with a chiding look toward Scott. "He just got carried away."

"My bad," Scott agreed. "I guess I'm just too excited to keep it to myself."

"Oh, that's so sweet," someone crooned while Tess fantasized about strangling him.

They took their leave as soon as they could politely do so. Dana's husband cracked a suggestive joke about the newly engaged couple wanting to be alone together, earning himself a cold stare from Nina that made him swallow visibly. Tess clutched Scott's arm in a white-knuckled grip and almost dragged him out the door.

A taut silence surrounded them in Scott's car as he drove through the gates of the neighborhood. Only when they were on the highway headed toward her condo did he sigh and say, "Okay, let me have it."

She twisted beneath her seat belt to face his profile. "I can't even come up with the words."

"Look, I'm really sorry, Tess. I know that was awkward for you—"

"Gee, you think?"

He winced. "It got away from me. That Glenn guy was grilling me about our relationship, talking about asking you out, brushing me off as nothing more than your boss, and I simply told him the truth. I didn't realize you and your family were within earshot, though I guess I should have checked before I spoke."

"Or maybe not have spoken at all?"

"Maybe."

She could tell he wasn't entirely sorry. Just what male ego button had Glenn pushed? Surely it hadn't been intentional; Glenn wasn't exactly the territorial type. For that matter, she'd never thought of Scott that way, either.

"Technically, I didn't say we're engaged," he added somewhat stiffly. "I told Glenn I'm going to marry you. I just didn't mention I haven't officially asked yet. You could have made it clear you haven't given me an answer yet if you didn't want everyone to start congratulating us."

"Oh, that wouldn't have been awkward at all."

"Sorry, Tess. But we knew when we started attending these things together that people would want to know what's going on with us. Like I said, Glenn asked about our relationship and I told him the truth. I want to marry you. I thought we'd already established that."

She couldn't quite define the emotions crashing through her. She wasn't surprised, exactly. Scott *had* made it clear that this was the direction in which his thoughts had been headed. All that talk of what a good team they made, what a brilliant idea he'd had about them, how nicely she fit in with his family, how well she understood his demanding obligations and responsibilities. Yet in all of that talk, not once had he mentioned love. He'd even had a hard time telling her he'd miss her while he was out of town.

She rode without speaking for the remainder of the drive, and he didn't push her to express her thoughts. He turned into the parking lot of her condominium compound. "Are you going to invite me in?"

With a little sigh, she reached for her door handle. "Of course. Come in."

They really did need to talk. The problem was that when they were alone together in her condo, talking was too often the last thing on their minds.

Inside her living room, she dumped her coat and bag on a chair, then turned to face him as he waited patiently for her to speak first. After a moment, she gave a wry laugh and pushed back her hair. "One thing about you, Scott—dealing with you is never boring. Neither at the office nor, it turns out, at parties."

"I hope that's a compliment."

"Not entirely. Every once in a while it might be nice to be prepared for what you're going to do next."

Taking a step toward her, he caught her hands in his, gazing somberly into her eyes. "I really am sorry I embarrassed you in front of your family, Tess."

She bit her lip, then couldn't resist saying, "Did you see Nina's face?"

A sudden grin tugged at his lips, though he seemed to be trying to contain it. "Yes. I'd say we surprised her."

"It's one of the few times in my entire life I've seen my sister struck speechless."

"How did that feel?"

"It didn't suck," she pronounced after another moment.

Scott chuckled. "She does like to get in her digs against you, doesn't she? I don't know how you keep from losing your temper with her."

She shrugged. "I have a few times. I learned long ago that it doesn't really accomplish anything. She gets all chilly and defensive and makes a grudging apology she doesn't really mean, and then everything goes back to the way it's always been. I've conceded that if I'm going to have any sort of relationship with my sister in the future, I just have to bite my tongue and accept the way she is."

He looked annoyed on her behalf. "But you don't have to let her push you around."

"I rarely do. I just let her speak her mind and then I pretty much do what I want."

Running a hand up and down her arm, he laughed softly. "Much as you do with me?"

She shrugged.

"I have always admired your quiet determination," he told her, and though his tone was still light, she could tell he was serious.

As always, his compliment touched her, weakened her resolve against him, dampened her annoyance. Releasing a low sigh, she shook her head slowly. "I guess you know word of this will be all over town by tomorrow. We had mutual acquaintances there, and Dana's love of gossip is second only to her passion for shopping."

"Then, we should probably tell my family. I heard you tell Nina you'd be at her house early afternoon tomorrow—why don't I join you for that and then you can come with me to my folks' house. We'll get it all out of the way in one day."

Out of the way. She frowned at him. "You're assuming quite a lot, aren't you?"

He grimaced. "I'm not trying to railroad you. I'm being clumsy again, I'm afraid. This really isn't my forte, is it?"

He drew a deep breath and asked, "What do you say, Tess? Will you marry me?"

She bit her lip.

"I'm lousy at the romance stuff, you know that," he said. "I'll probably forget birthdays and anniversaries and special occasions—hell, I've always depended on you to remind me of that stuff anyway. I'll cancel our plans when work issues come up. I'll get caught up in mulling over a dilemma and I won't hear your questions or comments. I'll be short-tempered and impatient sometimes when I let stress get the better of me."

"I'm used to all of that," she reminded him.

He smiled ruefully. "Yeah, I guess you are. I guess what I'm trying to say is you know me better than anyone. I can't be any different at home than I am at the office because that's just who I am. Other women didn't like that. They wanted more from me than I was able to give."

Lifting his chin, he added proudly, "And by the way, I think I have a hell of a lot to give. I can promise absolute loyalty and faithfulness. I'll be a good provider, a devoted father, a steadfast supporter of your dreams and ambitions. You can depend on me to be there for you whenever you need me. You and I have always gotten along amazingly well without either of us trying to be something we're not. We've proved that we have a strong, more than satisfying physical connection. I think we can carry our solid partnership into a marriage that will last a lifetime. I know what I want. But it's in your hands now. I can give you more time, even though I know I rushed things this evening. As much time as you need."

No, it wasn't a particularly romantic speech, but she couldn't deny that he'd laid out a very convincing argument. He was offering everything she'd looked for when she'd signed up with those online dating services hoping to make a connection. Well, almost everything. Maybe there was a bit more of the romantic in her than she'd realized. Most of the single women she knew would probably tell her she was crazy not to snap this guy up before he had even a chance to change his mind. And here she was dithering because there was some indefinable something missing from his earnest proposal.

Studying his face, she asked quietly, "What would you do if I were to tell you that I don't want to marry you? That I've decided we're not a good match after all?"

A muscle jumped in his jaw, but he spoke in an even tone. "I'd be disappointed. Very disappointed. But I would accept your decision and I'd continue to focus on my work. Maybe I was meant to be a workaholic bachelor. Whatever happens between us, I would still treasure our friendship and your contribution to my company."

"You honestly believe we could still work together if this experiment, as you called it, didn't succeed?"

"I'd like to think so. It could be a little awkward at first, but I think we could manage it. Which doesn't mean I wouldn't have moments of regret that it didn't work out," he added candidly.

Moments of regret. Hardly a description of a broken heart, but then they'd made a concerted effort from the beginning of this plan to avoid that drastic outcome, right? He'd steadfastly asserted that avoiding unrealistic expectations would protect them both from bitter disappointment. It sounded so logical and honest that she couldn't think of a sound argument.

"Is that what you're trying to tell me, Tess? That you don't think we're a good match?"

"I think we're a very good match," she replied, drawing a deep, bracing breath and lifting a hand to his cheek. "We'd never have made it through the past six years working together if we weren't. I'm willing to gamble with you that we're equally well suited outside the office."

The tension in his face eased. His smile broadened, as his face moved against her palm. "That's a yes?"

She swallowed. "Yes."

"We should seal the deal." He stuck out his right hand. "Put 'er there, partner."

A laugh sputtered from her. "I know you said you're no poet, but honestly, Scott...a handshake?"

Grinning, he swept her into his arms and spun her

around once. "I can do better than that," he said, and smothered her laughter with his kiss.

They took their time making their way to her bedroom. Whether because of their new status or because they were becoming more comfortable with their lovemaking, they weren't as frantic and impatient this time, but more deliberate, savoring every touch, every kiss, every slow caress. Clothes were smoothed out of the way rather than stripped off, falling softly to the floor beside the bed. Their bodies were illuminated by the dimmed light on her nightstand, an intimate circle of light in the otherwise shadowed room.

Scott frowned when he saw the bruise on her left shoulder that ran a few inches down onto her chest. He traced it very gently with one fingertip. "Does this hurt?"

"No, not really." Caught up in the pleasure of being snuggled against his warm, bare body, she couldn't care less about a couple of minor bruises.

"It's from your seat belt, isn't it? From the accident this morning."

"I guess. It locked up hard to keep me in my seat. I'm fine. I've just always bruised easily."

A lump formed in her throat when he pressed his lips very tenderly to the bruise. He lifted his head and smoothed her hair from her face, looking into her eyes with an almost fierce expression. "I don't want anything like that to happen to you ever again. But if it does, call me. Wherever I am, whatever I'm doing, I want you to call."

She'd had no idea it would bother him so badly that she hadn't called him that morning. She'd planned all along to tell him about the accident, of course. But she hadn't realized he would take the delay so personally. "I'll call," she promised.

He gathered her closer, lowering his mouth to hers. "Good."

Scott lay on his side, propped on one elbow as he looked down at the woman sleeping on the pillows beside him. He'd smoothed the covers over her and she'd snuggled into them, drawing them to her chin in her sleep. It was the first time she'd slept with him there. Was she growing more accustomed to his presence in her bed, or was she simply tired after a long week, a long day? He thought of the bruise on her shoulder and scowled, hoping she hadn't underplayed the physical effects of the accident. Should he be monitoring her sleep? No, he was overreacting. She hadn't hit her head. Even the bruise was mild, just a smudge of purple against her fair skin.

He was satisfied that she would remember to call him now should anything similar happen in the future. Now that they were engaged, he wanted to be the first one she thought to notify in an emergency, even a minor one.

Engaged. To be married. Tess Miller had agreed to be his wife.

He mulled the words over in his mind, getting used to the feel of them. They felt…pretty good, he concluded. Really good, he added, his body still warm and heavy with satisfaction.

He was still a little dazed by the way the evening had progressed. He hadn't intended to propose tonight, certainly not to announce their engagement before he'd even confirmed it with Tess. Hell, she'd have had every right to toss him out on his ear for his arrogance. Why hadn't she? Considering that Tess wasn't one to allow herself to be railroaded—not at work or in her personal life—he could only conclude that she'd accepted his proposal because she wanted to marry him. He'd made some good arguments in his own favor. Presented his case with the same enthusiasm and persuasion he used when making a pitch to a potential client. And he'd convinced her to say yes.

He always reacted to victorious presentations with pride, gratitude, personal validation. He supposed he felt those things now, but in a deeper, quieter way. Losing a bid, even a big one, was hardly devastating. Disappointing, perhaps, but there were always more jobs, more opportunities to make money. Having Tess turn down his proposal would have been harder to swallow. Since he'd concluded she was the perfect mate for him, he couldn't imagine anyone else in her place. He'd set his sights on convincing her and he'd been persistent. And now it was going to happen. He'd won again.

So why was there a nagging feeling deep inside him that something could still go wrong? That maybe he was forgetting something or overlooking some detail?

Perhaps it was simply all too new. Hadn't sunk in yet. Maybe it was the abrupt way the engagement had come about, as opposed to his usual practiced sales style. He'd been left with the feeling that something was still unfinished.

She stirred in her sleep and tugged the covers to her ears. He smiled. Tess was a cocooner. She'd probably nestle into his arms if he settled in beside her. Because that sounded so appealing, he did so, finding that she did, indeed, fit perfectly into the hollow of his shoulder. He hadn't intended to spend the night, but what the heck. He had no plans in the morning. It seemed like the right time.

He brushed a kiss across her warm forehead and closed his eyes. By tomorrow, he was sure this funny feeling inside him would be resolved.

Maybe he was just tired.

Tess wondered how long it would take for the novelty of waking up with Scott to wear off. She thought it might be a while. As for the novelty of having him join her in the shower and linger there with her until the water ran cold…well, she couldn't imagine that ever growing mundane.

They cooked breakfast together. She made French toast while he sliced fruit and brewed coffee. They didn't talk much as they prepared the meal, but worked in companionable silence in her small kitchen.

"So what time are we supposed to go to your sister's?" he asked.

"She sent me a text this morning. She ordered me to be there at two. I told her you'd be joining us."

"What did she say to that?"

"'Don't be late. I have plans for the evening.'"

"I can tell she's very happy for us."

She gave him a look over her coffee cup. "Delirious."

"Okay, two o'clock. That gives us time to stop by my place so I can change into clean clothes." He was wearing the slacks and shirt from last night.

"Plenty of time."

"Maybe we could run by the office, too. I have a couple of things I need to take care of there."

"Fine. But if we're late, you'll have to explain to Nina."

"Trust me. We won't be late."

She laughed in response to his fervent tone. Apparently Scott had decided it was best not to be on the receiving end of one of Nina's icy looks.

An hour later he ushered her into his house, a three-bedroom traditional-style home in a peaceful development filled with upscale professionals with families. Because it had begun to rain, and occasionally heavy downpours were predicted all day, he'd parked in the garage and brought her in through the kitchen. She had always admired the granite counters, the cherry cabinets, the state-of-the-art appliances. The room was almost exactly what she'd have designed herself, given the choice. Scott hadn't employed Stevie for the kitchen remodel because he hadn't yet met her at the time, but Tess doubted her friend would have any criticism of the beautiful and functional space.

Scott had bought the house at about the same time he'd been involved with Sharon, though Tess had gotten the impression even back then that Sharon hadn't been particularly enthused about living in this neighborhood with its families and minivans. Saying they could always flip the house for a profit and invest in something more to Sharon's tastes, Scott had boasted about having gotten a very good deal on the place. He'd had it remodeled to his own satisfaction after Sharon had taken off. Sharon had never lived there. Tess doubted Sharon had ever even spent a night in the house.

She was ruefully aware she found that fact gratifying.

The high ceilings and open floor plan gave the first floor an airy, inviting feel. Having toured the home previously, Tess knew a private office and the master suite were located downstairs while two smaller bedroom suites and a media room made up the second floor. He favored a traditional style inside, too, with matte walls, clean lines, leather and wood and stone. Not too masculine, but well suited to a nesting bachelor.

"You have a new sofa," she said as they entered the great room, nodding toward the large oxblood leather sectional positioned to face a big stone fireplace. Behind the sofa, glass doors led out to a travertine patio with teak furniture, a large fountain and a tidy expanse of privacy-fenced lawn beyond. He'd done little holiday decorating, but an artificial tree with multicolored lights and coordinated red and silver ornaments stood in one corner with wrapped gifts stacked neatly beneath. "Nice."

"Thanks. I'd had the old couch for ten years. It was ready to be retired." He motioned back toward the kitchen. "Can I get you anything?"

"No, I'm good. Go ahead and change. I'll make myself comfortable on your new sofa."

He moved toward the doorway. "Feel free to explore, if you want. After all, this will be your home, too, soon. Unless you want to sell both our places and find a different one," he added, pausing with a thoughtful expression.

She waved him on. "We'll talk about that later. Go change."

She pressed a hand against a little flutter in her stomach after he left. Glancing around the room, she pictured herself living here. Waking in the mornings, having breakfast with Scott, perhaps riding to the office together. Sleeping in that big master suite. She'd bet he had a nice big shower in there.

She cleared her throat and sank onto the new sofa. Very comfortable. Maybe she wouldn't have chosen leather, but she could get used to it quickly enough. She looked around. A beautiful house with a couple of extra bedrooms waiting to be filled, a handsome husband... Yeah, she could fit in here nicely, she assured herself.

He rejoined her a few minutes later wearing a royal blue shirt with khakis, clean shaven, his hair neatly combed. Her very own Prince Charming, she thought with a little smile, thinking of Stevie's nickname for him. "So what do you think?" he asked. "Do you approve of the couch?"

She patted the soft leather. "I approve."

He leaned over for a quick kiss. "We could always break it in," he murmured, waggling his eyebrows.

"Mmm." She ran a fingertip from his throat down the center of his chest to his belt buckle. And then she flattened her hand on his chest and pushed him away. "Later."

Scott groaned. "So cruel."

She stood and spoke with determination, "Okay, let's do this. We'll stop by the office and then find out exactly how our engagement is complicating my poor sister's life."

Scott gave one last wistful look at the new sofa, then turned with her toward the door. She paused on the way out to glance over her shoulder at the house that would be her home soon. She was sure she'd be very happy here. After all, she asked herself again, what more could she want?

Chapter Nine

The softly glowing numbers on the nightstand clock read 2:25 when Tess rolled over in the bed to check the time. She groaned and pushed at her pillows, trying to fluff them into a more comfortable position. It was a futile gesture and she knew it. Her sleeplessness wasn't caused by physical discomfort. It was too bad she couldn't unravel the tangled thoughts in her head as easily as she could smooth out the lumps in her pillow.

The sound of the rain hitting her windows should have been soothing, but it was only annoying instead. It had been raining on and off for hours. Turning over to put the clock behind her, out of sight, she found herself gazing instead at the empty pillow on the other side of the bed. She rested a hand on it, wondering fancifully if she could still feel Scott's warmth there. But no, it was cold. Claiming apologetically that he had a list of things to do to prepare for the to prepare for the busy upcoming workweek, he hadn't stayed tonight after they'd returned from dinner with his family. He'd left her with kisses and reluctance and a comment that he was looking forward to the time when they made their home together.

They still hadn't talked about a date for their wedding. Scott had implied that he'd like for it to be soon, which was no particular surprise to her. Once he had a plan in place, he was always impatient to get it under way. They'd talked about a wedding, both with her family and his, but had made no specific plans as of yet, agreeing that they should wait until Christmas was behind them to focus on the logistics.

Something about the word *logistics* made her wince. It was such a...businesslike word, taking the practicality of their engagement to an uncomfortable extreme. Scott could make her head spin with how smoothly and easily he transitioned from teasing, affectionate, even passionate to briskly realistic and deliberately prosaic. He claimed not to be the romantic type, and seemed to even take pride in the fact, but it was almost as if he were afraid of taking that final step into deep intimacy. Was it fear of being hurt? Of doing something wrong?

Now that she'd agreed to marry him, shouldn't he be more confident about it? Should she really have seen the faintest hint of panic in his eyes yesterday whenever anyone in their families had alluded to how romantic it was that their working relationship had turned into an engagement?

She thought about her sister. Maybe Ken had given Nina one of his rare lectures about how she should act that afternoon, because she'd been on her best behavior.

She'd served tea and pretty little cakes to Tess and Scott in her parlor and congratulated them on their engagement. True to form, Nina hadn't been able to resist a few complaints that she'd been left out of the loop and that she'd heard about their engagement in such an abrupt, public manner. Tess couldn't totally blame her sister for feeling slighted, which made her more patient in dealing with the censure. Nina had regally accepted Tess's apologies, then proved no more resistant than most to Scott's charming smiles and winsome contrition.

Nina had insisted she would do everything she could to help with the wedding—though of course her schedule was so very full, her presence so in demand, that she wasn't sure how much she could physically contribute. "We'll try to arrange lunches during the weeks ahead," she'd said to Tess. "You can bring photos and samples and I'll be happy to give you my input."

Tess could easily imagine how those meetings would go. She would potentially spend hours choosing colors and dresses and music and other details, and Nina would shoot down every option with an indulgent comment about how Tess's ideas were "cute," but perhaps she should consider Nina's much more fashionably inspired suggestions instead. Tess had smiled noncommittally and politely promised her older sister she'd let her know when she needed advice.

The only truly personal moment between her and her sister had come just as the visit was ending. Scott had dashed out in the downpour with an umbrella, having chivalrously volunteered to bring his car close to the front door for Tess. Waiting just inside the door with her sister, Tess had been surprised when Nina gave her a firm, apparently impulsive hug.

"I am pleased for you, Tess," she'd said. "I hope Scott will make you very happy. You deserve to have someone take care of you for a change."

Startled, Tess had almost replied that she was more comfortable taking care of herself, but sensing a rather touching sincerity in her sister's words, she'd said only, "Thank you, Nina."

Dinner with Scott's family could not have been more different. The whole Prince clan had been there, including the twins and baby Henry, all gathered around the big farm table in Holly's dining room, all talking at once, laughing, teasing, treating Tess as if she was already part of the family. They, of course, had already been aware of the change in Tess and Scott's relationship, so it was easier for them to process the announcement of their engagement.

"When's the big day?" Jake had demanded.

"We haven't set a date," Scott had replied, squeezing Tess's thigh beneath the table, "but I'd like for it to be soon."

"It takes a while to plan a wedding," Libby had warned. "You have to reserve a space for the ceremony and the reception. Caterers and florists and cake decorators and musicians are often booked well in advance, so as soon as you choose a date, you should start putting down deposits. I have a friend who's an excellent florist, Tess. I'd be happy to go with you to talk with her, if you like. Bet I can get you a discount."

"My cousin is a caterer," Christina had chimed in. "She did our wedding and it was great, wasn't it, guys? And I'll get you the number for our videographer and photographer. Jake and I were very happy with their services."

"I would love to help you with whatever you need from me," Holly had added eagerly. "I can make calls or address envelopes or anything else you want me to do. And I have a connection with a cake decorator who does some of the most beautiful work I've ever seen. I'd be pleased to introduce you to her, though of course I won't be offended if you decide to use someone else."

They had all been so excited, so eager to help, yet Tess hadn't felt at all as if they were trying to take over. They were just making themselves available to her in any way she needed them. She'd found that incredibly sweet.

All in all, it had been a very nice day. So why was she lying awake in the middle of the night, thinking back over the gatherings and trying to analyze why the more thrilled everyone seemed to act about them, the more Scott had seemed to withdraw into himself? Oh, nothing of the sort had shown in his behavior. He'd laughed and conversed as heartily as anyone else at his mother's table. He'd participated in the discussion of possible wedding venues and teased Tess about hiring an '80s-revival heavy-metal band for the reception. He'd kissed her good-night with the same heat and hunger that had made their previous embraces so exhilarating and he'd looked genuinely regretful when he'd made himself leave her.

Was she only imagining that he was holding a small part of himself back? Was she mistaken in sensing a tiny kernel of doubt deep inside him—or was that a projection of her own lingering misgivings? It had all happened so fast. She'd been swept along by his enthusiasm for his brilliant idea, his enticing verbal pictures of an ideal future together, her own yearnings and long-suppressed attraction. And now that everything seemed to be settled, now that everyone knew about their plans, now that it would be incredibly awkward to call it all off, now that she couldn't imagine not marrying Scott—a tiny part of her feared that she'd made a mistake.

With a groan, she punched her pillow again. She really was an idiot.

Maybe she was just tired.

Pulling the covers to her ears, she sank into the bed and squeezed her eyes shut, trying to push those silly doubts and foolish fears away. And wondering why she, who almost never cried, felt suddenly on the verge of tears.

Scott spent most of the following week out of town visiting job sites and attending planning meetings for the new year. Their hectic work schedule prevented them from spending much time together, but they spoke by phone every evening and managed to share a couple of pleasant nights together. By the beginning of Christmas week, both were tired and looking forward to the end of this hectic holiday season. Tess was ready to focus on their future together outside the office, something they'd barely had time to even think about since they'd become so unceremoniously engaged.

The shortened workweek ahead made Monday ridiculously busy in preparation. Wednesday was Christmas Eve, and Scott had announced the offices would close at noon that day and wouldn't officially reopen until the following Monday, which would also be a short holiday week. If any crises occurred, essential personnel could be called in, of course, but they all hoped the holiday would be problem-free.

The stressful day finally over, she was driving to Stevie's for a pre-Christmas celebration. But her mind was preoccupied by what had happened that afternoon.

Scott had called an early staff meeting to confirm the week's schedule. Then he'd wished everyone a merry Christmas as he handed out generous gift cards to an upscale local restaurant. End-of-the-year bonuses were included in their paychecks, but this was a little treat he'd been in the habit of providing on his own behalf for the past few years, telling his employees they deserved a nice night out to relax after working so hard and so loyally for him.

"Before we adjourn," he'd added, holding out a hand to Tess, "there's one more announcement I need to make. I'm sure the rumors have already begun and I want you all to hear the news from Tess and me."

Moistening her lips, Tess had pasted on a confident smile and taken her place at his side. Some of the staff looked puzzled, and she figured they wondered if a promotion or resignation was being announced. A couple others smiled knowingly, which meant the gossip had already made its way to the office.

After a slight nod of approval from her, Scott turned back to their team. "Tess and I are engaged," he said simply. "We haven't determined a date yet, but we're going to be married."

Amid the startled cries and happy claps, Scott held up a hand to add, "You all know how valuable Tess is to this company. Just so you know, we aren't making any immediate changes in her responsibilities here in the office. So carry on, and here's to another great year for all of us who make up PCCI."

She'd appreciated his attempt to make sure she was

treated no differently by the staff now that she was marrying the boss, but she knew some changes were inevitable. If there was any resentment, she didn't see it at the moment. Still, she and Scott would have to be very careful in the future to keep their personal life clearly separate from work, just as they had to this point.

The phones had begun to ring and everyone went back to work. Scott left soon after the staff meeting and was out of the office most of the day, though a series of terse phone calls and texts from him kept Tess and the rest of the staff busy trying to keep up.

He hadn't returned by the time Tess had to leave, so she sent him a text reminding him that she had plans with Jenny and Stevie, and that she'd see him at work in the morning.

I'll call you tonight, he texted back. Have fun with your friends. Tell them hello for me.

She arrived at Stevie's place for their own little Christmas celebration. A cozy bungalow, Stevie's house was the one in which she'd grown up with her mother and brother, located in a neighborhood that had briefly declined and was now undergoing a revival. Her white frame home sat on a corner lot, so her nearest neighbor was a '60s-style brick ranch on her west side, the one in which the widowed cat owner lived. Tess glanced automatically that way as she parked at the curb in front of Stevie's house. A dark car sat in the carport and lights burned in the windows, so she assumed Stevie's neighbor had returned from his business trip, though she caught no glimpse of him. She'd bet Stevie was glad to be done with her cat-sitting duties for now.

The neighbor hadn't decorated for the holiday, but other houses on the block were festooned with festive lights and oversize Christmas inflatables in their yards. Stevie had arranged a string of white lights around her little porch, and a Christmas tree with white lights was visible through the lace curtains at her front window. A big wreath with a red velvet bow decorated the front door, which was painted blue to match the shutters at the windows.

Stevie and Jenny both greeted Tess with such expectant expressions that she shook her head wryly. If they were trying to be subtle, they failed miserably at it. She'd told them individually about the engagement, sending messages to them both before they heard through the grapevine, and she'd promised to give them details tonight.

"At least let me set this stuff down before you start pelting me with questions," she said, handing over two wrapped gifts before peeling off her coat.

Jenny set the gifts beneath the tree while Stevie stashed away Tess's coat and bag. "Did Scott really blurt out that the two of you were engaged at Dana's party?" Jenny asked avidly. "Before you'd even told your sister?"

"Even worse," Tess replied with a groan, glad she could finally speak frankly about that night. "He told everyone we were engaged before he even got around to asking me."

"Oh, we definitely need to hear this whole story," Jenny said after a moment of stunned silence.

"Tell us while we eat," Stevie ordered. "I didn't cook all this food to serve it cold." She loved to cook, and she'd insisted on preparing the meal without any contributions from her friends.

An hour later, stuffed with delicious food and emotionally drained from talking, Tess sat with her friends in the living room, preparing to open gifts. Stevie was leaving the next morning to spend Christmas with her brother in Tennessee, while Tess and Jenny both had plans with their families here in Little Rock, so this had been the only night they could get together for their own little celebration.

"I'm so glad we decided not to have a big party this year. I prefer that it's just us," Jenny said as she leaned back against a throw pillow. "Though I would like for us to all get together soon to get to know Scott better. Gavin met him briefly when he responded to that break-in at your office earlier in the year, but they should get to know each other socially since I'm sure they'll be seeing quite a bit of each other through us. And Stevie will bring Joe, of course."

Stevie cleared her throat. "That's not an 'of course.'"

Tess and Jenny exchanged looks.

"Are you and Joe breaking up?" Jenny asked quietly.

"Looks like it." Stevie raised both hands to stave off any comments. "Would you mind if we talk about this later? After Christmas? I need some time."

"Absolutely."

"Whenever you're ready," Tess assured their friend.

Blinking rapidly, Stevie nodded. "Thanks. Besides, tonight is all about you, Tess. Jen and I hope you and Scott will be very happy together."

"Thanks, Stevie." But now it seemed completely wrong to discuss her engagement when her friend was obviously in pain. "You know, I have an idea. Let's not talk about men or relationship issues for the remainder of the evening. Let's focus on ourselves. Our friendship. Our jobs. Stevie, I want to hear all about this busy season for you. I know it's been great for your reputation and your bottom line. And, Jenny, tell us about your idea to open a store in Fayetteville. How exciting would it be to own a chain of three boutiques, maybe more? And I need to tell you about the new accounting clerk I hired this month."

Her eyes brightening, Stevie smiled. "I'd love to talk about my business, but first," she said, tugging impatiently at the red mesh bow on the gift Jenny had brought for her, "I have just got to see what's in here. I can't wait any longer to open presents!"

Laughing, Tess and Jenny ripped into their own gifts. They were still laughing two hours later when the night came to a close.

Stevie gave her a warm hug as Tess prepared to leave. Jenny had stepped into the restroom, so Tess and Stevie had the moment to themselves.

"Merry Christmas, Tess," Stevie said, pressing a kiss to her cheek. "Thank you so much for the bracelet. I love it."

"And thank you." Stevie had given her a hand-thrown pottery serving bowl. "It's gorgeous."

Her friend smiled with a little wrinkle of her nose. "I knew you'd like the colors. I hope they work in the new kitchen you'll be sharing with Scott."

She could already picture the bowl on the big island in Scott's kitchen. "It will work just fine. I'm sure he'll like it, too."

"I hope so." Stevie hesitated a moment, then blurted, "I know we said no more talk of relationships tonight, but I have to ask. Just for my own peace of mind..."

"What is it, Stevie?"

"Do you love Scott?"

"I—" It was such a simple question. It shouldn't have taken her by such surprise. And yet it occurred to Tess only then that Stevie was the first one since this had all begun to even think to ask.

"Tess?"

"Yes," she whispered as sweet memories of laughter and kisses, long conversations and leisurely lovemaking, flashed through her mind. "I love him."

Should that answer really make Stevie look only more worried? Shouldn't she have found it reassuring?

"Just one more question," Stevie said. "Does he love you?"

Tess swallowed. "He said there's no one else he'd rather marry."

Stevie held her gaze for a moment, letting her silence express a great deal, and then she reached for the door. "Thanks for being honest with me. I hope to God you're being honest with yourself. Good night, Tess."

Placing the bowl from Stevie and a beautiful spring cardigan from Jenny on the passenger seat beside her, Tess fastened her seat belt and started her car, her movements deliberate. Her gloved hands gripped the wheel tightly enough to cause pain in her knuckles as she drove away from Stevie's little house.

I hope to God you're being honest with yourself.

"So do I, Stevie." Her strained voice echoed hollowly within the darkened interior of her car. "So do I."

It wasn't uncommon for Scott to stumble into his house past 10:00 p.m., weary and ravenous yet satisfied after a long day of business operations. Particularly at this time of the year, he hardly had a minute to himself. Fortunately most of the professional and social obligations were out of the way now, with this week being reserved for family celebrations. He opened the fridge and drew out a container of yogurt, a little hungry but too tired to make a meal. He hadn't forgotten that he'd promised to call Tess that night, but he needed to catch his breath a minute first. He hoped she would still be awake by the time he finished his snack.

He was sure she'd had a good time with Jenny and Stevie. The three women had formed a tight friendship. A man would do well to keep in mind that he'd better not attempt to come between them, not that he would even want to try. He remembered before Tess met Jenny and Stevie. Though he hadn't given it much thought at the time, blindly ambitious as he'd been back then, he realized now that she must have been lonely, working long days while attending classes and taking care of her parents until she'd lost them so close together. He'd tried to be a supportive employer to her during those days, a good friend, even though he'd worked to keep the friendship professional. Perhaps getting involved with that guy James not long after her mother died had been a result of her loneliness. She'd done well to dump the jerk; Scott had met him only a couple times, but he hadn't liked him.

It was only during the past couple of years that Tess had really come into her own as a strong, competent, satisfied adult. Earning her degree, buying her condo, meeting her friends, taking on more supervisory responsibilities in the office, establishing her independence from her overly critical sister—all those things had contributed to a new confidence in her, a difference he'd observed and admired. She'd been looking for companionship on her own terms, unwilling to settle despite her expressed desire for home and family, and he was damned lucky she'd considered his proposal worthy of her. That she considered him worthy of her, despite his limitations when it came to romance.

How many women would have forgiven him for that boneheaded blunder at her cousin's party? Or would be so patient with his crazy schedule and his sometimes unpredictable moods? He hadn't showered her with compliments or gifts, as Sharon had pointedly and repeatedly informed him most women desired from a man. In fact, he hadn't given Tess anything at all, including an engagement ring, he thought with a frown. Hell, he hadn't even given her one of the restaurant gift cards he'd distributed to the staff.

Tossing the empty yogurt container in the trash and the spoon in the sink, he carried a glass of water into his bedroom to make the call he'd promised. He could at least do that, he thought guiltily.

"How was your evening with your friends?" he asked after they'd exchanged greetings.

"We had a wonderful time. Great food, good conversation, and we exchanged gifts. How was your day?"

"Long," he said with a sigh, and gave her a quick summary of what he'd accomplished since he'd last seen her. "Tomorrow's going to be just as long," he warned.

"Yes, I figured. I have a lot to do tomorrow myself. I'm hoping to finally have time to finish wrapping gifts and do my Christmas baking. I always take stained glass cookies and pear tartlets to my sister's house for Christmas dinner, and I haven't even started them."

"I've had your pear tartlets," he reminded her. "You made me a batch last year, remember? They were out of this world."

"I thought I'd make extras of everything to take to your family's house Christmas. Do you think they'd like them?"

"Are you kidding? They'll love them. Jake and Eli will probably arm wrestle for those tartlets."

She laughed musically in his ear. "That won't be necessary. I'll make plenty. Your mother was so insistent that as a first-time guest I shouldn't have to bring anything this year, but I feel as though I should take something."

"That'll be fine. It feels kind of strange to work around two family schedules for Christmas, huh?"

"It does. My social calendar was much busier this year than usual." Fortunately her family celebrated together on Christmas Eve, while his gathered for a big Christmas Day lunch, so the traditions hadn't overlapped.

"Mine's been packed, too," he said. "But I'm not complaining. I've enjoyed the past weeks with you."

"So have I," she said.

Had he heard something a little odd in her voice just then? He wished he could see her face. He wished he could touch her. Kiss her. The intensity of the hunger that shot through him so unexpectedly shook him. It had only been a few hours since he'd seen her, but here he was missing her as if it had been days.

"Tess? We can have as big a wedding as you'd like, but I'd like to put it all together fairly quickly. I don't know about you, but I'm hoping for a short engagement."

She hesitated only a beat, as if surprised by the abrupt change of subject, then replied, "I don't need a big wedding. Family and a few close friends are all I really want to be there."

"That sounds about perfect to me. The sooner the better."

"We'll talk about it."

"It's late. I'm sure you're tired. I'll see you tomorrow—though maybe only for a few minutes at a time."

"Okay. Good night, Scott."

The pause then felt oddly heavy, as if she was waiting for him to say something more, while he felt as though there was something he should say. He settled for "Sleep well."

And then he disconnected, feeling vaguely unsatisfied with the call's conclusion.

Don't screw this up.

Why did he feel the need to keep saying that to himself?

Chapter Ten

Christmas Eve was a great success so far, at least where Scott was concerned. For the first time, Tess had brought a bag and had spent last night at his house, a momentous occasion for both of them though they hadn't expressed it in so many words. They'd made dinner together in his kitchen, then watched a Christmas movie afterward while her pear tarts for the next day baked in the oven. They'd held hands during the movie like giddy teens in a theater. Afterward, she'd stashed the tarts in the fridge, playfully slapping Scott's hand when he tried to pinch a few. She had distracted him easily enough from the Christmas sweets by enticing him into the bedroom. It had been quite a while before they'd fallen asleep.

They'd talked of wedding plans that afternoon, and they'd agreed that a spring ceremony in his parents' sprawling backyard would suit them nicely. It was where Jake and Christina had exchanged vows, and Scott said theirs had been a very nice little wedding. Eli and Libby had married in the big Catholic church in which she'd grown up and had treated themselves to a lavish celebration with a couple hundred guests. Also nice, Scott had admitted, but not to his taste. He'd been relieved, but not particularly surprised, when Tess had heartily concurred.

Now, as it grew closer to time to leave for her sister's house, Tess donned the red dress she'd worn to the Holiday Open Home, and he was still struck by how good it looked on her. "You got your money's worth out of that dress," he assured her, looking at her in the mirror as he fastened his tie. "It's really pretty."

"Thank you. Sorry about the tie. Nina insists on fancy dress for her Christmas Eve meal."

He chuckled. "I don't mind. But tomorrow we get to be comfortable. My family's not nearly so formal."

"No surprise. I'm crazy about your family, by the way."

He grinned in pleasure. "Thanks. They feel the same about you."

It was all going so well, he thought in satisfaction. He must have misinterpreted whatever funny tone he thought he'd heard in her voice the other night. She seemed perfectly content with him now, visibly enjoying their time together. If there were moments when he caught her studying him with an expression he couldn't quite interpret, fleeting impressions that she was waiting for something he couldn't explain—well, this was all still very new for both of them, he assured himself.

It was only natural that it would require a bit of adjustment on both their parts.

When they were dressed in their finery, he asked her to wait a moment in the living room before they left. They'd already loaded his car with the gifts and baked goods they were taking to her sister's house, so all they had to do was collect their coats and her bag. She looked at him with a question in her expression.

"Have you changed your mind about going?" she teased, obviously knowing he hadn't.

Still, he gave an exaggerated shudder. "And risk Nina's wrath? I wouldn't dare."

She laughed. "Well, as least you're getting to know my sister. Since she's going to be your family, too, now."

"I can deal with your sister."

"Right."

His smile fading, he bent to pluck a small gift box out of the stack beneath the tree. "There's something I want you to open before we leave," he said, his heart beating just a bit more rapidly than usual.

Her eyes widened as she studied the gold-and-white wrapped box in his outspread hand. It would have been hard for her to mistake the size; he hadn't bothered with clever camouflage. She accepted it from him when he held it out to her, but didn't immediately open it.

"I have a gift for you, too," she said, her voice a little breathless. "I put it under the tree if you want to—"

Aware that she looked a little nervous—as he was himself, for some reason—he spoke gently. "I'll open mine later."

Moistening her lips, she nodded and tugged at the ribbon on the box. Moments later, she opened the hinged lid of the small velvet box she'd unwrapped to reveal the ring displayed in white satin inside. He'd selected a traditional round diamond engagement ring mounted in a platinum setting with three smaller diamonds on each side.

"I hope you like it," he said, growing a little anxious when she didn't immediately say anything. "It looked to me as though it would suit you—elegant but not too splashy, fashionable but not trendy." Again, he was quoting the jeweler, but the words had seemed to fit Tess. "If you'd rather have picked out your own rings—"

"This is beautiful, Scott. I can't imagine I'd have picked one any more perfect for me."

She looked up at him then and he was shaken by the sheen of tears in her eyes. He hoped they were happy tears. She'd said she liked the ring, so…

"Um, should I have gotten down on one knee?" he asked with a grimace. "Sorry, I—"

"No." With a misty smile, she placed a reassuring hand on his arm. "Please don't. We've said we aren't playing games, remember?"

Had he gotten on one knee when he'd proposed to Sharon? He couldn't remember. But come to think about it, he wasn't sure he had officially proposed at all to his former fiancée. He sort of suspected that an engagement had been mostly her idea. He'd just gone along for the ride because he'd thought himself ready to settle down and…well, because he'd been dazzled by her skills in the bedroom. A fascination that had worn off rather quickly when lust had turned to almost constant fighting.

But why was he thinking of Sharon now? Tess was nothing like his ex. He couldn't imagine his feelings for her ever turning as bitter and angry as he and Sharon had eventually become.

"No games," he promised. "We've already done the proposal and acceptance, even if I was fairly clumsy about it. But I will do this part right," he added, taking the diamond ring from the box. He slid the ring on her finger, then lifted her hand to his lips to kiss it in place. "There."

"It fits perfectly," she said in wonder.

"I guessed at your size, but the jeweler said it would only take a couple days to size it if it needs adjustment."

"I don't think it will. It's beautiful, Scott. I love— I love the ring."

He heard the little stammer and he attributed it to emotion. He thought that had gone very well. He believed Tess when she said she loved the ring. Seeing it on her hand gave him a wave of deep masculine satisfaction. From now on, he thought, all other men would know she wasn't free for New Year's Eve or any other night.

It occurred to him again that it wasn't like him to be the possessive type. At least he knew better than to say it out loud to Tess.

Don't screw this up.

"Let's see that ring! Oh, my gosh, it's so beautiful!" Clutching Libby's hand, Christina Prince turned to motion expressively. "Libby, Holly, come see. Scott gave Tess her ring and it's gorgeous."

While the men watched indulgently, Tess held out her hand for Scott's mother and sisters-in-law to examine the ring. All of them pronounced it exquisite, and just perfect for Tess.

"You picked it out all by yourself, Scott?" his mother asked in surprise.

"With a little help from the jeweler you've always used," he admitted.

"Patrick? Oh, yes, he has wonderful taste."

Tess couldn't help comparing this family's reaction to Nina's last night. Nina had studied the diamond with the shrewd eye of a well-trained jeweler, all but pulling out a loupe to assess the color and clarity before pronouncing it "very nice."

"Tess wouldn't have liked a big, gaudy diamond," she had assured Scott. "You were wise to choose such a pretty little stone for her."

Amazingly, Scott hadn't displayed any desire to strangle her tactless sister. He'd merely agreed that the ring seemed to suit Tess well.

Christmas Eve dinner with her family had been very nice, on the whole. With a newcomer in the midst, and with gifts on the line, the kids had been mostly on their best behavior. Scott had chatted easily enough with Ken, who was another college football fan caught up in postseason bowl hype, and it wasn't long before they'd drawn the boys into the conversation. Nina and her teenage daughter had spent the evening offering increasingly extravagant ideas for the wedding, from Nina's outlines for possible themes to Olivia's television-inspired suggestions of a Cinderella carriage with white horses, and doves for the guests to release after the ceremony. Tess had simply smiled and nodded a lot, mentally vowing to stick to the plans she and Scott had made.

Scott's family, on the other hand, seemed genuinely enthused about the ideas Tess and Scott presented, all agreeing that a wedding should reflect the individual couple's tastes and wishes.

"Both my sons had perfect weddings for them," Holly declared happily. "I know you and Scott will have just as nice a celebration."

"The wedding is just a party, really," Barry agreed, wrapping an arm around his wife's shoulders. "It's much more important to plan a marriage than a wedding. Holly and I were married by a justice of the peace in front of her grandmother's fireplace three days before I shipped out to Vietnam. We'll be married forty-four years next month. And I love her as much today as I did then," he added without embarrassment.

As if in echo of the sentiment, Eli and Jake hugged their wives. The love in the room was almost palpable. Tess swallowed a lump in her throat that seemed to be sharp edged. She glanced through her lashes at Scott and found him studying the back of his hand as if there were something fascinating to be seen there. He was obviously avoiding her eyes.

She was grateful when Madison—or was it Miranda?—interrupted the awkward moment. "We want to open presents," the little girl insisted. "Please, Grammy. May we please open presents now?"

"Lunch first and then presents," their grandmother said, smoothing the child's fine hair.

At the resulting protest, their parents reminded the twins that they'd already opened presents from Santa that morning and they had to be patient before opening the family gifts. They weren't happy about it, but the girls acquiesced and the family moved into the dining room to begin the meal.

Tess couldn't help watching the individual family members as they ate. She noted the little things—affectionate touches, shared smiles, teasing pats and pinches. She even heard a murmured "I love you" between Jake and Christina when they thought no one was listening.

As the day passed, she found herself working harder to keep smiling. She wasn't sure why, because she was having a lovely time with this endearing family.

"Tell us about when Scott gave you the ring," Libby said when the women were alone in the kitchen later. "Was it romantic? Did he get down on one knee?"

Tess forced a laugh. "I asked him not to do that. We've agreed that there's no need for pretense between us. We're just ourselves with each other. That has always worked well for us."

"Good idea," psychologist Christina approved. "You know each other so well after working together for so many years. It would be counterproductive to start acting differently with each other now. As long as you love each other for who you are, there's no need to try to change for unrealistic reasons."

"It's such a romantic story, though," the more sentimental Libby said with a sigh. "The boss who falls in love with his valued assistant and finds that she loves him in return. All these years you must have had secret feelings for each other. Now you can openly admit you're in love. That must be so liberating."

Tess twisted the ring on her finger, which suddenly seemed heavier than it had before. "Scott and I agree that we're very well suited," she said.

The brief silence that followed her words let her know it hadn't been an ideal response.

She was relieved when Jake barreled into the room.

"Tess, you have got to give us the recipe for these pear things. Man, they're good! Eli's been into them all afternoon, so I've hidden a couple for myself for later. Scott suggested we arm wrestle for the rest of them, but I know Eli would cream me at that, so I'm not taking the chance."

She was so relieved by the interruption that she spun to him with a too-bright smile. "I'd be happy to send you the recipe. They're really not that hard to make."

"These are good, too," Eli said, munching on a stained glass cookie as he followed his brother into the room.

His wife planted her hands on her hips. "Just how many sweets have you had today, Dr. Prince?"

Her husband grinned. "Calories don't count on Christmas, remember?"

"Sounds good to me," Christina said, heading for the dining room. "I'm having one of those pear things. You better not have hidden all of them, Jake."

Tess was smiling again until she looked around and accidentally locked eyes with Scott's mother. There was no mistaking the concern on Holly's face. It hadn't been there before that awkward conversation about Scott's feelings.

A hand fell on Tess's shoulders. "I told you your baked contributions would be a hit," Scott said with a laugh. "My brothers would marry you themselves if they weren't already taken."

She tried to laugh, failed, turned it into a cough. "I think I need a glass of water," she said, avoiding Holly's eyes as she moved toward the sink.

"You've gotten very quiet," Scott said in his car on their way back to her place. "You must be tired."

"A little," she conceded. She realized she was holding her hands in her lap, twisting the ring again, and she made herself stop before he noticed.

"Want some music?" He tuned the radio to an adult contemporary station, knowing from past conversations that she had a weakness for pop music, though his own tastes leaned toward classic rock. "I think we've had enough Christmas carols for a while, don't you?"

"Yes. This is fine, thanks." She was glad for the music, actually. She could pretend to listen and avoid having to make conversation for the duration of the drive.

Looking out the window at the passing holiday decorations, she let her head fall back against the headrest. A song ended and a new one began. She bit her lip when she recognized the opening piano notes to A Great Big World's "Say Something." The lyrics expressed the singer's longing to hear that his love was returned before he gave up on the relationship. He'd have swallowed his pride and followed his lover anywhere, he insisted in audible pain. All he'd needed were the words.

Say something, I'm giving up on you.

Funny. She'd heard this song dozens of times during the height of its popularity. She'd always liked it.

Only now did she fully understand it.

The last mournful note faded away just as Scott parked in the space beside the rental car. She'd have her own car back next week, she thought in relief. It was taking longer than she'd have liked, but that was probably to be expected this time of year.

Her car, at least, could be repaired. Brought back to its original condition, she'd been told, with no one the wiser at a glance to the damage that had been done to it. As for herself—well, maybe the damage wouldn't be visible at a glance, but she wasn't sure it would ever be fully repaired.

She and Scott both had their arms full of bags and gifts when they entered her condo. "Just dump it all on the couch," she said. "I'll put everything away later."

He turned to face her, his now empty hands planted on his hips. "All right, Tess. Spill it. What's wrong? Did someone in my family say something to upset you or make you uncomfortable?"

"Of course not." Not intentionally anyway. "Your family is wonderful. They were all so gracious to me."

"Then, what is it?"

She pushed a hand through her hair, her restlessly wandering gaze pausing on the Christmas tree. She hadn't turned on the tree lights so it was dark, the symbolism not lost on her. Should she wait? Was it horrible of her to do this on Christmas? But no. It would be worse to lie and tell him everything was fine. She and Scott had insisted on honesty from the start.

With her back to him, she slid the beautiful ring from her finger and looked down at it for a moment, struggling for composure. Only when she was sure she had her emotions under control did she turn to him, the ring closed in her fist.

"I asked you once what you would do if I told you I didn't want to go along with your plan. If I decided I'd rather not marry you."

His eyes wary, his expression guarded, he nodded. "I remember."

"Do you remember what you said?"

He nodded again. "I said I would be disappointed but I would do everything I could to put it behind me. I said I wouldn't let it affect our work relationship or our friendship. We could agree that it had been worth a shot and then go on with our lives just as we've been doing for the past six years."

She swallowed in pain before asking softly, "Do you still think you could do that? Even now?"

"Tess—"

He took a step toward her but she held up her free hand, palm out, and stopped him. "Please answer my question."

Lifting one hand to squeeze the back of his neck, he gave it a moment's thought before replying slowly, "I'm not saying it would be easy. As close as we've been the past month, as much as we've shared—hell, it'd be hard. But yeah, eventually, I could do it. Whatever happened between us, I would do anything I could to make you comfortable at the office, to assure you that your job would not be affected by any personal decision you make about us."

"And you'd be able to go back to seeing me as your office manager? Your employee?"

Again, a lengthy pause followed her question.

Say something, Scott.

"Yes," he said finally, the word a knife straight through her heart. "I could get to that point again. It might take a while, but we're adults, right? It would serve neither of us well to mope about our plans not working out."

"That's very...practical of you," she whispered. "You've always been so proud of your ability to compartmentalize your life. I guess that's part of what has made you so successful in your business."

She thought back to the end of his previous engagement. How long had it taken him to get over Sharon? A week? A day? She'd thought at the time he'd seemed almost relieved the relationship had ended, freeing him to concentrate again on the business he truly loved. Maybe it would take him a little longer this time.

But maybe not.

"Tess, you're really confusing me." He dropped his arm to his side. "I don't know where this is coming from."

She took pride in the fact that her eyes were dry when she looked at him. "I'm so very sorry, Scott. I wish I'd understood sooner what I wanted. What I needed. It wasn't your fault that I let myself get swept up into a fantasy. You did everything you could to warn me. You were nothing but honest with me from the beginning."

His eyes were wide now. Dark with dawning comprehension. "What are you saying?"

She held out her hand. Turned it palm up so that the ring was visible to him. "The life you've described would be a very good one. I'm sure you'd work as hard at being a husband and father as you have at running a business. Only a romantic idiot with totally unrealistic expectations would turn you down."

"You aren't an idiot, Tess."

"Apparently, I am."

The ensuing silence was almost suffocating. She drew a ragged breath into her aching lungs, her hand shaking a little as she continued to hold out the ring to him.

Say something. Please.

"What do you want from me?" He sounded honestly bewildered.

"Everything," she answered simply. "I needed to know that losing me would break your heart. But that's not something you were either able or willing to offer. And this pretty diamond isn't enough to make up for that."

"Tess, you don't understand. I can't... I'm not the kind who... I've tried before and I failed. And if I've hurt you now, I've failed again. I'm so sorry."

She took his hand and made him accept the ring. "It's not your fault," she repeated, tormented by his obvious distress. "You did nothing wrong. You offered everything you had to give. I'm the one who got greedy. Like I said, I'm an idiot. I fell head over heels in love with you, Scott. I've probably been in love with you for six years. Isn't that pathetic?"

"No." His voice was a little choked as his fingers closed hard around the ring. It would probably leave a mark on his palm. "Not pathetic."

"But foolish."

He couldn't seem to argue with that.

"I think you'd better go now," she said with a strained, sad smile. "I'd hate to complete my humiliation by bursting into tears. Neither of us would care for that."

"I don't want to leave you like this."

"Please." She almost flinched at the entreaty in her own voice. The one thing she was determined not to do was to beg. "Just go."

He walked slowly to the door. "Will I see you at the office next week?"

"I'll come by to get my things and to make arrangements for a replacement. Maybe Damaris could take over my duties until you can hire someone permanent. Actually, you'll probably have to hire a couple of people to replace me," she added with wry candor. "You'll need an office manager and a human resources manager."

"You're quitting?" So many emotions swirled in his face that it was hard to identify them all, but she saw the first glint of anger then. Good. Maybe it would make this easier if he got mad. At least that was a real, honest emotion. "You're seriously giving notice?"

"Yes. Unlike you, I can't go back to the way it was before. I can't just stop loving you. And I won't punish myself for it by working with you every day and watching you get over your disappointment and then move on. I deserve better than that."

"Yes. You do. You deserve everything you want." With that quiet statement, he turned and let himself out. He didn't look back as he closed the door behind him.

She didn't know how long she stood there just staring at the door, unable to move, unable to cry, unable to think beyond the dull realization that she had just ended her relationship with Scott and quit her job. She knew which loss was more devastating—but she'd loved her job, too. She would miss it almost as much as she would him. Or had she loved the job so much because of him?

The numbness began to wear off and the pain came in waves that crashed through her, slammed the breath from her lungs. A sound escaped her that was part sob, part moan. Nothing had ever hurt her as badly as this.

She needed not to be alone. But Stevie was out of town and she couldn't crash Jenny's first Christmas with her new husband. On an impulse she snatched up the keys to her rental car, tucked her bag under her arm and headed for the door.

Somehow she made it to her sister's house without being in another car crash. Shivering in the cold that seemed to be coming more from inside her than outside, she huddled into her coat and rang the doorbell.

Having checked through the security window, Nina opened the door. "Tess, what on earth are you doing here? It's nearly ten o'clock. On Christmas night! We're already getting ready for— Oh, my God. What's wrong? What's happened?"

The tears had started, and there was no way she could stop them now. "Can I—can I come in? Please."

"Of course." Nina took her arm and drew her inside. "Let me make you some tea. You're freezing. You can tell me all about it once you're warm."

Tess allowed her big sister to lead her toward the kitchen, even though she wasn't sure she'd ever be warm again.

Chapter Eleven

Scott hated failure. Hated it. He'd spent his entire life doing everything he could to avoid dealing with it, which meant he'd never really learned how to handle it. Failure had been such a rare thing in his life. Oh, sure, there'd been the broken engagement to Sharon, but that had been easy enough to wave off. Maybe because he'd never really considered that failure his fault. Sharon had demanded too much from him, made it impossible for them to continue. She might have been the one to officially call it off, but he would have done so eventually if she hadn't. So he'd always told himself that had all been more of a misstep than a failure. Still, it had left a few scars, along with more determination than ever to avoid future potential failures at all costs.

He'd been so confident that he'd minimized all the risks with Tess. That he'd looked at every angle, foreseen every potential problem, dodged any complications. With the experienced skill of a successful entrepreneur, he'd presented his case, brought her on board with his plan, followed a step-by-step progression from first date to engagement, a path that should have continued on to the cozy little wedding and a couple of kids to fill those empty upstairs bedrooms. He'd pretty much won over her sister, and his family had all but adopted Tess. The staff at work seemed okay with their arrangement, so that potential complication had been avoided. He'd done everything right. She'd said so herself.

But still he'd hurt her, the one thing he had vowed from the start not to do. He'd lost her as a fiancée, as a friend, even as an office manager. He hadn't just failed, he had failed spectacularly.

On Saturday, two days after Christmas—a month after he'd come up with that so-called brilliant idea—he sat in his empty office staring at a phone that wasn't ringing, looking at a doorway no one would be walking through today. The job sites were idle, his business associates all busy with their holidays, so there was nothing to distract him from his glum thoughts.

He hadn't broken the news to his family yet. He'd managed to avoid calls and respond to texts in brief, nonspecific replies, so they probably thought he and Tess were utilizing the time off to celebrate their engagement. Which was exactly what they should be doing, had it not all fallen apart.

He shoved himself to his feet, unable to sit still any longer. He didn't know what he was looking for when he wandered into the lobby. Everything was as tidy as they'd left it at early closing time on Wednesday.

The garland and other decorations still hung in place. He'd always thought there was something forlorn about Christmas decorations hanging around after the holiday passed. Today was no different. The tree sat in the corner, lights off because he hadn't wanted them on. Tess had been sitting right there under that tree when his brainstorm had hit.

The door to her office was open. Her desk was clean, organized. He tried to picture Damaris sitting there, or some other future employee. His brain just couldn't process it. Tess was the only one who'd ever sat at that desk. How could he ever find anyone to replace her? Here—or in the rest of his life?

Why would he want to replace her?

He could go on, he told himself. He could put it behind him. Shake off this misstep and focus on what he was good at. His business. He didn't need a wife he'd probably just neglect, or kids he didn't have time for anyway.

For Tess and the kids they'd have made together, he'd have made time.

He thought of the upcoming Kilgo job, the new Best Burger restaurants on the long-term plan, the apartment complexes and strip malls and other construction jobs waiting to be bid on and won and implemented. Maybe he'd get back his enthusiasm for the projects before long, once he figured out how to tackle them without Tess at his side.

Maybe he just had to get through that stages-of-loss thing. He'd already dealt with shock and denial. He was still struggling with bouts of anger.

What the hell more had she wanted from him? He'd

offered her his home, his business, his family, his future. What more could he have given her?

I needed to know that losing me would break your heart.

There wouldn't have been any need for heartache if she'd just gone along with the plan. She'd said she wanted the future he'd outlined, the same things he desired. Why had it mattered so much to her to hear the words, the things so many people said and didn't really mean? How many of his friends had tumbled into love, rhapsodized about their undying devotion to their new someones, thrown themselves headfirst into fairy-tale weddings, only to end up angry and disillusioned, bitter and resentful? Words held no guarantees. Actions were what counted. And he'd been prepared to follow through on all his promises.

I fell head over heels in love with you, Scott. I've probably been in love with you for six years. Isn't that pathetic?

What was more pathetic? The one who confessed love—or the one who was too cowardly to surrender to it?

I deserve better than that.

Yes. You do. You deserve everything you want.

He'd meant what he'd said. He wanted her to be happy. She did deserve it. He was sure there were plenty of men who'd be more than willing to offer Tess everything he had held back. Men who would think they'd just won the lottery of a lifetime if they were lucky enough to earn Tess Miller's love. Scott doubted that the boring Glenn was the only other man smart enough to figure out what a treasure she was. And choosy as she was, she would find someone worthy of her someday.

Maybe someday soon. And then he'd have lost her for-ever. That stupid plan of his would have cost him every-thing. More than he'd even known he'd placed at risk.

He leaned his throbbing head against the doorjamb of her office and pressed a hand to his aching chest. He'd never had his heart broken before, so he didn't know what that felt like. He suspected it felt a hell of a lot like this.

"You didn't turn on the security system. Don't you know just anyone could break in?"

He froze, his wounded heart clenching in his chest. And then he turned, very slowly, wondering if he'd only imagined her voice because he'd wanted so badly to hear it.

But no. She was here, standing in front of him look-ing a little pale, a little worn, but her chin held high and her shoulders square. Tess might have been hurt by his stupidity, but she would spring back to her feet. She was a survivor. He suspected she was a hell of a lot stronger than he.

"Why are you here?"

"I thought I'd start cleaning out my desk," she said quietly, dashing his hopes that she'd come to find him. "It's not something I want to do in front of the staff."

"You're really quitting."

She nodded. "I think it's best."

"I don't want you to go."

"I know. It won't be easy for you to replace me," she said with a frank shrug. "But you'll manage."

"And if I don't want to manage?"

"I'm sorry," she said, but he could tell she wasn't going to change her mind.

He pushed his fingertips into the pockets of his jeans. "I respect your decision."

"Thank you."

He moved to one side to allow her to enter her office. She set a tote bag on the desk. He hadn't even seen it in her hand. She opened her desk drawer. "Are you going to stand there and watch me?"

"Tess." Exploding into action, he reached around her and slammed the drawer shut. "Damn it, this is wrong. You can't do this."

He heard the edge of desperation in his tone, but there was nothing he could do about it.

She looked for a moment as though she was about to snap at him, but something in his expression must have caught her attention. She went still. "Why can't I do this?"

"The company needs you."

She shook her head. "Not good enough."

"*I* need you."

Her expression didn't change. "You'll find another office manager. No one is irreplaceable."

"You are," he said roughly. "Maybe I could replace you here in the office, though I'd never find anyone as competent and dedicated. But I could never replace you in my life. I don't even want to try."

"Why, Scott?"

"Because I love you, damn it. I don't want to lose you."

The words echoed in his ears as she studied him in silence. He grimaced. He'd screwed up again. That was probably the least romantic declaration she'd heard since…well, since he'd made such a mess of proposing to her.

"I really am hopeless at this," he muttered. "I can't

blame you for wanting to get as far away from me as you can, but I'm asking you to stay. If it means getting down on one knee—hell, on both knees—I'll do it. Don't give up on us, Tess. Don't give up on me."

She'd said she loved him. Had she changed her mind? Had she come to her senses?

She took a step toward him, searching his face intently. "You've really suffered the past two days, haven't you?"

"Yes," he admitted in a growl. "Hell, yes."

Incredibly, she smiled. "Good."

"Well, I'm glad that makes you so happy," he grumbled.

She threw her arms around his neck so abruptly he staggered backward. He righted himself quickly, gathering her close. "Tess?"

She drew back just far enough to gaze fiercely into his face. "I don't want to be married because we make a great team. I don't want to be the one you choose because I'm practical and sensible and fit in well with your family. I don't want you to marry me because I'm low maintenance or easygoing or understanding. I want the romance, darn it, just like any other woman. You don't have to get down on your knees, but you'd better be willing to admit you don't want to lose me. You'd damned well better fight for me if you want me."

He studied her flushed face and wild eyes, utterly fascinated by this new side of her. How could he ever grow bored with Tess or take her for granted when she never ceased to surprise him?

"I'd fight dragons for you," he said in growing wonder. "I'd give up everything I own to keep you, including this company. I'll give you every material thing I own because none of that matters. You already have the rest of me."

"Including your heart?"

"You're the only one who's ever had it. I was just too damned scared to admit it."

Rising on tiptoes, she lifted her mouth to his. He kissed her thoroughly, intensely, pouring all the emotion she demanded from him into the embrace. All he wanted to give her.

"You'll have to be patient with me," he said when they could finally speak again. "I'm going to make a lot of stupid mistakes."

She nodded. "I'll probably make a few myself. We'll deal with them together."

He set her a few inches away and dug into his pocket. Holding out his hand, he offered her the ring on his palm. The ring he hadn't been able to put away since she'd returned it to him. She hesitated only a heartbeat before smiling and reaching for it. Scott caught her hand and slipped the ring on her finger himself. Once again, he kissed it into place.

"This time it stays," he said in steadfast resolve.

Cupping his face in her hands, she brushed her lips against his. "This time it stays."

Feeling whole again for the first time since she'd sent him away, he grinned and swept her into his arms.

They really did make the perfect team. In business. In love.

It turned out he'd had the perfect plan all along.

* * * * *

MILLS & BOON®

Why shop at millsandboon.co.uk?

Each year, thousands of romance readers find their perfect read at millsandboon.co.uk. That's because we're passionate about bringing you the very best romantic fiction. Here are some of the advantages of shopping at www.millsandboon.co.uk:

* **Get new books first**—you'll be able to buy your favourite books one month before they hit the shops

* **Get exclusive discounts**—you'll also be able to buy our specially created monthly collections, with up to 50% off the RRP

* **Find your favourite authors**—latest news, interviews and new releases for all your favourite authors and series on our website, plus ideas for what to try next

* **Join in**—once you've bought your favourite books, don't forget to register with us to rate, review and join in the discussions

Visit **www.millsandboon.co.uk**
for all this and more today!

MILLS & BOON®

Cherish™

EXPERIENCE THE ULTIMATE RUSH OF FALLING IN LOVE